The Secret of
Dragonhome

The Secret of

Dragonhome

JOHN PEEL

SCHOLASTIC INC.
New York Toronto London Auckland Sydney

No part of this publication may be reproduced in whole or in part, or stored in a retrieval system, or transmitted in any form or by any means, electronic, mechanical, photocopying, recording, or otherwise, without written permission of the publisher. For information regarding permission, write to Scholastic Inc., Attention: Permissions Department, 555 Broadway, New York, NY 10012.

ISBN 0-590-59680-2

12 11 10 9 8 7 6 5 4   5 6 7 8/0

Printed in the U.S.A.
First Scholastic printing, July 1998

The Secret of
Dragonhome

Prologue

"Lord of all I survey," mused Sander to himself as he stared from the battlements of Castle Dragonhome. The sun was setting, throwing a bloodred glow across everything. It seemed to be particularly appropriate. Below him, Sander could see the jutting stones of the dragon gate that guarded the approach to his castle. Cold, hard stone, matching the cold, hard feelings in his own heart. "And is it worth it?" he asked himself.

He looked down at the courtyard behind him. His son, Corran, was walking slowly across the space, heading for the dining hall. Corran was five years old, but he walked like an old man, slightly bent and with a burden of cares on his childish shoulders. Sander wished that there was something he could do to help his son, but he didn't have a clue. He couldn't help himself — how could he help the son he barely knew?

Sander ran a gloved hand across the stone wall. Cold, hard, and lifeless. Like so much of his life. He had almost become one with his ancestors' castle, he supposed. And, like the castle, he guarded its secrets.

His eyes flickered across the forbidden wing. It was slightly ruined, and gave some credence to his lie that it was dangerous. Nobody in the castle would dare try to enter that area. Only he had access. Only he knew the truth of what lay within. It was dangerous, certainly, but not in the way that the servants believed.

If anyone ever discovered what it hid, Sander would have no choice but to kill them. Even if it was his only son.

The secret was too dangerous for any other human being to know. It was almost too dangerous for him.

Slowly, he descended the steps to head for the dining hall himself. Food wouldn't be served until he arrived, and he didn't wish to keep everyone hungry, even though he had no appetite himself. As Lord of Dragonhome, he had responsibilities. Again, he looked toward the forbidden wing. And, tonight, he would have to venture in there once again. He would have to confront his responsibility, his guilt, and his future.

Alone. Always alone. There was nobody he could ever trust with what he knew.

Slowly, brokenly, he walked alone across the courtyard, to where warmth and friendship awaited. The warmth and friendship he would never know.

The secret he held made certain of that.

Chapter One
The Raiders

Melayne could tell by the sky that a huge storm was on its way. The dark clouds had a slightly surreal touch to them, a kind of smoky grayness, that showed they meant business. They had been increasing most of the morning, piling dark mass upon darker masses. When this storm broke, it was going to do some very serious damage. Melayne knew that she and her brother, Sarrow, should be heading home, but it was hard to resist the urge to stay out for just a few more minutes.

"Why do we always have to be alone?" Sarrow asked suddenly. "Why can't we ever go into town?"

Looking up from the books she had been using to teach her eight-year-old brother, Melayne smiled fondly at him. He was such a handsome boy, with his sandy-blond curling hair, blue eyes, and easy smile — so very different from Melayne. He took after their father, while she had all of her mother's looks — long dark hair, and eyes the same smoky gray as the rain-bearing sky. Perhaps that was why she was so reluctant to leave the hill. She felt a kinship with the sky.

"It's because of the war," she explained. Sarrow was young, but very quick-witted. Melayne had learned a long time ago that there was never a need to talk down to him.

"The war's very far away," Sarrow complained. "Greenholt isn't."

"True, the war is far away, but it touches on the lives of everyone in the Five Kingdoms." Melayne turned back to the map of the world she had open in front of her, and showed it to him. "Our continent is split into the Five Kingdoms," she reminded him, tracing each one. "There's Vester, then Farrowholme. Here's Morstan and Pellow. And this small piece that juts out here is Stormgard, where we live."

"I know all of that," Sarrow said, with the contempt of an advanced student. He tapped the extreme south of the promontory. "And here's where we are, right at land's end." He gestured to the south. "And the sea is out there, leading to nowhere, just flowing forever. What does any of this have to do with us going into town?"

"Because the Five Kingdoms have been at war for almost as long as anyone can recall. Vester and Farrowholme against the rest of us. Since the war's been going on so long, they always need people to fight in the armies. So the kings take them."

Sarrow frowned. "Even people as young as me?"

Melayne nodded. "Not because you're ready to

fight, mind you," she told him. "But because you have a Talent."

"I *don't* have a Talent," he argued stubbornly. "Not like you."

Melayne smiled. "No, not like me. But you're very young yet. Sometimes Talents manifest themselves when you're a child. Mine came when I was five. But at other times, it takes until you reach puberty."

"What's puberty?"

Laughing, she shook her head. "I don't think you're ready for that one yet!" And she wasn't sure that she was the one who should tell him about it, either. Mother had explained it to Melayne when she was nine; at the time, it had sounded like a very strange change to go through. But it was nothing like she'd been expecting when it had happened almost three years ago. Now, at fifteen, Melayne enjoyed being a young lady. She'd enjoy it more, though, if there were some young men around. . . . Which brought her back to Sarrow's original question.

"Anyway, the armies all want Talents to do the fighting. There are very few Talents born, compared to other people. Maybe one in twenty. And nobody knows why somebody becomes a Talent. Sometimes one person in a family has a Talent, and the rest don't. Mother and Father don't, for example, but both of us do. And Kander did, too. So I guess our family is special."

"I don't *feel* special," Sarrow answered. "I feel *lonely*."

"You have me, Sarrow."

"I know," he said, adding with the terrible honesty of childhood: "But you're my *sister*. I want some *other* people to be with. I want some friends."

A pang of desire went through Melayne as he said that. He couldn't know that she felt exactly the same way. She longed for company, for someone new to talk to — and, perhaps, more. Her mother had an old romance story back at the house, *The Tale of the Forlorn Knight*. It was about a handsome but sad knight who went all over the Five Kingdoms doing great and heroic things, even though he was cursed always to lose whatever he loved. It was such a sad story, and Melayne adored it. She often fantasized that the knight would come to her one day, and she would be doomed to fall hopelessly in love with him. She longed to stare soulfully into someone's eyes, and have them stare back, entranced.

But it could never be. With a sigh, Melayne shook her head. "It's too dangerous," she explained. "Because we both have Talents, if anyone found us, they would have to turn us in to the Royal Courts. And then we'd be taken away from our parents, like Kander was. He was only seven when he was taken, and we never saw him again. That was when Mother and Father decided that they would bring me up somewhere alone and safe, where nobody could betray me. They were both rather surprised when you were born. But they had to make you safe, too. That's why we live out here, beside the sea, and without neighbors. And why only Mother or Father ever goes into town. If anyone knew we were Talents, we'd be taken away. And that would break our parents' hearts. You wouldn't want to do that, would you?"

"Never," Sarrow declared. "But I can't help wishing to meet other people. You did, once. What are they like?"

"I was only five years old," Melayne replied. "I don't remember too well. There were some other children I know I enjoyed playing with. And adults, like our parents. Most of them were very solemn, but some of them were nice. And some were a little bit mean. Most of them were a bit intimidated by Mother and Father. Not everyone can read, Sarrow, and they're a little insecure around those who can. I think they viewed our family as outsiders. So when Kander's Talent erupted, they were only too glad to turn him in."

Sarrow frowned. "Don't other people like Talents?" he asked.

"Most don't. You see, we have something extra inside of us somehow. Something that shines through as our Talent. There are many different Talents. Not all are like mine. But they're all special gifts. And those without such gifts are jealous of us. Because they don't have a Talent, they think we shouldn't have one, either. Still, they feel Talents are very useful in the war, so the kings all try and recruit every Talent that they find into their Armies."

"I see," said Sarrow thoughtfully. "They dislike us, but they'll use us when it suits them."

It was a very cynical thought, even for Sarrow, but it was true. "Yes," Melayne admitted. "That's it, exactly. So, you see, if you went into Greenholt, and anyone there found out that you were a Talent, they'd turn you in straightaway."

"They wouldn't find out," Sarrow said contemptuously. "I could hide it so that nobody would know. Even you could do that."

"Yes," Melayne agreed, ignoring the subtle insult. Sarrow never meant anything by his casual slights. "But there are tests that can be done to see if a person has a Talent. And if we were put to them, we'd fail."

"What sort of tests?" Sarrow demanded.

"I don't know. Just tests. That's what Mother and Father said. And they said it so grimly that I didn't want to know any more."

"That's because you're just a girl and don't have a brave heart. When we go home, I shall ask them and I shall listen to all of the answers without fear. I'm not scared of hearing the truth."

That stung Melayne a little. "I am *not* afraid," she replied coldly. "I just don't see any need to know what the tests are. We're never going to have to face them."

"Never say never," Sarrow snapped back, using one of her own favorite expressions against her. "One day, we'll have to go back to the outside world."

"Why?"

Sarrow sighed. "Because Mother and Father won't live and be strong forever. Haven't you noticed that Father has more aches and pains these days? Being a farmer is tiring work, and it's wearing him down."

Actually, Melayne *had* noticed. But she'd tried to ignore it. Father's limbs were growing stiffer, and it was taking him longer to do the farm chores than it had a year ago. She helped out, of course, and did Sarrow and Mother. But Mother's hair was going very gray now, turning the color of her eyes, and her face was growing lined. Melayne hated to think about it, but Sarrow was right. Their parents wouldn't live forever.

And then what? She and Sarrow might be able to run the farm between them, especially if they had years to go before anything serious happened. Melayne had a strong constitution, and a grim determination that helped her endure. Sarrow would survive, too, no doubt. But the farm couldn't provide everything that they needed to live. One or the other of their parents took a trip into Greenholt once a month to trade some of their surplus food for other things that the family needed — matches, candles, a little oil, some food they couldn't grow themselves. Sometimes they even managed to bring back a new book, which Mother and then Melayne would devour greedily.

Someone would have to do that, if anything happened to their parents.

"You're right, Sarrow," she agreed reluctantly. "I'll ask about the tests, too, when we go home. I'm the oldest, so I'll have to be the one to start taking such risks. I'll always protect you, I promise."

"I know you will," he said simply.

Melayne looked up at the sky. She was very good at reading the weather, and she could tell that there was only about a half hour until the storm started to rage. "We'd best be going home," she said. "I don't mind getting wet, but the books will."

"And we can ask about the tests," Sarrow said firmly. He wasn't going to let the subject drop.

"Yes," Melayne agreed. She had a gentle nature, and didn't want to think about what sort of things the tests might be. But she remembered the chapter in *The Tale of the Forlorn Knight* in which a woman was accused of witchcraft. They tested her by throwing her into a lake. If she floated, she was a witch, and if she sank, she was innocent. This woman sank, and it was only the bravery of the knight — who dragged her from the lake bed — that saved her life. If that was how people tested for witches, what sorts of things might they do to test for Talents?

And could she really hide hers from other people, anyway? Surely she'd betray herself without thinking. Her Talent was so much a part of her, how could she keep it secret?

Overhead, a gull wheeled, looking for shelter from the coming storm. It glanced down at her and smiled. *Storm's coming, chick,* it called out to her. *Best you head for your nest and stay warm.*

I will, she called back. *Thank you!* There was no need to tell the bird that she'd been planning on doing that anyway. Gulls were kind enough, but not too bright, and they couldn't follow explanations very well.

How could she hide this gift she had? If she didn't Communicate with animals, then she'd be even more alone than she was now. With a shudder of guilt, she realized that poor Sarrow didn't even have this comfort. He couldn't Communicate like she could. To him, a rabbit was only a potential meal, not a potential friend. That was why he felt so lonely, having no animals to share joy and laughter and excitement with him. Melayne was so blessed, she knew, and she felt sorry for Sarrow.

Of course, it was possible that he might develop the gift of Communication, too. But the odds were against it. Kander had been a Fire Raiser, able to start fires burning just by wishing it. Sarrow would probably have a different Talent, too. Maybe one even more interesting than Communication. Melayne couldn't think of a better Talent, even though she knew of several. Levitation, for example. To be able to fly, just like that gull — there would be a Talent indeed! Or Lifting. That could be very handy, picking things up without having to touch them or strain yourself.

But there was no telling when Sarrow would develop his Talent, or what it might be. They would just have to wait and see.

Melayne gathered up the books and slid them into her shoulder bag. Then she stood up, brushing the grass from her flowing skirt. Sarrow leaped to his feet, heedless of the grass on his trousers. He was always so full of energy, she was sure he was about to race her back to the house. But today, for some reason, he didn't. He walked slowly beside her, his face a mixture of emotions. He was obviously thinking about the tests for Talents, and what he might someday be forced to endure.

They were only about a mile from the house. The place was built on a small spit of land overlooking the sea. Father had a small boat in the inlet that he used to go fishing. He would take Sarrow with him, and Sarrow was turning into quite the fisherman, already almost as good as Father. Melayne couldn't go. She could hear the fish screaming as they struggled to escape, and howling as they thrashed about on deck, dying. It wrenched hard at her emotions, and she could never bring herself to harm any living creature. Or to eat them, though the others did. Melayne ate only vegetables and fruits, and she was glad that they didn't have spirits. What must they feel on being wrenched from the ground or dragged from bushes and trees? She didn't want to know. She had to eat something, after all.

It didn't bother Sarrow, hunting and fishing. He wasn't old enough to be very good with a bow yet, but Father said he was showing progress and would be a great hunter one day. Sarrow was proud of that, almost as proud as Father was of him. Perversely, Melayne was a wonderful bow-woman, much better even than Father. But she would never, ever, aim at a living creature.

"Such a waste," Father would sigh. She supposed it probably was, but how could she ever kill a deer or a wild boar, one that she might have spoken to only the day before? It was absolutely unthinkable to her.

Sarrow stopped so suddenly that she bumped into him. "What's the matter?" she asked.

"Smoke," he said, pointing.

Coming back to the present, Melayne stared ahead. Sarrow was right. There was smoke in the air from the direction of their house. Far too much for it to be coming from the chimney.

"The house must be on fire," she gasped in sudden realization. What was going on? Were Mother and Father all right? "We'd better hurry! They might need our help!"

Sarrow grabbed her arm with surprising strength. "It might not be their doing," he cautioned her. "We shouldn't rush in blindly."

That hadn't occurred to her. She was lucky that Sarrow was so cautious. But he could be wrong. "We have to go," she insisted.

"Yes," he agreed. "But *carefully*."

Melayne nodded. There was a sparrow settling down in the hedgerow nearby, getting ready for the coming storm. *Friend*, she called out to him. *Would you do me a great favor? Would you fly on ahead of me and look out for my nest?*

It will rain soon, the sparrow complained. *I want to stay dry.* Sparrows were rather selfish creatures.

Please! she begged. *There may be danger for me, and you can so easily fly around. I need a brave helper.*

Oh, very well, it agreed ungraciously. *But I'm not*

11

hanging around. It shot off like a crossbow bolt, and Melayne felt better.

She and Sarrow hurried along, staying close to the trees. Melayne felt sick to her stomach with worry and fear. What was happening? Were their parents hurt? There was a turmoil of questions, but no answer until she saw the sparrow skimming back.

Men, the sparrow informed her, panting. *They set fire to your nest, and they're burning everything they find. Just like humans! I'm off.* And it shot into the woods.

"Men," Melayne gasped to Sarrow. "There's some sort of raid in progress."

"Then we'd better head away from it, not toward it," Sarrow answered.

Melayne stared at him in anger and pain, and then realized that he was too young to understand what was happening. "Our parents may be injured," she explained. "We can't just abandon them."

Sarrow snorted. "What can *we* do? If there's a raiding party, that means lots of big, well-armed men. A girl and a child would only be more victims for them."

There was certainly some truth to what her brother was saying, but Melayne knew she couldn't do what he suggested. "I have to *know,*" she told him. "Stay here while I look. I'll be very careful, and I'll be back as fast as possible."

Sarrow considered it, and then shook his head. "I'd feel safer with you," he replied. "I don't want to be left alone if there are raiders around."

"Fine," Melayne agreed. "Come on, then, and keep quiet. We'll take a look from the edge of the wood and see what's happening."

They hurried on cautiously. Melayne wished there were more intelligent creatures around that she could question. But the storm was almost upon them, and everyone was in hiding, wanting to stay dry. Maybe the raiders would have horses she could talk to. That would be a big help. They'd know a lot about what was going on.

As they carefully approached the edge of the trees, Melayne and Sarrow could look down on the small bay where their home lay. Melayne gave a stifled gasp of shock as she saw what was happening there.

A boat lay in the bay, its prow and tail carved in the manner of some grotesque beast. It was medium-sized, with room for about forty people. She could see about a dozen men milling around their farm, most of them loading food from the barn into their ship. They had taken whatever they wanted from the house already, and had set the rest of it ablaze.

Melayne's heart fell as she saw two ragged red bundles by the house. She recognized her parents only by their clothing. The redness was their blood.

"They're dead," Sarrow said sadly. "Those men killed our parents."

"Yes," Melayne agreed, fighting not to cry. It was so hard . . . to see those shattered, bloodied bodies, and to know that these were her parents . . . the stern, but gentle father who had taught her so much about so many things. Her kind, persistent mother, who had nursed and guided her, shaping her beliefs and teaching her the joys of books and learning. Their happy faces swam in her eyes, making them tear uncontrollably. Almost angrily, she wiped at her face, as if brushing at the tears would somehow wipe away the pain that was stabbing at her heart and soul.

Gone . . . dead . . . murdered . . .

This was no time to break down! Melayne breathed deeply, trying to drive the images and pain from her heart. She had to act, not to cry. The crying could wait until later. It *had* to wait until later. There was too much that was urgent now.

"There's nobody to protect us now," Sarrow said.

Melayne clutched him to her chest, struggling with her emotions. "I'll protect you," she vowed. "They won't hurt you."

"They don't have horses," Sarrow pointed out, his voice a bit muffled from being held against her. "There's nothing you can do."

She pushed him out to arm's length, and then wiped away the tears that clung to her eyes. "We have to escape," she informed him. "That's a large raiding party — too large just to be aiming at our home. We have to get to Greenholt and warn them."

"Why?" Sarrow asked. "They've never tried to help us. Why should we help them?"

"These men have already killed our parents. They'll kill a lot more people in Greenholt if we can't get a warning there. Other children will lose their parents. These barbarians might even kill the children. Or worse."

Sarrow shrugged. "I guess. Maybe they'll let us stay with them in town, then. They could protect us."

"Yes," she agreed, glad for any excuse not to argue further. "Come on!"

Even though she'd never been to Greenholt, Melayne knew the way. It wasn't really a town, since there were only about fifty families living there. Mother had said that there were real towns further north. "My sister lives in Halden," she'd once told Melayne. "That's a place where thousands of people live. You can't imagine what that's like." That was true; she couldn't. So many people, all in one place . . .

Melayne hurried along the path to Greenholt, Sarrow clutching her hand tightly for comfort. She tried not to think about Mother and Father lying dead outside the house, with nobody to help them or even bury them. Once the raiders were beaten off, perhaps some men from the village would come and help Melayne to give her parents a decent grave. She didn't want to think about it, though, because it brought a terrible pain to her chest and made her eyes tear so much she couldn't see where she was hurrying.

Cry later, she ordered herself, sniffling and wiping her eyes on her sleeve. Now there was more important work to do.

A huge finger of lightning broke the sky, making

her gasp in shock. She'd forgotten about the storm, but as the thunder roared about them, the rain began — a cold, hard, merciless downpour. She pulled Sarrow in closer to try to protect him a little, and they hurried along. Though it was only a little after noon, the clouds made it almost as black as midnight. Only the fiery trails of lightning lit the scene.

Melayne's clothes were sticking to her now, soaked through and chilling. Her hair was streaming water. Her skin was cold from the downpour, and still it continued.

Now the ground was starting to get muddy, too, slowing them down even further. Melayne tried to ignore it and struggle on, but it wasn't as easy for Sarrow.

"We have to get to shelter," he begged. "We can't go on like this."

"We're almost there," Melayne assured her brother. "We should be able to see the town from the top of the next ridge. Be brave, Sarrow, and press on."

He might be brave, but he certainly wasn't happy. He grumbled to himself, but at least he did come along, as fast as his tired feet could make it. Melayne was feeling the strain herself by now. Still, they were only about five minutes from Greenholt, and then they could find somewhere to rest and get dry and warm.

They reached the ridge, panting, and looked down at the village.

She had thought that she couldn't feel worse. She had been wrong.

This was why they had seen only a dozen raiders at their home — the rest had headed straight for Greenholt.

The town was ablaze, dirty clouds of smoke hanging uncertainly over the wrecked homes. There were dead bodies in the street, and Melayne was thankful they were too far away to make out any details. The raiders were dressed like the ones back at the farm — in thick furs, which kept them warm and served as a kind of armor. They all wore metal helmets and carried swords and shields. Some had long spears, and others had war axes. Even at this distance, Melayne could hear them laughing and howling as they went about their dreadful work. They were looting whatever they could find from the houses.

In the center of the town was a small square, and here the survivors were huddled. Melayne was a little surprised that there *were* any survivors. She could just make out that they were the children and teens from the village. They were roped together. With a further chill, she saw that some of the girls' clothing was in shreds. She knew that some men did terrible things to women.

"We can't warn them," Sarrow said practically. "And they can't help us."

"No," she agreed sorrowfully. "We can't free them. And we can't stay here. We have to go, now."

"Go *where*?"

"I don't know. But we can't stay, with those men here." Melayne turned back to the woods and gasped.

Coming into view farther down the path were some of the raiders from their farm. They must have finished loading up the stolen food, and were on their way to help their companions. One of the men spotted Melayne and Sarrow and gave a yell.

"Quickly!" Melayne cried, and she dived into the woods, dragging Sarrow after her. They had to escape! Sarrow didn't complain this time. Instead, he ran alongside her, grimly concentrating on moving as fast as he could. But it wasn't easy in the mud and pouring rain.

Melayne chanced a glance back and saw that two of the raiders were coming after them — big, brutal men, laughing, with their swords at the ready. Despite the rain and mud, the two of them were moving faster than Melayne and Sarrow. In just a few moments, they would be caught. . . .

Chapter Two
The Helpers

What could she do now? Melayne knew that she and Sarrow wouldn't be killed. The raiders were taking the younger folk as slaves. And the girls to abuse. She had knowledge of what was likely to happen to her, and she was resolved not to let them take her. There had to be *something* she could do. But what? What could a fifteen-year-old girl do, unarmed, against two savages with swords?

She wasn't entirely unarmed, of course. She had her Talent. But how could that help her? If the men were on horses, she could have talked to the horses and convinced them to help. But the men were on foot, and her Talent didn't work on people.

Is there anyone who can help me? she called, using her Talent to its fullest extent. *We are in grave danger from men who want to hurt us.*

There was no reply. All that there were this close to Greenholt were squirrels and songbirds. No wild boars or anything like that. People didn't allow dangerous animals to roam so close to their homes. Although she hadn't really expected help, Melayne had been *hoping.* . . . What else could she do?

And then, amazingly, there was a reply.

We are here, a voice called back. *Little one, we do not love men. We will help you. Be brave!*

Melayne's heart leaped at this reply, even though she had no idea what kind of an animal had called out to her. It was a voice like none she'd ever heard before. There was a great deal of intelligence in it, and an underlying power. It was so different from the chattering rabbits or the nervous, hungry squirrels. It was harder and colder than a horse, and more determined and cunning than a cow. She couldn't imagine what it might be.

But she had no time to wonder; the raiders were virtually on top of her now.

"Girl!" one of them called, in the thick accent of a Morstan man. "There's no use in running. Stand and wait."

"Aye," his companion laughed. "And we'll give you something worth waiting for!" Both men laughed loudly at this joke.

Melayne knew exactly what he meant, and she had no intention of stopping. But could she possibly get away?

Sarrow's foot slipped in the mud and he went sprawling. Their hands were interlinked so tightly that Melayne was dragged off her balance, too, and she splattered down beside him in the mud.

"What an obliging girl," the first raider laughed. "She's even laid herself down to make things easier for us."

Melayne struggled to get up again, absolutely terrified. The men were going to catch them and rape her, and she knew she would never be strong enough to fight them off. Only a short while ago, she'd been wanting to see other human beings, and she'd been granted her wish. Only it was not the way she would have had it.

She would fight, though. Perhaps she couldn't hurt them, but she would never give in without a fierce struggle.

The two men loomed over her as she and Sarrow finally regained their footing. Melayne looked around for a fallen branch or anything that she could use to fight back, no matter how pitifully. Sarrow clung tightly to her, hampering her movements even more.

The first man laughed and lunged for her.

Suddenly *something* whipped out of the trees to Melayne's left, snarling. She had a momentary glimpse of fangs and gray fur as the startled raider was felled by his attacker. The second man turned to face the trees, expecting attack.

It came — but from the opposite direction. Two more gray shapes slammed into the man's back, throwing him to the ground.

The first attacker snarled, and the fang-filled jaws snapped together across the man's throat. Melayne shuddered as blood gushed from the terrible wound while the creature ripped out the raider's throat. The man shook, and then lay still, the wound steaming.

The second man was winded, and flat on his stomach. He'd seen what had happened to his companion, and he didn't aim to die so swiftly. With a growl from deep in his throat, he tried to swing his sword up to deal with his attackers.

It didn't work. Sharp teeth latched onto his wrist and bit deep. The man screamed and tried to shake free. It was the opening that his attackers needed One darted for his exposed throat and ripped it apart. The raider died quickly and noisily.

And then it was all over. Melayne held Sarrow close to her. She didn't want him to see the bodies; he was too young for that. And she wasn't certain that she could actually trust her rescuers not to turn on them next.

The first one moved to stare up at her. Now that the fighting was over, Melayne could see they were three large gray wolves with golden eyes. The leader blinked and then said, *You are the one who called for us?*

Yes, she replied. *Thank you for your help. They would have hurt us terribly.*

They're men, the wolf answered, as if that was all the explanation needed. *But so are you. Why did you need help from us? Would your own kind not help you?*

They are all dead or captured by the friends of these men, Melayne explained. *There are many more such raiders. We should not stay here.*

No, the wolf agreed. He turned to his companions and barked an order. The two of them ran off, vanishing into the dark, rain-drenched woods. Then he turned back to Melayne. *You are wet, man-child, and the other is even colder. You had best accompany me.*

Thank you, Melayne replied sincerely. She let Sarrow loose and explained to him what had happened. He stared in awe at the wolf, and nodded.

"They'll help us," he said with conviction.

"Yes," agreed Melayne. Unlike people, animals didn't understand the concept of lying. Whatever they said, they would do. She faced the wolf again. *We're ready.*

The wolf shook itself like a dog, spraying water everywhere. *You're very slow,* he said. *So this is going to take a while. And I hate rain.*

It was kind of you to help us, Melayne told him.

I hate men more than rain, the wolf answered honestly. *Men hunt us and fear us for no reason. They kill us whenever they can.* He grinned, tongue lolling. *It was good to kill them for once.*

"Wait," Sarrow said, as they started to move off. "We should see if these men have anything on them we can use."

Melayne shuddered at the thought. "I'd rather not."

"It might make the difference between living and dying," Sarrow said. Melayne conveyed this thought to the wolf.

He has a good point, the wolf agreed. *Never refuse the chance to take what might help. And they're hardly likely to object.*

The thought of touching one of the bodies made Melayne's skin crawl. But she could see the wisdom in it. It didn't seem to bother Sarrow at all. He went to the nearest man and started to rummage through his clothing and possessions. Fighting down her urge to vomit, Melayne did the same with the other man. She avoided looking at his ripped-open throat. The constant rain was washing away most of the blood and stench.

She found a pouch with matches that she slipped into her shoulder bag. Also a small knife in the man's boot. It was well looked-after, and could be handy. He had nothing else that she could use, though. She eyed his sword and shield, but the idea of even trying to lift them up was ludicrous. The men were savages, stronger than normal people. And even if she could somehow lift the sword, she had no idea what she'd do with it. It would only slow her down.

"He's not carrying any food," Sarrow complained, having finished with his own man. "And I'm starving."

Melayne's stomach growled at the mention of food, but she didn't really feel hungry. She was too sick to think of eating right now. The wolf laughed.

I know humans better than to suggest that those two dead ones could be used for eating, he said with a silly grin. *Well, maybe we can find something that even a delicate human stomach can stand. Come on.*

They set off into the woods, well off the path. Melayne was already feeling a little safer. If more raiders came and found their dead friends, they wouldn't know which way to look for the killers. The rain was washing away all signs of their trail. Another advantage of plunging into the woods was that the thickly leaved branches overhead helped to keep out a lot of the rain. Melayne wasn't getting quite as soaked.

Why did you decide to help us? she asked the wolf as he led the way.

Because you asked, he replied. *And you sounded . . . interesting.* He gave her an odd look. *Humans don't normally talk to us, so I always listen when they do.*

You've spoken to others like me? Melayne asked, excitedly. Were there more Talents around?

Three, the wolf answered. *None of them were as interesting as you, though. They only spoke on a very simple level. You . . . go deeper.*

Melayne wasn't sure what he meant. She knew that other people could Communicate with animals. It was not an uncommon Talent. *I don't understand,* she confessed, feeling very simple.

The others could talk to me, the wolf explained. *But with you, it's different. Your heart is open to me, as mine is to you. You know that I mean you no harm, and I know the same of you. You have an inner nobility. Wolflike, in fact.* He gave an almost human shrug. *I like you.*

Melayne was amazed. Was he right? Did she somehow have a slightly different Talent than other people? He was certainly right in one way: She *did* know him. She could feel his character as she spoke to him. He was bold, aggressive, and domineering. But he was fair, amusing, and a devoted father, too. There was a deep curiosity inside him. She didn't know how she knew all of this, but she knew that it was true. And, apparently, the Talent worked both ways; he knew her, as well.

This had never happened to her before. Well, not exactly. She understood other creatures well enough, and felt their personalities. And she could coax or flatter them into doing whatever she required of them. They, however, didn't seem as drawn to her as this wolf was, or have so much depth and intelligence. Not even the hawk, who was one of her favorites.

The wolf turned its golden eyes on her again. *We wolves are not common animals*, he informed her. *We are linked to men, though we do not like it. There is some kind of common blood between us. There are tales among wolves of were-men — wolves who are forced to turn human at certain times of the moon.*

I've heard something similar, Melayne admitted. *Though we call them werewolves.*

No doubt, he agreed. *Somehow, then, we are linked. Maybe that's why I like you. I'm not so fond of your companion, though. He's very cold.*

It's the weather, Melayne protested.

It's not that sort of cold, the wolf replied. *There's ice in his soul.*

He's very young still, Melayne said, confused. *He'll learn as he grows.*

I hope so. The wolf scratched himself, and then shook off more water. *We're almost there, thank goodness. I hate traveling this slowly. My fur's soaked.*

So am I, Melayne added.

Yes, but you can take your furs off to dry, the

wolf pointed out. *I'm stuck inside mine.* He nodded ahead. *Just up there.* Then he stared at her again, his golden eyes burrowing into her mind. *I'm called Tane.*

I'm Melayne, she replied, pleased by the exchange. No other animal had ever told her its name before. Perhaps the others didn't have names. Perhaps only wolves did, because they were so like humans in some ways.

Trudging on through the rain, Melayne realized that the ground had started to rise. Ahead, she could barely make out a hill in the gloom, and a small stream beside them. Tane led the way up the hillside a short distance, and then nodded ahead.

Here, he said kindly. *Shelter. Enter slowly, though.*

Melayne nodded and moved on. She could just see the entrance to a low cave. Stooping, she moved out of the rain — thankfully! — and into the gloom. She stood there, Sarrow beside her, until her eyes adjusted.

The cave was about twenty feet deep and eight wide. The roof was only six feet tall and her head bumped it in places, so she walked with a slight stoop. There were more than a dozen other wolves inside, some sleeping, others awake and staring at the humans. Melayne felt a twinge of worry as she was stared at. But she fought it down, knowing that they were safe here. The wolves would not hurt them; Tane would not allow it.

None of the other wolves spoke. Tane moved forward.

These two man-children come among us for a short while, he said. *They need our help, and I have promised it. Treat them kindly. They will do the same to you.* Then he turned to Melayne. *Come.*

He led the way to the rear of the cave. Here another wolf was resting, this one a female. Around her were six small puppies, all of them quiet and intent on watching the two humans.

My mate, Sashah, Tane introduced. *And my pups.*

They're lovely, Melayne said sincerely. *I'm pleased to meet you all.*

Likewise, Sashah replied, smiling. *Child, you are chilled to the bone. So is the other cub. You must get warm and dry.*

Tane shook himself, spraying water everywhere. *Me, too,* he said. He looked at Sarrow. *Tell this one to come with me. One of the other wolves will help him. He must take off his wet clothes, or he will catch a chill. So must you.*

Melayne repeated Tane's message to Sarrow, who looked worried. "Can we trust these animals?" he asked.

"Yes," Melayne promised him. "They will help us. Go with Tane; you'll be looked after."

"All right," Sarrow agreed. He went off, still apprehensive, but at least trusting her. And Melayne was certain that the wolves would be kind to him.

Get out of your skins, Sashah ordered. *Then cuddle next to me. I have plenty of warmth for two.*

Melayne felt rather self-conscious taking off her clothing, but she knew she had no choice. If she didn't, she'd catch her death of cold. The dress was absolutely soaked, and her shift just as bad. She spread them out on a rock to dry, knowing she was blushing. She knew that it was wrong to be naked with other people, but wolves weren't really people, and she shouldn't be embarrassed. But they *felt* like people, and she couldn't help herself. Then she moved to join Sashah, and cuddled in next to her.

The she-wolf *was* warm, amazingly so. Sashah snuggled close, and Melayne felt her hot breath across her face. Then a rough tongue licked her nose.

Cheer up, child, Sashah said. *You're among friends here.*

Melayne nodded, hugging the female wolf tightly. Now that things had calmed down, she could feel all of her emotions flooding through her body. Everything that had happened crashed like a tidal wave against her soul.

Both of her parents were dead, slaughtered by the Morstan raiders. Greenholt was destroyed, the men killed, and the children taken captive. And Morstan was supposed to be their ally! To do such horrible deeds . . . Melayne simply couldn't understand it. All she could understand was the pain in her mind and soul. Never to see her parents again, or her home again. She was alone now, with Sarrow to look after. . . .

And seeing those two raiders killed by the wolves . . . that had been a shock. Even though the men had intended to hurt her, she hadn't really wanted them dead — just stopped. Well, they *had* been stopped, and she had seen their throats being torn out.

It was all too much for her; Melayne couldn't keep back her tears any longer. She shook and cried, her face burrowed into the warm fur of the she-wolf. Sashah licked her tears gently away. *Cry, child,* she advised. *Let the sorrow out. That way, you can deal with it.*

Melayne didn't know how long this lasted, and she didn't really care. All the pain and hurt had welled up inside her, and was flowing out with her tears. She cried for all of her losses, and they were many. Finally, though, she simply had no more tears left, and she sniffled and stopped.

I'm sorry, she told Sashah. *You must think me very weak to cry like that.*

You're only human, the wolf replied. *Of course you're weak. But I don't hold that against you. We all must be what we can be. It's unfortunate that you weren't born a wolf, but we can't all be lucky in this life.*

That almost made Melayne smile. *Thank you for your understanding,* she said, straightening up. Her cheeks were still wet from her tears, but at least the rest of her had dried off. Her clothes, though, were still soaking, and would be for a while. There wasn't much she could do to dry them without a fire, and she wasn't sure how the wolves would take to one in their home. After their kindness, she didn't want to upset them.

Sarrow was sitting beside one of the other wolves, his face unreadable. Not for the first time,

Melayne wished her Talent worked as well on people as it did on animals. What was he thinking? There was no way to know for sure. Sometimes he seemed very mature for his age; at others, he proved he was still only a child.

"Did you cry, too?" she asked him.

"Cry? Not me. That's for girls."

Where had he ever heard that? Melayne had no idea. Certainly she had never taught it to him. Perhaps Father had. "If you hurt badly inside, I don't think even a boy should be ashamed of tears," she said.

He shrugged. "I don't hurt much. But I *am* hungry. We haven't eaten for *hours*."

That reminded Melayne of her own hollow stomach, and she heard it growl loudly. "I know. But I didn't get a chance to bring any food with us."

Tane is hunting, Sashah informed her. *You may share our meal later.*

Thank you, Melayne replied. *But . . .*

The she-wolf's golden eyes bored into her own. *Is something the matter? Don't you want to eat with wolves? To share our food is to be a part of our pack forever.*

It's not that, Melayne explained hastily. *I would be greatly honored to be accepted as a part of your pack. It's just that . . . well, Tane will be bringing meat.*

Ah! Sashah laughed. *And humans dislike eating meat raw, the way it should be. You like to use fire to sear it and make it lose its flavor. Well, if you can, you could build a small fire in the corner.*

Thank you, Melayne said gratefully. *I know that will be fine for my brother. But I don't eat meat.*

The wolf simply couldn't understand this. *Not eat meat? Why not?* Melayne could feel her confusion.

I can communicate with all animals, Melayne explained. *Not just wolves. I would never feel right about eating something that I can talk to.*

Sashah was obviously having a problem understanding this objection. *It is the way of the world*, she said, puzzled. *There are animals that eat plants and berries, and there are those who eat meat. We have no choice but to eat meat. Our stomachs cannot tolerate other food.*

I understand, Melayne told her. *But it's not like that for me. I can live on fruits and vegetables, so I don't eat meat.*

Huh! The she-wolf leaned forward. *Let me see your teeth*, she ordered. Melayne obligingly opened her mouth. Sashah radiated smugness. *Your teeth aren't for eating plants*, she said. *Those are the teeth of a meat eater.*

Perhaps, agreed Melayne, wondering how she was managing to lose an argument with a wolf. *But I choose not to.*

While you are with us, there will be nothing else to eat, Sashah pointed out. *It would be foolish of you to refuse the food that you need simply because you think it wrong. The animal will still be dead; why not make use of it?*

I don't know that I would be able to do it, Melayne said honestly.

Well, it's up to you, Sashah answered. *But Tane*

might be annoyed if you refuse to share food with us. It would be an insult.

Oh, dear . . . Melayne didn't know what to do. She couldn't afford to offend their friends, who had shown them such kindness. But, at the same time, she really didn't think she'd be able to make herself eat meat. She would be thinking of the poor animal all the time. It would be like cannibalism for her. So, to do something while she was thinking, she decided that she'd have to build a fire.

"What did she say to you?" Sarrow asked.

Melayne had forgotten that he couldn't understand the wolves. "That we can build a fire," she replied. "Tane has gone hunting, and he'll bring something back. We'll be allowed a share of it, and we can cook it if we get the fire going."

"Good," he replied. "I'm really hungry. Almost hungry enough to eat raw meat."

"If we can't get a fire started, you may have to," Melayne informed him. There were dry twigs and moss in the cave, which would be great for starting a small fire. What they needed now was dry wood to keep it going. She didn't know if she'd be able to find any outside in the storm, though. She crept to the cave mouth and peered out.

She must have been crying longer than she thought, because the storm had stopped. There was that steamy freshness in the earth now, and a faint haze as the water was evaporating. Through a break in the trees, she could see that there was a little sunlight, but that it was now late afternoon.

What are you doing? asked a small voice. Melayne looked down, and saw it was one of Sashah's cubs.

Looking for dry wood, she told him. *I have to build a fire.*

What's a fire? the cub asked.

If I find enough wood, I'll show you, she promised.

Okay, he agreed. *We'll help.* He turned and raced back to his brothers and sisters. A moment later, the six of them hurried out of the cave, yapping and playing.

Melayne smiled at their enthusiasm, and set about hunting herself. She found some fallen sticks that had been sheltered by bracken and bushes from most of the rain, and that would probably burn. It took a while, but she managed to gather a handful that should do. Then she went back to the cave.

The cubs had done surprisingly well, having gathered between them as much as she had. One ran in with a stick in her jaws to add to the pile. Sarrow had been busy, too, and had kindling all together. He took one of the matches from his pocket and struck it on a stone. The cubs all gasped as the match flared to life, and then Sarrow added it to the kindling. Snapping and sparking, the moss caught fire. Melayne helped him to feed small twigs to the fire, and watched it grow.

The cubs were amazed, and Melayne had to warn them to stay back. *It can hurt you very badly*, she explained.

But you've tamed it, the first cub protested.

Not tamed, just controlled, Melayne informed him. *It can still fight back.*

Neat, the cub said with respect.

Little by little, Melayne and Sarrow built up the fire. She was glad of its warmth. The adult wolves stayed on the other side of the cave, but the cubs were quite entranced by the fire, dancing about it and daring each other to get just a little bit closer to show how brave they were. Melayne had to constantly shoo them away to prevent them from singeing their fur. Sarrow was a little contemptuous of them, but she thought they were delightful.

And then Tane was back, dragging a small deer in his mouth. Its neck was broken. Melayne felt a pang of pity for the poor creature. Tane seemed to understand.

It is the way of the world, he informed her gravely. *We must honor its memory, and thank it for the gift of life that it passes on to us.*

Melayne nodded, trying to accept this. She knew that animals killed one another to survive, even though that seemed harsh to her. She couldn't condemn the wolves for killing what they needed to live on. But she wasn't sure that she could eat any of the poor deer. Still, Sarrow was licking his lips and he was younger than her and needed food badly.

You must burn the flesh before you eat it, Tane said with a laugh. *Take a portion of the leg.* His sharp teeth tore at the skin. Despite her revulsion, Melayne accepted the portion she was given. Once Tane had passed on this piece, it seemed to be the signal for the rest of the wolves to close in.

Melayne kept her back to the sight, not wanting to witness it. She heard the tearing of the flesh, and the chewing, as well as the gnawing of bones. *It's their way*, she reminded herself. She kept occupied by sharpening a stick with her stolen knife and then using it to jam the leg portion over the fire to cook. She felt terribly unclean, and wished she could wash her hands. But to do so, she'd have had to leave the cave, past the grisly feast going on behind her. She simply couldn't do that. So she huddled by the fire as the meat cooked.

"It smells great," Sarrow said with enthusiasm. "My stomach's so empty, I could eat it all."

"You may have to," Melayne told him. "I don't think I could bring myself to touch it."

Sarrow laughed. "You can't be a vegetarian in here," he told her, unconsciously echoing Sashah's earlier words. "You have to keep your strength up, Melayne, so you can look after me. You *have* to eat some."

Melayne glanced at the roasting meat again. There *was* a kind of enticing smell coming from it, and her stomach growled loudly again.

"There!" Sarrow said triumphantly. "Even your body agrees with me. You *must* eat some of the meat."

He had a point, actually. She *did* need to keep her strength up. And the poor deer was dead anyway. Until she could get back to her proper food, this was all she had. And it would be a terrible insult if she didn't accept the kindness of the wolves.

"All right," she said with a deep sigh. "I don't have much choice, do I?"

"No," Sarrow agreed. "Is it done yet?"

"Maybe." Melayne had never cooked meat before, so she wasn't certain. She pulled it from the fire, and saw that the outside was almost charred. Using her knife, she cut off a large slice for Sarrow. He started to scarf it down instantly. She took a smaller piece for herself, and looked at it.

She couldn't help knowing that it had been alive only an hour earlier. It must have run for its life — and lost. Melayne felt sad for the poor thing. But . . . well, its suffering was over, and she really *needed* food. . . . "Forgive me," she whispered, and then gingerly bit some of the meat.

It tasted wonderful. She'd been half-afraid she'd choke on it, but instead it tasted heavenly. She ate the chunk hungrily, and her stomach called for more. Despite her feelings, she cut more for herself and Sarrow. She didn't eat a lot of the meat, but she ate what she could. Sarrow, being a growing boy, did indeed almost finish their share alone.

By then, the wolves seemed to have settled down. Most of the adults were already sleeping off their meal. The young cub from earlier ambled over, a bloody bone in its mouth.

You finished? he asked her, settling down to gnaw at the bone.

Yes, she replied. *I feel better now. But very tired.*

Adults are like that, the cub answered. *Always sleeping.* He looked up at her, and there was laughter in his golden eyes. *I like you, even though you're human.*

I like you, too, she told him honestly. *I'm Melayne. What's your name?*

Greyn, he informed her. Then he concentrated on his bone, and she took the hint. Sarrow had settled down to sleep, too.

Melayne put her wet clothing and Sarrow's together as close to the fire as she dared. That would help them to dry out by morning. Then she went back to Sashah, who was already asleep. Melayne cuddled against her for comfort and warmth, and closed her eyes.

What was she going to do in the morning? The pack had saved her life, but she couldn't stay with them forever. She had to decide what would be best. She had Sarrow to look out for now, and she was all the protection he had in the world.

There had to be something that she could do. There *had* to be. . . .

Chapter Three
The Journey Begins

Melayne awoke and stretched. Her arms connected with something warm and furry, and for a second she was completely confused. Then she remembered what had happened the previous day, and she opened her eyes to find them sore from all her weeping.

Come on! a young voice said impatiently. *You're as bad as the adults, sleeping the day away.*

Greyn was bouncing impatiently beside her, and Melayne had to smile. The cub seemed to have decided to adopt her as an older sister. He was obviously wanting to be out and moving, and Melayne saw that the other cubs had already vanished. So had one of the adults, almost certainly to watch out for the cubs.

Her clothes had dried beside the fire, which had died out in the night. Slipping them back on, Melayne followed Greyn out into the morning light. The sky was bright, and the clouds from the previous day had all vanished. The ground was still very muddy, but it didn't seem to bother Greyn, or any of the other cubs who were bouncing around like little maniacs. The six of them were mock stalking, pouncing, and fighting.

Come on! Greyn invited her. *It's fun!*

Melayne shook her head. *I'm not a wolf,* she replied. *I'll lose every time.*

Oh, right, Greyn agreed, somewhat sadly. *I forgot you're handicapped.*

That wasn't *quite* the way Melayne would have put it, but she could see why the cub might think that. Leaving them to play, Melayne walked to the nearby stream she could hear bubbling over rocks. It was slightly flooded with all the rainwater runoff, and crystal clear. She knelt to drink a couple of handfuls of the cold, delightful water, and then splashed her face.

Then she sat back, thinking. What was she to do now? She had to look after Sarrow — that was her first priority. What would be best for him? And what had happened to the Morstan raiders? Were they still nearby, or had they retreated with their loot and slaves? She needed to know. Glancing about, she saw a crow in a nearby tree.

Sir Crow, she called to him gently. Crows were very vain, and needed to be flattered in order to get anything from them. *Since you are such a wise bird, I wondered if you might be able to enlighten me.*

The crow blinked one eye and hopped closer. Obviously, it liked the way she talked. *Ah, human child. I would be happy to do my best to pass along some of my great knowledge. What is it you need to know?*

Thank you for your kindness, Melayne replied. *I wonder if you happened to see the human fighters yesterday who attacked the nearby village.*

Those! the crow replied scornfully. *Savages! They ruined the place, and then retreated to a floating nest. Thankfully, they are gone. Still,* he added thoughtfully, *they did leave lots of juicy little tidbits for us crows.* He swelled up in pride. *I myself gorged on eyeballs.*

Trying not to show her disgust, Melayne politely thanked the crow, who then shook himself and flew off. Reminded of the dead bodies, he had clearly decided to look for a spot of breakfast. Melayne didn't want to imagine what it might be.

Still, she at least had some information. Greenholt was totally destroyed, but the raiders had left. That meant that she and Sarrow should be safe enough for the moment. But what were they to do? They needed some way to live. To be honest, she didn't have a clue as to how to go about this. Although she'd worked on the farm all of her life, she didn't know whether she could use these skills anywhere else. Should she go back home and see what she could salvage? Try to start again? But the raiders had burned down their house, and undoubtedly either killed or stolen all of their livestock. All that was left for her there was to bury their parents.

There was a flash of gray and Tane was beside her, lapping cautiously at the stream. Then he eyed her thoughtfully. *What are you planning to do, man-child?*

I'm not sure, she replied. *I have to look after my brother, but there doesn't seem to be any way to do it here. And I have to return home to bury my parents now that the raiders have gone.*

Gone? the wolf asked. *They are not gone. They have simply moved on.*

Moved on? Melayne felt alarm. *But the crow said —*

You can't believe everything a crow says. Tane answered rather scornfully. *All he sees is the boat leaving, and thinks it's gone. While I was hunting last night, I saw them move it to another cove. They are simply preparing to attack another town. This area is not safe for you. You must leave.*

But . . . my parents! Melayne said wildly. *I must bury them!*

Tane bowed his head. *I understand that this would honor them. But it would also get you and your brother captured or killed. And there's no honor in that. You must leave.*

Sighing, Melayne realized that the wolf was right. If she were on her own, she might risk stealing back to bury Mother and Father. But she had to look after Sarrow, and she knew that her parents wouldn't want her to risk his life for that. She had to flee the immediate area. But where could she go?

Struck by an idea, she hurried back to the cave. Sarrow had woken up and dressed. Melayne smiled, and hurried to where she had placed her shoulder bag the previous day. Inside it were the books she had been using to teach Sarrow, including the geography text. She moved outside to study it.

"What are you doing?" Sarrow asked her, yawning and stretching.

"We have to leave," Melayne replied. "The raiders are still around. So I was trying to decide where we should go." She tapped the map of Stormgard. "Mother told me she has a married sister in Halden, which is here, in the north. I think we should go there. They're blood kin, so she should help us."

Sarrow nodded. "I'm sure she will," he agreed. Then his face fell. "But it looks like a long journey."

Melayne shrugged. "Stormgard's not that large," she said. "It couldn't be more than a couple of weeks."

"It sounds like it could be rough," Sarrow complained. "I don't like the idea of walking that far. Isn't there somewhere closer we could go?"

"We're Talents," Melayne reminded her brother. "If we tried to go anywhere else, we're likely to be spotted and taken. Family will take us in. I doubt the same would be true of strangers."

"I guess," he agreed reluctantly. "But what will we eat? Where will we stay?"

"I can ask the animals and birds for help," Melayne pointed out. "They'll be able to tell us what to do."

"I'm not sure I trust them," Sarrow said, frowning. "And what if something happens to you? I can't Communicate with animals. I'd be in real trouble then."

"Nothing will happen to me," Melayne assured

him, praying that she was telling the truth. "Sarrow, this is the best thing we can do. Now, go and get some water and wash your face. It's all dirty. I'll thank Tane, and we can be on our way. The sooner we're out of this area, the safer I'll feel." He ran off, and Melayne turned to see Tane watching her.

I think you have made a wise decision, he informed her. *But you will need to be careful as you travel. Humans have such dull senses. You cannot hear or smell or see very well. It is likely to get you into trouble.*

Judging by wolf standards, Melayne was sure he was telling the truth. *I know*, she agreed. *But we will do as best we can.*

Tane nodded. *I will escort you today*, he offered. *Farther from my pack I cannot go. But at least you will be safe for one day.*

She stroked his head affectionately. *Thank you, Tane. You have all been very kind toward us. I shall not forget you.*

The wolf chuckled. *And I doubt the cubs will forget you*, he commented. *I have to keep reminding them that not all humans are like you. Your brother, for example, is still afraid of us, and doesn't trust us.*

He's very young, Melayne replied. *And he cannot speak with you as I can. He's simply frightened.*

Sarrow returned at that moment, and looked bothered to see her standing with her hand on Tane's furry neck. "I'm hungry," he complained.

"I'm sure I can find us some food on the road," Melayne told him. "You'll just have to wait a while."

To be honest, she was hungry, too. And the meat she had eaten last night sat heavily on her conscience. There had been no choice, but she still wasn't happy about it. *Tane,* she added, *please thank Sashah and Greyn for me later. Now, we had better go. I think the farther we travel today, the safer we'll be.* To Sarrow, she added: "Come on."

They set off northward, through the woods. Sarrow tramped along beside her, lost in his thoughts. No doubt he was thinking about their losses, as Melayne was. Though she was cried out for the time being, there was still a tremendous sadness in her heart. She had loved her parents dearly, and for them to be killed that way really hurt. And not even being able to give them a decent burial was even worse. There was no sense of closure, merely of abandonment. It didn't assuage her guilt that she really had no choice in the matter.

Melayne knew she couldn't allow her thoughts to get in the way of being careful. Tane had slipped off into the trees, scouting the way ahead and only showing himself from time to time to assure her that they were on the right track and safe. While he was gone, she questioned a squirrel and found some berries that she and Sarrow could eat. Sarrow grumbled that it wasn't enough, but there wasn't much else that she could do.

At any other time, she might have enjoyed herself. The woods were thick and beautiful, and Tane had found them an old pathway leading pretty much in the right direction. The path enabled them to make speed, away from the ferns and bracken that had been slowing them down. Tall trees shaded their path, preventing the sun from appearing too hot or bright, and the day was warm. Melayne had always loved walking in the woods. The sights and smells always excited her, and the chance to chatter with the animals had helped her to learn so much. But today she was too sad to be able to enjoy the walk. It was simply a chore that had to be done, and she spoke only sparsely to the animals they encountered.

She spoke just as little to Sarrow. He was brooding, undoubtedly hurting as well. But Melayne didn't know how to console him, because she couldn't console herself. Their lives had been savagely ripped apart, and there was no easy fix. She hoped that this wouldn't emotionally scar him, but how did one try to heal such wounds?

Finally, whenever she looked at Tane, Melayne's emotions were mixed. She was grateful to the gray wolf and his pack for their kindness, but he also served to remind her of how helpless she was. Without his aid, she and Sarrow would have been captured or killed. For all of her Talent and learning, she was so helpless. She didn't know how to defend herself, how to fight, or even how to hunt her own food. There had never been any reason to learn any of these things on the farm. Taking care of the animals and looking after the crops had been all that she'd known. And then all the learning she'd done from books. She knew a lot of useless information, Melayne realized, and very little of any practical use.

She'd somehow always expected to remain on the farm, and had never prepared for any other kind of life. True, she'd always hoped that one day she would meet a nice boy and fall madly and passionately in love. But that had always been a *someday* kind of thing, nothing that she'd ever planned. Fantasized about, certainly, but never actively sought. She'd always been too worried about the hypothetical boy's reaction if he discovered that she was an undeclared Talent. While she'd dreamed that he wouldn't care — or, even better, that he would be a hidden Talent of some kind himself! — she had always really known that it would be more likely that he'd turn her in rather than face problems with the king's Seekers.

So, here she was, on the road north, with her younger brother to care for and absolutely no training for the life she was about to lead. She tried to sound confident to Sarrow, but she couldn't lie to herself. They were not going to have an easy time of it.

By midmorning, Melayne's stomach was complaining almost as loudly as Sarrow. She couldn't blame her brother, but his constant demand for food was irritating her slightly. The berries and fruits she scavenged weren't what he wanted, of course. And it was late in the season, so there wasn't even a lot to be had when she could find any.

Thankfully, Tane seemed to have picked up on Sarrow's distress. He showed up with a bloody rabbit dangling from his jaws. *It's for the two of you*, he said. *I've already eaten.*

Can we risk a fire? Melayne asked the wolf. *Hungry as Sarrow is, I don't think even he will want his meat raw.*

A small one, Tane suggested. *I'll patrol back down the path while you cook and eat. Be very careful.*

Melayne was. She made the fire as small as possible, while Sarrow skinned and prepared the rabbit. He claimed it wasn't too different from preparing fish to be cooked, and Melayne hoped he knew what he was doing. She'd found a few tubers that she wrapped in wet leaves and set to cooking with the rabbit. Even though she knew she'd have to give in again and eat some meat, she was going to do so as sparingly as possible.

They ate in silence, Sarrow attacking the rabbit ravenously while Melayne nibbled at it and the tubers. When they were full, she wrapped the leftovers in leaves and slipped them into her bag. She didn't want to think about the mess the leftovers would cause, but it was better than having Tane kill them something later. The less animals lost their lives, the better she liked it.

Tane reappeared just as they were finishing. Either he had been watching them, or else he had a really good instinct for timing. Either way, he was impatient to be on the move again, even though he'd detected no signs of pursuit. Melayne carefully put the fire out and scattered the ashes, hoping that it might at least disguise their trail a little. It was probably useless against skilled raiders, but it made her feel a little more like she was doing something positive. Then they set off again.

Melayne had no idea how much ground they had covered by the time night started to fall, but her legs were insisting that it was way too far. Tane had managed to find them a sheltered spot close to water where they could camp.

There are no signs of any dangerous animals, he informed Melayne. *Including men, of course. You should be safe here for the evening. Keep going north tomorrow. The woods will end by tomorrow night, and you'll be on the edge of human lands. I don't know what comes after that. I'm sorry I can't help you further.*

You've done much more than I could ever have asked, she replied with affection, stroking his muzzle. *Thank you, Tane. You saved our lives.*

Then take care of them, human cub, he replied, licking her hand. *The forest gods go with you. If you can, come back some day, and we shall talk of all of your adventures.* Then, with a short bark, he vanished into the gloom.

"I'm glad he's gone," Sarrow said. "He gave me the creeps."

Melayne felt stung by this remark. "He saved our lives and helped us to escape," she chided her brother. "Don't be so ungracious."

"He didn't like me," Sarrow answered sullenly. "He only helped *me* because I was with *you.*"

"Perhaps," Melayne conceded. "But he *did* help you, nevertheless, and you should show some gratitude. Especially if you want some more of the rabbit he caught for us earlier."

"Oh, all right," Sarrow agreed. "I'm really hungry again."

"It's your age," Melayne informed him with a slight smile. "You're a growing boy, and you need a lot of food." She handed him the leftovers, contenting herself with munching on the tubers.

Night came as they ate. Because they were in a hollow, the sky overhead was clear. All signs of the storm had vanished, and the stars were sprinkled across the ebony sky, sparkling and cheerful like old friends. Melayne looked up, enjoying the view, and tried to remember the various constellations. Appropriately enough, the Wolf was just starting across the cleared sky.

Suddenly, something flew out of the trees, slamming into Melayne and knocking her to the ground. Panicking, she started to struggle until a familiar voice said: *Gotcha!*

Greyn! she exclaimed, sitting up and staring at the wolf cub now grinning back at her. *What are you doing here?*

Stalking you, he replied, rather self-satisfied. *You didn't hear me coming, did you?*

No, she said honestly. *But why did you do it? You shouldn't be here! Your father's already gone back.*

I know, Greyn agreed, licking at his paws. *I figured you'd need someone to take care of you, so I decided to come along. You're the most fun thing that's ever happened to me.*

"What's *he* doing here?" Sarrow demanded, tired

of being left out of the conversation. "Can't you tell him to get lost?"

"He seems to think we need his help," Melayne answered. "And I'm trying to get him to go home." She turned her attention back to Greyn. *You're just a cub. You should go home.*

A wolf cub, Greyn said smugly. *I'm old enough to look after myself. And you, too. Wait and see.*

Greyn, she insisted. *You have to go home. If I have to, I'll take you home myself.*

Back toward the raiders? the cub asked perceptively. *That would be a very foolish thing. Anyway, your cub brother wouldn't allow it.*

It's not his decision, Melayne said firmly. But Greyn did have a point. Going back would endanger Sarrow, and she didn't want to do that. On the other hand, she didn't want to have to look after Greyn as well. . . . What was she to do? Melayne wasn't used to having to make her own decisions, and this was taxing her too much. Since the decision affected Sarrow as well, she explained the problem to him.

"The wolf's right," Sarrow said immediately. "It's too dangerous to go back." He scowled at the cub. "If he won't get lost, then I suppose he'll *have* to come with us. But I don't like it."

"Nor do I," admitted Melayne. But she suspected that it was very different aspects of the situation that each of them disliked. Sarrow had never been an animal person, and had absolutely no interest in her friends. He was certainly none too keen on sharing his journey with a cub. But, Melayne realized, they really didn't have much choice. She could hardly force Greyn to go away. All he'd do was to walk out of sight and follow them anyway. He was a very determined young wolf.

I suppose you had better stay, she told Greyn.

He licked her nose. *Come on,* he said, his golden eyes staring into hers. *Aren't you glad to see me just a little bit?*

Yes, she admitted grudgingly. *But I still think you shouldn't be here.*

I know I should be, Greyn replied. *Back soon. Got to get food.* He vanished into the night, off hunting.

Melayne sighed. Well, now she had another child to look out for. At least, she realized, Greyn could probably fend for himself as far as food went. Still, it was one more responsibility that she really didn't need. She settled down to sleep, wondering what further problems the morning would bring.

Chapter Four
Flight

The next few days were surprisingly better. Melayne wasn't actually enjoying herself, but at least she wasn't quite as miserable. She seemed to have cried as much as she could for the moment, and the memory of her parents was now a constant, dull hurt rather than a sharp, excruciating pain. Her legs were strengthening as they walked, and she wasn't as tired when they were forced to stop in the evening. The weather stayed clear, though there was a slight nip in the air to show that summer was definitely gone and winter was just over the horizon.

Greyn had proven to be correct, too. He was absolutely no trouble to them, able to catch his own food, and often extra for the two humans, too. He seemed to be full of boundless energy and good humor, and constantly stalked and attacked Melayne. She was getting more alert to him now, and he wasn't catching her by surprise quite as often as before. Oddly enough, this seemed to please him.

I'll make a wolf of you yet, he promised, grinning, tongue out. Then he dashed off again into the woods.

He never played with Sarrow. He and her brother tolerated one another, but it was clear that there was no affection between them. Each put up with the other only because Melayne wanted it to be so. Melayne knew there was no helping it, but she wished it could be different. She really liked Greyn, and it was obvious that the young wolf was devoted to her for some reason of his own. Maybe simply because she could talk to him, and obviously enjoyed his company. Plus, of course, she could scratch him where he couldn't quite scratch himself. This always left him blissful.

Sarrow was complaining less, but, Melayne suspected, this was more because he knew there wasn't any point to it than because he had nothing to complain about. He was only eight years old, and she sometimes forgot this when he acted more maturely. It had to be a lot harder for him that it was for her.

They left the woods on the second day, and skirted a human town. Melayne thought it was the one marked Felham on her map, which meant they were making very slow progress. At this rate, it would take them weeks to get to Halden. Still, now that they were out of the woods there were trails they could follow, and the occasional road. This sped them up a little, but there was a downside to it as well. Whenever there were signs of other people on the road, the three of them would have to seek out a place to hide until the other travelers had passed. Sarrow thought this was kind of silly, but Melayne wasn't willing to take any chances. Maybe the other folk wouldn't be too interested in her and Sarrow, but she couldn't be certain of this. It was best simply to avoid them and have done with it.

Still, her heart ached as she watched from hiding as people passed by. She still wished that she could meet other people and have fun, or simply a conversation. She'd been alone with Sarrow for long enough, and it would be lovely to have a few fresh voices to talk to. But she didn't dare. Would she ever be able to risk a conversation?

And so they traveled on, covering the ground. Melayne didn't really know how far they had gone because she wasn't sure that all of the towns and villages that they passed were actually on her map. The only way to be certain would be to go up to someone and ask them, and they couldn't do this.

"Then how will we know when we reach Halden?" Sarrow asked her rather pointedly. "If we don't ask someone where we are, then we could walk right past where we're going and not know it. We might *already* have gone past it."

"I really don't think so," Melayne replied. But she was worried. Sarrow did have a point, even if it was a dangerous one. They *had* to know where they were. They had just passed a small village a few miles back, and Sarrow had started complaining again.

"I want some *real* food," he said. "Not half-burnt

meat all of the time. I want some fresh, hot bread and a bowl of stew. Something hot to drink. A bed to sleep in again, not a pile of leaves. I *hate* this."

"It's not exactly my idea of fun, either," Melayne snapped. "Don't you think I'd love the same things? And a hot bath? Fresh clothes to wear? But there's no point in wishing for what we can't have. We're doing what we have to do, that's all."

"I think we have to take *some* chances," Sarrow repeated sullenly. "We have to find out where we are."

Melayne gave an exasperated sigh. "I *know* what you think. But we can't just walk up to the next village and start asking questions. It'll get us into trouble, and noticed. And maybe they'll spot us for Talents."

"Maybe they *won't*," Sarrow countered. "We don't know that there's any way for people to tell Talents just by looking at them. We never had a chance to ask about it, remember?"

"I know," Melayne agreed. "It's just that —" She broke off as they reached the brow of a hill. The sight down below them looked almost familiar. There was a small house, with a larger barn, and several acres of fields. They had been freshly harvested, and there were people working out in the farther reaches of the farm. It looked so much like their own home in its way that it made Melayne's heart ache.

And it gave her an idea.

"Maybe we could ask there," she said slowly. "It's far out of town. There's probably just a farmwife in the house, and maybe a girl or two. Even if they spot us for Talents, I'm sure the two of us could outrun any problems with ease."

Sarrow nodded eagerly. "And maybe they'll spare us some food," he said hopefully.

"It's possible," she agreed, though she was not so certain about this. Still, it did seem to be the least risky method of finding out where they were and what might be happening. Maybe the farmer had even heard news about the raiders by now.

Greyn padded up to them. *I'd better take off for now*, he said. *I don't think I'd be very welcome there. On the other hand, maybe they have chickens.... I'd love a nice, juicy, plump chicken for supper.*

Don't go stealing from them! Melayne begged. *They'll never help us if you do that.*

Spoilsport, Greyn complained. Then, with a sigh, he added, *All right, I'll be good. See you later.* He disappeared again.

Melayne led the way down to the farmhouse, feeling less and less sure of herself every step of the way. Was this *really* a good idea? How would the farmwife react to the sudden appearance of a couple of skinny and slightly dirty children? Would she be able to tell them for Talents? Every step forward she took made her want to call the whole thing off and flee.

"Momma!" a young girl's voice called from the yard. "There's people coming!"

It was too late to retreat now. Melayne managed to settle what she hoped would pass as a friendly smile on her face. The house was larger than their own had been, which suggested a larger family. There was also the delightful scent of fresh baking wafting from where the kitchen had to be.

A large, stout woman with graying hair popped out of the closest door, wiping her hands on an apron. She stared at Melayne and Sarrow — first in suspicion, and then in puzzlement.

"Hello, ma'am," Melayne said politely. "My brother and I were wondering if you might be able to help us with a few directions. We're not quite sure where we are, you see."

The woman blinked, her eyes opening wide. "Mercy!" she exclaimed. "I don't believe I've seen either of you before. Are you from around these parts?"

Melayne decided that the best thing to do would be to tell as much of the truth as she dared. "No, ma'am," she admitted. "We're from Greenholt."

"Greenholt?" The woman shook her head. "And where might that be?"

"By the coast," Melayne explained, gesturing back the way they had come. "Several days' walk."

"Several days?" The farmwife peered closer at them. "You've been walking for several days? Whatever did you eat?"

"Whatever we found," Sarrow said, putting on a pathetic pity-poor-me act that had the woman clucking and muttering curses under her breath.

"And you a growing lad, too!" she exclaimed. "Mercy, that's not the right thing to do!" She put an ample arm around his shoulder. "You two come along with me right now. I won't hear another word out of either of you until I've put some good food into you!"

And she meant it, too. She shushed them both to silence, hurrying them into the kitchen. The delightful scent of cooking made Melayne's stomach rumble. There was a young girl — perhaps a year or two older than Sarrow — looking at them with obvious curiosity.

"Ketty!" the woman snapped. "Get me two cups of cider, straight away!" To Sarrow and Melayne she said, "Sit, sit here." She cleared away space at the edge of the table where she had been preparing vegetables. Then she hurried to a pot over the fire and drew two bowls of a thick soup, which she brought them with chunks of warm bread. The girl, Ketty, came over with two mugs of cider.

Melayne was relieved to discover that the soup was a thick vegetable broth, and she started in on it with a will. Sarrow ate as if he had grown two extra stomachs. The farmwife filled his bowl for him a second time, a fond smile on her face. Finally, though, she decided that her guests were quite full enough.

"Now then, young lady," she said, settling into a chair opposite them. "Perhaps you can explain yourselves." Ketty hung around, obviously just as intrigued as her mother.

"Raiders," Melayne answered. "They attacked our village several days ago. They killed the adults, and captured all of the children as slaves. My brother, Sarrow, and I managed to escape. Our parents were killed."

"Raiders?" The woman was shocked. "Well, that

probably explains the King's Men we've been seeing these past few days riding south. On their way to put a stop to such horrors once and for all. I'm sorry for the both of you, losing your kin and all that. But whatever are you doing on the road like this?"

"We have an aunt who lives in Halden," Melayne answered. "We're going there to see if she'll take us in."

"Halden?" Again the woman seemed puzzled by the name. "Where is that?"

Taking the book from her bag, Melayne opened it to the map. "It's here, in the north," she explained, pointing.

"You can read?" asked the woman, interested. "Never learned it myself. There isn't much need for it when you work the land. But I can see that it does have its uses."

"Perhaps you can tell us the name of the village we just passed?" Melayne suggested. "If it's on our map, then I'll have some idea how far we have to go."

The farmwife looked puzzled. "Why didn't you just stop in and ask as you were passing?" she asked. "There are even a few folks there who can read, and they'd have been more use to you than I can be."

Uh-oh . . . Melayne cringed slightly. "We . . . didn't want to be any trouble," she lied, trying to look as pathetic as Sarrow.

"Trouble? After what you've been through, you poor darlings?" The farmwife shook her head. "Anyone would have been glad to help you." Then, smiling, she added, "It's called Brach. Is that on your map?"

Melayne studied it for a moment before she found it. It was there, a bit off to the west, and not as north as she'd been hoping. "Yes," she said. "It looks like we've still got a long way to go, though." She smiled at the woman, relieved that she seemed to have accepted her excuses. "Thank you so much for the food, ma'am. It was really wonderful. But we'd better be moving again. We've a lot of ground to cover."

"You could stay here with us for a few days," the woman suggested in a kindly voice. "It's the end of the harvest, and my husband could probably use a couple extra pairs of hands."

Melayne was touched by the offer, especially since she was sure that they really didn't need any more helpers. The farmwife was simply trying to be kind to them. "Thank you," she said. "But I really would feel better to be on the way again. We ought to get to our aunt's house as soon as we can."

"I understand." The woman smiled again. "Then let me give you a little food to take with you, you poor things." She scurried about the kitchen, putting things together.

Ketty came over to stare in awe at Melayne. "You really going to head all the way north?" she asked. When Melayne nodded, she asked, "Aren't you scared at all?"

"We can look out for ourselves," Sarrow said, slightly scornfully. "We escaped the raiders and we've made it this far."

"Ketty, don't you bother them," her mother said.

She had a bundle of things wrapped up in an old cloth, which she handed to Melayne. "Here you go, love. It's not a lot, but it should last you for a few days. And don't you worry about the road north. Like I said, the King's Men have been coming and going for the past few days. They'll make sure it's safe for you to travel. They might even be able to give you a ride."

The last thing Melayne wanted was to run into the King's Men, but she couldn't let the woman know that. "Thank you so much," she said, genuinely grateful. "You've been wonderfully kind."

"It's the least I could do," the farmwife said, smiling happily. "Now, both of you take good care. May the good God watch over you as you journey."

"Thank you," Melayne said again. To the young girl, she added, "Bye, Ketty. Thanks for the cider."

Sarrow was clearly reluctant to leave. He'd been enjoying the attention. Still, he understood that they couldn't stay. Waving to the woman and her daughter, Melayne and Sarrow headed back to the main pathway.

"King's Men riding," she murmured. "Sarrow, that could mean a lot of trouble for us. The Seekers might be among them, and *they'll* know what we are for sure."

"But *she* didn't," Sarrow pointed out. "She didn't know we were Talents. So we don't have to hide from everyone we pass, after all. However they spot Talents, it can't be obvious."

"She didn't know how to read, either," Melayne

replied. "She's been stuck on a farm all her life, I expect, and doesn't know much outside of that. Other people might be better educated than she is."

Sarrow scowled. "You're always looking for trouble," he complained.

"No," she answered. "I'm trying to *avoid* trouble. I think we're still better off staying out of the way of anyone on the road."

"Well, we did all right out of this," Sarrow pointed out. "Hot soup, and cider, and some more food for the next few days. We should try finding another farm after that. It's nice to eat properly again."

Humans never eat properly, Greyn said, slipping back to join them now that they were out of sight of the farm. *You do horrible things to good food, instead of eating it raw and bloody, as it should be.* There was a little blood still on his muzzle, and Melayne realized he'd been taking a little snack, too. She just hoped it wasn't one of the chickens he'd been aching for. It was probably better not to ask.

And, she had to admit, it had gone a lot better than she'd worried it might. Maybe Sarrow was right, and she was being too cautious. Then again, it was better to be unnecessarily careful than to be caught. And simply because they'd lucked out once didn't mean it would happen a second time.

"From what that nice woman said," Sarrow added, as they walked along, "these King's Men aren't something to be afraid of. They've been heading south to stop the raiders."

"They're something *normal* people don't have to be afraid of," Melayne corrected him. "We're *Talents*."

"But how do we *know* they'd do anything to us?" Sarrow asked her.

Melayne looked at her brother in shock. "Because Mother and Father told us so!"

He gave her an odd look. "And how do we know they were right?" he asked. "That farmwife didn't say anything about Talents at all. Maybe they just don't care."

Melayne didn't know what had come over him. "Sarrow, how could you say that? Our parents would never have lied to us! They kept us hidden because they were afraid of what would happen to us. What *did* happen to Kander, remember?"

"We only have their word about that," Sarrow said sullenly. "And maybe they didn't tell us the truth. Maybe they were just hiding us away because they didn't like other people or something."

"Sarrow! You're talking about *our parents*!" Melayne was stunned. "They would *never* do something like that!"

People will do all sorts of odd things, Greyn said. *Wolves wouldn't, of course.* Melayne ignored him.

"Look," Sarrow said, "you're the one who always says we only learn by asking questions. So I'm asking one. Okay, our parents told us that the King's Seekers will take away all Talents. But who *else* says that? Do any of your books say that?"

Melayne was caught off guard by that question. "No," she admitted. "But we have so very few books, mostly textbooks Mother thought we could best use."

"In other words, books *she* picked out," Sarrow pointed out. "And even they don't back up what she told us. Melayne, I'm not saying that our parents lied to us. Just that we don't *know* if what they said about Talents is true."

"Sarrow, I'm shocked that you could even *suggest* such a thing," Melayne told him firmly. "I don't want to talk to you while you're in such a horrible mood."

"Fine," he snapped. "Don't talk, then. And don't think for yourself, either." Sullenly, he stomped on ahead.

Melayne was very disturbed by his line of thinking. He couldn't possibly be right. Mother and Father would never have lied to them. She could never think of a time when either of them ever had. How could Sarrow distrust them so badly?

And then she realized. He must be missing them, and must feel that they had somehow let him down. Sometimes young children blamed parents for irrational things when they felt betrayed or hurt by them. Sarrow must be feeling lost and helpless without them, and he was just questioning their word because of this. He didn't *really* think they'd been lying. How could he?

Should she try to comfort him, or just give him time to calm down a bit? She decided that it wouldn't hurt him to be on his own for a while. Let him sulk; maybe he'd realize how foolish he was being. He'd certainly want to talk as soon as he became hungry again.

They traveled on for most of the afternoon in silence. The sun was getting low on the horizon and Melayne was thinking of finding somewhere to spend the night. Then she saw a cloud of dust on the road ahead of them.

"Riders!" she called out to Sarrow, who was about twenty feet ahead of her. "We'd better get off the road."

"Why?" he called back, the hurt and irritation still in his voice. "We don't have anything to be afraid of."

"You only *think* that," she snapped, hurrying to catch up with him. "We can't take a chance on it."

He whirled on her. "I'm *sick* of all this walking, and all this horrible food," he exploded. "I want to stay in a house again and be comfortable. I want somebody like that farmwife to look after me. I don't want to be on the road all day, sleep in the filth at night like an animal, and do what *you* want me to do." He folded his arms. "You go and hide in the dirt if you want. *I'm* not doing it anymore."

Melayne didn't know what to do with him. She saw that the dust was getting nearer. They had to hide, now! "Sarrow, listen to me!"

"No!" His face was set and stubborn.

Should she drag him into hiding? She didn't know what was best. But she was certain that he was wrong: They *did* have to hide. The problem was that she'd never lifted a hand against her brother in her life, and she didn't want to start now. All that they had left was each other.

Greyn jumped in, teeth bared at Sarrow. *Endan-*

ger yourself if you like, he growled, even though Sarrow couldn't hear his words. *But you will not endanger Melayne while I live. Hide now, or I'll drag you into hiding!*

Melayne was going to translate for Sarrow, but she could see from the pale, shocked expression on her brother's face that he had understood without the need for words. "Call it off!" he yelped. "It's going to bite me!"

Not if you behave, Greyn snarled.

"He just wants you to listen to me and hide," Melayne said. "Please, Sarrow, just do it."

Sarrow didn't really have any choice. He could see that Greyn wasn't bluffing. Pale and trembling, he followed Melayne off the road and into a stand of trees. Melayne thought he was scared. Then he spoke and she realized he was shaking with anger.

"I *hate* that creature!" Sarrow yelled. "And he hates me! Get rid of him, Melayne!"

"He's just protecting us," Melayne assured her brother. "He doesn't hate you."

Guess again, Greyn told her, flopping down beside her, eyes fixed on the road.

She could hear the riders approaching. Peering through the branches, she watched the road with interest. A moment later, they rounded a bend and came flashing toward the hidden watchers.

There were eight riders. Seven were on horses — warhorses, by the look of things. They were large animals, very muscular. The men were in leather armor, and all had spears and long-handled axes strapped to their mounts. Each man had a sword, too, clanking at his hip. They didn't pause, but were riding hard, obviously King's Men on their way to help fight the raiders.

It was the eighth rider that held Melayne spellbound. Clearly, he wasn't a knight — and the creature he was riding was *not* a horse.

The eighth man carried no weapons, and he wore a long, embroidered cloak that whipped in the wind behind him. His blond hair was long and flowing free. He looked very regal, as if used to giving commands. Melayne figured that he had to be a minor noble at the very least. And the animal he rode . . .

It was like a huge lizard, with mottled, leathery green and brown skin. Its neck and tail were both long and snakelike, its legs splayed and odd-looking. Despite a strange gait, the creature was keeping up with the horses without showing any signs of strain.

Melayne held her breath as the riders went over the edge of the hill, down toward the farm the travelers had so recently left. The sound of hooves and lizard feet died away, and Melayne slowly came back to reality.

"What *was* that thing?" Sarrow asked in a small voice. "I've never seen anything like it."

"Nor have I," Melayne admitted. "At least, never alive. I've seen a drawing of one, once, in one of Mother's books. It's a firedrake."

"A firedrake? What's that? I never heard of one." Sarrow seemed to have forgotten that he had sworn he wouldn't talk to her.

"A firedrake is a relative of dragons," she explained, remembering what she had read. "Only nonmagical and less nasty. They can be tamed to do work, but they're quite rare. They only have one baby every four or five years, so there never will be very many of them."

"But dragons don't really exist," Sarrow protested. "They're just a story, aren't they? That's what Father always told me when we went fishing. There never were dragons, people just made them up."

"I don't know," Melayne answered. "If they ever did exist, they died out a long time ago." She remembered her favorite book of the knight errant and mentioned it to Sarrow. "They were horrible, vicious creatures that hated people and ate them. The King's Men went out, along with knights, and killed them all. The men were very brave, and even though many of them died, they made certain that all of the dragons were killed off so that they couldn't hurt anyone ever again."

Sarrow shrugged. "It's just a children's story," he said. "I don't think it could really have happened."

And what does he know? scoffed Greyn. *He's only a pup — and a human pup at that. Thinking he knows all about how the world works! Hah!*

Melayne turned to the cub. *Do you know anything about dragons?* she asked him eagerly.

Not me, he answered. *I never met any, and my parents never talked about them. Maybe they never did exist. But if your brother thinks that, then I'm going to believe that they did. I don't want to share any of his opinions.*

Oh, well. Melayne had been hoping that the

69

wolves might have known something about dragons. Still, what Greyn said made sense: Why talk about something you were never likely to meet anyway? All the dragons were dead — either because they had been killed off, or because they never existed in the first place. All that did exist were the harmless and useful relatives of dragons, like the firedrakes. Despite the "fire" part of their names, they couldn't breath fire. They were actually just very large and very strong lizards, Melayne believed. Of course, she didn't know for sure. She'd only read it in a book.

Now that they were safe again, they moved back to the road. The sun had almost set by now, so they needed somewhere to stay the night. Melayne knew Sarrow was getting fed up with sleeping on the ground, but she had no idea what else they could do. Then, on the hillside, she spotted the broken shell of an old house.

"We can spend the night there," she suggested. "It's a bit open, but it should be better than sleeping on leaves again."

"Then I'm all for it," Sarrow agreed, starting off up the hillside. "Maybe there will be some abandoned furniture or something."

"Who knows?" Melayne was glad that her brother seemed to have cheered up again. Greyn padded along beside her, sniffing like crazy for any signs of trouble. Obviously there were none, because he didn't speak a word.

The house must have been abandoned for a very long time. The walls had partially collapsed, and all of the roof was gone. Sarrow was obviously disappointed that there was no furniture, but Melayne wasn't too bothered. At least it was somewhere to spend the night, and it felt good to have walls around her again, even if they weren't in very good repair.

She and Sarrow shared some of the food the farmwife had given them, while Greyn turned his nose up in disgust at it and went hunting for fresh meat. Melayne wondered how Sarrow was feeling. At least he seemed to have forgotten his earlier mood, and was willing to talk to her again.

"How much longer is this journey going to take us?" he asked.

"I don't know," she admitted. "We're traveling more slowly than I'd hoped. Maybe a couple more weeks."

"I don't think I can take it," Sarrow confessed. "I really hate this. It's so dirty and uncomfortable." He tapped the piece of bread he was eating. "I like good food, and being able to lay in a bed. I *hate* having to rough it like this."

"It won't be much longer," she promised him. "As soon as we reach our aunt's house, things will be better."

"How do you know that?" he demanded. "Just because she's our aunt, do you think she'll be glad to see us? She never came to visit. She probably doesn't care about us at all!"

This had been Melayne's own worst fear, but she'd managed to keep it hidden from Sarrow — and, almost, from herself. *Would* their aunt take them in and look after them? Simply because she was kin didn't mean she'd be nice and considerate. Or that she'd even want them. But Melayne couldn't let Sarrow think along those paths. "She *has* to take us in," Melayne insisted. "The only reason she never visited was because it was so far."

"But what if she doesn't?" Sarrow insisted. "What if she's got ten kids of her own and doesn't need any more?"

Melayne slumped down, totally demoralized. "I don't *know*!" she snapped. "I don't know! I'm just doing the best I can! I didn't ask for this to happen — it just did. All I can do is what I think is best! I don't need constant criticism from you every step of the way!"

"It's just wishful thinking!" Sarrow accused. "We're only going to our aunt's because *you* think it's best. Well, you've never been away from the farm before, either. So what do *you* know?"

"Sarrow!" she cried, hurt and confused. "We mustn't quarrel! We're all we both have now. Each other."

"No," he said, rather spitefully. "You've got that dumb wolf, too. All I've got is you, and I'm not sure you're really smart enough to look after me."

That really cut her to the bone. Melayne was on the verge of tears. "Sarrow, you *know* I'm trying my best to look out for you."

"Yes," he agreed. "But is your best good enough?"

She didn't know what to reply, because she honestly didn't know the answer. *Was* her best good enough? She was just a simple girl, with no real skills except for her Talent. And here she was, out in a world she didn't know, with her younger brother to look after. She was doing the best she could. What more could he ask of her? He was just being selfish and mean and nasty, and trying to hurt her for some reason. Well, he was tired and discouraged, and so young. He was just missing all of the comforts he had grown up with. She couldn't really blame him.

"Sarrow," she said gently, "I'm going to take care of you. I promise."

"I'm not sure I want you to," he replied. "Maybe there are other people who could do it better."

Greyn materialized through a broken window and growled low in his throat. Sarrow glared from the wolf to his sister, and shook his head.

"I don't think I want you looking after me anymore," he said. "I want to be somewhere where I can eat properly, and have a real bed, and meet people. I don't want to be running and hiding all of the time."

"That's good," a fresh voice said from the doorway. "Because that's what I had in mind for you both."

Shocked, Melayne whirled around. Someone had crept up on them. She stiffened in shock as she saw who it was.

The richly embroidered cloak swirled slightly as the blond man stepped into the broken room. His eyes moved from her to Sarrow to Greyn. "Talents," he murmured. "I knew I smelled Talents. It's unmistakable."

Melayne was on the verge of hysteria. "Talents?" she gasped. "What makes you think we're Talents?"

The man snorted, good-humoredly. "Aside from the fact you've got a pet wolf?" he asked, sarcastically. "I know because it's my job to know. I'm a King's Seeker, child."

A Seeker . . .

Melayne's heart was thundering. She could see that Greyn was getting his hackles up, ready to throw himself at the intruder. *No!* she yelled at him. She wasn't entirely sure why she did, but she was absolutely convinced that attacking the Seeker would be a very bad move.

"A sensible decision, my dear," the blond man said approvingly. Seeing her shocked look, he added, "Oh, no, I can't read your mind. But I can tell when a wolf wants to bite me." He laughed. "I'm sure he's a friend of yours, and I wouldn't want to upset you by having to kill him." He didn't appear to be armed, but Melayne had no doubt that he had some way of protecting himself if he needed to.

"What are you going to do with us?" she demanded, trying to sound braver than she felt.

"What should have been done with you a long time ago," the Seeker replied. "Take you to the Royal House, where you can be with others like you, and can be trained." He smiled. "Trust me, you'll like it. You've been hiding and running for a long time, haven't you? I can't imagine why you've been doing it, but it's all going to be unnecessary now."

Melayne was confused by what he was saying. It

wasn't what she had expected. "You're taking us away to die," she said flatly.

"Die?" He laughed. "My dear, somebody *has* been filling your head with nonsense! I'm going to take you to *live*! You're *much* too valuable to kill."

Sarrow smiled slightly. "What do you mean?" he asked. Melayne noticed that he'd moved forward slightly.

The Seeker smiled again. "You're a Talent, I can tell. Talents are very special people, and need to be trained and looked after. We're fighting a long war, and only people like the two of you can help Stormgard to survive."

Something clicked in Melayne's mind. "*You're* a Talent, too!" she exclaimed. "And your Talent is spotting other Talents!"

The Seeker nodded approvingly. "Quite right, my dear. I knew you were a bright one. That's exactly it — I find other Talents, so they can be trained."

"And we'll be treated well?" Sarrow asked wistfully.

"Very well," the Seeker promised. "You're very valuable. All Talents are. What's your Talent?"

"I don't know," Sarrow admitted. "I think I'm too young for it to have started yet."

"That's possible," the Seeker admitted. "Well, no hurry. I'm sure it will be a fine ability." He turned to look at Melayne. "Your pretty sister obviously has the Talent of Communication, otherwise that wolf wouldn't be here."

Melayne blushed when he called her *pretty*. Was

it possible that she was pretty? She didn't really know, never having had other people to relate to.

"Food?" Sarrow asked.

"Real food," the Seeker promised. "And a bed. A place to stay and train." He smiled. "Friends."

"It doesn't sound so bad," Sarrow admitted. He looked at Melayne. "Maybe we should go."

"I'm not so sure," Melayne answered, though she was torn herself. This man seemed friendly enough, not the horrible person that her parents had always made Seekers out to be. And he was a Talent, too. Why would he be working for the king if the king hated Talents? Still, all they had to go on was his promise. And what did that mean? He could be lying.

I don't trust him, Greyn said firmly.

I'm not sure I do, Melayne admitted. *But can we get away?*

Greyn's nostrils flared. *No. I was stupid and inattentive. The soldiers are here as well, outside. They will stop us all if we try to escape.*

The soldiers . . . Melayne felt a pain in her stomach. It really didn't matter what she wanted now. There was no way to escape from so many people. "We don't have any choice, do we?" she asked bitterly.

"No," the Seeker admitted cheerfully. "But don't make it sound like a prison sentence. Trust me, you're going to find that this is very different from whatever you've been led to expect."

Melayne wasn't so sure of that. She looked at

Greyn. "Will you let my wolf go, at least?" she asked. "He shouldn't be locked up."

I'm staying to look after you! Greyn snapped.

"Locked up?" The Seeker spread his hands. "Nobody's being locked up! Trust me, once you've been in the King's House for a few weeks, you won't ever want to leave. And if that wolf is your friend, then you should bring him along. We don't want to separate friends. You must *really* think we're cruel! He'll be well looked-after, I promise you."

He was doing a lot of promising, Melayne reflected. And there was no reason for her to believe a single word of it. On the other hand, there wasn't really a lot of reason for her to distrust it yet, either.

Maybe her parents *had* been wrong. This Seeker didn't seem like such a bad person. Maybe the King's House wasn't so bad, either. Still, since she and Sarrow were as good as captured anyway, what difference did it make? They'd find out sooner or later.

"I guess we're going with you," she said reluctantly.

"That's the spirit!" the Seeker said happily. "Come on, it's not a sentence of doom. You're going to meet others of our kind. It'll be fun for you, wait and see!"

Melayne could wait, all right; she just wished the wait could last forever. Only it wouldn't. Their escape was now over.

Chapter Five
The King's House

Since it was already evening when the Seeker found them, he decided that they might as well stay in the broken house that night, and start on their way in the morning. Melayne was very disturbed by the man. He *seemed* to be very friendly and helpful, but she wasn't certain how genuine this was. Not for the first time, she wished she could read people the way she could read animals.

This wish gave her an idea. She glanced at the man, and saw that he was chatting happily with Sarrow. Her brother had taken to the Seeker, that was obvious. The seven soldiers had elected to spend the night outside the building, and had made themselves a roaring fire, roasting something they had killed. The seven horses and the firedrake were tethered close by.

"I've never seen a firedrake before," Melayne said to the Seeker. "Would it be all right if I went and looked at yours?"

"Of course," the man replied. "I don't need to tell

you to be careful with her, of course. Since you can Communicate with animals, you know that."

He didn't seem to be bothered that she might run away into the night. Well, why should he, since Sarrow was here as hostage for her good behavior? Or was she simply being unfair to the Seeker? Did he genuinely mean them well?

Troubled, Melayne went outside. Two of the soldiers glanced at her, and then went back to their feasting and talking. They didn't seem to be bothered by her, either. She moved over to where the animals were tethered, greeting and rubbing the noses of each horse before working her way to the firedrake.

Close up, it was even more impressive. It was certainly a lizard, and a huge one, but it had some interesting details she hadn't spotted earlier. It had ridges above each eye that ran in bumps over its head and down its neck. There were small horns on its head, too, and it had large, deep, purplish eyes.

Hello, she said to it. *I've never seen a firedrake before.*

There was a moment's pause as the lizard looked back at her. Melayne had the impression of a well, with something peering at her from the depths. *Welcome, child,* the firedrake finally said. *It is not often I find someone who can speak with me. Not even among the Talents.*

Really? Melayne asked. *Surely there must be many who can Communicate?*

There are, the firedrake agreed. *But not with such skill. It is . . . difficult . . . to reach our minds.*

Melayne stroked the firedrake's skin. It was dry and slightly warm to the touch. *I'm glad I can talk to you,* she confessed. *You're so fascinating! According to stories, you're related to dragons. Is that true?*

There was a feeling of amusement. *I can hardly say,* the firedrake replied. *I have never met any dragons, nor met any of my kind who has.*

Melayne felt disappointed. *Then do you know if there ever were really any dragons?*

How can I say for sure? The firedrake paused. *In the Mountains of Morning, there are vast numbers of ancient bones. They are very large, and worn smooth by the winds of time. The local people claim that these are the bones of dragons once slain by knights. It is possible, I suppose.* The firedrake paused. *It is also possible that the bones are from other animals, and that nobody knows for sure. I have seen huge elephants in the north that wear coats of long fur. They are tall and strong. Perhaps their bones might be taken for those of dragons by people who do not know any better.*

Perhaps, Melayne agreed. She found herself liking this firedrake. Maybe it wasn't really a minor dragon, but it was still very interesting. *You must have seen a lot, being the steed of a Seeker.*

It takes me far and wide, agreed the lizard.

Have you met many Talents?

The firedrake nodded. *That is the purpose of the Seeker — to find the hidden Talents.*

Hidden? Melayne asked sharply. *There are many hidden Talents?*

Yes. Many human parents hide their children when they know that they have Talents. It is the Seeker's task to search them out.

So it wasn't just her own parents who did this! Melayne felt as though she were on the verge of an important discovery here. *Why do they hide their children?* she asked eagerly.

I cannot say, the firedrake replied. *It is a human thing, and I do not understand humans very well.*

Disappointment washed through her; Melayne felt sure that this was important. If the Talents were treated so well by the King's Seekers, then why would anyone want to hide their children away? And why were Seekers so necessary?

What happens to Talents? Melayne asked it.

They are trained for war, the firedrake replied. *Then they go off to fight it.* It shrugged. *I do not understand "war." It is another human thing. Firedrakes fight one another for mates, and sometimes for land. But it is one firedrake against another. Humans, I believe, gather together in hundreds and attack hundreds of other humans. I think it is sometimes for land, but it is very rarely for mates. It is something I do not understand. And I don't think I want to understand it.*

I don't understand it myself, Melayne admitted. *I don't want to fight and kill anyone, for any reason.*

You will have no choice, the firedrake warned her. *All Talents are forced to fight. But do not ask me why, because I don't know. Ask the Seeker. In his own way, he is a kind man. He will tell you what he knows.*

Perhaps that was a good idea. Besides, it was getting late, and Melayne was rather tired. Walking all day did that to you. She wished the firedrake and the horses a good night, and then walked back to the house, past the soldiers. One of them looked at her with interest. Perhaps the Seeker was right, and she *was* attractive. Then the man looked away again, and Melayne wondered if she was simply noticeable, rather than pretty.

Inside the house, Sarrow had fallen asleep. Melayne noticed with surprise that the Seeker had covered her brother with his own cloak. It was a kind act, and made her feel slightly more at ease with him.

"Did you enjoy talking with my steed?" he asked her quietly, careful not to waken Sarrow.

"It was . . . interesting," she admitted. "She doesn't think like a human being."

He laughed. "No, I didn't think she would. She's got quite a personality, though. What did you ask her?"

"If she was related to dragons."

The Seeker raised an amused eyebrow. "And did she claim descent from a dragon king?"

"No," Melayne admitted. "She said she'd never seen a dragon, or met anyone who had. Do *you* know about them?"

"Only the usual tales, my dear," he admitted. The fire outside cast strange shadows across his pale, handsome face. "Whether they ever truly existed, I can't say. In any event, they don't exist now, and it's a good thing. I gather they used to be partial to a nice, skinny virgin girl for supper. They wouldn't give you the chance to talk to them — just a quick gulp, and you'd be in their gizzards."

Melayne shivered at the thought. Changing the subject, she added, "The firedrake also said that we're to be taken to train as soldiers."

"That's true enough," the Seeker agreed.

Melayne shook her head. "I don't want to fight or hurt anyone. I won't do it."

"Not even the raiders that killed your parents and burned down your home?" the Seeker asked. He nodded toward Sarrow. "Your brother told me what happened to you. The raiders attacked Greenholt, murdered the men, and enslaved all the children. Then they attacked two more villages before the King's Men counterattacked. Surely you can see that killing such men is a good thing."

"Yes," agreed Melayne. "They are savages, and deserve to die. But those are not the sort of men I would be trained to fight. You're talking about the war with Vester and Farrowholme, aren't you? The raiders were from Morstan, and they're supposed to be on our side."

"I think they've gone over to the enemy side now," the Seeker explained. "Such things happen from time to time in war."

"Then we have only Pellow on our side?" asked Melayne. "Surely, we can't stand against the other three kingdoms?"

"It's not quite that bad," the Seeker informed her. "According to the latest reports, Vester might be coming over to our side."

Melayne frowned. "This doesn't make any sense," she complained. "What is the War all *about*?"

The Seeker shrugged. "Politics, I imagine. Wars usually are. Kings falling out, border disputes, that kind of thing."

"But don't you *know*?" she demanded.

"It's not my business," the Seeker answered. "That's the business of kings and knights, not of lowly Seekers."

Melayne felt a flash of anger and frustration. "Since you're responsible for finding Talents to put in the war, I would have thought it was very much your business. If you expect me to go off and fight for some king or other, shouldn't you know *why* we're fighting?"

The Seeker sighed and laughed. "My child, you're very young and very naive. Kings don't explain their reasons to the likes of us. If they order you off to fight, then you'll go off to fight. And if they order me to find Talents, then I'll go off and find Talents."

"They can't make me fight," Melayne said stubbornly.

For the first time, the Seeker showed an emotion other than amusement. Melayne was surprised to see that it was worry — for her. He laid a gentle hand on her arm. "They can put you to death if you refuse their orders," he informed her. "Melayne, you have no option but to do what you are told to do. Otherwise they will kill you."

"They don't sound very nice anymore," Melayne said bitterly. "If I won't obey the orders of a king who will not explain himself to me, I'll be killed! Oh, that's a wonderful incentive!" She gazed at him levelly. "I will not be forced," she vowed.

"You can't do anything about it," the Seeker warned her. He gestured outside. "Those soldiers are friendly now. But if you tried to escape, they would seek you out and catch you. And then they would punish you."

"They might *try*," Melayne replied gently. "But I do not think they would succeed."

"You've been caught once," the Seeker reminded her. "You would be caught again."

"You caught us this time because we did not know what you could do," Melayne answered. "I don't think you'd have such an easy time of it again. And if Greyn hadn't been distracted, you'd never have been able to sneak up on us."

"Perhaps not," the Seeker agreed. "Your wolf has been keeping a wary eye on me ever since I arrived. I've no doubt that he'd attack me if you asked him to." He leaned forward slightly. "So, why haven't you asked him to? Why not seize your chance and run for it? I'm sure you could convince the horses and even my firedrake not to help catch you again."

Melayne squirmed uneasily. "The idea had crossed my mind," she admitted. "But you know where we'd be heading, don't you? You found out from Sarrow. So we'd never be allowed to make it. And you might even punish my aunt if we tried to reach her. And I don't know if you're telling the truth about the King's House or not, but it seems to me that I'd have to go there to find out. And, anyway . . ."

"Yes?"

"Sarrow is tired of running," Melayne admitted. "He doesn't like this life. He wants somewhere where he'll be fed and given a bed. He's only eight, and he needs somewhere to stay. I know he's already made his mind up that he wants to go to the King's House. So, I have to go along with that."

"A wise decision," the Seeker said approvingly. "Melayne, you'll like it there. There are others like us — other Talents. You'll be able to make friends."

"And learn to fight and kill," Melayne added bitterly. "And be sent off to fight for a king I don't know in a war I don't care about."

"There's a price for everything."

"Yes," she agreed. "And some prices are too high to pay. And there are some things that should never be bought and sold. Like our consciences."

The Seeker laughed easily. "My dear child, usually our conscience is the first thing we sell off. It makes life so much easier."

"I imagine it must," she shot back. "After that, you can take money for doing anything. Even selling out your own kind."

That made him scowl. "I'm not betraying you," he assured her. "I am helping you."

"If I could, I'd believe you," she informed him. "But you don't know enough to be able to say that. If you don't know what the war is about, then you don't know that you're helping me. You may only be setting me up to be killed. And I could do that by walking back to the raiders, thank you very much."

The Seeker shook his head. "Child, if you talk like this at the King's House, you will get into serious trouble. They're not as easygoing as I am."

Melayne's eyes flashed angrily. "And you're *helping* me by taking me to such people?" she sneered. "I don't want your help."

"Perhaps not at this moment," he agreed. "But it's better in the long run."

"Better?" she snapped. "Better for *who*?"

"You," he assured her. "Though it may take you a while to understand that." He yawned. "Pardon me. It's been a hard day, so we should rest now. After we've dropped you off at the local King's House, my men and I still have to ride south and help beat those raiders. So it's going to be a tough day for all of us tomorrow. Good night, Melayne."

"Good night," she said, grudgingly. She moved to where Greyn was dozing, and curled up beside her friend. He stirred enough to lick her cheek, and then fell back asleep. Melayne didn't disturb him. For a while she lay awake, wondering what the morning would bring. Finally, she would not be able to hide any longer. In one way, it was a bit of a relief. But she was still scared about what would happen to them all.

The following morning, the soldiers were eager to be going. Melayne heard them joking about wanting to kill themselves a few raiders. She didn't really blame them for their mood — the raiders were killers and abusers, after all — but she didn't like the way it made the soldiers act. She helped them to feed and water their horses simply because she enjoyed being around the animals. Greyn had to wander off, though, because the steeds were nervous when he was around, despite Melayne's assurances that he was safe.

The firedrake ate meat, and she saw that it had pointed teeth in abundance. It was moody and withdrawn again, so she didn't try talking to it. And she had little enough to say to anyone else. Sarrow seemed to be getting along famously with the Seeker. The two of them were laughing and chattering away together. Melayne felt a pang of irritation, along with her suspicions of the man. Why couldn't Sarrow be like that with *her*? Why did he always have to whine and complain to her, and be so friendly to the Seeker?

Because he was male, of course, and she was only his sister. There was a strong chauvinistic streak in Sarrow. Melayne imagined it had to be common in all boys his age, but she couldn't be sure of that, since she didn't know any other boys, his age or any other. But it wounded her to see Sarrow taking so well to a man who was, after all, turning them in.

Melayne couldn't really blame the Seeker. He was only doing his job. But why did he feel that he *had* to do it? He'd proven that he didn't even understand the reasons for what he was doing. So she paid him back in the only small way she had — ignoring him.

When everyone was ready, the Seeker mounted his firedrake and pulled Sarrow up to sit in front of him in the saddle. "You'll enjoy this," he promised the boy. Turning, he called, "Captain, you must take the girl."

The captain cantered his horse forward with ill-concealed irritation, and then reached a hand down toward Melayne. She studied the man for a moment. He couldn't be more than twenty-five or twenty-six, and was quite handsome in a rugged, battered sort of way. The only thing marring his features was his scowl.

"Hurry it up, girl," he snapped. "We don't have time to waste coddling a Talent."

She grasped his hand and swung up behind him on his saddle. She had to adjust her long skirt to sit comfortably, and then she held on to his waist as he indicated for them all to begin.

As they left, Melayne saw Greyn move through the woods. He was coming with them. She had wanted to tell him to go home, but she wasn't sure he could make it alone. On the other hand, she was glad he was still around. A sudden thought struck her, and she cleared her throat.

"Excuse me, Captain," she called. "But will there be any problem with my bringing my wolf with me to the King's House?"

"Your wolf?" The soldier sounded surprised. "I doubt it. If that's your Talent, they'll expect you to practice it. Though wolves aren't the most popular animals around. Couldn't you have decided to bring a dog or a cat?"

"I'm afraid the wolf did the choosing, not me," Melayne apologized.

That actually seemed to amuse the soldier. "Don't

worry, they'll tell you all of the rules when you arrive. They'll look after you." He sounded as if he were trying to be kindly, after all.

"I'm sorry we're preventing you from carrying out your mission," she told him. "I know you must be wanting to save the villagers and stop the raiders. We didn't mean to detain you."

"No, I'm not sure of that," the captain snapped. "You just wanted to shirk your responsibilities and hide away selfishly."

That stung! "What responsibilities?" Melayne demanded. "To fight in a war I never asked for, and don't understand? How is that *my* responsibility? And what's so selfish about wanting to live a peaceful life? Don't most people want that?"

"Most people," he informed her, "aren't Talents."

"And what is *that* supposed to mean?" she demanded. "That I'm somehow less human because I'm a Talent?"

"My brother's a Talent," the captain replied coldly. "And I love him dearly. I'm not prejudiced against your kind, as some are. But you have extra abilities, powers that can help other people. To hide away and deny their use to other people is the height of selfishness. You should want to use your Talent to do good."

"I do want that," she informed him. "But I don't see that going off to war and killing helpless soldiers is going to help anyone at all."

"Helpless soldiers?" He laughed scornfully. "You won't be fighting soldiers. You'll be fighting enemy Talents."

Melayne was shocked again, even though she knew she shouldn't be. *Enemy Talents!* That had never occurred to her! Of course, it made perfect sense — you pitted a Talent against another Talent, not against a common soldier. "Fighting my own kind?" she asked weakly.

"Girl, they're *not* your own kind!" the captain exploded. "They're the *enemy*! They're less than human!"

"Really!" she asked, flushing with embarrassment and anger. "And who *is* the enemy? Last week, it would have been Vester, but the Seeker tells me that they might be our allies soon. And last week, Morstan would have been our ally, only now they're our enemy. Does that mean that everyone we liked last week we have to hate this week?"

"Don't try to get smart with me, girl," the soldier replied. "A soldier's job isn't to think, it's to follow orders."

"But I'm not a soldier," she pointed out. "*You* are."

"You will be when the King's House is done with you," he informed her. "And by then you had better stop talking so smartly and asking such foolish questions." His voice softened slightly. "Look, girl, I know this is a bit of a shock to you. You don't seem like a bad child, just sort of foolish. Take my advice: Shut your mouth, except to say *Yes, sir!* when you need to. Don't argue, don't ask questions, just do as you're told. And you'll be fine."

"In other words," Melayne said bitterly, "just act

like I have no mind or personality of my own? Thank you *so* much for that advice."

That annoyed the captain so much that he refused to speak for several hours. It was just as well, really, because Melayne didn't have anything else to say to him. She'd learned as much as she could for now, and there was so much for her to think about.

They had taken a side road, traveling farther west than she and Sarrow had walked. She had very little idea where they were going, or how long it might take. She refused to ask the captain, though. She didn't want him to think she needed anything from him.

After three hours, the Seeker called for a rest. They'd reached a small, clear stream, and the horses were all in need of rest and drink. Melayne's head reeled slightly as the captain stopped his horse. Twisting, he offered her his hand to help her down. Melayne accepted, and almost stumbled when she felt solid ground beneath her feet again. She couldn't help wincing from the pain in her behind.

The captain smiled slightly. "Sore?" he asked, almost sympathetically. "It's always hard, if you're not used to it. Don't worry, we've only about another hour of traveling left us before we reach the King's House."

"That's good news, but a little late for some parts of my body," Melayne answered.

"Here — take some food," the captain told her, handing her a chunk of bread and some cheese. "You look as though you could do with some food inside of you. I can see your bones all over."

She attacked the food happily. This soldier seemed to be changing moods quickly. One moment he disliked her, and the next he was helping her kindly. Were all adults this changeable? Melayne suspected that she'd soon get to know. And, while he was in a good mood, she decided to get more information from the captain.

"Do you work with many Talents?" she asked him, as he munched his own bread and cheese.

"Me? No." He shrugged. "The Talents are assigned to the war, you see. My men and I are internal patrols. We don't go to the front."

"You don't?" Melayne was confused again.

"Only the Talents fight in those battles." He studied her hard. "You really don't understand, do you? A normal human being can't face a Talent and win. Some of them — some of *you*," he corrected himself, "have terrible powers. Like Fire. They can make a person burst into a pillar of flames. How could a normal man face that?"

Melayne shuddered. "How could *anybody*?" she asked. "Even another Talent?"

"I don't know," the captain admitted. "But it means that we normal troops are kept well away from the Talents. We patrol Stormgard and look for any trouble. Like the raiders."

"I see," Melayne answered. She nodded at the Seeker. "Is he always in charge of you?"

"Him?" The captain looked offended. "*He's* not in charge. *I* am."

"But he gives you orders," Melayne protested.

"Only when it comes to Talents," the soldier explained. "When we find Talents, he has unquestioned authority. The rest of the time, I'm in charge. He's with us because we haven't had a sweep of the southern coast for Talents in a few years. You two are the first he's found this trip."

"Oh." Melayne thought about this for a while. "So there's no way a normal human would have known we were Talents then?" she asked. "Only the Seekers can tell?"

"Only they know for sure," agreed the captain. "Otherwise, you seem to be perfectly normal." He chuckled. "Except when you run around with a wolf following you like a sheepdog," he added. "That's a bit of a giveaway." Then his eyes narrowed. "You're not thinking again of trying to run away, are you?"

"No," Melayne replied, though in truth the thought had more than crossed her mind. It was good to know that there wasn't anything that betrayed their true nature to average people. If they *did* escape, that meant that they could hide out without fear of being discovered.

Soon it was time to move on again. Melayne sat behind the captain once more as they set off, and Sarrow sat with the Seeker. They seemed to have gotten very friendly, and this disturbed Melayne. Sarrow seemed to be forgetting that the Seeker was not their friend, but the man who had captured them.

As the captain had promised, the rest of the journey didn't take long. They followed a river to a small village, and then went on beyond that. About a mile outside of the village was the King's House.

It must have once been a castle, Melayne realized with a thrill. She'd read about castles in her books, but of course had never seen one. And now, here she was, about to be staying in one! It was made of heavy gray stone, with a large wall. Built into this were towers with small windows. There wasn't a moat, though, just a large gate that was wide-open. They rode through it, nodded to by the soldiers on duty. *To guard the castle?* Melayne wondered. *Or to stop the Talents from escaping?*

Inside, the grounds were large and sprawling. There were several small buildings, most made of wood, though some were of stone, set against the walls. At the far end of the yard was a large building set right into the walls. It was three floors tall, and there were more guards outside of it.

There were more people here than Melayne had ever imagined could be in one place at a time. There had to be a couple of hundred, at least. Most of them were children, some as young as Sarrow, and very few as old as she was. Many of them were training to use swords in the center of the courtyard. This forced the travelers to circle around them as they headed for the large building on the far side. Melayne watched the trainees, and saw that most of them had very grim expressions on their faces. Even eight-year-olds were fighting with grim determination. It seemed horrible to her.

"Don't worry, you'll soon be that good," the captain informed her, mistaking her look.

She didn't ever want to get like *that*, but she realized that there was no point in saying this. Instead, Melayne looked all around.

There were soldiers everywhere. Some, obviously, were the ones training the Talents. But there seemed to be a lot more of them than just teachers. She was sure they were guards.

I don't like this place, Greyn called up to her. The wolf was staying very close to the horse she rode on.

Nor do I, Melayne admitted. *But we don't have any choice in the matter.*

There's always a choice, Greyn informed her. *But I suppose that you're right — for now.* Unhappily, he padded carefully along.

The Seeker drew up outside the main building. "I'm sure the administrator will want to see you," he commented, helping Sarrow down. "I'll just drop the two of you off, and then we have to be on our way."

The captain helped Melayne down. "Thank you," she told him. "You've been very kind."

"You look after yourself," he told her gruffly. "Don't let them bully you. And choose your friends here carefully. Not all will be on your side."

Melayne wasn't sure what he meant by that, but it seemed well-intentioned. There wasn't time to ask him, and he seemed reluctant to say any more. So she just waved slightly, and followed the Seeker through the doorway. Greyn padded along beside her, sniffing loudly. She didn't need to Communicate with him to know he was disturbed. She couldn't blame him, because she was pretty disturbed herself.

The Seeker seemed to know exactly where he was going, striding along confidently, one arm loosely over Sarrow's shoulder. Sarrow seemed content, almost eager, as if on the verge of a great adventure. Melayne followed, Greyn beside her, his fur on edge. There was something about this place that she didn't like, but she couldn't quite work out what it might be that was worrying her. The people she saw didn't seem antagonistic or anything — indifferent, for the most part.

The Seeker knocked at a door and entered. Melayne saw it was a small office of sorts, with a desk, chairs, and a case of books. A man stood up from behind the desk as they entered, and Melayne studied him carefully.

He was a large man and well-built, even though his hair was graying. He had the look of a soldier about him, the carriage of a man who knew what he was capable of, and what he expected of others. He wore a simple outfit of dark trousers and a jerkin. His only concession to ornament was a wrist guard about both arms. There was some kind of decoration on them, but she couldn't quite make it out.

"Magwyn," the Seeker greeted the man politely, inclining his head.

"Seeker," Magwyn responded. His voice was deep and seemed to echo slightly in his massive chest.

"Two more recruits," the Seeker explained, indicating Melayne and Sarrow. "The young girl can Communicate. The boy's a little too young to demonstrate a Talent yet."

Magwyn nodded slightly, and his cold gaze swept over Melayne. It made her shudder. "She's a bit older than we're used to," he complained.

"Their parents hid them out," the Seeker answered. "She's a good girl, but with a few wrong ideas in her head."

"They'll be knocked out of her here," Magwyn said simply. He looked at Sarrow with complete disinterest. "Very well, Seeker, I'll see to them now. Good hunting."

The Seeker nodded, and then turned to smile once more at Sarrow. "You'll be taken care of here," he promised. "You'll soon make friends and be lonely no more." To Melayne he added, "Study well, and you'll find everyone here will be your friend." Then he left the room, closing the door behind him.

"He's wrong, you know," Magwyn said abruptly. "Not everyone here will be your friend. *I* won't be. I'm the administrator here, and that makes me no person's friend. It is my job to see that you are trained in combat and in the use of your powers. As soon as that is accomplished, you will be assigned to an army post and then leave here forever. How long you are here and how much you see me will depend on your progress." He smiled coldly. "But I can promise you, you will want to see me as little as possible."

Melayne didn't doubt him. She could tell without question that Magwyn was not the kind of man to fight. He only understood winning. There didn't seem to be any need to reply, so she kept quiet.

Magwyn stared at Greyn, and frowned slightly. "Since your gift is Communication," he said slowly, "I see no problem with you keeping the wolf here. It will help you to develop your Talent better. But it will be your responsibility. If it does anything wrong, you will be punished. Do you understand me?"

Better than you think, Melayne thought, but wisely kept this to herself. "Yes," she replied simply.

"Yes, *sir*," Magwyn stressed. "You're training for the military now, and you must always address a superior officer as *sir*. Do you understand *that*?"

So that was how it was to be? Melayne felt a burst of rebelliousness. Even though she knew she shouldn't indulge it, she was too annoyed with the situation to care. "And how am I to recognize a *superior* officer?" she asked. "As opposed to an inferior one?" And, after a beat to show her attitude: "Sir?"

Magwyn stared at her with his cold eyes. "Any officer is superior to you, because you are a recruit," he informed her.

"I am *not* a recruit," Melayne objected. "I am a conscript. I was given no choice in the matter. Sir."

Magwyn moved around his desk to stand in front of her. Close up, he was even more of a mountain, and extremely intimidating. Melayne was scared of him, but she wasn't going to let him see that. Unless, of course, he already had.

"I can tell that you're going to be a trouble-maker," Magwyn said softly. "I don't like troublemakers, because they come to see me too often and take up my valuable time."

"Then let us go, and we'll take up none of it," Melayne suggested. "Sir." She was making the word sound like an insult each time she said it.

"It is the law of the king that all Talents be a part of the war effort," Magwyn explained. "And I am loyal to my king. Are you?"

Melayne shrugged. "I don't know him," she replied. "And anyone who wants my loyalty has to earn it. What's he done that would make me be loyal to him? Sir."

The administrator glared down at her. "He is your king," he replied coldly. "That is enough."

"For you, perhaps," she agreed. "I'm a little more demanding, obviously. All this king has done for me so far is to say I must fight for him whether I like it or not. That doesn't make me very loyal to him. Sir."

"Then we'll have to see about forcing some loyalty into you, won't we?" Magwyn studied her. "I'm giving you the benefit of the doubt because you're obviously an idiot. But I warn you that if you persist in such nonsense, you will be punished for it, and punished quite severely." Abruptly, he turned to his desk and rang a small bell.

There was a rap on the door and a young soldier entered, saluting smartly.

"Take these two youngsters to their barracks," he ordered the young man. "And then see that they get to training."

Again, the soldier saluted crisply, touching his

heart and holding his palm outward. Melayne could see that it was meant to symbolize the willing gift of his life in Magwyn's service.

"Pay attention to his salute," Magwyn informed her. "You will be expected to do the same when given orders."

So, it was to be a combat of wills. Melayne shook her head. "No," she replied quietly. "You will never make me do what I don't wish to do." She turned and smiled sweetly at the waiting soldier. "Weren't you ordered to take us somewhere?" she asked politely.

The soldier was caught now. He looked to Magwyn for help, and the administrator nodded. The young man marched toward the open door. Melayne, a slight smile on her face, followed, with Sarrow and Greyn in tow. Outside the room, the soldier closed the door and then glowered at her.

"It's a serious mistake to try and make fun of the administrator," he informed her. "You will not win."

"I already have," she answered cheerfully. "Didn't you notice that I stopped calling him *sir*, and he didn't object?" She smiled at him. "What's your name?"

"Names are irrelevant in the army," the soldier replied stiffly.

"Suit yourself," Melayne agreed. "Just don't expect a card from me on your next birthday. Now, wasn't there some talk of a bed?"

The soldier flushed, considered speaking, and then simply led the way instead.

Melayne wasn't fooled for a moment. She was winning with a few tricks right now, but that was simply because the real war had not yet begun. When it did, she knew that she was going to come under considerable attack.

Could she possibly stand up to it — and win?

Chapter Six
Training

Their first stop was a long dormitory room. Their guide nodded to it. "This is where you will sleep," he informed Sarrow. "You will be assigned a bed by your squad leader, and will be expected to look after it."

"He's not really very good at making his own bed," Melayne apologized. "I usually do it for him."

"This is the army," the soldier snapped. "He will make his own bed or be punished."

Melayne gave him a glare. "Haven't you ever heard of positive reinforcement? Why not simply offer him a second dessert if he makes his own bed well? Sarrow *loves* desserts, and you can get him to do almost anything if they're part of the bribe."

"The army doesn't bribe people," the soldier answered. "They *order*."

"Well, maybe you should think about it," Melayne suggested. "So, do you have two beds together?"

"Two?" That had caught their guide off balance. "Well, you don't think I'm leaving him here alone, do you?" Melayne asked him, as though the idea were unthinkable. "I have to look after him."

"That's out of the question," the soldier replied in horror. "This is a *boy's* dormitory."

"I don't mind slumming," Melayne replied.

"Do you have any idea what would happen to you if you were left in this room with fifty boys and young men?"

Melayne deliberately blanked her face. "I'd probably be the center of attention," she said. "That's fine by me." She lowered her voice. "Confidentially, I'm a bit of a show-off and I'd love that."

The soldier swallowed. "They would *attack* you," he protested.

"Then you're not training them properly," Melayne said firmly. "Why, even I could make sure that young men know how to treat a lady properly. Couldn't you just *order* them to be nice and polite to me? You order them to do everything else."

The poor man was starting to turn scarlet. "It would be bad for morale to have a pretty young woman alone with fifty men."

"I'd hardly be alone if I were with fifty men," Melayne pointed out. "Do you really think I'm pretty?"

"It's not done," the soldier spluttered. "You have to sleep with the other girls and women."

Melayne sighed loudly. "Oh, very well." She turned to Sarrow. "You don't mind sleeping with fifty women, do you?"

"You *can't* stay together," the soldier insisted. "You have to obey orders."

Melayne raised her eyebrows. "Well, when I hear one that's sensible enough to actually obey, I will," she promised. "So far, I haven't." She shook her head. "Didn't Magwyn say something about you taking us to the person in charge? Maybe I can talk some sense into him."

The soldier looked scandalized again. "That's the *administrator*," he protested. "You can't call him Magwyn."

"Of course I can, if that's his name," Melayne said firmly. "Really, you aren't very bright, are you? Did you become a soldier because you couldn't qualify for any other job?"

The young man flushed again, and grabbed at her arm angrily. Greyn growled, low and with a promise that Melayne didn't need to translate to know it included blood spilled. The soldier hastily withdrew his hand and stared at the wolf.

"Well, you're not quite as stupid as I thought," Melayne said approvingly. "Shall we be off?"

Giving Greyn a filthy look, the soldier set off out of the main building and into the courtyard. The boys and girls who had been exercising when Melayne arrived were now resting. The soldier led her and Sarrow to the officer in charge. He saluted, and then started to explain that these were two new recruits who had to be integrated into the company.

Melayne studied the instructor. He was in his thirties, she estimated, and had hair cut short and an air of no nonsense about him. He was lean and muscular, not as imposing as Magwyn but clearly a fighting man. He also looked to be very rigid and a man who shouted rather than talked. She didn't see that she would have any problems with him.

On the other hand, she didn't envy him his job right now.

Being told that she *had* to become a soldier and *had* to learn to fight had brought out Melayne's bad side. Her mother had always complained that Melayne was as stubborn as a rock when she was sure she was right. And her mother ought to know. This whole thing had rubbed Melayne the wrong way, and she was utterly determined to fight back. If they didn't want her to enjoy this, then she'd make absolutely certain that they would enjoy it even less.

The instructor whirled on her. "Ten-shun!" he snapped.

"There does seem to be lots of tension, yes," she agreed. "You really should relax more. You'll make yourself sick like that."

A couple of the younger recruits giggled at what she said. They shut up when the instructor glared at them. He was well on the way to training them, obviously. Well, she would have to see what she could do about that.

"Do you think you're funny?" the instructor growled.

"Well, *they* seem to," Melayne answered. "I really don't want to brag, but —"

"Shut up!" the soldier roared.

"If you don't want me to speak, then don't ask questions," Melayne snapped. "Make up your mind."

The instructor glared at her. "Drop and give me twenty," he ordered. "NOW!"

Melayne cocked her head. "What?"

"Push-ups," the instructor snarled. "Do it."

"Whatever for?" she asked innocently.

The instructor glared down at her. "Because I gave you an order."

"Oh. Thanks, but I'd rather not, if it's all the same to you." Melayne smiled at him sweetly.

There was a deathly hush from the recruits. They had been quiet before, but this was like something had sucked all sound possible from the area. The instructor leaned forward, pushing his face into hers. "You will do as you are told!"

Melayne took a step backward and batted at the air between them. "What did you eat for breakfast? A skunk?" she asked him. That got a few more sniggers and the instructor glared everyone into silence again.

"You are in the army now," he informed Melayne coldly. "And you will obey orders or else be punished. Twenty push-ups, now."

"Oh, that's *really* mature of you," Melayne answered. "Do what you tell me, or you'll punish me? Didn't your mother ever teach you to be polite to young ladies?"

The instructor raised his fist, ready to strike her. Greyn growled and leaned forward. The man paused and looked down at the wolf.

"So you can Communicate?" he asked her coldly. "Do you think that makes you better than me?"

"No," Melayne said truthfully. "Just different. I can think for myself," she added. "*That* makes me better than you."

"If you want that wolf to stay alive," the instructor told her, "you'll call it off."

"If you want to be able to eat with that hand again," Melayne answered, "you'll lower it now."

The instructor considered what she said and slowly lowered his hand.

"That's better," Melayne said cheerfully. "See, if we just try, we can all get along fine."

The man had a knife out of his belt and held at the ready, a smile in his eyes. "Now see what your wolf friend can do, if you want it to die," he sneered.

Melayne sighed. She was obviously not getting through to him. Glancing up, she saw a passing pigeon. *A small favor, please,* she called.

A large white dropping landed on the instructor's head. He gave a startled cry and jumped back. Greyn leaped, slamming into the man's hand and sending the knife spinning away.

Don't hurt him! Melayne said urgently. She knew that she could press her act only so far without causing real trouble. Greyn backed off, having picked up the knife in his mouth. He handed it to Melayne, who took it gravely.

"You dropped this," she said to the instructor, offering it back. His hair was stained with pigeon droppings, and he was furious. Having to take back his own knife didn't improve his mood.

"Archers!" the man snarled. "Target the wolf!"

Three of the trainees leaped to their feet, whipping arrows into place and centering them on Greyn. Melayne felt a second of panic, but they didn't fire. Which meant that she was still in charge, whatever the instructor thought. She called to several more pigeons, holding them ready to strike if need be.

The instructor still thought he was winning, and smiled coldly at her. "Now, give me those push-ups, or your wolf friend will be wearing an arrow overcoat."

"This isn't going to work, you know," she warned him. "You can't beat me by force. Why don't we just sit down and talk this over?"

"Archers!" the instructor called, raising his hand.

Melayne knew she'd forced him into this. He couldn't back down without looking foolish to the trainees. On the other hand, neither could she back down. It would be setting a bad example to everyone else. Reluctantly, she called on the pigeons for help.

Six of them flew down at the heads of the archers, while three more whizzed past, their beaks opening and closing faster than the recruits could move. Three bowstrings were snapped instantly, the arrows falling uselessly to the ground.

The instructor was stunned. He'd clearly never seen anything like this before. The problem was, this was likely to escalate out of control unless Melayne took firm command of the situation. She wasn't used to dealing with people yet, and she knew that there had to be a better way to handle this. The main thing was to stop the problem from getting worse.

"Well, this is certainly one way to train me to use my Talent as a warrior," she said cheerfully. "But don't you think you've done enough for now? I wouldn't want to tire out all of your troops."

The instructor glared at her. "You have to learn to obey orders," he informed her. "I gave you an order that you still haven't obeyed."

"The twenty push-ups thing?" She sighed. "Does it really mean that much to you?"

"Yes."

"Oh, all right." Melayne had made her point by now. She moved to obey and did the push-ups quickly. Then she stood up, breathing easily. "Are you happy now?"

"No," the instructor answered. "But you *will* learn to do as you are told."

"Perhaps," Melayne agreed, not wanting to start fighting again. She glanced over at where Sarrow was standing, where he must have been watching her, wondering how he was doing. To her surprise, he wasn't even looking in her direction. He was watching the soldiers, almost enviously. Melayne was puzzled. Did he think that this was some kind of a game they were caught in? Or did he see the men as offering more protection than his sister? Sarrow was understandably obsessed with survival. He was still only a child, and the thought of dying had to scare him. Especially after all they had been through.

Still . . . it hurt Melayne more than a little to know that he wasn't even paying that much attention to her.

But perhaps this was what he really needed: contact with others like himself, and his own age. Not being mothered by an older sister.

The instructor turned to the rest of the recruits. "That's enough of a rest!" he yelled. "On your feet. It's time to practice combat again. And our two newest members can join in." He turned to the soldier who had guided them. "Dismissed!" The youth saluted and left — very quickly, Melayne noticed.

The rest of the afternoon went quickly. Melayne and Sarrow were given practice swords, which had their edges blunted so that nobody would get cut. All of the recruits were forced to practice attacking and blocking. Sarrow seemed happy enough to learn, and since the whole thing was supervised, Melayne wasn't too worried about him. She concentrated on trying to learn the drill. It hurt her wrist to have to fight with another of the girls, but she started to get the hang of it by the time the instructor called a halt.

"You're a sorry bunch," he complained. "But I aim to make real soldiers out of you. For now, though, it's time for supper. Trainee Corri, you will take charge of this . . . young woman." He nodded at Melayne. "Brakka, you look after the boy. Explain what is expected of them." He moved to glare at Melayne again. "I expect better behavior from you after that."

"Once I know the rules, I'm sure we'll get along

better," agreed Melayne pleasantly. "By the way, my name's Melayne. What's yours?"

"Sir!" he snapped. "You have no need to address me as anything else."

"Whatever," Melayne agreed. "But we can't possibly be friends if you won't tell me your name."

"I am not going to be your friend," the instructor informed her. "I am your commanding officer. Dismissed."

Corri grabbed her arm before she could say anything else, and urged her to go along with the rest of the recruits toward the barracks. Melayne complied, after telling Greyn to go and find some food. He was a little worried about her, but realizing she could take care of herself, he loped out of the main gate to go hunting.

"Are you *crazy*?" Corri hissed to Melayne as they hurried along. Melayne looked at the young girl. She was dressed like everyone else in a tunic top and trousers, with her blond hair cut neck-length.

"Possibly," Melayne agreed. "I'd like a second opinion on that, though."

"You *are* crazy!" Corri informed her.

"Well, there we go, then," Melayne said, with mock sadness. "I guess I am crazy. What gave me away?"

"Teasing old Cotra like that!" Corri said, scandalized. "Don't you know what he can do to you?"

"Not very much," Melayne answered. "Look, do we have to talk about him? Can't we talk about something nicer? Are there any really cute guys here? I haven't dated much — well, not at all, actually, so I'm sort of interested in learning how to go about it. You look like a cute girl, so I'm sure you have lots of experience. I'll take all the help I can get."

"She *is* crazy," another girl offered. "You got stuck with rotten duty, Corri."

Corri nodded glumly. "I'll be punished, too, if you don't learn," she explained. They had come to the entrance to the barracks, and the troops split into male and female, each to go their own way.

"Hold on a second," Melayne said to Corri. She turned to Sarrow and Brakka. "It looks like they're splitting us up for now," she told her brother. "I don't like it much, but I guess you'll be okay. I'll talk to you later." She turned to Brakka. "You look after my brother," she informed the other boy. "If you don't, you answer to me."

"I answer to Cotra," the boy said proudly. Sarrow looked rather embrarrassed by her concern. His chauvinism was showing through again.

"You answer to *me*," she repeated, giving him a hard look. "And, believe me, you don't want to annoy me." Then she turned to Corri. "So, what's for supper?"

The meal wasn't very good, but it was edible — even if that was something of a close call. Melayne was so hungry that she cleaned her dish. Corri had been quiet, like everyone else, during the meal. Afterward, she led Melayne upstairs to the girls' dormitory.

"This will be your bed," she informed Melayne. "Next to mine."

"Good," Melayne replied. "I hope we can become friends. I've never had a best friend before, and I kind of like you."

Corri's face cracked slightly with a smile. "I kind of like you, too," she admitted. "But I think you're likely to be a target for trouble. Being your friend could be dangerous."

"Yes," Melayne said honestly. "But it could also be fun." She flopped onto her bed. "So, what's your Talent?"

"I can Fly," Corri said modestly. "I'm not really very good at it, though."

"Fly?" Melayne echoed, enthralled. "Wow! That's terrific. Come on, show me! I'm dying to see this!"

It took a bit of coaxing, but after a few minutes, blushing, Corri lifted her feet off the ground, and then moved through the air in a figure of eight before landing again.

"That is *wonderful!*" Melayne said, honestly impressed. "That's a terrific Talent. I'll bet you have a lot of fun with it."

"Talents aren't *fun*," Corri protested. "They're responsibilities and possibilities. It's our job to learn to use them to their fullest potential."

Melayne made a face. "I'll bet I know where you heard that. You people are crazy to submit to this nonsense."

Another girl glared at her. "It's all very well for you," she snapped. "But we don't all have the ability to Communicate."

"Maybe not," Melayne agreed. "But you've all got Talents. What's yours?"

114

"Finding," the girl answered, sullenly. "That's not much use."

"Finding?" Melayne laughed happily. "I should say it is! If you can Find things, I'm sure we could all use your help." She looked around the room. "I've never met any other Talents before. This is so exciting for me! I want to know what everyone here can do!"

The next hour passed happily, as each of the girls was quite eager to demonstrate her Talent. There were several Fire Makers, two others who could Communicate, three who could Fly, one who could Change — that delighted Melayne, seeing the girl change a stone into a jewel — and many other Talents, most of which she had never heard of before. The mood in the room lifted considerably, and the girls stopped being grim recruits and became young girls again. Most of them were between eight and twelve. Only Corri was her own age, and none older.

Then there was a call from the window: *Hey!*

Oh, Greyn! Melayne called. *I'm sorry.* She hurried to the window and opened it. Greyn bounded inside, looking rather pleased with himself and obviously well fed.

"Is he . . . tame?" asked Corri nervously.

"Tame?" Melayne shook her head. "Certainly not! He's a wolf. But he's *safe*. He wouldn't hurt any of my friends."

"Oh." Corri seemed cheered by the news. "Can I pet him?"

Be my guest, Greyn commented. *Don't worry about fingers — I'm really quite full.*

"He says it's fine," Melayne translated, hoping none of the others who could Communicate would feel she had to be more accurate. Corri knelt down and started to stroke Greyn's fur, which made him hum with pleasure. Pretty soon, most of the girls had overcome their nervousness and were scratching or petting the wolf. Greyn was radiating smugness, which amused Melayne. It looked as if things weren't going to be totally bad here. All she had to do was to get the rest of the team to loosen up a little, and life might become endurable.

Of course, she didn't imagine for a second that the people in charge would approve of such a thing. They were bound to fight back. To Melayne's surprise, she discovered that this prospect didn't worry her. They all had rigid minds, used to thinking in one way only. Besides, she had realized that the officers were not Talents.

Which raised an interesting point.

"Corri," she asked, "are any of the Talents ever given positions of power? Apart from the Seekers, I mean?"

Corri stopped scratching Greyn a moment to think. He nudged her to continue with a paw. "Not that I know of," she admitted. "All of the officers are just normal humans."

"Isn't that odd?" Melayne asked. "I mean, there should be *some* Talents who are good enough to get promoted."

"Get real," the girl who had Finding said. She seemed to be the grouch of the group. "The normal humans are scared of Talents. They'd never give us any authority over them."

"I guessed as much," Melayne admitted. "But surely they wouldn't mind Talents giving orders to other Talents?"

The girl shook her head. "They don't like Talents giving orders to *anybody*. We're just supposed to *obey*. That's our job."

"It doesn't sound fair to me," Melayne objected.

"Fair?" The girl laughed. "Humans aren't *fair* to Talents. *Humans* aren't forced to fight in the army if they don't want to. Humans are allowed a choice. *We're* not."

"Well, we're better than them," Corri said simply. "Because of our Talents. It's our responsibility to look after them."

"Says who?" the other girl challenged. "Says *humans*, that's who."

It looked to Melayne as though she had an ally, of sorts. This girl, though very angry, had the right attitude. "Exactly," Melayne agreed. "We shouldn't just accept what we're told without thinking about it. That would be very foolish."

The angry girl looked interested at last. "I'm Devra," she said, giving her name at last. "I have to admit, I liked the way you stood up to old Cotra."

"But it got her into trouble," Corri pointed out. "If she keeps on like that, she'll be severely punished."

"Nonsense," Melayne insisted. "They can't do anything to punish me. I don't want to be here at all, and I won't let them turn me into a killer. There's no reason for any of us to fight in their war."

There was a shocked silence at this. Finally, one of the younger girls said, "But if we don't, the enemy will overrun our country."

"How do you *know* that?" asked Melayne. "The only overrunning I've seen so far was a group of Morstan raiders — and they were supposed to be our allies. I'm not so sure that the war's being fought for any good reason. Besides, we'd only be fighting other Talents, and I don't want to hurt somebody who's just like me."

"They're not just like *us*!" another girl protested. "They're the *enemy*."

"Says who?" Devra asked bitterly. "Cotra? Can you trust *his* word? He's a sadistic bully. Magwyn? He hates Talents, and he's not going to give us any good news."

"The king has declared them our foes," Corri said. "And we have to believe him."

"No, we don't," Melayne argued. "This is the same king who made a law saying we *have* to fight and kill and die for him, isn't it? Well, that doesn't sound like the sort of king I'd like to obey."

"You don't have any choice," a younger girl argued. "He's the *king*. He can do whatever he likes."

"Not with me, he can't," Melayne said firmly. "I refuse to obey any orders I'm given that don't make sense to me."

"You can say that in here," Devra said, "but it'll be different when you're outside, being trained. Cotra will force you to do whatever he wants."

"I'll say the same thing outside, too," Melayne promised. "I don't care what they do to me. I'm not going to obey any stupid or wrong orders. It's as simple as that."

"*You're* simple, if you ask me," Devra replied. But there was a tone of odd respect in her voice.

It was soon time for bed. Corri showed Melayne where she had to get ready and found her a long nightgown to wear like everyone else. Melayne was absolutely exhausted, and fell easily into a dreamless sleep. She was awakened early by Corri shaking her.

"Wash and breakfast," she said. "We have to start early."

Melayne considered objecting, but it wasn't worth it. She let Greyn out to hunt, and told him to take his time. There wasn't much he could do inside the King's House anyway, and it was probably better not to have him underfoot. After she'd washed, Melayne was given a set of trousers and a tunic like the others wore. It was dark green.

"Don't they have any brighter colors?" she asked.

"We all wear the same," Devra informed her. "To remind us that we're not individuals, just trainees."

"Well, *I'm* an individual," Melayne objected. "I'll have to think of some way to brighten it up." She put the clothing on. It wasn't very comfortable, but there didn't seem to be any point in complaining. At least it meant she could wash her other clothes at last.

Then they all headed outside to the courtyard, where Cotra was already waiting for them, looking grim. Did he ever lighten up? Melayne couldn't imagine it. He had everyone begin by doing exercises. Melayne quite enjoyed them, as they warmed her up nicely. She saw Sarrow with the boys and waved to him. Sarrow winced and looked away. He seemed to enjoy being with the other males.

"None of that!" Cotra snapped.

"None of what?" Melayne asked, puzzled.

"Recruits are not to make unnecessary gestures," he informed her coldly.

"That wasn't unnecessary," Melayne argued. "He's my brother. It would be very rude of me not to say hello to him. You aren't trying to make me into a rude person, are you?"

"I'm trying to make you into a *soldier*!" the instructor replied. "And it doesn't matter to a soldier whether he's rude or not."

"Well, you certainly live down to your own standards," Melayne informed him, which made several of the girls giggle. "But I'm sorry — I can't live like that."

"You will live any way I tell you!" Cotra told her.

"I will not," Melayne answered. "I will live according to my conscience. You'd better get used to it."

Cotra was actually speechless for a moment. Then he said, "Soldiers obey orders, and you will obey mine. There will be no disobedience."

Melayne shrugged. "I don't want to be a soldier, so that really doesn't concern me. If you give me reasonable orders, I don't have a problem with it."

He glared at her. "Well, *here's* a reasonable order," he snapped. "Twenty push-ups. Now."

"You really have a thing about push-ups, don't you?" Melayne asked. "All right." She set to work on them.

"And you won't speak to me unless I tell you to do so!" he added. "No backtalk."

"If people talk to me, I talk back," Melayne answered, ignoring the command. "It's only polite. But, oh, yes, you're into rudeness. Sorry, I forgot." She finished the push-ups and stood up, breathing a little hard. It was a good thing she was healthy. This could get to be a problem otherwise.

They were set to doing more sword practice. Melayne wasn't very good at it, but Corri was worse, so it wasn't a problem for her. Melayne noticed that Devra was very good, though. There was a short break for food, and then they were all led out of the courtyard and beyond the walls. Here a set of archery targets had been placed. Each of the girls was given a bow and a quiver full of arrows.

"I trust *this* suits you?" Cotra smirked at Melayne. "You're going first."

"No problem," Melayne said cheerfully. She might not be able to handle a sword, but a bow was another matter. She strung the bow, nocked her first arrow, and let it fly. It was a little heavier than she'd expected, and missed the bull by a couple of inches. She corrected for the next shot, and placed three in a row all inside the inner target.

Cotra's smirk had vanished completely. "I suppose you think you're really something," he complained.

Melayne shrugged. "Not really. It's just something I happen to be good at." But she could tell he was not happy at her success. He'd been hoping she'd fail miserably and make herself look like a fool.

Frustrated, Cotra went in search of another victim. The other recruits were lined up and the practice began in earnest. Melayne shot off all of her arrows and then went to help Corri, who was having trouble hitting any part of the target.

"You're too tense," Melayne explained. "And you're jerking your hand when you release the string." She put her own hands over Corri's. "Keep them like this, and don't panic. You'll be fine." Corri smiled her thanks and tried again. She had to fight the urge to move her hand when she released the string. This time, she actually hit the target.

"What do you think you're doing?" Cotra demanded.

Melayne looked at him, puzzled. "Helping Corri get it right," she explained. "She needs a little hand, that's all."

"I didn't order you to help her," the instructor snapped.

"Well, you didn't order me *not* to, either," Melayne replied. "Honestly, there's no pleasing you, is there?"

"All you have to do," Cotra said in a low voice, "is to obey orders. Nothing else. Don't think for yourself, and don't do anything I haven't told you to do."

Melayne sighed. "Look, that's fine for a six-year-old. But I'm old enough to act intelligently without having to be watched every second, okay? Do you want Corri to be able to handle a bow or not? If you do, just let me work with her for a while, and I'm sure she'll be terrific."

"That's not your job," Cotra insisted. "Stop doing it."

"If you're going to take this attitude," Melayne told him, "you'll never get anything done, will you?"

"I've had more than enough from you," Cotra decided. He gestured for one of the soldiers, who came running. "Take this . . . recruit to the dungeon," he ordered. "Let's see how happy she is after a night in the cells with no food or water."

The soldier grabbed Melayne's arm roughly, and jerked her into motion. "Hey!" she protested. "There's no need for that. I'll be happy to follow you."

"Come on," the young man snapped.

They entered the grounds again, and Melayne was led to a set of steps by the main wall leading downward. There was a slightly ripe smell as they descended. "Needs airing out," Melayne decided. At the bottom was an unlocked door, and beyond that a short corridor. There were several doors leading off this corridor, and the soldier let go of Melayne's arm to open one of the doors.

"In here," he ordered.

Melayne examined the room beyond. It was made from cold stone, gray except where moss was growing. There was filthy straw on the floor and a small hole in the floor to one side. The only light came from another small hole high in the wall. There was a stench of stale urine that turned her stomach.

"In *there*?" she said, incredulously. "It's disgusting. You can't be serious."

"You're being punished," the man answered, smiling at her disgust. "You're not supposed to like it."

"Punishment is being sent to my room without dessert," Melayne complained. "This is inhumane."

"Tough." The soldier shoved her hard, and she stumbled into the cell. He slammed the door shut behind her, and turned a key. "This will teach you better behavior."

Annoyed, Melayne called out, "I'm not staying in here, you know. This is beneath my dignity."

"You're a soldier," the young man replied. "You don't have any dignity."

"I'm not a soldier," she informed him through the small grille set into the door. "And I'm going to have strong words with Cotra about this."

The soldier laughed. "Dream on!" He placed the key over a hook on the wall. "I'll be back for you in the morning." Still laughing, he marched down the corridor. A moment later, Melayne heard the outside door close.

The smell was awful, and she was quite serious in not intending to stay in the cell a second longer than she had to. Cotra was just being spiteful, and she wasn't going to put up with it.

Hello, she called out to any animal that might be around.

There was a twitchy sort of feeling, and then a cautious: *What do you want?*

It was a young rat, curious and hungry. She peered through the grille in the door and saw the rat emerge from one of the other cells. Melayne had never spoken to a rat before. On the farm, her father had always considered them vermin and exterminated them. But this one seemed to be friendly enough, so Melayne replied, *I don't like it down here, and I'd like to be out.*

Wouldn't they all? asked the rat. *Easier said than done, though.*

All? asked Melayne. *There are more people down here?*

Oh, yes, lots, the rat answered. *More than three.* He obviously couldn't count very high.

That's terrible, Melayne decided. *Well, would you mind giving me a little hand? I just need you to scurry over and fetch me that key from the hook there.*

The rat studied the key. *What's in it for me?* he asked.

Fair enough question. *I'll bring you some food tonight,* Melayne promised. *I'm not sure what it'll be, but it has to be better than what you'll find down here.*

True enough, the rat agreed. *Okay.* It scuttled across the floor, and then bounced off a convenient stool to get some height. He hit the wall beside the key, knocking it off the hook with his nose. Then he dragged it across to her cell and shoved it under the door. Melayne took the key and opened her cell.

Thank you so much, she said politely. *I'll see you later, I promise.* Then she went to the next cell and peered inside. She gasped as she saw two young girls, both looking filthy. The stench was even worse than the one in her cell. Grimly, she unlocked the door. "Come on," she said. "I don't know why they did this to you, but enough is enough."

The two girls looked amazed. Both couldn't be more than ten years old. They came to her nervously. "We were locked up for trying to escape," one explained. "We've been down here ... three weeks."

"Three weeks?" Melayne was appalled. "Here? Well, that's far too long. I'm going to give that Cotra a strong talking to."

"Are you crazy?" the other girl asked. "He'll kill you! I'm not leaving here until he says I can! He'll lock me up forever otherwise."

Melayne realized that neither of them intended to come with her. She couldn't see why they'd want to stay down here in the filth and stink, but if they wouldn't come, she was hardly going to force them. She left their cell door open, and checked out the other cells. There were three boys in the remaining cells, and all of them proved to be too scared to follow her out.

"This is abuse," Melayne said firmly. "And I'm going to put a stop to it right now." She spun around and marched to the exit door. Throwing it wide, she stormed up the steps and into the courtyard. Angrily, she looked around and saw that the trainees were back inside again, once more at sword practice. Cotra was there, with his back to her. Her rage boiling up, Melayne stomped across the courtyard toward him.

When they saw her, the recruits dropped their guard, staring in astonishment. Melayne didn't know why they found her appearance so odd, unless it was because she was finally angry.

Cotra realized something was going on and he spun around. He looked stunned. "You! Why aren't you still in your cell?"

"Didn't *he* give you my message?" Melayne asked, indicating the soldier who had locked her up. "I told him I wasn't staying in that terrible place. It's too disgusting for words. And now I've discovered that you've got other people down there, too. People who are too scared to come out unless you tell them to. So, go right on down and order them to come out." She folded her arms across her chest and glared at him.

"Who do you think you are?" Cotra demanded, going pale with anger. "You're *nobody*. I'm the one who gives the orders here. Those people stay down there because they're being punished. And you're going back down to join them again immediately."

"I most certainly am not!" Melayne informed him. "That place is not punishment — it's abuse. I'm going to report you to Magwyn and have this stopped immediately." She started to turn away.

"You don't get to speak to the administrator," Cotra snarled. "He's too busy to talk to dumb recruits."

"He'll talk to me," Melayne assured him. As she was about to start for the offices, she saw Cotra move. He reached for her, grabbing her arm so tightly it hurt. "Let go of me!" she told him. "You're only making things worse."

"You must be insane!" Cotra gasped. "Shut your mouth, or I'll shut it for you." He raised his free hand high, and then slapped downward.

The blow slammed Melayne's head back, and stinging pain lanced through her cheek. She cried out in anger and shock, and her whole cheek burned. When her vision cleared, she saw that he had his hand raised for a second blow.

"If you ever want to be able to pick your nose with that hand again," she said, her voice charged with tears, "you won't lay another hand on me."

Snarling, he slapped her a second time, across the other cheek. The pain was terrible, but her anger was greater. Melayne reached out with her power, and called, *To me!*

Cotra raised his hand for a third blow, but this one never landed. Instead, a dark shape hurtled down from the sky, screaming in anger. The hawk had been passing when Melayne's call for help had reached it. Claws and a sharp beak slammed into Cotra's upraised hand and he screamed louder than the hawk as it lacerated his palm and fingers. His grip on Melayne loosened, and she jerked herself free.

The hawk rose, pleased with itself. *I'll stay for a while*, it promised. *In case you need me.* It perched on a corner of the roof, watching the scene below.

Cotra was holding his hand, which was dripping blood badly. He seemed to be in shock.

"You should learn to listen," Melayne told him coldly. Turning to the soldier who had locked her up, she said, "Get him to some medical help before he bleeds to death." The youth hurried to do just that. Cotra didn't complain as he was led away.

"Now you're going to be in serious trouble," Devra said, though there was awe in her voice. "They're really going to punish you for that "

"For what?" Melayne demanded. "I was only defending myself. And you all heard me warn him. It was his own fault."

"Melayne!" Corri protested. "This is the *army*! They're not going to see it like that. Cotra has the right to punish you."

"And where did he get that right?" Melayne asked scornfully. "He's not my parent, and nobody else has ever had any right to punish me."

Another officer was hurrying across the courtyard to join them. With him were three more soldiers. "Which one of you is responsible for attacking Captain Cotra?"

Melayne moved forward. There wasn't really any need, since every one of the recruits was staring at her anyway. "I was defending myself against him," she replied. "I warned him not to attack me. I seriously hope you have no intention of doing the same. Because if you do, I'll have to defend myself again."

"You may have caught Cotra off guard," the officer snarled, "but you won't catch me that way." He drew his sword and moved toward her. His three men followed his actions. "If you resist arrest, you're going to get very hurt."

"I'm not going back in that dungeon," Melayne promised him. "So don't even think it."

You want me to peck out his eyes? asked the hawk, eagerly.

That's a bit extreme, Melayne decided. *Let's try something a little less violent first.* It was clear that the soldiers weren't going to stop. Melayne looked across to where two mounted men sat, watching. *Horses,* she called politely. *Would you be kind enough to stop these men?*

Of course, came a joint reply. The two riders catapulted backward as the horses shot forward. The four men advancing on Melayne suddenly became aware of movement out of the corners of their eyes, and they started to turn.

The horses slammed into the startled men, knocking them aside without effort. All four men hit the ground hard and stayed there, groaning. Melayne politely thanked the horses and then marched over to where the officer lay, his arm at a funny angle.

"Now," she said, "will you please stop trying to bully me? I've had more than enough of this nonsense, and it isn't getting either of us anywhere. I'm going to have a little talk with Magwyn and get this all straightened out." She turned back to Devra and Corri. "Maybe you two had better keep an eye on the rest for now," she suggested. "I hope they'll leave everybody alone, but I'm sure you can look after yourselves if they don't."

"What are you talking about?" Devra demanded. "We can't fight the soldiers. That's crazy!"

"But she just did," one of the younger girls protested. "If she can, we can. I'm sick of following their dumb orders, too."

"So am I," a third girl decided, one of the Fire Raisers. "If any of them tries to make me, I'll set his pants on fire!" That got a chorus of laughs.

"You're all talking mutiny!" Devra said loudly, appalled. "They'll kill us for this!" She whirled on Molayne. "This is all your fault! You're going to get us all killed!"

"Don't talk nonsense," Melayne said, slightly unsure of herself. "All I'm doing is saying that they shouldn't be allowed to bully us. What's wrong with that?"

"It's not the way the army is run!" Devra explained.

"Well, I never *asked* to be in the army," Melayne replied. "If they want me that badly, then they'll just have to take me on my terms."

"You *are* crazy!" Devra protested. "All they'll do is kill you."

"You think they'd go that far?" asked Melayne, confused. "Just because I'm standing up for my rights?"

"They'll flay you alive and *then* kill you," one of the injured soldiers told her. "Filthy Talents, all of you! I hope they kill the lot of you!"

The girl who was a Changer glared at him. "So, you're like the others," she said. "You think we're less than human because we're Talents. Well, Melayne's showed us we don't have to take that." She Changed all of his clothes into stinging nettles.

Screaming with pain, the soldier leaped to his feet, strewing the nettles as he ran for cover and protection. The girl smiled at Melayne. "I'm with you," she said. "I'm taking no more stupid orders."

There was a slight smile on Devra's face. "You're going to get us all killed," she warned Melayne. "But I don't think we have much choice now. We're with you, too, I suppose."

"With me?" Melayne didn't know what the girls were talking about. "What do you mean?"

"Mutiny!" Corri said happily. "I'm sick of this training, and the bullying, too. You're right, Melayne — they don't have the power to make us obey them anymore. I say we all just quit."

Melayne looked at the rest of the recruits. Some of them moved eagerly to join the protesting girls, including a few from the boys' section. Others hung back, looking scared and uncertain. Sarrow was one of those, and this upset Melayne. She had to do her best for him, and staying here would only endanger his life. It had become time to leave, she decided.

But how would Magwyn take that decision?

Chapter Seven
Mutiny

Melayne crossed to Sarrow and looked down at him sadly. "I'm sorry," she informed him. "I know you were probably enjoying it here — a bed, friends, and meals. But it's not safe for us. They're crazy, and they're trying to make us just as bad."

Sarrow shook his head. "It's okay, I don't want to stay anyway. I think this whole thing is a trap."

"A trap?" Melayne couldn't understand him.

"Yes." He looked around at the boys with him. "I've been asking everybody, and do you know something? Not one boy in my dormitory has ever seen an adult Talent. Not one, ever. I don't think we're expected to survive the war."

Devra looked shocked. "You think they're doing all of this just to kill off the Talents? How could you even *suggest* such a thing?"

"Have *you* ever seen an adult Talent?" Sarrow challenged her. "Or *anyone* here, except for the Seeker? And all he's kept for is to sniff out other Talents. Isn't it odd that only the Talents seem to die in this dumb war we're supposed to fight."

Corri was pale. "Well, I know that some of the normals are scared of us. . . . But to try to *kill* us all like this . . . it doesn't make any sense."

"Yes, it does," Melayne said sadly. She had a strange suspicion that Sarrow had discovered something important. "If they're that scared of us and our abilities, they don't want us to grow up. This way, they can get rid of us."

"But why go to all of this trouble?" asked Devra practically. "Why not just kill us off when they know we're Talents?"

"Because they daren't," Melayne realized. "Look, even though you're Talents, you have parents and a family that loves you. They wouldn't just let soldiers come in and kill you. So, instead, the king insists that Talents have to fight his war, and that we're heroes and all. Now your families think it's a good thing that's being done to you. And when you die in the war — well, it's the enemy's fault, isn't it? Not the king's."

Devra sighed. "I hate to say it, but you're making some sense. And making me even more certain that I'm not fighting and dying for the king."

There was another chorus of agreement that broke off as Magwyn stormed out of the office building followed by several soldiers, all carrying bows.

"Trouble," Devra said. "I think we'd better get ready to use our Talents."

"Talk first," Melayne said hastily. "But a couple of Fire Raisers — keep an eye on those archers. If they look like they're going to start shooting, set fire to their bows."

Melayne swallowed nervously, realizing that this was unlikely to be easy. If Sarrow was right about what was going on — and he was very perceptive at times — then Magwyn wasn't going to allow them to walk free.

"What's going on here?" the administrator demanded, halting about ten feet from Melayne. "Do you have any idea how much serious trouble you're in, young lady?"

"No," Melayne replied honestly. "And it will all stop as soon as you let us go. We don't want to be here, and you obviously don't really want to keep us here."

"What any of us *wants* is irrelevant," Magwyn informed her. "By the king's decree, all Talents must be trained for war."

"We're trained," Devra said coldly. "So you've done your job. Now let us go."

Magwyn gave her a stony glance. "So, you're all in on this little rebellion?" he asked. He looked back at Melayne. "It appears you're a bad influence on the rest of the trainees."

"I think I'm a good influence, actually," Melayne replied. "You're trying to dehumanize them, and I don't think that's helping anybody."

"You're *not* human," Magwyn said flatly. "You're Talents. Freaks."

Corri's face was red. "So that makes it all right to send us out to die?" she demanded. "You don't intend for *any* of us to survive the war, do you?"

135

"It's your duty to fight for the king," Magwyn informed her.

"And what about what *he's* supposed to do for *us*?" Devra asked. "Isn't he supposed to look after us? Sending us off to be killed deliberately isn't my idea of protection."

Magwyn looked across the grim faces, and shook his head. "You're all going to be severely punished for this, I promise you."

"You *can't* punish us," Melayne told him. "We're Talents, remember? We won't let you bully us anymore. We have the ability to stop you."

"Stop this, then," Magwyn growled, raising his hand.

Instantly, the archers nocked an arrow each and moved to fire. As they did, all of their bows burst into flames. Screaming, they dropped their weapons and started to bat at their burning hands. Magwyn didn't seem bothered by the men's screams, but his eyes narrowed.

"So . . . that's how you want it, is it?"

"No," Melayne replied. "We just want to leave. But if you try to stop us, you'll give us no choice. We're not taking your bullying any longer."

"Tadron!" Magwyn called. "To me!"

A thin scarecrow of a man ran from the office to stand beside the administrator. Magwyn smiled coldly. "I have my own Talent at my service," he purred. "One you won't be able to stop."

Melayne felt uneasy as she looked at the gangling man. What sort of Talent did he possess? Still, maybe she could appeal to him. "Why are you siding with him?" she asked gently. "Tadron, you're a Talent and should be with us."

"Oh, no," Tadron answered, his voice oddly pitched. He sounded as if he were slightly crazy. "I know Magwyn's my friend. I'm on his side. Do as he asks you, or I'll be forced to hurt you."

"And he can," Magwyn assured her. "Tadron, do it, now!" He smiled at Melayne. "He's a Pain Caster."

For a second, Melayne didn't know what this could be. Then it felt as if every nerve in her body was on fire. Screaming, she fell to her knees, feeling nothing but the terrible agony in every part of her body. It was as if she were burning up from the inside out.

And then it was over. Tadron was panting slightly, Magwyn smirking.

"Surrender now," the administrator demanded. "Or the next time he'll fry your brain completely."

Still hurting, Melayne looked at Tadron. "You would inflict such pain on your own kind?"

"I do as I'm told," Tadron said, drooling slightly. "And I'll kill you if Magwyn tells me to."

"Let me get him," one of the Fire Raisers said quietly.

"No," Melayne answered. "This is my fight. Just wait." She realized that Tadron was a little retarded, and Magwyn had preyed on this. "I'm sorry, Tadron, but I have to show you that you can't get away with what you've done."

Tadron frowned. "Your Talent is Communication," he said, puzzled. "I'm not an animal. You can't hurt me."

"Don't believe it," Melayne told him. She'd recovered enough strength to act now. "Your clothing is full of fleas and lice. And *they're* animals." To all of his bugs, she ordered, *Bite!* Bugs have very small minds and they do as they are told.

Tadron screamed as all of the creatures sank their teeth into him at the same second. He fell to the ground, writhing about. Melayne felt a twinge of guilt as she staggered back to her own feet.

That's enough, she told the insects. Glaring down at Tadron, she added, "Did you know that there are tiny creatures inside your body called germs and bacteria? I can command them, too. If I tell them to, they'll start eating at you from the inside. You might take hours to die, in terrible agony. If you try to hurt me or any of my friends again, I'll do it."

"No," Tadron whimpered. "I can't stand pain. I can't. Just leave me alone." He'd curled up in a ball on the ground, sobbing. Melayne felt bad for him, but she'd been left with no choice.

Turning to face Magwyn, she said coldly, "I think we've just shown you that you can't stop us. Neither with soldiers, nor with renegade Talents. Let us leave in peace, and we'll do no more damage."

"Leave?" Magwyn spat on the ground at her feet. "You're loathsome Talents. I don't negotiate with Talents. I whip them when they don't obey me. I thank God every day that the wars serve to kill you all off. If you were left to infect society —"

"So, it *is* true," Devra interrupted furiously. "You train us to kill so that we can die! Well, never again! We're leaving here, and if you don't like it then you'll suffer." She concentrated, and then turned to the Changer. "That stone there," she said, pointing to the office. "Change it to sand."

The other girl grinned and concentrated. Melayne had no idea what was going on, and she stared as the rock simply melted away.

Then the wall started to crack and groan. The stones shook, and then began to tumble.

"That was the corner stone I Found," Devra said with satisfaction. "The one that holds everything else up."

The wall crumbled, collapsing in a crashing heap of rocks. People inside howled, thinking it was an earthquake, and dashed for safety. Desks and other furniture shattered in the collapse, and papers were flying everywhere. Dust sprayed the courtyard.

"Do you want more?" Devra asked Magwyn. "I can bring this whole place down on your head, if you insist."

"And I can burn it — and you," the Fire Raiser added.

"And then I can make the horses stomp on your smoking bodies," Melayne finished. "Don't you understand, Magwyn? It's over. You can't beat us when we won't allow you to. You ruled through fear and bullying, but I've made everyone see that this is all it was. You have no power over us that we won't grant you. And we grant you *nothing*. Let us go, because we're going anyway. The only question is whether we leave you anything — including your lives."

Devra grinned. "You taught us how to kill," she said. "You never expected us to use it on you, though, did you?"

Magwyn had gone pale as he'd witnessed what the Talents had done. "How far do you think you'll get?" he yelled at them. "I'll have soldiers in to hunt you down and wipe you out! All of you! None of you will survive! I'll kill every last freak among you!"

Devra shook her head. "I don't think he's understanding our message," she said. "We're going to have to start shouting."

Reluctantly, Melayne agreed. Turning to the Fire Raisers, she said: "Start burning everything. But give people the time to get out. We don't want to hurt anyone if we don't need to." To the Changer, she said, "More sand, I think." She herself called out to every animal inside the area: *Flee, now!*

A stream of rats, cockroaches, and dogs shot out of the buildings. Mice, owls, and bats fled the rafters. Horses bolted from the stables, all of them just ahead of igniting straw. The buildings started to smoke and shake. People ran from the buildings as they started to collapse. There was the sound of howling, of breaking stones and burning materials, and a thick smoke started to fall everywhere. Animals and insects swarmed past them, heading for safety. Melayne calmed a couple of the horses, and they trotted to her side.

"We're leaving," she informed Magwyn. "All of us. If you're very smart, you'll forget about trying to come after us. But I know you're probably not that smart. So I'll just tell you now that *anyone* who comes after us to hurt us is going to be in serious trouble." She gestured at the ruins all about them. "*This* proves we can do it." She pulled herself into the saddle of the horse and swung Sarrow up behind her. Devra jumped into the saddle of the other. Several more of the riders among the Talents caught and mounted the rest of the horses. Everyone else fell in with them, including those who had been unsure before. They all had grins on their faces and hope in their hearts.

Magwyn simply stood there watching them, his mouth slack and his eyes glazed. He was obviously having trouble understanding what had happened. Tadron still lay at his feet. The soldiers waited, uncertainly, for orders that never came.

Melayne whirled and led her small army out of the burning, shattered King's House. Smoke obscured their way, until they were clear of the buildings.

"We did it!" Devra said, enthusiastic for once. "Melayne, you're incredible."

"It wasn't me," Melayne replied, blushing at the praise. "It was all of us, working together for a change. They can't stand against us if we stand up in support of each other."

"But you gave us all the example," Corri added. "We never tried standing up to them before. And now we're free!"

"It's not that simple," Melayne said. "We're out of their hands, but where will we go? They're not going to let us simply walk away. If they do, they'll never be able to recruit any more Talents. And you heard Magwyn — this whole war *is* a plot to dispose of Talents. We all know it, and we're not going to fight. They're going to try to kill us again. They're afraid of us."

"Then perhaps we should give them a reason to be afraid of us," one of the Fire Raisers suggested. "Show them what will happen if they mess with us. *Force* them to leave us alone."

"I don't think that will work," Melayne objected. "For one thing, if we start a fight, they're going to *have* to kill us all. For another . . . well, it's one thing to take on Magwyn and his bullies. If anyone deserves hurting, they're the ones. But I couldn't attack innocent people. The people in the towns and villages think that they're doing the right thing by turning Talents over for the war. If we start attacking them, they'll only start believing that Talents *should* all be killed."

"Then what else can we do?" Devra demanded. "We have to do *something*."

"We have to stay together," Melayne said firmly. "Set up a community of our own. A community of Talents. Look out for one another, and be nice to the normals who live near us. Make them like us. Help them. Show them they have nothing to fear."

"And where could we do that?" Devra asked. "Where could we go?"

"Why ask me?" Melayne replied. "You're the one whose Talent is Finding. Why not Find us somewhere to go?"

Devra looked astonished. She'd clearly not considered the idea before. Now she blinked, and then looked hopeful. "Why not?" she agreed. She concentrated, using her powers, and then smiled. "Melayne, you were right! I've Found us the perfect place! It's a small island off the coast. Nobody lives there now, but there are villages on the mainland, close by. We could be by ourselves, somewhere we could defend, and yet close to normal people so we could interact with them. It's perfect!"

Melayne laughed. "See? We're working together again, and getting places. That's what we need to do. We'll start our own village, and a new life."

At that moment, Greyn came running up, panting slightly. *Melayne,* he said, urgently, *we have to talk.*

Of course, she agreed, puzzled. *What is it?*

You're in serious trouble, the wolf answered. *I stayed behind to listen to what that snake, Magwyn, was planning. He's sent for the Seeker, who, it seems, can track you down. Magwyn wants to kill both you and your brother. He's going to put troops after you.*

Melayne was shocked. She'd expected retaliation, but not this soon and not this well planned. *We're going to have to fight,* she decided.

No, Greyn argued. *You have to run. Just you and Sarrow. If you stay with the other Talents, they'll all be involved and possibly killed. Magwyn's sent for a large number of troops.*

Melayne was silent, thinking this over. Corri touched her arm, concerned. "What is it?" she asked gently.

"Magwyn wants me dead," Melayne explained. "He's getting the Seeker to track me, and is sending a large force with him."

"We'll defeat them," Devra said, full of confidence. "They can't stop us."

"No," Melayne decided. "There's no need for it. Sarrow and I will go off in the other direction. We can lead them away from you, because it's me they'll be following. That will get the rest of you time to reach the island before they can intercept you."

"A decoy?" Corri asked. "But, Melayne, that puts you in danger!"

"Not really," Melayne replied, with considerably more confidence than she actually felt. "We're on horseback, and can travel a lot faster than the rest of you can. It'll be a day or more before the Seeker arrives, giving us a head start. They'll never catch us, and they'll just waste time trying. It'll give you the time that you need."

Devra scowled. "But where can you possibly go to get away from them?" she demanded. "There's nowhere in Stormgard that you'll be safe."

"Right," agreed Melayne, making her decision. "So we won't stay in Stormgard; we'll cross the border into Farrowholme."

"Farrowholme?" exclaimed Corri. "But they're our *enemy*! They'll kill you, too!"

"Not if they don't know where we're from," Melayne insisted. "I'm sure we'll be able to fit right in. And if the king lied about the reason for the war, maybe he lied about what terrible people they are, too. If we reach there, I'm sure Sarrow and I can hide out. And I don't think the Seeker will want to lead a small army over the border. It would be the same as asking to be killed."

Devra looked stricken. "Do you really have to go?" she asked plaintively.

"I do." Melayne touched the other girl's arm. "Devra, you can lead the Talents. You've got the ability, and you know the way. Corri and the rest can help you. You'll be better off without me, since I'll be leading the true enemy in the wrong direction."

"I'm going to miss you," Corri said, looking like she was about to weep.

"I know I'll miss all of you," Melayne replied. "You're the first friends of my own kind I've ever had, and I'll never forget you. Be strong, and make me proud of you. As soon as I can, I'll return and come and find you."

"I'm the Finder," Devra said, tears in her eyes. "Maybe I should come and Find you."

"Maybe." Melayne looked at her friends with reluctance. "Take care of one another," she said, feeling the tears on her own cheeks. She had really started to like Corri and Devra and the rest, and it was breaking her heart to leave them. But she had no option. Almost angrily, she whirled the horse around. "Be brave!" she yelled as she rode off, away from the Talents. Greyn followed closely.

"Take care!" Devra called.

Melayne rode hard for several minutes on the road toward the border. Tears stung her eyes, but she didn't wipe them away. She wanted to feel the pain of parting. She'd just begun to feel like she finally had friends and a place to fit in — and now this! It was so hard to go through with it. But it was the only possible way. She had to buy time for her friends to escape, and Magwyn would track her and not them.

"It's safer for us to split off from them, too," Sarrow said with satisfaction. "We can travel faster this way. I like your plan."

"I'm glad to hear it," she said numbly. At the moment, she didn't care. She was missing her friends already. And, if she were honest with herself, scared about the choice. What if the professional soldiers caught up with them? She could stop a few of them, but not a whole force.

They had to get away. They *had* to!

She rode the horse as hard as she could. Greyn seemed to enjoy the run, keeping pace with her effortlessly. He did seem to be filling out into a strong young wolf. And he'd proven himself several times over already by helping her and saving her life. He, at least, could still stay with her. And Sarrow, of course. And now they had a steed, so they'd cover ground faster like this.

They rested a little later, before continuing again. Melayne and Sarrow were both hungry, but they didn't dare stop to try to find food until they were farther from the hunters. They were worse off than before in some ways. Melayne had been forced to leave her bag behind, so they didn't even have the map to guide them. And she didn't have her real clothing, just the trousers and tunic from the King's

House. She hated wearing them, but she had very little choice for now. She wished she were back in her skirt and blouse, and more like a girl rather than a soldier. Well, that was something to worry about later.

It was getting late in the day before Melayne called a halt so they could rest. Her stomach was growling loudly, and Greyn took off alone to look for food. Despite the running he had done, he still seemed to have enough energy left. Melayne didn't.

Sarrow, at least, provided a small help. He still had the matches he'd taken from the raider, so they were able to have a small fire crackling when Greyn returned with a large hare dangling from his mouth.

I tried catching you some tubers, he said to Melayne. *But they were all too fast for me.*

Melayne had to smile at his weak joke. *Thanks for the thought. It looks like I'm back on my meat diet again, for now.*

Greyn took half of the hare to devour where his table manners wouldn't offend the humans. Sarrow skinned their half and started it roasting. Then he looked up at his older sister.

"People are funny," he announced. "I'd always wondered what it would be like, meeting other people and getting to know them. Some of them were okay. Brakka was a bit silly, though, and not really mature."

"Most eight-year-olds are," Melayne informed him affectionately. "You're rather special."

"I know," he agreed, without blushing. "I guess I could get along without people if I had to, though. On the whole, I don't like them as well as I thought I might."

Melayne laughed. "Wait till you meet some more," she advised him. "You might like them better. I liked Devra and Corri a lot. We could have become very good friends."

"Girls!" Sarrow snorted.

"You're picking up some bad attitudes," Melayne cautioned him. "There's nothing wrong with girls. If it wasn't for girls, you'd still be at the King's House now, being trained to be killed. I didn't see many of your boys helping me out."

There wasn't any answer to that, of course, so Sarrow pretended he'd had enough talking for a while. Melayne didn't mind, since she was still worried about her friends. Would they be able to make it to their island retreat without her help? She felt responsible for them, since she'd started all of this, even if she hadn't intended for it to happen.

Greyn seemed, as usual, to know what was on her mind. *They'll be fine*, he told her. *They're Talents, and know how to use their powers now. I pity any humans who get in their way or try to stop them.*

I know, she agreed with a sigh. *But I can't help worrying about them.*

If you want something to worry about, Greyn advised, *then worry about us. We're going to have half an army on our trail tomorrow morning.*

That hadn't escaped her, of course. She simply didn't like to think about their chances. Still, they had a head start and a horse, so she felt that they had a good chance. Even with professional hunters on their trail. And it couldn't be too far to the border. Once they were over that, they'd be safe.

Except from whatever lay *over* the border. There was no way for her to know what conditions would be like in Farrowholme until they reached it. Melayne refused to worry about that, however. It was enough for now that they would be able to escape the troubles that she already knew about; anything else could wait. There was no need to seek trouble; it would arrive unbidden, she was sure.

She ate a little of the hare, even though she still disliked eating meat. She needed her strength, and Sarrow was depending on her. She couldn't allow her scruples to wear her strength down. Sarrow didn't share her worries, and he seemed to have developed a ravenous appetite. Melayne was quite glad to let him eat the majority of the food.

They settled down quietly for the night, Greyn promising to wake her just before dawn. Melayne wanted to be on her way well before the soldiers could be on their trail. If she remembered her map properly, they should be able to reach and cross the border by tomorrow afternoon. She didn't really have any idea what the border would consist of. Was it fenced off? Patrolled by armed soldiers? It could be anything. She'd simply have to wait and find out, and then decide what to do about it.

Right now, she had to sleep and conserve her strength — for whatever would happen tomorrow. . . .

Chapter Eight
Farrowholme

Greyn woke Melayne while it was still dark. Groggily, she woke Sarrow, who grumbled as usual. They made their way to the stream they had camped beside, washed their faces, and took a drink. Melayne filled the canteen that had been fixed to the horse's saddle, and as soon as the first rays of dawn tinged the sky they were moving again. Greyn went ahead of them, scouting the way. Sarrow yawned and snuggled in against Melayne's back.

Until the sun was fully above the horizon, Melayne let their horse pick its way carefully. Once they could see, however, she urged it to greater speed. Since she'd explained their situation to him, he understood their urgency. In response, he took off in a fast but not too energy-intensive way.

Melayne's behind was still sore from the previous day, but she attempted to ignore the pain as they traveled. Thanks to Greyn, they were able to stay away from any villages. Melayne didn't think that there had been any messages sent out about them, but there was little reason to chance passing too close to other people who might be able to help their trackers later.

Taking breaks only when they absolutely had to, they traveled through the morning. They were forced to stop at noon, since they were all in desperate need of their second breath, especially the poor horse. He was doing the bulk of the work, of course. Sarrow was impatient with the delay, and even more surly because there was no food for them. Greyn hadn't been able to hunt, and he had little sympathy for Sarrow's empty stomach. Melayne didn't think that going without a meal would really hurt any of them right now; certainly not as much as stopping to find food might harm them.

As soon as the horse felt ready, they were on their way again. They were still moving through woodlands and meadows, and making good time. With any luck, they would reach the border very shortly.

Melayne was more comfortable in the saddle now. She'd started to adjust to the rhythm of the horse's movement, and it no longer hurt her quite as much. And her behind was starting to become numb anyway. She realized that she'd probably never get used to riding, but with luck there wouldn't be much call for it after today.

The landscape suddenly opened out before them as the last of the woods died away. They had crested a small hill, and at the bottom of it was a river. Melayne gasped at the sight — it was huge! It had to be at least a quarter of a mile across, and she could see even from here that it was moving quite swiftly.

That's probably the border, Greyn informed her.

Melayne agreed. It certainly looked like it split two countries. So that meant they'd have to cross it somehow if they were going to flee Stormgard. *Can you swim that?* she asked their steed.

He whinnied his uncertainty as they drew closer. As they approached, Melayne could see it was pretty deep.

"Now what?" asked Sarrow. "This wasn't such a great idea, was it?" He scowled at his sister.

"It was our only chance," Melayne informed him. "And it still is. If we can get across it, I'm sure we'll be safe."

"But will we be safe crossing it?" he asked her. "You know I can't swim very well."

Melayne could swim quite strongly, but she knew she wouldn't be able to cross this river. Instead, she stroked their steed gently. *Do you think you can make it?* she asked him. *I won't ask you to do it if you don't think you can.*

The horse eyed the rushing water, and his uncertainty was obvious. Then he shook his body. *I can do anything,* he assured her. *Not a problem.* Melayne knew he was just putting on a brave face for her, and she hugged his neck.

Thank you, she said. Turning to Greyn, she asked the cub, *What about you? Can you cross here?*

He eyed the water suspiciously. *No,* he finally decided. *It's too strong for me here. But that's not a problem. I can go upstream and find somewhere that's easier. The soldiers aren't after me. You two cross here. I'll catch up with you later.*

That was a sensible decision, but Melayne knew she'd miss the wolf's help. *Take care*, she called as Greyn started to pad away.

I'm not the one running the risks, he called back. *You are. Stay well, and look for me.* Then he was gone.

Their steed moved slowly down to the edge of the water. *This is going to be a bit rough*, he warned Melayne. *You and the other human hold on tight. If you're washed out of my saddle, I won't be able to come after you.*

I understand, Melayne agreed. She wrapped the reins around her hand tightly. "Hold on, Sarrow!" she ordered her brother. His grip tightened, and she could feel him shaking from fear. The horse plunged forward.

Six steps in, he was swimming. The current tore at him, trying to drag him downstream with all of the water. The horse fought hard, even as he was being carried downstream. He struggled toward the far shore. Melayne was absolutely soaked by now, water flowing and cascading over them. Sarrow clung to her, and she held on tight to the horse. Panting, muscles straining, the steed pushed inch by inch across the river and toward the far side.

Melayne could feel the energy he was expending in his effort. His heart was racing, muscles fighting. The river tore at them all, trying to drag them along with its wild flow. The steed refused to give in, struggling all the while to stay afloat and on course.

Melayne could see very little, as her face was constantly getting soaked, and she couldn't free a hand to wipe her hair from her eyes. All she could do was trust that the horse was doing his best.

The struggle was terrible, and the force of the river almost beyond imagining. It tore at her clothes, it tried to pry Sarrow from her body, tried to drag the reins from her numb fingers. It pushed and battered at the poor steed, trying to draw him down to his doom or drag him with the flow downstream. Single-minded, the horse plunged on, swimming with all of his strength.

Then, finally, he found footing again and surged toward the shore. It took all of his remaining strength to drag himself out of the grip of the river and onto solid land once more. Then he simply collapsed.

Melayne had known this was about to happen, so she had let go of the reins and thrown herself and Sarrow to safety first. The horse, panting like crazy, his heart throbbing wildly, couldn't help it. He was so close to the end of his strength. Melayne was exhausted herself from the crossing, and could only imagine what the poor animal was going through. *Thank you*, she called, stroking his heaving neck. *You saved our lives*. He couldn't reply, of course, being far too tired, but he knew her gratitude.

"I'm soaked," Sarrow complained. "I hate being wet. And hungry."

"We'll worry about it later," Melayne told him, a little curtly. "Right now, our horse needs to rest. It's the most important thing."

"Not quite," Sarrow answered. "Look." He was pointing back across the river.

There were riders there, staring back at them. One of them was the unmistakable, cloaked form of the Seeker. They had been found already!

"Do you think they'll try to cross?" asked Sarrow, worried.

"I don't know," Melayne admitted, feeling panic starting to grow. If they did, she'd never be able to stop them. There had to be at least twenty men, all of them armed and trained. They already knew what she was capable of, so they might well be ready for her. "I think it's time we left."

"On *that*?" Sarrow asked, gesturing to the still-exhausted steed.

"No," Melayne agreed. "He's much too tired." She bent over the animal again. *Stay here and rest*, she told him. *We have to leave*. "On foot," she added to Sarrow.

"We can't outrun soldiers on horseback," Sarrow objected.

"We don't have to," Melayne answered. "Even if those soldiers do try to cross the river, their horses will be at least as drained as ours. They'll have to rest before chasing us. Anyway, they might not even try to follow us. This has to be Farrowholme we're in now, and they won't be welcome here."

"Will *we* be?" Sarrow asked.

"There's only one way to find out. Come on." Squelching in her watery boots, Melayne started up the small hill, heading for the summit. Sarrow, grumbling, fell in beside her. Melayne didn't know what they would do now, but they couldn't stop running just yet, no matter how badly she wanted to rest.

Sarrow grabbed her arm and pointed back. "They're going to try it!" he exclaimed.

Melayne looked back, and shivered. About half of the riders had plunged into the river. The other half were heading upstream, presumably hoping to find an easier place to cross. The Seeker was with this group; he obviously didn't intend to chance the river crossing. Melayne was shocked; she honestly hadn't expected them to follow. Now that she was in Farrowholme, she'd hoped that they would just give up. She'd obviously underestimated their rage and hatred.

She wished she had the strength to run, but the crossing had taken too much out of her. It was all she could do to plod on up the hill. Behind them, the soldiers' horses were swimming furiously.

Maybe she could ask the horses to turn back? No, she realized; it wouldn't work. They were too far away for her to call to them. And as much as she wanted to escape the soldiers, she didn't want to endanger their horses by interfering with their swimming. Once they reached this shore and got closer, then she'd be able to do something about them.

Melayne and Sarrow pushed forward. When they reached the brow of the hill, Sarrow whimpered in shock.

There were six soldiers there already, staring down at them in surprise.

Melayne panicked, clutching Sarrow close to her.

"Stay away from me!" she exclaimed. "You'll be sorry if you don't!"

"What are you talking about, girl?" asked the group's leader. "We don't mean you any harm. Why are you so wet?"

Melayne suddenly realized what was going on. These were *Farrowholme* soldiers. And they didn't know that Melayne and Sarrow were from Stormgard. "That's marvelous!" she exclaimed happily. She gestured back down the hill. "My brother and I were down by the river. We saw soldiers swimming over from Stormgard! We panicked and fell in, and then tried to get away."

"Stormgard, you say?" The leader tugged on his horse's reins. "You two stay out of this; we'll see to it. Head down into the village. You'll be safe there." Then he and his men spurred their way past Melayne and Sarrow, and started down toward the river.

"That was a stroke of luck on our side for once," Sarrow said with relief. "Those men will stop the ones after us. And there's a village close by. That means food and warm clothes!"

Melayne felt a surge of hope at the thought. "But we can't pay anyone," she noted.

"Let's worry about that later," Sarrow replied. The news had given him a little more strength, and he started to follow the pathway the soldiers had been traveling. Melayne hobbled along behind him, not wanting to dash his hopes. Maybe he had the right attitude after all.

Behind them, she heard the sound of yells, and

then the ring of metal on metal. The two forces had met, and engaged in combat. Melayne was almost certain that the Farrowholme men would win — there were fewer of them, but they hadn't been swimming across the river so they were a lot fresher. Plus, the hunters had to be disheartened at this turn of events. A few moments later, she discovered that she was correct. The soldiers came back up the crest of the hill, their bloody swords in hand. One of them was missing, and one was slightly wounded. The leader rode up to Melayne again.

"That's fixed their stupid attempt," he said. "Did you see any more of them, girl?"

"There were about another ten who rode upstream," Melayne informed him. "I think they were looking for somewhere easier to cross."

The man nodded. "Sensible of them. Well, we'll cut them off. You've done us a great service today, young lady. They were obviously spies sent to infiltrate our country. Brant!" The wounded man rode over. "You need that hand seen to. Go with these youngsters to the village." He looked down at Melayne again. "Are you from the village?"

"No," Melayne replied, knowing that if she lied she'd be caught quickly enough. "We're from the south. We were traveling with our parents, but they were killed. We're trying to get to our aunt's home farther north."

"Poor things," Brant said sympathetically. "Well, you helped us today, so I'll make sure they help you in the village. Come along."

Melayne fell in beside the horse as the other soldiers wheeled about and set off upstream. Brant was only about eighteen, and a little pale from the blood he'd lost from his cut hand. "Let me see it," Melayne ordered, as he rode gently beside her and Sarrow. He held his hand out, and she saw that a sword blow had cut across the back. Wincing at the thought of how much it hurt the young soldier, Melayne tore a strip from her soggy top and then wrapped it around his hand. "It's not much," she apologized, "but it should stop some of the bleeding."

"Thank you," Brant said.

"We're the ones who should thank you and your friends," Melayne said. "If you hadn't come to our aid, those soldiers would have killed us."

"Probably," he agreed. "They couldn't have let you go, knowing you'd seen them." He obviously believed the theory that the soldiers were spies. Maybe this sort of thing happened a lot. Melayne didn't know. All she knew right now was that they were safe for the time being.

They walked on in silence. Soon, Melayne could make out houses ahead of them. This had to be the village they were heading for, and she felt excitement and apprehension at once. Would anyone realize that they were actually from the enemy side of the river? Or that they were Talents?

As soon as they were spotted, several women hurried from the houses to meet them, accompanied by some of the younger children. Brant called out, "I need the Healer! And some kind people to look after these poor orphans."

"Timmin," one of the women called to a young boy. "Go fetch the Healer, instantly." The youngster shot away like a hawk after its prey. The woman hurried up to meet them. "Welcome, patrolman." She caught sight of Melayne and Sarrow. "Mercy, have you been swimming the river?"

"Being dunked in it," Brant replied for them. "They spotted soldiers from Stormgard, and fell in the river."

"Soldiers!" the woman exclaimed, shocked. "Coming here?"

"Not now," Brant assured her. "These two brave souls alerted my patrol, and we stopped them with a welcome of cold steel."

"And probably saved us all from being massacred in our sleep!" the woman exclaimed. It was certainly an overreaction, but Melayne wasn't going to set her straight.

"They can come along with me," a second woman said in a kindly manner. "I've dry clothes that should fit them from my own children, and some food for them. Do you think you could eat it?"

"Just try me," Sarrow challenged her, and the woman laughed.

"That's the spirit for young heroes," the woman said approvingly. "Come along with me, then, while your soldier gets tended to." She bustled them along to one of the stone-built houses. Once inside, she called out, "Ysane! Come here, you lazy thing, this instant."

A young woman about Melayne's age and size ran into the room. "Yes, Mother?"

The woman pushed Melayne gently. "Take this girl and give her some dry clothes. Then bring her back here while I fix a meal." To Sarrow, she added, "You come with me, and I'll find you some dry things."

Melayne reluctantly allowed herself to be led off. She didn't think anything bad would happen to Sarrow, but she didn't really like letting him out of her sight.

Ysane grinned at Melayne, taking her to a room in the back of the house. There were three beds, each with a large chest at its foot. Ysane opened one of these, and pulled out a skirt and shift, and a fresh top. They were brightly colored, and, above all, dry. "These should fit you," she said cheerily. "Get out of those wet things, and I'll get you a towel to dry off with."

Melayne was glad to obey, and even happier to towel off when Ysane returned. She had been wet and cold, and was already starting to warm up again. As Melayne started dressing, Ysane picked up her discarded trousers and tunic.

"Why were you dressed like this?" she asked, puzzled. "Don't you like girls' clothing?"

"Oh, yes!" Melayne said gratefully. "But I've been traveling with my brother for about a week on our own. I thought I'd be less likely to be attacked if people thought I was a boy."

"With *that* lovely long hair?" asked Ysane. Her own was short-cropped and blond.

"I had it up under a cap," Melayne lied. "It was washed away in the river."

Ysane looked at her with admiration. "You must be very brave," she said. "I wish I had the courage to do that."

"I'm glad you don't have the reason to do it," Melayne replied. "Our parents were killed, and we're trying to get to our aunt's. Otherwise, I'd have definitely stayed at home."

"That must be hard," Ysane agreed sympathetically. "I'd hate it if my parents were dead. Come on, you have to eat, remember?"

"How could I forget?" Melayne asked, smiling. "My stomach's been complaining all day."

In the kitchen, Ysane's mother had a slab of cold pie, along with potatoes, a mug of cider, and some wonderfully warm, fresh bread. Melayne was salivating just looking at it, and the woman insisted that she start eating immediately. Melayne didn't need further urging, and she began ravenously. Sarrow, dressed in dry clothing, joined her a moment later, matching her own keen appetite.

As she ate, Melayne gave a fabricated account of their adventures, explaining that they were from Darrien, a town she remembered from the map book. She explained that they had been traveling with their parents to visit their aunt, and that they had been attacked by bandits, who had killed their parents. Since then, she had tried to get Sarrow to their aunt's. Ysane and her mother listened and clucked at the appropriate places. It wasn't exactly the truth, but Melayne didn't dare tell that.

"Well, you can stay here the night," Ysane's mother said firmly. "And if you insist, you can travel on again tomorrow. We'll make sure that you have some supplies, at least."

"Thank you," Melayne said, grateful. Whatever anyone in Stormgard believed, it was obvious that the average person in Farrowholme was just as nice as they were back home. These people weren't monsters; quite the opposite, if anything.

After she was full, Melayne asked if there was anything that she could do to help around the house. "Our parents were farmers, too," she explained. "Sarrow and I know what to do."

"There's no need to work," Ysane's mother protested. "You've had a terrible shock."

"I'd prefer to help out," Melayne insisted. "You've been so kind to us, and I wouldn't feel right, lazing while you work."

The woman chuckled. "Very well," she agreed. "Why don't you help Ysane with her chores, and the youngster here can help me with dinner. Do you think you'll be ready to eat again in a couple of hours?"

"Definitely!" Sarrow said, and that made her laugh happily.

Melayne followed Ysane, and helped her with her jobs. They worked out in the barn, where Ysane was transferring apples from barrels into the cider press, to make more of the common drink. With the two of them working at it, the job went quickly. Ysane was a chatterer, which suited Melayne very well. It meant that she didn't have to talk too much, lessening the chance that she'd slip up and say the wrong thing. It also meant that she could learn what life was like around here, and what the locality was like.

Because now she had a decision to make. They were out of Stormgard and safe in Farrowholme. But where would they stay? They didn't have any relatives here, and Melayne honestly didn't know where they might go. Perhaps something Ysane would say might give her a clue.

It was starting to get dark by the time the two girls had finished pressing the apples and storing the cider. There was a call from the house, and they went across together to join the family for the day's main meal. There was a father, three boys — one Sarrow's age, the other two almost old enough to be married — and two girls slightly older than Ysane. It was a cheerful family, and they made Sarrow and Melayne feel right at home. The meal even started with the father giving thanks to the good God for the food, just like her own father had always done. A tear touched the edge of her lashes, but she brushed it away without spoiling the mood.

To her surprise, she was ready to eat again. She avoided the meat, sticking to vegetables and more of the delicious warm bread. Sarrow, of course, ate everything he could. He seemed to have fit right in, and everyone made a point of including him in the general conversation. Ysane's mother must have told the family Melayne's story, because nobody asked about it, beyond one of the brothers asking if it had been scary seeing the enemy soldiers.

"Horrible," Melayne admitted. "That was why I

lost control of the horse and we fell in the river. We were very lucky we weren't swept away."

"It was pretty brave of you to warn the patrol, though," the boy said, his admiring look lingering on her for a moment. With a rush of awareness, Melayne realized he was sizing her up. She blushed slightly at the attention. This had never happened to her before. Well, *of course* it hadn't; she'd never sat down with a boy like this before. She discovered that she liked the feeling of being looked at and admired. The boy, Falma, made sure to pass her whatever she needed, and tried to include her in what was being said. Melayne discovered that she didn't know what to reply, though, and was quieter than normal. Still, Sarrow more than made up for her silences.

Ysane seemed to have realized what was happening, and she took every opportunity to mildly tease her brother while winking slyly at Melayne. Falma stumbled a bit at this, but didn't let it deter him. All in all, it was a pleasant meal in good company. Melayne was more certain than before that the prejudices of Stormgard against Farrowholme were baseless. This was a lovely family who cared for one another and had compassion for strangers. What was there not to like about them?

Besides, Falma was kind of cute, in his own way. Having grown up on a farm, he was muscular, and he had a sort of rugged good looks, with hair as blond as Ysane's and almost as long. He had kindly eyes, too. Melayne couldn't help meeting their gaze from time to time, and then she would have to look away, blushing.

After the meal, she helped the mother clean up. She and Ysane washed the dishes between them, and Falma and his brother dried and stacked them. Once that was done, the chores were finished for the day.

"Would you like to sit outside for a while?" Falma asked her, a little nervously.

"Is sitting all you have in mind?" asked Ysane, giggling slightly. "We all saw how you've been looking at Melayne all evening."

"You're not too old for me to smack your backside, you know," Falma informed her, blushing slightly.

"I don't think it's *my* behind that you're interested in," Ysane laughed, not at all bothered by his threat.

Melayne realized that the two of them might go on like this for quite some time. "I'd love to sit and talk," she said to Falma.

"If you need help, holler," Ysane said in a stage whisper. "I can still wrestle him to the ground in twenty seconds, if he gets fresh."

"I'm sure he won't," Melayne answered.

"Me, too, to be honest," Ysane replied quietly. "But you can always hope, can't you?" Grinning, she wandered off.

Melayne left the house with Falma. He led her toward the well behind the house, where there was a large bench. He sat close to one end, shyly. Melayne sat in the center, and looked up at the sky. Stars shone down brightly, masked only by thin veils of clouds. "It's lovely out here," she said. "It reminds me so much of my own home."

"I'm sorry about what happened to you, Melayne," Falma said. "It must be very hard for you. But I admire the way you cope."

"It is hard," she agreed. "But I've discovered that there are a lot of nice people in this world. Like your parents. They are very kind." She sighed. "I seem to be meeting either very nice or very nasty people, and not much in between."

"At least there are some nice people in your life," Falma said gently. "You deserve to be treated nicely."

Melayne smiled at his sweetness. "Thank you. But I'm afraid we have to be on our way tomorrow. We have a lot of ground to cover. So don't get too used to having me around."

"Do you *have* to go?" Falma asked her. "Couldn't you stay — at least for a while? Sarrow seems to be at home here and . . ." He stumbled slightly. "I think *you* could get to be at home here, too."

Melayne patted his hand, which raised a fierce blush in his cheeks. "Perhaps I could," she agreed. "But it simply isn't possible. Not that I'm not seriously tempted." And she was; this was a lovely family, and she and Sarrow might well fit right in. Falma's interest in her was apparent, and she couldn't help feeling an attraction of her own for him.

But . . . there was *always* a "but," it seemed. What would happen when the family discovered the truth about her and Sarrow? She could lie about their background for a while, but the truth was bound to come out sometime. Especially if Falma pressed on with his romantic interest. Well, they were nice folk, and they might be able to forgive Melayne and Sarrow the accident of their being born in an enemy country. Maybe. However, there was still the problem of being Talents. There was absolutely no way for them to hide the truth for very long. Melayne could no more stop Communicating than she could stop breathing.

So, hard as it might be, she and Sarrow had to move on. And there was no way that she could possibly explain this decision to Falma, or to Ysane, as much as she liked them both.

Her decision wasn't to Falma's approval, that was clear. But he was too polite to argue much. Instead, he chattered on about his work, and life in the village. Melayne let him talk, knowing that he was simply trying to make her feel comfortable here and change her mind about leaving. She let most of what he was saying pass over her head with barely more than a smile and an affirmative comment.

Until something he was saying caught her attention with a jolt.

"It's a big castle," he said, gesturing to the north. "But very run-down. It used to be very powerful thirty, fifty years ago. But now it's not. Hundreds of people used to work there, but there's only a handful now, with the current lord. They say he's crazy, and very few people will work there."

"Really?" Melayne was intrigued. "What's the place called again?"

"Dragonhome," he answered, amused by her interest.

"Dragons . . ." she breathed, entranced.

"Not *real* ones," Falma added with a chuckle. "I've not seen the place myself — we tend to avoid it — but one of my friends says that there's a big stone dragon guarding the gate. That's why it's called Dragonhome." He shrugged. "Me, I think they call it that just to make it sound big and scary. I mean, would you stay away from a castle that called itself something like Pigsty?"

Melayne laughed. "No," she agreed. "Dragonhome certainly makes it sound fierce. But I always thought it was a shame that there aren't really any dragons."

"Good riddance to them," Falma answered. "You'd like to have man-eating monsters around? I'm glad they were all killed off — *if* they ever really existed. You're too soft, that's the problem."

"Is it a problem?" she asked gently.

"No," he admitted. "It makes you even more attractive. But you have to choose your sympathies with care. I think you should be glad for us humans that there aren't dragons around to gobble us all up." He grinned. "I hear they're partial to pretty young virgins, which would make you a *very* tempting target."

"For the dragons . . . or for you?" Melayne asked, and was rewarded with another furious blush. She smiled; she couldn't help liking Falma. "I think it's about time for us to go back inside. Otherwise your family might suspect you're trying to eliminate me from being potential dragon bait." When he looked a bit confused by her comment, she added: "The *virgin* bit." That made him blush furiously once again. He obviously was very attracted to her.

Well, she liked him, too. She knew that she could do a lot worse for herself. He was a good person, and clearly a hard worker. He'd be starting his own farm and family one of these days, and Melayne had no doubt he'd be a good and decent man. And he was good-looking, pleasant, and just inexperienced enough to be very appealing. If she could stay, she was sure she could get to like Falma a lot.

But she couldn't stay; it was out of the question. So, regretfully, was a relationship with the handsome youth. Melayne led him back to the main house, and discovered Ysane was just inside the kitchen, dying with curiosity.

"So," she asked eagerly, "are you staying?"

"Only tonight," Melayne replied. "Sarrow and I must be on our way tomorrow, I'm afraid."

Ysane's face fell. "I was hoping . . ." she said.

"So was I," Melayne agreed. "You have a lovely family. And a really cute brother I think I could get to like. But we can't stay."

Ysane wasn't about to give up, Melayne could see, so Melayne pleaded that she was too tired to stay up longer and needed to get some rest. It wasn't really a lie, either. The day had been very long, and she was almost completely exhausted. And, as with all farm families, bedtime was early in this house.

She was to share Ysane's bed for the night, and was loaned a gown for the evening. It was strange for Melayne to share a bed with anyone — even another girl — and she realized that her life was changing in so many different ways. It was hard to keep track of what had happened to her in just one week.

Ysane wanted to talk for a while, of course, mostly about the possibility of Melayno staying. Melayne managed to switch her attention by asking the other girl about Dragonhome.

"It's *haunted*," Ysane answered promptly. "There are so many ghost stories about the place. They say the current lord is very handsome and totally insane."

"They say?" Melayne asked. "Doesn't anybody know?"

"Are you serious?" Ysane asked, her eyes wide in the moonlight from the window. "Nobody goes near the place! And he never comes to the village. Sometimes his cook does, and she's strange enough. She's kind of creepy, and doesn't care about fitting in at all. She won't talk about the castle, or him, but there are tales."

"I'm sure there must be," agreed Melayne. She was intrigued now. People always gossiped, and the worst possible stories always were believed. Melayne knew that from the stories she had read. The more she heard about Dragonhome, the more perfect it sounded to her. A lonely place where nobody much went. A lord who kept to himself. She and Sarrow might be able to hide out forever there! If there was only some way to be allowed into the castle . . .

Ysane talked about some of the ghosts that were rumored to live there, mostly of former owners or their wives or children who had died in gruesome ways. Melayne wasn't too bothered by these stories, since she didn't really believe in ghosts. Her mother had always insisted they were only overactive imaginations at work, and Melayne was inclined to agree with her. Ysane, however, clearly believed that they were real, and to be avoided.

It was a perfect place to hide. Provided, of course, that the stories about it weren't true. . . . What if it really *was* haunted? Melayne tried to dismiss the thought, but it kept returning. Maybe there was some substance to the gossipy tales after all.

She hoped not, because she was getting more and more certain that this might be a place to hide out. *If* she could get in . . .

It was something to work on tomorrow. . . .

Chapter Nine
The Dragon Gate

Melayne had a hard time not crying as she and Sarrow said their good-byes to Ysane's family the following morning. She was amazed at how close you could get to another person in a very short space of time. She seemed to have a knack for making friends easily — but not being able to keep them. Ysane cried a little, and Falma looked rather unhappy. Their mother insisted that Melayne and Sarrow keep the clothing they had been given, and gave them a bag of food, enough to last several days.

"If you can," Falma begged her, "come back and see us."

"If I can," Melayne promised. She *would* like to see the family again, even though the risks were rather great. They had been so kind.

Sarrow felt the same way, evidently. He'd kicked up a fuss about leaving when she had told him that they must. However, once she'd explained her reasons, he quickly agreed that she was doing the right thing. "They treat me nicely," he complained. "I don't like going. But I guess we have to."

Ysane insisted on walking with them part of the way as they left the village. They learned from the local women that the soldier, Brant, had had his hand seen to and had ridden on the previous afternoon. Melayne was glad to hear that he was fine.

At the edge of the village, Ysane gave Melayne a hug, and said good-bye again. Melayne hugged her back, and then deliberately walked quickly away. It was better to go now, before either of them grew more weepy. There were tears in the corners of her eyes, though, as she and Sarrow marched down the road.

"Girls!" Sarrow said scornfully. "You don't catch me crying."

"That's because we're taking with us what you cared most about in that house," Melayne replied. "Food."

"True enough," he agreed, with an impudent grin. He seemed to be in good spirits, so Melayne explained her plan to him as they walked.

"You wouldn't be frightened of going to a haunted castle?" she asked him.

"Not me!" Sarrow boasted. "Only a girl would be afraid. I'll face any ghost, any day."

"Good," Melayne said. "You may have to." Then she sighed. "There's no guarantee that this mysterious lord will have a job for us, though. Or that he'll be sane enough that I'd chance staying."

"He'll let us stay if he sees us," Sarrow said with confidence. "All the young men seem to enjoy fawning over you. Falma was really sickly with it last night." He gave her a critical look. "I guess that must mean that you're pretty or something."

Melayne smiled as his naiveté. "I suppose I must be," she agreed. "So you think I could charm this lord into letting us stay?"

"Only if he isn't blind," Sarrow answered. "Some men will do anything to impress a girl. Not me, though. I'm not that stupid."

"No," Melayne agreed. "But maybe you're just too young. Wait till you're Falma's age; I'll bet you'll be making eyes at all the young girls then."

"Not me," vowed Sarrow. "I've got more sense than that."

He's got very little sense of any kind, a familiar voice said. Greyn loped out of the woods. *Miss me?*

Melayne stooped to give the cub a hug. *Of course I did! It's not the same without you.*

"Why did *he* have to come back?" Sarrow complained. "It's much nicer without him."

Some things don't change, I see, Greyn replied. *He's still as nasty as ever.*

He's not nasty, Melayne insisted. *He's just a boy.*

You can't use that excuse for him forever, the wolf answered. *And I don't think he's going to change much, no matter how old he gets.*

Don't be jealous, Melayne cautioned him. *Anyway, are you all right?*

Oh, I'm fine, Greyn assured her. *I crossed the river a few miles upstream. It's a lot quieter there. Then I saw something interesting. The soldiers who were after us found the same spot and came over.*

175

They started heading this way, so I followed them to see if they would find you. But other humans from this side of the river found them, and they fought. The one they called the Seeker ran away, but the others were killed. So I don't think there's anyone after you at all right now.

That's good news, Melayne agreed. *And I think I might have found us somewhere to stay.* She told the cub about the castle.

Sounds like my kind of place, the wolf agreed. *If it's big and run-down, there must be somewhere I can stay where I won't be spotted. If I'm with you, people will know you're a Talent. But I don't want to be too far away from you. You lead such an interesting life.*

Melayne was amused, but Greyn was correct: They shouldn't be seen together. She didn't like having to ask Greyn to hide, but the wolf seemed happy enough with the idea. He decided to explore ahead, and ran off again. Sarrow was glad to see him go.

Ysane had been a bit vague as to where Dragonhome actually was, but she did know it was to the north of the village, and only about four or five hours' walk. Melayne stopped a passing raven, and asked him if he knew where the castle was.

Can't miss it, the bird answered. *It's straight ahead. You can just about see it from here. Well, you would if you had good eyesight, like mine.*

Just ahead, the trees thinned out again, and a few minutes later they could make out the castle. Melayne had been a bit disappointed with the King's House, thinking it wasn't like a real castle. This one, however, lived up to her imagined picture — and more.

It was obviously large, even from a distance, and made of gray-brown stone. There were towers at the corners, and two more midway along the longest sides. The walls were high, with narrow windows, and there was a moat surrounding the castle. The drawbridge, at least, was down, so they could approach.

But the most impressive thing about the castle was the main entrance. As Ysane had mentioned, it was shaped like a dragon, made of heavy stone. In fact, the castle looked as though it were growing out of the back of some immense dragon that had been magically converted into stone centuries before. As Melayne and Sarrow drew closer, they could make out more and more details. The dragon's head jutted out toward the drawbridge, its mouth open as if roaring or breathing fire. Carved "teeth" hung down and jutted up from the ground. With a shudder, Melayne realized that to enter the castle you had to walk between the stone jaws. The massive head looked strong and aggressive, and the two eyes were windows, for guards to examine visitors. The short neck led to a squat body, and it was from this that the castle rose. Twin stone paws were walls, preventing anyone from getting around the head.

"It's not exactly welcoming," Sarrow complained. "Are you sure this is a good idea?"

"I'm fairly sure," Melayne replied, swallowing. It *was* rather oppressive, which it was no doubt meant to be. Anyone trying to attack this castle would certainly feel this way. It looked almost impregnable. Maybe this hadn't been such a good idea, after all.

It wasn't until they were closer that they could see the castle was no longer in the best condition. Some of the stonework had tumbled from the walls, and one of the towers looked rather rickety. Melayne imagined that it must cost a fortune to keep the castle in good repair, and maybe the local lord's family had lost money and could no longer afford to keep it in prime condition.

Somewhat nervously, Melayne led Sarrow toward the drawbridge. It was then that she realized that it wasn't a true drawbridge after all. There was no way to raise it, because of the dragon head. Instead, it was simply a ten-foot-wide bridge that pivoted at the far end. It could be turned to open a gap across the moat. The water was green and slightly scummy, and Melayne imagined she'd probably be in grave danger of catching a disease sooner than a fish in it. Sarrow gripped her hand, and they walked across the bridge and up to the dragon's-head gate.

There was a grille across the mouth, blocking access. Melayne stopped, looking around. There was no sign of anyone at all.

"Hello!" she called. "Is there somebody here?"

"Maybe there's nobody living here," Sarrow suggested. "It looks pretty crumbly and deserted."

"Ysane said that there's a lord and a cook, at least," Melayne answered. "So —"

"Go away," a slightly cracked voice said from above them.

Melayne gave a start, and then looked up. There was a man in one of the dragon's eyes, glaring down at them. He was some sort of a soldier, that was clear, but he looked like he was in his twenties, at least.

"Oh," Melayne replied. "Hello. We're just here —"

"I don't care why you're here," the soldier answered. "No visitors are allowed, by order of Lord Sander."

"Maybe we should go," Sarrow suggested. He seemed to be very nervous about this place.

"No," Melayne whispered back. Smiling at the sullen guard, she said, "We're not visitors. We've come to see if Lord Sander could use a couple more people on his staff."

"Looking for jobs?" the guard asked, obviously not expecting that reply. "Nobody comes here looking for jobs."

"Nobody plus two," Sarrow replied, a little annoyed.

The guard considered this for a moment. "I don't think Lord Sander wants any more help," he finally decided.

Melayne refused to be put off. "But you don't *know* that," she pointed out. "Maybe you'd better send somebody to ask him. You wouldn't want to turn us away, and then discover he *does* need help, would you?"

Again, the guard thought. "You may as well wait," he finally decided. Then he vanished from the window.

Sarrow sighed. "This castle is oppressive," he decided.

"It *is* a bit intimidating," Melayne agreed. "But it means that there won't be anyone coming here looking for us. And I'm sure we could get used to it, in time."

"If we're given the time," Sarrow said. "It's more likely they'll just send us away, if this Lord Sander is anything like this soldier."

"Well, we'll just have to wait and see." Melayne refused to allow Sarrow's pessimism to contaminate her. She was almost certain that what she was doing was right. She couldn't quite decide why she felt so confident, but she was.

Sarrow, on the other hand, seemed nervous. He was fidgeting, which was something he normally didn't indulge in, and he had an almost tangible air of gloom over him. It was as if he was expecting the dragon to suddenly come to life and swallow him.

"There's nothing to be afraid of," she told him, trying to comfort him.

"You can't possibly *know* that," Sarrow replied. "It's just that you're always expecting the best. Even after all that's happened to us. Well, I'm expecting the worst. And if it doesn't happen, I'll be happy."

There was no point in talking to him if he was going to be in this sort of mood. Melayne ignored him, looking around instead. Though there was a certain amount of neglect obvious — the grass and undergrowth about the castle needed trimming, for example — she saw that the bars across the gate were cleaned, and the stones were in good repair. Nobody could get into the place without an invitation. A couple of men in the dragon's eyes could hold off an invading army if it was necessary. And the tower and walls that needed repair were well above ground level. The main walls were sturdy enough.

Was this Lord Sander expecting trouble, then? Or did he simply like his privacy?

Then the soldier was back, looking down on them. "Lord Sander has graciously decided that he will see you," he called down.

"That's very kind of him," Melayne said politely.

"Yes," the soldier agreed. "It is. I told him not to bother, but he never takes *my* advice."

"Why should he?" Sarrow asked rudely. "You're in his employ, not the other way around."

"Sarrow!" Melayne said, shocked. "That was uncalled for!"

"Aye," the soldier agreed. "But accurate, for all that. Hold on." He bent to some mechanism. With a groan and a clatter of metal, the grille began to rise from the ground. The edges of it were finished in sharp spikes that Melayne eyed nervously. There was the sound of a ratchet, and the grille stopped in place, some five feet from the ground. "Just duck under it," the soldier advised them.

Melayne didn't like the thought of bending under those spikes, but there wasn't really much choice. Swallowing, she ducked under the grille quickly and straightened up beyond it. Sarrow scowled, but followed her lead.

From above, she heard the ratchet release, and the grille slammed back into place, grinding at the stone flaggings. Melayne shuddered, imagining how easily it could have crushed her body if she'd been under it when it fell.

A door beside the grille opened, and the soldier came out. "I'll show you the way," he said. "Don't dawdle, and don't deviate from the path. Parts of the castle have seen better days, and if you wander off, I'll not be held responsible for your safety."

"Charming," muttered Sarrow. Melayne nudged him, and they followed after the soldier. She was a little nervous as they passed through the stone throat of the dragon. At the end was a second grille, but this was already raised and locked into place. The soldier passed below it without a thought, and Melayne followed with considerably less confidence. Another short passageway led them into the inner courtyard.

As in the King's House, the courtyard was large. But this was mostly open. There were buildings beside the walls, but some of them had been abandoned. At least one was a stable, for Melayne caught the unmistakable scent of horse manure. There was only one other person in sight, hurrying between two of the buildings and ignoring them.

The soldier led them across the courtyard to a large door. They went inside, and the walls felt cold around them. The stone was hard and dark, and there were burning torches set into sconces in the walls at long intervals. Melayne and Sarrow were led down the passageway, and then the soldier rapped on a door and held it open. "In you go," he said.

Melayne nodded, and led the way, Sarrow hanging back unhappily. Inside the doorway she paused uncertainly.

It was a smallish room, about ten feet across, and circular. It had to be the base of one of the towers, she realized. There was a fireplace opposite the door, with a brisk fire burning. A pot of some kind hung on a metal arm above it. There were only two windows, one small, one larger, not allowing in much light from outside. Most of the light came from the ruddy glow of the fire. The walls were hung with tapestries, quite nicely woven, primarily green and gold. There were three in all, and each of them showed dragons. One had a dragon perched on a rock, looking down at the world. A second showed a dragon flying over a landscape. The third showed a dragon in some sort of mountainous nest.

The only furniture in the room was a desk, three chairs, a table with a wine jug and fruit bowl on it, and a larger chair — not really a throne, but ornately carved — that was the only one occupied. The man clearly had to be Lord Sander himself.

He was sitting, but Melayne could tell that he would be tall if he stood. He was well-built, though not overly muscular. He had dark hair that hung to his shoulder. His clothing was expensive but not garish — a dark tunic and darker trousers. His boots were almost up to his knees and well-made, if slightly worn. He had gloves on each hand that stretched up to his elbows. He wore no weapons, and there was no smile on his face. His eyes were dark and intense as he looked over first Melayne and then the uncomfortable Sarrow. He couldn't be more than in his midtwenties, Melayne realized. She'd been picturing someone older.

Melayne wasn't sure if it would be polite to speak first, but she decided that politeness couldn't hurt her cause. She curtsied instead.

"It's not often we get strangers here at Dragonhome," Lord Sander said. His voice was modulated, projecting well without effort. He leaned forward, his chin on his right hand, looking at Melayne once again. She felt self-conscious as his eyes examined her. "Why do you come here?"

"If it please your lordship," she replied, "my brother and I are orphans."

"So am I," the lord answered. "What of it?"

"Since my parents are dead," Melayne went on, refusing to be put off, "I have to look after my brother. We need somewhere to live, and some work to do. My brother needs to be safe, to have regular meals and a bed at night. I thought you might have need of extra workers here."

Lord Sander nodded slightly. "And you can do . . . what?"

"Our parents were farmers, my lord," Melayne answered. "We can both do farmwork. I imagine you have fields to grow food for this castle and its inhabitants."

"Its inhabitants are fewer than you might think," the lord replied. "But you are correct — we do have fields." He inclined his head slightly. "And we do have enough farmers already. Is there anything else that you can do?"

"I'm a willing worker," Melayne said hastily,

sensing problems. "But I admit that I have no great training for other professions."

"I see," Lord Sander said. "No skills that may be of use to me?"

"No," she admitted in a quiet voice. She couldn't tell him about her Talent! And there really wasn't anything else she could do. She and Sarrow were going to be thrown out after all. She knew it.

The Lord nodded, as she confirmed what he had guessed. He looked at Sarrow. "You're very quiet," he commented. "How does your sister treat you?"

"She looks after me," Sarrow replied, almost defiantly. "She's good at it. She's kept me safe and alive since our parents were killed. And she thinks you might be able to help her."

"Do *you* think that?" Lord Sander asked.

"No," Sarrow admitted honestly. "I think she's silly to even ask. But she does what she thinks is right." Sarrow shrugged. "Most of the time it is."

"Most of the time." The lord seemed to be slightly amused. He looked back at Melayne. "Your brother speaks well of you."

"Not always," Melayne felt compelled to admit.

That made Lord Sander smile. "If he spoke well of you all the time, he wouldn't be a younger brother." He considered for a moment, and Melayne was certain that the most they could now hope for was a meal and perhaps to be allowed to stay the night before being sent on their way. "You're both honest, at least," he said. "Though I think you underestimate your skills, girl. This is a harsh world, and if you've been able to bring yourself and your brother this far, then you have some abilities. Perhaps even ones that I can use."

Hope surged within her again. "Then you have a job I can do?" she asked.

"No." But, before her hopes crashed and burned, he added, "I have a job that *both* of you might be able to do. Corran!"

Melayne was confused, but guardedly optimistic. What was going on? The door opened behind them, and a young boy entered the room. She looked him over, and saw that he was younger than Sarrow — five, probably. He was small, thin and dark, and he looked sad.

"This is my son, Corran," Lord Sander said gently. "He is the only child in Dragonhome." He looked at Sarrow. "Until now. He has been very lonely, and needs companionship and caring." He stared intently at Melayne. "You've done rather well with your brother, girl. Do you think you could do as well with my son?"

Melayne looked at the boy, and he looked back at her. She could sense a hollowness in him, a void that needed filling. "What about his mother?" she asked.

"I'll show you her grave someday," Lord Sander answered. "She died in childbirth. Corran had a wet nurse from the village, but the woman . . . didn't fit in. Since then, he's had to make do. I feel ashamed to admit that — I'm not all the father I ought to be. But I have . . . responsibilities that do not allow me to act as I wish toward him. So — my first question for you, girl, is: Do you think you could look after him?"

"Yes," said Melayne without hesitation. "He needs someone, and I think I can help. So can Sarrow — he'd have a playmate then."

"Good." The lord nodded his approval. "My second question: Are you discreet? Life about my castle is . . . unusual, shall we say? You may have to go into the village, or visit others on my behalf. Can I trust you to keep my secrets?"

Melayne had no idea what he was talking about, but it wasn't a hard question to answer. "Yes," she informed him. "And I can keep my own just as well."

That made Lord Sander smile. "A fine reply. Perhaps I shall have to try and discover what secrets they might be. You look like an . . . interesting challenge." Melayne shuddered at the thought of his discovering her Talent. "The final question." He leaned forward. "What is your name? I can't keep calling you *girl* if you're to look after my son."

"It's Melayne," she answered, smiling.

"A pretty name for a pretty girl," Lord Sander replied. "Very well, you're hired on a trial basis. Whether you stay depends on how Corran takes to you. And how I do." Before Melayne could thank him, he called out: "Bantry!" The soldier who had brought them to this room entered and saluted smartly. "Take these youngsters over to see Hada. They'll be staying with us, at least for a while."

"Aye, my lord." The soldier — Bantry — held the door open.

Melayne turned back to Lord Sander. "Thank you, your lordship," she said. "I'm very grateful."

"Look after my son for a week," he replied, a smile twitching at his lips. "Then we'll see how grateful you are. Go with Bantry. If I need you, I'll send word. First, however, a final warning." He held up a hand. "Bantry and Hada will explain which regions of the castle you must stay within. The rest is off-limits. Much of it is dangerous."

"I understand, my lord," Melayne answered. She curtsied again for good luck, and then held out her hand to Corran. The young boy took it without a word. Melayne led him out of the audience room, Sarrow following.

The first obstacle, at least, had been overcome. They were in Dragonhome, and she had a job. Melayne was excited at the prospect, despite the signs of problems ahead. She smiled down at the serious boy beside her. "This will be fun," she promised him. "We'll get along."

He didn't reply.

Chapter Ten
A New Life

Melayne couldn't help feeling excited as she followed Bantry down the passageway. Her hunch had paid off, and she and Sarrow were now in the castle! Lord Sander seemed to be very withdrawn, though not as much as his young son. . . .

Bantry opened another door, and gestured for Melayne to go inside the room. Melayne obeyed, and realized that they had reached the kitchen. It was a large room, with a huge fireplace and chimney. There were small ovens built into the walls of the fireplace, and lots of metal armatures so that pots could be pushed into the fire. There were two already in place, bubbling away, being watched over by a teenage boy.

In the center of the room was a large table, where a middle-aged woman was working chopping vegetables. Along the walls various cooking utensils, barrels of foodstuffs, and bundles of vegetables were stored. A door at the far end of the room probably led to the larder and root cellar, Melayne guessed.

The only other person in the room was a tall woman who seemed to be in her late twenties. She had honey-gold hair caught up on her head, and wore a simple but pretty flowing dress. Melayne couldn't see her feet.

"Hada," Bantry said, gesturing at Melayne and Sarrow, "the lord has decided that these two will be working for him, looking after Corran. You're to get them settled and explain things to them."

"How am I ever going to get all my work done if I'm constantly interrupted?" Hada asked with a sigh. "Oh, very well, very well. Off you go, Bantry. You're lazy enough, without any encouragement to stay in the kitchen." She shooed the soldier out, and then turned to Melayne with a pleasant smile. "Welcome to Dragonhome, child. I am Hada. I look after the household for Lord Sander."

Melayne smiled back. "I'm Melayne, and this is my brother, Sarrow," she replied. "We're very pleased to be here." Sarrow looked less than sure that he was pleased. He was glaring at Corran rather scornfully.

"Good." Hada turned back to the cook. "Well, I trust you can manage without me for a few minutes?"

"I can manage without you a lot longer than that," the cook answered sullenly. "I know how to run my own kitchen without your help."

"Mind your tongue!" Hada said sharply. Then, shaking her head, she turned back to Melayne.

"Some people," she commented. "Come along, then. Let me show you where you'll be staying." She examined the two of them carefully. "No belongings?"

Melayne shook her heads. "We lost everything when bandits killed our parents."

"Poor things. Well, I'm sure I can find you a few things around the place. Come along." She led the way out of the kitchen, and down one of the ever-present corridors. Melayne was paying careful attention, so she could find her way around the castle later. She was starting to suspect that a map would be very useful. Even though there weren't many people here, it was a large place. Sarrow simply followed silently, ignoring almost everything around him. Corran was withdrawn into himself.

Luckily, they didn't have to go far. Hada led them out into the courtyard, and to one of the smaller buildings by the wall. Just inside the door, she opened a second. "This will be your room, Melayne," she said. "Sarrow can have the room next door."

Melayne peeked in, and saw that the room was small but neat. There was a bed, a chest, a table, a washbasin, two chairs, and a reasonably large window with drapes. It certainly wasn't pretentious, but it would be fine.

"I'll have the bedclothes sent over for you," Hada assured her as Melayne eyed the unmade bed. "Along with some spare clothing for the both of you. The latrine is at the end of the hall, last door on the left." She looked serious for a moment. "Now, you can go where you like in this building — except other people's rooms, unless you're invited — and also in the main castle. But stay away from the rest of the place. Money's been tight for a while now, and a lot of the castle isn't in very good shape. You could get injured or killed if you go poking around. Lord knows it's happened a couple of times since I came here, and I don't enjoy having to bury people your age. So be careful. If you've any doubts, don't enter. Ask." She rubbed her hands together. "Well, I've a lot to do, and it won't get done standing around chattering, however pleasant it may be. Corran will no doubt tell you when it's time for meals. He's got a healthy appetite, despite the way he looks."

"Thank you," Melayne said politely.

"Not at all, child," Hada answered. "We're like a family here in Dragonhome, and I trust you'll fit right in. If you have any problems, feel free to seek me out. But, as I've said, I am very busy, so I'd prefer it if it wasn't for frivolous reasons." Then she laid a hand on Melayne's shoulder. "A word with you alone, please. Sarrow, you can keep an eye on Corran for a moment."

Hada led Melayne outside again, and lowered her voice. "You've a tough job ahead of you," she confided. "Corran is a strange one. Very withdrawn. Doesn't speak to many people, and likes even fewer. But his father loves him, so take care of the boy. Just don't expect much response from him."

"I'll do my best," Melayne assured her, worried. It didn't sound as though things were going to be easy.

"That's all we can ask, girl." Hada smiled again. "Is there anything else you need to know?"

"I think that's all for now," Melayne decided. "I'm sure I'll have lots of questions later, though."

"Fine. Well, I must be about my business." With a final half-smile, Hada hurried off across the courtyard, back to talk to the cook again, no doubt.

Melayne hesitated a moment. Hada seemed to be friendly and helpful. It was nice to have someone in the castle like that. It would certainly make settling in here easier. Melayne smiled to herself, and was about to collect Sarrow and Corran when she heard a familiar voice.

You seem to be doing quite well for yourself.

Happily, Melayne turned to greet and hug Greyn. *How did you get in here?* she asked him.

Wolves can find a way, he answered, licking her face. *I know, I've got to stay hidden when anyone else is around. That's not a problem. There are dogs here, and they always make me sick.*

I like dogs! Melayne protested.

Wolves who were, sneered Greyn. *Pale shadows of the real thing.*

They're just different, Melayne answered. *You're just prejudiced. I'll bet you could get to like them if you only tried.*

I have no intention of trying, Greyn informed her. *I'll have nothing to do with domesticated animals. Unless they're tasty.* He licked his lips.

I have to get back to Sarrow and Corran now, Melayne told Greyn, bringing him up to date on her situation. *Can you stay hidden until tonight?*

You have to ask a wolf that? Greyn snorted. *Don't worry.* Then he sniffed and frowned. *There's some-*

thing . . . odd here, he announced. *Something I don't know, that I don't understand. An odd smell . . .* He shook his head. *It's probably nothing. I'm not really all that experienced yet. Maybe I'll figure it out later.* He ambled off back into the shadows.

Glad of his company, Melayne returned for the two boys. Both of them were simply waiting, neither looking at or speaking with the other. "Right," Melayne said cheerfully, "Corran, what do you normally have to do with your day?"

The boy simply shrugged. "Whatever I like."

"Oh. That sounds rather undisciplined to me." Melayne smiled. "So — what do you like?"

"Anything."

Not exactly communicative. Melayne refused to allow it to bother her. "That's good. Very general. Right, is there a library in this castle?"

"Library?" Corran looked blank.

"A place where they keep books," Melayne explained. "Can you read and write yet?"

"No." It didn't seem to bother the boy. Well, he *was* very young.

"Then I can see there's one thing we can do together," Melayne said. "But we need books to do it with. Do you know where there might be some?"

"No," Corran answered.

This wasn't getting her very far. "Maybe we should look around," she suggested. "I'm sure your father must be able to read and write, if he's such a great lord. So he must have some books somewhere."

"Then ask him," Corran suggested simply.

"I don't think we should bother him," Melayne replied. "I'm sure he must be a very busy man. He's very important."

"He's never very busy," Corran said. "Mostly he just sits and thinks. I don't know what he thinks about." Then, with the brutal honesty of youth: "I don't think it's about me. He doesn't care for me very much."

"Oh, I'm sure that's not true!" Melayne exclaimed, horrified. "I'm sure your father loves you very much."

"No, he doesn't," Corran insisted. "He hates me because I killed Mother."

Melayne stared at the boy in shock. "How did you kill your mother?"

"Being born." Corran shrugged. "I don't know what it means, really, but everyone in the castle knows I did it."

The poor child . . . Melayne started to understand why he was so withdrawn. She knelt down in front of him and took his small shoulders in her hands. "Listen to me, Corran. I don't care what anyone else told you. You *didn't* kill your mother. It was simply a terrible accident that she died."

Corran shrugged. "Daddy thinks I killed her, and so does everyone else."

"Well, then, they're all wrong," said Melayne firmly. "Just because people believe something doesn't make it true. You pay attention to what I say, Corran. I won't lie to you, so you can believe me when I tell you something. And I tell you that you didn't kill your mother. And I'm sure your father

195

doesn't hate you. If he did, why would he want me to look after you?"

The boy shrugged again. "Maybe he hopes you'll kill me, and he won't have to put up with me anymore," he suggested unemotionally.

"Well, that's a silly idea!" Melayne exclaimed. "As if I'd even hurt you. No, I'm sure he wants me to look after you because he cares for you, Corran. It's just that sometimes men don't really know what to do with children, and women do."

"Are you a woman?" asked Corran. "Everybody calls you *girl*."

"I'm *almost* a woman," Melayne answered. "Though sometimes I do feel like I'm still a little girl inside. One day, though, I know I'll feel like a grown-up woman." She grinned. "Probably not for a long time yet, though. Anyway, let's try your idea then, and ask your father about books. Now, I *think* I remember the way back to his room properly, but you'll have to tell me if I get it wrong. I may be looking after you, but you're going to have to help out by looking after me, too."

Corran considered the idea. "Is that my job?"

"It is," she informed him. "And it's likely to keep you *very* busy. I sometimes need an awful lot of looking after."

"Okay," he agreed. "That sounds fair."

Melayne laughed, and took the two boys by the hand. "Let's see if I did remember it right."

She almost did; Corran had to correct her only once before they were back before the wooden door to Lord Sander's room. Melayne hesitated slightly, and then knocked on the door. She pushed it open and timidly looked inside.

"What's wrong, girl?" asked the lord. He was still in the chair, his chin resting on his hand. He didn't look as if he'd moved since they had left him. "Had enough already?"

"Certainly not, your lordship," Melayne replied. "It's just that I thought I ought to be teaching Corran some lessons, and wondered where I might find some books to use."

"Teaching him?" Lord Sander asked, as if the thought had never occurred to him. He stared at his son. "Isn't he a bit young for that? How old are you?" he asked Corran.

"Five, last birthday, Father," Corran replied.

Melayne was amazed. "What kind of a father doesn't know his own son's age?" she demanded indignantly.

The lord frowned at her accusation. "I've been . . . busy," he said evasively.

"Too busy for your own son?" Melayne asked him, her temper rising. "Look, your lordship, I'll take care of him, but he needs attention from *you*. You're his father, and he needs you."

Lord Sander rose to his feet, and stared coldly at her. "Are you daring to lecture me?" he demanded.

Drat her temper! Now she'd put her foot in it. This could get her kicked out already — not even a day into the job! But she simply couldn't back down now. "Yes, I am," she said bluntly. "And you deserve it."

Looking at his silent son, Lord Sander abruptly

sat down again. "You're right," he agreed surprisingly. "I do." He considered for a moment. "I promise to set aside some time each day for Corran's benefit. Now are you happy?"

"Almost," Melayne answered, breathing a silent sigh of relief. "The books I asked about? Are there any?"

"Oh, yes." The lord clambered to his feet again. "This way." He led the three of them from his room to the next door. Here he hesitated. "This was your mother's study," he informed Corran. "I don't normally allow people into it. But you're her son, and you should know it." He looked at Melayne. "And you're to teach him, so I have little choice but to allow you in, too. But —" he held up a hand. "Disturb as little as you can. It is all I have to remind me of her."

"No it isn't," Melayne said. She laid a hand on Corran's shoulder. "You have her son, too."

"Yes," Lord Sander agreed. "Sometimes I forget that. I remember that he's my son, but forget that he's hers as well." He turned back and opened the door. It led to a flight of steps that circled the inside wall, leading upward. He led the way, and at the top of the stairs opened a second door. He moved inside, and waited for them.

It was a room directly above his own, and the same size inside. There was a large fireplace, but without a welcoming fire. There were more tapestries on the wall. One was of a rampant unicorn, one of women gathering flowers, and the final one was of a dragon, sitting beside a stream. There were several benches in the room, and four tables. Books were piled on three of the tables, and there were further piles on the floor and stacked against the round walls. Light came in from a large window facing the courtyard, and a smaller one facing the world outside the castle.

"I shall have to send a boy up with wood," Lord Sander said. "It is quite chilly in these rooms without fires." He turned to go.

"Thank you, my lord," Melayne commented. "We will be very careful in here."

He nodded, and his dark eyes met hers briefly. She felt a shock, as if she were staring into a very deep well, with water way below the surface. Then he was gone.

Corran was looking about the room, showing interest in something for the first time since she'd met him. Ignoring the cold in the room, Melayne went to the closest pile of books.

"Right," she said cheerfully. "I'm sure there must be some good things to use in all of these. Let's see what we've got." The first few titles were books she'd never heard of and they sounded quite dull. Something about natural history, and one about religion. Then she started to strike gold. She found a geography book that included several maps, and then a copy of *The Tale of the Forlorn Knight*. With a cry of joy, she pulled the book from the pile. "This is wonderful!" she exclaimed. "This is my favorite book ever," she told Corran. "It's filled with great stories and wild adventures. I'm sure you'll come to love it, too."

Corran just shrugged as usual. "I guess."

"It *is* fun, I promise you," Melayne told him. "Isn't it, Sarrow?"

"It's pretty good," her brother admitted. "If you have to read, then that's one of the best." Sarrow lowered his voice and whispered to Corran, "And you'll *have* to read. Once Melayne makes her mind up about something, you can't talk her out of it. She makes me read, and she's going to make you do it, too."

"I certainly am," Melayne informed them both. "I'm going to make sure that you two get as good an education as possible." Then she smiled. "But it's going to be *fun*, too," she promised. "And I think that this book is a very good place to start." She led the two boys over to one of the benches. "Sarrow, I know you've heard some of these stories before, but you can stand hearing them again. They teach you all about honor and courage and chivalry."

Sarrow snorted. "I've not seen much of that in the world as yet," he said. "It doesn't sound too practical to me."

Melayne frowned at him. He was in one of his difficult moods, which might make it hard to get Corran interested. "There's plenty of use for such things," she insisted. "I always try to abide by them, and so should both of you. Especially you, Corran."

"Why pick on me?" asked the boy.

"Because you're the son of a great lord," she explained. "And that means that you have to look out for those who need your protection when you're older."

"I can't protect anyone," Corran objected.

"Not now," she agreed. "But when you get older you will be able to protect lots of people, like your father does. He has to look after everyone who lives in this castle, and one day you'll have to do the same. So you have to learn now how you can do that. This is why you should pay attention to the story of the Forlorn Knight."

"What does *forlorn* mean?" asked Corran.

Melayne thought she was detecting just a little enthusiasm in him now, which was good. "It means sad," she explained. "He's a very unhappy knight."

"Then why don't they just say that?" asked Corran, confused.

"Because *forlorn* means more than just sad," Melayne explained. "It means he's heartbroken, and troubled. *Forlorn* is a very deep sadness."

"Oh." Corran thought about that. "Like my father?" he asked.

"Probably," agreed Melayne. Lord Sander was obviously a deeply sad man. He was greatly troubled. "So, in a way, this book could almost be a story about your father. It's about a knight who's very sad, but who still does what he knows is right because it's his duty."

The door opened and the young boy from the kitchen entered, carrying a pile of wood and a small bucket of coals. He quickly started a fire going, and a little warmth crept into the air of the room, dispelling some of the chill Melayne had been feeling.

"Why is he so . . . forlorn?" asked Corran.

"Well," Melayne said, smiling, "that's where the story begins." She opened the book up at the first chapter, and started reading.

The afternoon flew by as she read the story. Sarrow tried to pretend he wasn't really interested, but Melayne could see from the corner of her eye that he was listening to every word. Corran made no effort to hide his own fascination and excitement. He laughed and winced and jumped up and down as the story progressed, totally engrossed in the knight's adventures. Melayne was glad that he was having so much fun; he was such a serious child, it was clear that this wasn't his normal kind of life.

After she had finished the first adventure, Melayne took out the atlas and opened it up. She spread it on the floor, and showed Corran where the story had been taking place. Then she showed him on the map where Dragonhome stood, and explained what all of the symbols meant.

"Using a map like this," she told him, "you could go anywhere in our world and know where you were and how to get to where you want. And it would tell you the sort of land you'd have to cross to get there, so you could plan what you might need. It's very helpful."

"But it doesn't tell you about the people you'll meet," objected Sarrow, speaking for the first time in a while. "There's no telling what they'll be like."

"I'm not sure I like people very much," Corran said seriously. "I don't know very many, and most of them don't seem to like me."

"*We* like you," Melayne said firmly. "Don't we, Sarrow?"

Sarrow shrugged. "He's okay, for a child," he said, from his own vantage point of being three years older.

"I guess I like you, too," Corran decided. "Can we read some more story now?"

At that moment, there came the sound of a pealing bell. Melayne looked around. "What does that mean?"

"Dinnertime," Corran answered. "No story, then. We have to join my father for the meal. Come on."

"About time," Sarrow said. "I'm starving."

Melayne realized that she was hungry, too. She'd been so absorbed in reading *The Tale of the Forlorn Knight* that she hadn't realized how much time had passed. Seeing the excitement seize Corran had completely distracted her. Now she hurried down the stairs after the two boys.

The dining room was quite spacious, but mostly empty. There were only two tables in the room, which was illuminated rather poorly by a large fire in a huge fireplace ten feet from the tables. Lord Sander was already seated at one table, alone. As Melayne, Sarrow, and Corran came in, he gestured them to the other table, wordlessly. Corran seemed to know the drill, and he took his seat.

"You sit here, Melayne," he said softly, gesturing to his right. "And Sarrow there," gesturing to his left. Melayne obeyed, staying quiet. Obviously, not much talking went on during meals here.

Hada entered the room by another door, which presumably led to the kitchen. Seeing that everyone was present, she turned and nodded over her shoulder before joining them at the secondary table. Evidently she was the only other person who was to eat with them. Melayne wasn't sure how many other people there were in the castle, but they evidently ate somewhere else.

The young boy who had fetched the wood and the woman Melayne had seen in the kitchen served the food. Each of them had a bowl made of pewter, a spoon, and a knife. The boy brought out a steaming vegetable soup, serving Lord Sander first, then Hada, and finally the younger ones. He then brought freshly baked bread, while the cook brought out flagons of cider for all.

Melayne ate eagerly. The bread was delicious, and still warm. The cider was spiced and tasty. After the soup, a meat dish was served with steamed vegetables. Melayne was the only one who took no meat. Sarrow happily took her share as well. Melayne glanced up from her plate to see Lord Sander's piercing eyes staring at her. She blushed and looked away, but he didn't. She wondered why he was paying her this attention, and realized she wasn't likely to discover the answer.

The final portion of the meal was some kind of stewed apples, mildly spiced, that were a little tart, but delicious. The cook here was obviously very good at her job. Melayne hadn't eaten so well in a long time. Even Sarrow cleaned his plate, and he wasn't much of a fruit lover.

Melayne sat silently, wondering what happened next. After a moment, Lord Sander pushed back his chair, stood up, and walked over to their table.

"An excellent meal, Hada," he complimented her. "I suspect our cook is attempting to impress our new arrivals with her skills."

"If she was, it worked," Melayne said. "She's very good."

Hada beamed at the praise, "She is a good workon, and I'm pleased with her myself. Thank you, my lord."

He nodded, and then turned to Corran. "And how was your afternoon?" he asked his son.

"Enjoyable," Corran answered. He seemed to be uncomfortable around his father. Considering what he had said earlier about Lord Sander hating him, Melayne couldn't blame the boy. But his father seemed to be genuinely interested in what Corran had done.

"We started to read *The Tale of the Forlorn Knight* together," Melayne added.

Lord Sander nodded slightly. "That was one of my wife's favorite books," he said reflectively. "I am pleased to hear that you like it, too." Abruptly, he stared at her again, in that disquieting way of his. "We shall have to talk later," he decided. "For now, good evening." He turned and strode from the room.

Hada tapped Melayne's arm gently. "He seems to like you," she informed Melayne. "He doesn't take to everyone, so you should be pleased."

"I am," Melayne answered, slightly distracted by the memory of those dark eyes. "And I like it here."

"I think you'll fit in very well," Hada decided. She gave Melayne an encouraging smile. "If I can do anything else to help you, let me know. Now, I must get busy again, I'm afraid. Work seems never to be done."

Corran came over to her. "Can we read some more story before bed?" he asked her.

"I don't see why not," she replied, smiling. "The next chapter is where he goes up against a monstrous bird that's tyrannizing a poor village. It's very exciting."

The evening passed quietly, as Melayne read the story. Corran was enthralled, not used to this kind of thing. He admitted that he'd never been read to before, and he obviously loved it. He had a good imagination, and Melayne could see that he was entering into the spirit of the tale with enthusiasm. It felt so good to raise a smile on his childish lips, and Melayne was pleased with her efforts.

In contrast, Sarrow stayed aloof, as usual. He never seemed to be able to enter into stories in the same way that Melayne did. He always held back, and his imagination never seemed to be very keen. Melayne was used to this, though, knowing he had other strengths instead. Not everyone could appreciate a good story.

Soon it was time for bed. Darkness had descended on the castle while they were reading, and Corran yawned. Melayne put the book away, promising to get back to it the following day. She sent Sarrow off to get ready for bed on his own, and then escorted Corran to his room. There was a young servant boy waiting there to prepare him for bed, so Melayne turned to leave.

"I like you," Corran said abruptly.

Melayne smiled in delight. "I like you, too."

"Promise me you'll never leave," Corran begged her.

She hesitated, troubled. "I'll stay as long as I can," she promised.

"That's no answer," he complained, his face falling.

Melayne hugged the young boy to her. "It's the best I can give," she apologized. "Corran, I'll never lie to you, so I can't promise I'll always stay. But if I leave, it won't be because I want to. I can promise you that. I *want* to stay here, with you, very much."

That seemed to make him happy again. He nodded, and turned toward the servant. Then he glanced back. "You should marry my father," he suggested. "That way you could always stay."

Melayne colored at the thought. "Corran! I can't just do that!"

"Why not?" he asked. "Don't you like him? He likes you, I can tell. He kept looking at you during dinner, and he hardly ever looks at people."

Melayne couldn't stop blushing. "I'm sure there was a good reason he was looking at me," she murmured. "He was probably just checking that I've been treating you right. Anyway, he's a lord, and I'm just a homeless girl. Lords don't marry girls like me."

"One of them did in your story," Corran objected.

"But that's just a *story*," Melayne explained. "It's not real."

Corran shook his head. "You told me that the story teaches me how to behave, and that it *is* real. You can't say it isn't now." He grinned at her, with the childish certainty that he'd caught her. "So, you see, you can marry my father after all."

Melayne had to smile. "Well, that's up to your father, I think," she said. It seemed to be the safest thing.

"I'm sure he'd like it," Corran said. "It might even make him happy again. He hasn't been happy since Mother left. Not even when she comes back."

Melayne frowned. "Comes back?" she repeated. "Whatever do you mean? Corran, I'm afraid she died."

"Yes," he agreed cheerfully. "But she still comes back some nights. I hear her."

A chill stroked Melayne's spine. He was talking about his mother's ghost. . . . "I think it's just your imagination," she said uncertainly.

"No, it's not," Corran answered. "You'll see. You'll hear her, too. She's quite loud."

Melayne stared at her young charge in confusion, but he'd had enough talk. He went to the servant boy and started to get ready for bed. Melayne left, wondering what he could have meant. She didn't believe in ghosts, so she wasn't exactly scared. On the other hand, Corran had seemed so *certain*. . . .

Crossing the courtyard to her room, Melayne

shivered. There was a slight chill in the air, but that wasn't what had touched her.

Was it possible that Corran was right? Was this why Lord Sander was so sad? Was he still haunted by the spirit of his dead wife?

Melayne stood still, looking around her. The night had wrapped itself about the castle, only the faint gleams of torches inside the building showing. Overhead, the stars splashed across the sky. There was a faint breeze, hardly enough to cool the air.

And then, echoing about the walls and towers, there was a faint keening sound. It was the noise of someone in pain and despair, crying aloud to bewail their wretched state. The sound was low and heartfelt, seeming to come from everywhere. Melayne shuddered as she heard the cry, her eyes darting around, trying to discern the direction.

Was this the ghost of Corran's dead mother?

There was a sudden movement, and Melayne gasped in shock as a shape drifted next to her.

Chapter Eleven
Haunted?

Melayne's heart was beating wildly until she suddenly realized that the shadow was actually Greyn. Unusually, the wolf looked very worried. *What is that noise?* she asked him, clutching him to her side for comfort. He was actually shaking.

I don't know, the wolf replied. *I've never heard any creature make a sound like that.*

Is it an animal? Melayne wondered. *Or could it be . . . a ghost?*

Ghost? Greyn's teeth flashed in the starlight. *I'll try my jaws on it, whatever it is. If it will just come out here.*

The crying sound continued, thin and airy but chilling. Greyn continued to tremble. Melayne had to be strong, for both of them. He was, after all, little more than a cub, no matter how grown he might look. *It might just be the wind,* she suggested. *Blowing in a collapsed hallway.*

You don't believe that any more than I do, Greyn

corrected. *The wind never makes noises like that. It's something living. Or once alive.*

Melayne was afraid he was correct. She really didn't believe it was the wind. There was some kind of intelligence behind the sound, no matter how terrible its pain. Whether it was alive or dead she couldn't say. But, whichever it was, it was clearly in some kind of physical or spiritual pain.

Can't you tell if it's an animal? Greyn asked her. *You have the Talent of Communication, don't forget.*

Melayne hadn't forgotten. *It's making no sense,* she replied. *Just noise. Pain. Either it's not an animal, or it's an animal that I can't Communicate with. And I've never found one I couldn't talk to before.*

Perhaps you were right, then, the wolf decided. *Perhaps it is an unresting spirit. Some tortured soul.*

There was the sound of a door opening, and Melayne stiffened in shock. If anyone saw her with a wolf, they would suspect her Talent! *Quickly!* she ordered Greyn. *Hide!* He was reluctant to leave her, but understood the need. He loped into darker shadows, and Melayne shivered as she turned to see who it was.

The soldier, Bantry, ambled across the courtyard to join her. He was trying to look casual, but Melayne could see the tension in his face. "Now you know why so few people stay here, miss," he told her, eyes hollow. "That's our resident ghost."

Melayne shook, and he put a comforting arm

about her. "Are you sure it's a ghost?" she asked in a soft voice, not wanting to perhaps attract its attention.

"Listen," he said. "Could anyone living make a sound like that? There's no need to shake, though — nobody here has ever seen it. It never comes into the light. It just stays in the darkness somewhere and howls out in loss and pain." He sighed. "It wears a man down, hearing that sound."

"Do you . . . have any idea whose ghost it might be?" Melayne asked him nervously.

"There are those who say it's Corran's mother," Bantry answered. "You know that she died birthing the boy?"

"Yes, he told me." Melayne considered a moment, and added, "He thinks his father hates him for that."

"Lord Sander?" Bantry snorted. "He hates nobody, miss. To hate someone, you have to have passion, and all passion was burned out of him years ago. He really loved his wife, you know, and her death was a terrible blow to him. He built a wall inside his soul so that nothing could ever get in to gain power over him like that again."

"I don't understand you," Melayne confessed.

"When you love someone so deeply," the soldier explained, "you give them power over you. Power to love, and power to hurt. When Lady Cassary died, it hurt the lord so much we thought he would go mad with despair. But he recovered instead, by blocking off his passion. Now he doesn't love or hate. He just exists. He won't let anyone else get close enough to him for him to start loving them."

"The poor man," murmured Melayne, feeling desperately sorry for Lord Sander. To love so much, and lose so much . . . It *had* to be terribly hard to bear. No wonder he seemed so listless, concerned so little with what went on about him. He was afraid of losing people again. It was probably why he seemed to have so little love for his own son. It wasn't that he hated the boy. It was simply that he was afraid of loving him, for fear of the consequences.

There came another wailing cry, tearing at Melayne's heart and courage. "And they say that is the spirit of Lady Cassary?" she asked in a whisper.

"People say all kinds of things," Bantry admitted. "But that's the most likely, if you ask me. Lady Cassary, wailing for her lost life and child."

"Poor Corran," Melayne said. "This must hurt him badly."

"He's a sensitive boy," agreed the soldier. "But it's not likely he can hear this from his room. And nobody will speak of it while he's around. He's probably oblivious to it all."

"And what of Lord Sander?" asked Melayne.

"Oh, he knows about it, all right." Bantry grimaced. "I've seen him some nights when the crying begins, heading for the west wing. That's the unsafe area, so be sure you stay out of it. But that's where the crying seems to come from. Maybe he's looking for his lost love again." He shrugged. "They say she was very beautiful."

"*Say?*" echoed Melayne. "Didn't you ever see her?"

"Few people did," Bantry informed her. "She was

beautiful, but frail. She had to stay in her rooms most of the time. Only Hada and a few of the servants ever got to meet the lady. Not me. I'm just a humble soldier, and it's not my place to go visiting my betters."

"Oh." Melayne thought things were starting to make sense now. Lady Cassary had been ill to start with, and becoming pregnant with Corran must have been a strain on her poor body. No wonder she died giving birth. It was terribly sad.

The door behind them opened again, and another person came out into the night. "Bantry!" It was Hada's voice. "What are you doing with that poor girl?"

"Just comforting her," the soldier answered, shuffling his feet. "She heard the ghost and —"

"Ghost?" Hada's voice was suddenly sharp. "That's no ghost, you goose! Stop trying to fill her poor head with all the nonsense in your own. I know you, Bantry — foolish and shiftless as ever. Any excuse to get your arms around an innocent girl! Let her go this instant, and get along with you."

Bantry released Melayne as if she'd suddenly become red-hot, and retreated. "Sorry, miss," he said. "I didn't mean anything by it, honest."

"I know you didn't," Melayne whispered back. "Thank you."

Hada joined her under the bright stars. "Pay no attention to his foolish stories," she said firmly. "He is as superstitious as the rest of the servants. A ghost indeed! Don't start believing that nonsense."

"I don't, really," Melayne assured her. "But . . . well, it *is* very uncanny."

"Not to those of us with scientific minds, my dear," Hada assured her. "I don't know if Bantry really believes all those foolish tales of ghosts and hauntings. I *do* know he has an eye for a pretty girl, though, and you're prettier than most. You shouldn't allow him to become so friendly with you. At least, not unless he's offering a wedding hand, too."

Melayne found herself blushing. "He wasn't being improper," she assured Hada. "I was just nervous, and he —"

"Was making you even worse," the overseer finished. "Melayne, that sound is nothing more than the wind echoing through the old well and water system. There's nothing unnatural in it at all."

Melayne smiled in relief. "Are you sure of that?" she asked.

"Quite sure," Hada answered. "Now, I think it's time you were in bed. You have a lot of work to do in the morning. I'll see you to your room, if it makes you feel better."

Melayne nodded her thanks, and they walked across the courtyard together. Greyn had slipped into the shadows and wouldn't be seen. The howling continued, but there did seem to be something of the wind in its makeup now. She'd simply allowed her imagination to get the better of her, that was all. It wasn't a creature, nor a wandering ghost. It was just the wind in the pipes. Perfectly natural, and nothing to be frightened of.

"You seem to be getting along well with Corran," Hada remarked. "He doesn't normally take to strangers, but he's taken to you. I swear, I even saw him smile today, and that's something he hasn't done for a long time. You seem to be good for him."

"He's a delightful child," Melayne replied. "I think he's good for me, too. And it will give Sarrow someone to play with."

Hada nodded. They had reached the door to the sleeping block now. "I think you'll fit in here very well, Melayne. And you have friends here. I am one of them. If you can bring some joy back into that poor child's life, then we shall all be grateful to you. If there is anything I can do to make you happier, please tell me."

"Thank you," Melayne answered. "I'm sure I'm going to be very happy here. Good night." She entered the building. Before going to her room, though, she peeked in on Sarrow. Her brother was fast asleep in his bed, completely unbothered by the wailing. Now that she was indoors, in fact, she noticed that the sound was almost completely deadened. She felt a lot happier herself.

Returning to her room, she saw that Hada had kept her promise. There were other clothes there now, simple but sturdy, that she could wear. She placed them in the trunk at the foot of her bed, keeping only the nightgown she needed for now. Her bed had been made, and there was a pitcher of cool water beside it. Melayne hurriedly changed into the nightdress, and slipped between the covers. It was cold in the bed, and she shivered for a moment. Gradually, though, she began to warm up, and the ice in her skin thawed to a pleasant warmth. She lay there in the darkness, thinking over the events of the day.

She fell asleep thinking about dark eyes, dark hair, and a rich, gentle voice. . . .

The next few days were almost relaxing for Melayne. Corran was attentive and eager to learn. She managed to start him on his alphabet, holding out the promise that he could soon start reading books by himself to motivate him. It worked; he studied diligently and with a natural aptitude. She rewarded him by reading aloud further installments of *The Tale of the Forlorn Knight.*

Even Sarrow seemed to be relaxed. He'd made friends with Bantry, and the young soldier was giving him lessons in swordsmanship. Melayne wondered about the value of these lessons, since Bantry didn't seem to be exactly proficient himself, but they kept Sarrow amused and out of trouble, and she didn't object. Sarrow also seemed to like playing games with Corran, which gave her a rest from time to time from both of them.

Bantry seemed to enjoy being around Melayne, too, even though he was somewhat shy. He did seem to be attracted to her. Melayne wasn't sure how she felt about him. She'd never had a boyfriend before, and this whole business was new to her. But she liked the attention, and Bantry's fumbling attempts to compliment her. Hada didn't exactly approve, of course, but Melayne discovered that this was because she was quite straight-laced.

"She's the daughter of a squire," Bantry explained helpfully. "Not exactly noble blood, you understand, but a cut above us peasants." He grinned to show he meant no disrespect by including Melayne in the peasant category. "So she likes everything to go just right, and thinks that anyone who doesn't act the way she does is some sort of lesser being. She likes you because you carry yourself well, and you're gentle and respectful. And I'm sure she's got a good heart underneath all of her stuck-up ways. But she doesn't half get on my nerves some days."

Melayne laughed. She found Hada to be a little aloof, but kind in her own way. Still, she did insist on things being done her way, and if she came across Melayne running or playing or just dancing quietly to no music she could hear, a tiny frown would crease the supervisor's forehead, and Melayne could tell she disapproved. Hada never actually criticized her as such, but she'd make "general" observations like, "Young people are so boisterous today. It wasn't like that in my day." Melayne knew she was being told off in a polite way, but it didn't really bother her.

She saw Lord Sander only at mealtimes. The rest of the days, he would be off alone somewhere in the castle, no doubt brooding and hiding out from the human race. Melayne couldn't help feeling sorry for him. He was still a young man, though probably ten years older than she was. And he was definitely good-looking, if you could ignore the brooding. "Why hasn't he ever remarried?" she asked Bantry one day.

"There's three schools of thought on that matter," he informed her. She wasn't surprised to hear that the servants had been speculating. "First, there's those who think he still misses the Lady Cassary too much ever to take up with another woman."

"It's a shame and a waste if that's truo," Melayne answered. "I'm sure ho'd make somebody a wonderful husband, and there have to be some ladies around who need a good man."

"I'm sure there are," Bantry agreed, scratching his neck. "The problem there may be that he's not got a whole lot of money left. His father lost a lot of the family fortune, I hear tell, through bad investments, and our lord has only enough left to keep up Dragonhome. Well, that doesn't make him a really good prospect for marriage now, does it?"

"It didn't seem to bother Lady Cassary," Melayne pointed out.

"Ah, well, that was a love match, that was." Bantry grinned. "Smitten with one another they were. She'd have taken him if he were a pauper. Or even a common soldier, like myself. Not that there's anything common at all about Lord Sander."

"She must have been a lovely woman," Melayne said dreamily.

"So they say." Bantry shrugged. "Of course, then there's the second belief as to why he's never remarried. Those that believe it say that the wailing you hear every night is the spirit of Lady Cassary, and that she still pines for her lost love. They reckon that the ghost scares off any girl who even looks twice at his lordship, because she can't stand the thought of sharing him with another woman. That's the one I believe myself, in fact. You've heard the cries, so you know that they must be of someone in terrible torment."

Melayne shivered at the thought. "But if she loved him, wouldn't she want him to be happy?" she objected. She was thinking of her own attraction to the dark lord. Would the ghost come after her for such thoughts? Or did she only go after those who actually stood a chance with Lord Sander?

"It may be so," Bantry agreed. "But, well, she's dead. And who knows *what* the dead really think? Maybe she feels that he's still hers, and nobody else should have him. It's hard to say."

Wanting to get away from this idea, Melayne asked, "And what's the third thought?"

"It's pretty silly, really," the soldier admitted. "But a couple of the cook's assistants believe it. They think that Lady Cassary isn't really dead, and that it's not her ghost we hear at night, but the lady herself, locked away in the west wing."

"Not dead?" Melayne was completely confused. "But, surely, there's no doubt about it . . . is there?"

Bantry looked uncomfortable. "Well, you see, like I said, nobody saw much of the lady, because she was sickly. And when Corran was born, the doctor said she'd died. There was a funeral and all, but the coffin was closed, so nobody saw the body. According to these assistants, the lady didn't die, but she suffered horribly during childbirth. They had to take water up to the lady's bedroom, and they say Lady Cassary was screaming something dreadful, like she was out of her mind. They reckon that she didn't die from birthing Corran, but instead went completely mad. And that she can't stand to be around normal people now, and might hurt herself. So Lord Sander had her taken to the west wing and locked away. And that the wailing we hear at night isn't her tortured spirit, but her real screams because she's completely mad."

Melayne shuddered deeply at the idea. Lady Cassary, completely mad, locked away in the castle, howling insanely at night ... It was worse, even, than the thought of her being a vengeful ghost. To be unable to think rationally, just to howl and scream ... "That can't possibly be true," she objected uncertainly. "Could it?"

"Well, like I say, I don't place much belief in it myself," Bantry admitted. "But there are two telling points in its favor. Lord Sander has been seen late at night with a large key ring, entering the west wing. He never explains why he's been there, and nobody dares ask him, of course. And the second thing is that the cook's assistants say that there's fresh meat that goes missing from the kitchen when the lord has been around. Quite a lot of it."

"Raw meat?" Melayne asked, shocked. "But why?"

"Well, those that believe this story say it's because Lady Cassary has regressed to a primitive state, where she'll eat only raw, bloody meat, like some wild creature of the forest."

The idea almost made Melayne sick. She had a picture in her mind of some beautiful, frail lady, acting like a beast, tearing chunks of bloody meat, dribbling blood down her tattered clothing, and then howling at the moon . . . What a terrible idea! It couldn't be true . . . could it?

Hada scoffed at all of the tales, of course. "Stuff and nonsense," she said, when Melayne asked about them. "Really, I had expected better of you, child. Those foolish servants have nothing better to do with their time but gossip and make up the most outrageous stories. There's not an ounce of truth in any of them, so don't think about them for a second. I told you, the so-called ghost is just wind in the water tunnels. And Lord Sander only goes into the west wing to check that it's safe. He doesn't want it crumbling in and killing anyone." She mellowed slightly. "And, to be honest, I think he goes in there to dream about repairing it and opening it up again. There was once a beautiful ballroom there, where music and laughter and dancing were heard. I'm sure he'd love to restore those days to this castle." She sighed. "We all need dreams and plans to give our lives meaning, young lady. Even such as I."

"What do you dream?" Melayne asked her, curiously. To her surprise, the other woman blushed slightly.

"I would like an advantageous marriage," she replied.

"But you'll meet nobody here to marry," Melayne answered. She couldn't resist adding mischievously,

"Except for the likes of Bantry, of course. You aren't soft on him, are you?"

"That ragamuffin?" Hada sniffed. "Certainly not!"

"Somebody in the village, then?" Melayne persisted. Hada was the one who went there to shop, after all.

"Those commoners? Never." Hada shook her head. "I haven't set my mind yet," she added, not meeting Melayne's gaze. "But one of these days . . ." Her voice trailed off. "That's enough nonsense," she said firmly. "I'm sure we both have work to do."

Melayne was amused, but didn't press the point. She liked Hada, and didn't really want to make the older woman uncomfortable. Let her keep her secrets! After all, it wasn't anything dangerous like Melayne's own secrets.

Luckily, nobody seemed to even suspect that she was a Talent. Everyone she met simply accepted her as she was. Melayne made certain not to Communicate when anyone was around to see or overhear. She met Greyn quietly at night, in the shadows, and talked to virtually no other creature. Greyn was growing stronger and larger every day. He was a handsome wolf. She kept trying to convince him to leave her and go back to the forest where he belonged.

No, he replied, keeping one wary ear on the sounds of the wailing. He never got used to it, even though Melayne sometimes didn't even notice it now, it was so commonplace. *You need someone around to look after you. It may seem safe here, but there are still dangers you cannot understand. I won't leave you.*

It was frustrating, but Melayne was secretly glad Greyn wouldn't go. She loved the wolf, and she always felt better knowing that he was around somewhere, keeping his watchful golden eyes on her. But she felt guilty that he was giving up his own life to lurk in shadows and look after her. He needed to meet a nice she-wolf, and settle down to start his own pack. But she couldn't figure out a way to get him to agree to this.

And then there was Lord Sander himself. He kept mostly to himself, speaking very rarely at mealtimes. She saw little of him, and understood even less. His dark eyes would sometimes rest on her, and Melayne would feel a thrill shake her body. What was he thinking when he regarded her like that? That she was pretty? Or a puzzle? Or a nuisance? He never said anything to her of a personal nature, and when he spoke it was concerning his son.

To her surprise, then, she was teaching Corran to read one day when the door opened into Lady Cassary's room. She assumed that it was the cook's boy, fetching more wood for the fire, and spoke without turning. "You can put the wood down. We'll see to the fire when it needs banking."

"I have no wood," came back Lord Sander's voice, sounding slightly amused. "But I would have brought some had I known it would make you happy."

Melayne blushed, and spun around. "Oh, I'm sorry, your lordship," she apologized. "It's just that I thought you were the cook's boy . . ."

He nodded. "A common error. We've often been confused for one another."

Considering the cook's boy was thirteen, slightly plump, and sandy-haired, Melayne realized that he was teasing her. "Did you want something, my lord?" she asked, anxiously.

"I came to see how my son was doing," Lord Sander replied. He moved closer, leaning over Corran's shoulder. His eyebrows rose. "Can you actually read that book?" he asked his son. "Or are you simply trying to impress me?" He eyed Melayne. "Or your pretty teacher?"

"I can read it," Corran answered indignantly. Then honesty forced him to admit, "Well, some of it, anyway."

"Excellent. Show me."

Hesitantly, Corran read, "The knight rode down the road, ast . . . ast . . ." He broke off and looked at Melayne. "That's a hard one."

"Indeed it is," she agreed. "It's *astride*. It means he's got a leg on either side of the saddle."

"Oh." Corran pressed on. "*Astride* his noble steed."

"Very good," his father said approvingly. "You really are doing well, Corran. I'm proud of you."

Corran's face shone. "Really?" he asked, as if he hardly dared to believe it.

"Really," Lord Sander assured him. "You've made great progress since Melayne arrived here, haven't you?"

"Yes," Corran agreed. "She makes everything so much fun."

"So I noticed," his father answered. "Now, I want you to run a quick errand for me. Go down to the kitchen and tell Hada that I want her to arrange a special dessert for tonight, so we can celebrate how well you're growing up. And you can pick what it shall be."

"Really?" Corran shot to his feet, the book forgotten. "Terrific!" He ran from the room.

Melayne looked at Lord Sander approvingly. "That's what he needs," she said gently.

"What? More desserts?"

"No," Melayne replied, knowing she was being teased again. "Your attention. Children are like flowers; they blossom when attention is paid to them."

"I shall have to make a note to rain on him more often, then," he answered. Then he gestured to her chair. "Please, sit. To be honest, I sent Corran off not so much for his sake, as for it allowing us a short time to talk. Judging from the speed he was traveling at, we will have only a very short time."

Melayne sat, puzzled. Lord Sander lowered himself onto the bed, and looked at her. She didn't have a clue as to his intentions. He rubbed his gloved hands together, as if he were nervous, for some reason.

"You seem to be fitting in here quite well," he said abruptly. "The servants like you, and Corran obviously adores you. You're getting so much out of him."

Melayne found herself blushing slightly at the praise. "He's a good student," she answered. "Anyone could do the same."

"No, they couldn't." His dark eyes focused on her face again. "*I* couldn't, for one."

"That's because he's just a bit scared of you," she answered.

"A bit?" Lord Sander shook his head. "He's terrified of me. Or, rather, he used to be. Now ... there's been a change in him, and I can only assume it's due to you. Whatever you've done to him, I'm truly grateful."

"He simply had a ... wrong belief about you," Melayne answered. "I cleared it up, and he's happy."

Those dark eyes burrowed into her soul again. "What did he believe?"

Melayne had to shake herself mentally to be able to concentrate. "He thought that you hated him. That you blamed him for your wife's death."

"A foolish notion," Lord Sander agreed, thoughtfully. "But one that I can quite understand. I've not been a very ... emotional man for a long time, Melayne. I find it hard to express my feelings."

"Since your wife died?" she asked, sympathetically.

"Yes," he agreed. He looked around the room. "She loved being here, and I kept this room locked off, to remind me of her."

"Perhaps we shouldn't be in here, then," Melayne suggested. "I could teach Corran anywhere."

"No. If anyone has a right to be here, it's him." Lord Sander smiled sadly. "I've been living in the past," he confessed. "Brooding on what once was, and is no more. It's foolish of me, and I can't help it. If I close my eyes, I can still almost feel the touch of her skin beneath my fingertips..." His hand twitched.

After a moment's silence, Melayne said gently, "You must have loved her very much."

"Yes." He shook his head, as if to drive out memories. "And I know I will never stop, even though she has been gone for five years. But the living must live, mustn't they? I've been infecting poor Corran with my own loss and despair, and he needs joy and strength — two things I have been unable to supply. But *you* have managed to give him those things, and I am more grateful to you than you can ever know, Melayne. You've brought my son back to life, and that's a gift I cherish."

"Then don't allow him to slip away," Melayne begged him. "Stay in his life. Be involved with him. Let him know that you love him."

"I shall," Lord Sander agreed. "Perhaps not as much as I would wish. I have ... other responsibilities, too. But I shall not neglect him again. You have my word on it." Abruptly, he reached out and took her hand. Raising it to his lips, he kissed her gently on the knuckles. "Thank you."

Melayne knew she went horribly red at the touch of his lips on her skin. She wished she could think of something to say, but her mind was simply whirling confusion.

And, naturally, at that moment Corran dashed back into the room. "It's all set," he said happily. Then he saw his father holding Melayne's hand. "Oh. Are you two going to get married?"

Melayne jerked her hand free from his glove.

"Your father was just ... thanking me," she stammered.

"Indeed," Lord Sander agreed, rising to his feet. "I hardly think such a lively young woman would want to be married to a dark-spirited old man like myself."

"You're not old," Melayne protested. "Or dark-spirited." Then she shut up, realizing that Lord Sander was simply being gracious, trying to avoid telling his son that he'd never marry a peasant. She blushed again, and looked away from the lord's amused smile.

"I think you should marry her anyway," Corran told his father. "That way, she'd have to stay here, wouldn't she?"

"Yes," Lord Sander agreed. "I suppose she would." He looked at Melayne, and she could see that he was enjoying something about all of this. "Why? Were you thinking of leaving us? Aren't we treating you well enough?"

"Oh, no," she protested. "It's not that! I love it here. But, well ... you never know what the future might bring, do you?"

"No," the lord agreed. "But sometimes it surprises you by delivering a rare gift when you think that all you ever get is misfortune." Then he looked at his son. "I hope you've chosen wisely for dessert."

"Wait and see!" Corran said mischievously.

"All right, I shall," Lord Sander agreed. He looked back at Melayne. "If that is all ... ?" he prompted.

An idea suddenly popped into her head, something she'd been pondering since before she had arrived at the castle. "Perhaps you can answer a question," she said slowly. "I wondered why this castle is called Dragonhome."

He raised an eyebrow. "A good question," he murmured. "Come to the window." He led them both over to it, and pointed out at the mountains. "See those peaks? They were once where dragons dwelled. There were dozens of them up there, flying, and fighting, and feasting—until we humans killed them all off. The mountains were known as the Dragonhome Mountains, and my ancestors named this castle for them. While the dragons were alive, nobody dared go up against the Lord of Dragonhome. They were terrified of getting too close to the dragons. Once the dragons were slain, however . . ." He shrugged. "People stopped being frightened of us. The castle was attacked about seventy years ago. My great-grandfather fought the raiders off, but it left the castle weakened, and his treasury slightly impoverished. Since then, we've never had the money to rebuild the damaged sections."

It was a lovely story, in one way at least, but Melayne couldn't believe it. Even the firedrake had said there were no such things as dragons, and he was surely one who should know. But she wasn't going to say that in front of Corran. Let him believe in dragons if he wished. *She* knew better, but she wouldn't wreck his faith.

Lord Sander soon left them, and Melayne nursed her confusion and questions for the rest of the day.

She wasn't at all sure of the lord now. He seemed to have loosened up a bit, and he was making Corran very happy by actually paying attention to him. It was what he was doing to Melayne that confused her. Why had he kissed her hand liked that? Was it simply a noble sort of thing to do? Was that how all lords thanked women? Or had he meant something by it?

Impossible! He couldn't possibly be interested in her at all. Still, he *had* called her pretty . . . Maybe . . .

It was all too confusing. Especially those dark eyes of his. She couldn't *think* when they were focused on her. She just didn't know what to believe. She knew what she *wanted* to believe, but that was something she hardly dared admit to herself, let alone believe in its possibility . . .

Somehow, she made it through the day and down to dinner with Corran and Sarrow. Sarrow was happy, having been out hunting with Bantry. He seemed to be getting along very well with the soldier, and Melayne was glad he was making friends. He seemed to be so much more at ease these days.

Lord Sander was quiet as usual during the meal, speaking sparingly with Hada on matters concerning the day-to-day operations of the castle. From time to time, though, his eyes turned to Melayne, and she found herself blushing stupidly, without any real excuse.

Dessert turned out to be an apple and berry pie with hot yellow custard, and Lord Sander eyed it with delight.

"An excellent choice, my son," he said approvingly. "It's one of my own favorites, too." Corran beamed at the praise, basking in his father's approval. Melayne was happy to see him so glad.

And the dessert *was* excellent.

Later that evening, Melayne slipped out into the courtyard to meet with Greyn. The wolf materialized from the shadows, licking her face in greeting. There was the faint scent of fresh blood on his breath that she ignored.

Good hunting? she asked him.

Yes, he agreed. *Once I got away from that clumsy brother of yours. He and his soldier friend were scaring away the game.*

Sarrow's learning, Melayne answered. *He's bound to be a little clumsy at first. Don't pick on him.*

At that moment, the wailing began, echoing about the ruins. She looked up and steeled herself against the noise.

Someone's coming, Greyn told her, his senses much more acute than her own human ones. He slipped back into the shadows, and she moved with him. She crouched beside him, her hand on his fur, stroking it for comfort. Here in the darkness, nobody would see either of them.

There was a brief flare of light from the door, and Melayne could see that the person coming out was Lord Sander. He closed the door gently behind him, and then hurried across the courtyard, carrying a large and bulky sack.

What was he up to? Melayne frowned and concentrated. He moved slyly to the locked door of the west wing. Bending over it, he must have used a key, because the door soon swung open. Carrying the sack, he entered the doorway, and then shut it behind him.

Puzzled, Melayne slipped from the shadows and moved soundlessly across the courtyard to the door. She tested it gently, but it was locked once more. What was going on here?

That's odd, Greyn said, sniffing at the ground. *Blood.*

Blood? she asked him, confused.

That human was carrying a sack full of raw meat, Greyn informed her. *The scent was unmistakable.*

Raw meat? Melayne stared at the locked door, her mind filled with confusion. So one of Bantry's stories had turned out to be true! Lord Sander had a key to the west wing, and he was taking raw meat into it. She pressed her ear to the door. Was it just her imagination, or was the keening sound even louder here? Whatever Hada said about it coming from the drains, they weren't in this section of the castle.

Was it possible that the cook's apprentices were right? Was Lady Cassary, mad and driven back to a primitive state, imprisoned in here? And was her husband taking her the only food she could eat — raw and bloody meat?

The secrets of Dragonhome grew deeper.

Chapter Twelve
The Seeker

Melayne didn't know what to do. She was simply too confused to be able to think straight. The door was locked from the inside, so there was no way to follow Lord Sander. But . . . did she *want* to? Did she *really* want to know what that meat was for?

Yes, she decided, she did. It wasn't simply curiosity — though, to be honest, that was a large part of it — but also for her own security. If there was something in this castle that could be dangerous, she had to know about it. She had to look out for Sarrow, and now Corran as well. She didn't think that Lord Sander would be harboring any secret that might harm his own son, of course, but there was no way to know if it could hurt Sarrow and herself until she knew what it was.

Could it be Lady Cassary, driven mad, as the cook's assistants believed? Melayne wished she could laugh at the thought, but she simply didn't know enough. Could people be driven that crazy? Melayne wished she'd been exposed to more people while she was growing up, so she might know if such a thing was possible. The books all claimed various kinds of madness might come about in people — through pain, or torture, or even unrequited love — but books often romanticized life. She couldn't trust their testimony.

But if it wasn't a madwoman in the west wing, what was it?

I don't like it here, Greyn announced. *Something smells wrong.*

Even with all that raw meat around? Melayne asked him. *I thought you'd like the smell.*

Oh, I like the blood well enough, the wolf agreed. *It's that other smell I don't trust. The one under the blood. I told you about it the other day. It doesn't smell right.*

Is it some kind of animal? she asked him.

I don't know, he admitted. *If it is, it's one I've never encountered before. But it may not be any creature.*

Melayne shivered. *Could it be . . . a ghost?*

I don't know, Greyn repeated. *I've never smelled a ghost before, so I've nothing to compare it to. For all I know, it could be.*

That wasn't very reassuring.

Melayne realized she was getting nowhere with all of her questions. She simply had to get some more information. And there was only one way to do that — to get into the locked west wing somehow. She turned to Greyn. *Is there any other way into the west wing?*

I don't know, he told her. *And, to be honest, I have*

no intention of looking. I don't like that place. Why don't you ask one of the other animals? There must be a rat or something that lives in there. They have no class. I'm sure one of them could tell you.

That was a pretty good idea, Melayne realized. Concentrating, she called out to any creature within hearing: *Hello! I'm a friend and would like to talk to you. Please come out!* Then she waited, trying to see if anything was nearby.

There was absolutely no response, which was very odd. Greyn was right — there should at least have been rats in the west wing, and they tended to be chatty creatures. Yet . . . no reply. This was very odd. Feeling spooked once again, Melayne retreated from the wing toward the main body of the castle. She called out again, and a moment later a rat popped its head out of the stones, nose twitching, eyes carefully watching Greyn so as not to end up as a midnight snack.

Hello, it said, guardedly. *I don't often hear from humans. Much too busy to pay attention to me — except when they try to kill me. What do you want?*

Not to harm you, Melayne assured the little gray rat. *I'm just after some information*. She gestured at the west wing. *Are any of your friends and relatives inside there?*

There? The rat shook its head. *No chance. Nobody ever goes in there and comes out alive, young human. You don't know much about this castle, do you?*

No, I don't, Melayne admitted. *I'd be very grateful for anything that you can tell me. I know that you roam all over, and you must know a great deal about this castle.*

True enough, the rat agreed, settling itself down to chat. *But I can tell you only this about the west wing: Anyone who goes in there never comes out. Oh, except for that tall, dark human, but humans don't really count.* It grinned. *No offense. I don't really think of you as human. You're much too intelligent.*

Thank you, Melayne said dryly. *So, there are no animals at all living in the west wing, then?*

They might be living there, the rat admitted. *But if they are, they keep to themselves. Personally, I don't think there's anything alive in there. Now, I can tell you plenty about the rest of the castle. It's a nice place to live, especially if you know where the cheese is hidden.*

I'm sure it is, agreed Melayne. *But it's the west wing that interests me.*

The rat eyed her critically. *Maybe you are as foolish as all of the other humans after all,* it commented. *Didn't you hear what I said? Stay clear of the place; it's death to wander in there.*

Not for Lord Sander, Melayne objected.

Perhaps he's struck a bargain with whatever is in there, the rat suggested. *But simply because he survives is no guarantee that you will.*

There was more than a grain of truth in that observation, and Melayne couldn't help worrying about it. Was she asking for trouble, probing into the secrets of the castle?

Melayne thanked the rat for its kindness, and the

little creature dashed away. Greyn pretended he was going to chase it, but his heart wasn't in it. The wailing noise clearly disturbed him, and Melayne knew he was only staying in the castle right now to look after her.

It's all right, she told him. *I'm going to bed now. You don't have to wait around to make sure I'm safe.*

That made him a lot happier. He slipped through the shadows, watching her until she entered her room, and then left. Melayne got herself ready for bed, and then, instead of getting immediately between the sheets, she sat beside her window, peering out across the courtyard. She pulled a blanket around her so she wouldn't freeze to death, and tucked her cold feet under her bottom to keep them slightly warm. Then she waited, watching.

Lord Sander couldn't stay in there all night, she was sure. And she wanted to see what he would do when he left.

Hours passed. Melayne had to massage her feet, which were turning into blocks of ice, to keep her circulation going. And she was growing very tired. But she refused to give up. Finally, the door to the west wing opened quietly and Lord Sander slipped out. The bag he'd carried in before was gone, and he carefully locked the door behind him. Melayne couldn't make out much in the gloom, but he seemed to turn and look her way for just a second before he hurried back to the main part of the building.

After all that waiting, she'd hadn't really learned anything. Except that he'd left the meat behind in the west wing. She struggled to bed, and lay there shivering. She might as well have gone to bed earlier for all the good her vigil had done. All she had were questions, and her only hope of getting them answered had to lie in entering the west wing herself. But how could she do that? And, more important, could she survive such a trip?

Melayne fell asleep eventually, and her dreams were filled with terrible creatures that tried to rip her flesh from her body and drink her warm blood. She woke early shivering from fright instead of cold this time. She couldn't recall the exact nature of her dreams, but she knew they'd been born of her fears. Maybe going into the west wing was a really stupid idea after all.

But what option did she have?

Sarrow vanished after breakfast again. He'd made friends with several of the people in Dragonhome, and he was welcome all over the place. It was one of his skills, and Melayne rather envied him. She still felt uncertain of herself around other people, and liked to keep up a slight barrier to let them remain at a distance. But Sarrow was happy to plunge in and make friends with everyone. Melayne was pleased, because it was good to have a little rest from him from time to time. And she had Corran to look after and teach. She knew she should be teaching Sarrow, too, but one active youngster was about as much as she could handle some days.

The lord's son was doing well with his reading, and he was genuinely keen to improve. He concentrated **as best** he could on the words, and he was progressing. Bantry was impressed. Like so many of the common folk, the soldier could neither read nor write. He alternated between a slight contempt for what he considered a useless skill and guarded envy for someone who could do something he could not.

Since it was an unseasonably warm day, Melayne and Corran went out in the courtyard to read, and Bantry ambled over. "I can't see much point in this reading myself," he admitted, staring upside down at the page Corran was struggling to decipher.

There was simply no getting through to him. Melayne smiled sadly. "Being able to read and write has helped me a lot. After my parents were killed, it was my being able to read a map that got us here. And some of the things I learned from books helped Sarrow and me to survive. If I'd not been able to read or write, I might not be alive today."

"Then maybe it does have its uses, if it kept you alive," Bantry agreed grudgingly. "But it's still not for the likes of me."

"Then you should be glad Lord Sander hasn't asked me to educate you as well," Melayne answered with a smile.

"Believe me, I am," the soldier assured her. He grinned down at her. "And I still know plenty of stories, most of which haven't been written down. Do you know those mountains out there, for example?"

"Yes," Corran said, getting interested in the conversation at last. "My father says that dragons used to live there."

"That they did," Bantry agreed. He leaned on his

spear. "And terribly cold and harsh they were, too. Mean, vicious creatures that hated men."

Corran frowned. "That's not what my father says," he said, puzzled. "He says that the dragons were just animals, and that people hunted them because they were afraid."

"Aye, well, your father wasn't as affected by them as we peasants were," Bantry replied. "But those dragons came after the villagers who lived hereabouts in those days. They used to pounce on anyone who was daft enough to be out alone, and — snap! Crunch! Down the dragon's throat they went. It was a horrible way to go, and there was no way to protect yourself against them."

"Why not?" asked Corran, spellbound. Like most children, there was a grisly streak in him.

"Because they had such thick skin," Bantry explained. "Almost like armor it was. Hard and scaly, so tough you couldn't even cut it with the best of swords. The knights who lived in those days had to come up with a new way to kill the dragons, so people could live in safety. What they did was to make themselves long lances. They're kind of like spears, only they're made completely of metal, so they're stronger. A wooden spear would just break on a dragon's hide, you see. But a metal lance would stand the strain. And the knight would ride a big, powerful horse, called a charger. Because they would charge right at the dragons. The lance would be driven into the dragon's scales, and pierce it straight through, if the knight was skilled enough.

"Anyway, a whole body of knights was formed, all with special orders to kill the dragons. They went out all over the Five Kingdoms, and they hunted out every dragon that they could find and slew them. All the common folk were extremely grateful to them. But it was dangerous work, and many of them died in the doing of it."

"They went all over the Five Kingdoms?" Melayne asked with interest. "Do you mean that there wasn't any war back then?"

Bantry shrugged. "There was war, right enough. I reckon there's always been war. After all, you can't trust anyone who isn't Farrowholme-born and bred, can you?"

"I suppose not," Melayne said, her irony lost on both Bantry and Corran.

"All of the others are dreadful people, who lie and cheat and steal and kill," Bantry added. "You two don't know how lucky you are to be living here. Anyway, the war was going on, but the dragons were such problems that anyone who was out after slaying dragons was allowed to go where they needed, and everyone made them welcome. People were so glad to be rid of the dragons that it didn't matter if a man was born in Farrowholme, or Stormgard, or Vester — if they were out to slay dragons, they all got a hero's welcome. And rightly so.

"Anyway, eventually all of the dragons in the Five Kingdoms were dead, except for the last few. They hid out in the Dragonhome Mountains. And Lord Sander's father's father's father led the battle to slay the last of them. He and six knights went into the mountains. They were gone for almost two weeks, but when the lord returned, the dragons were all dead. And so were five of those six knights, all perished in terrible combat with the wicked dragons. Only the lord and one knight came back alive. And, since then, there hasn't been a single dragon seen in the world." He smiled down at Corran. "So you see, young fellow, you come from a great line. You should be proud of the past lords of Dragonhome. They were a brave bunch, and noble as they come."

"And my father's just as good as them," Corran declared. "And when I'm grown up, I'll be even better." Then his face fell. "Only there aren't any dragons for me to slay," he complained.

"There are other evils in this world," Melayne assured him. "Perhaps not as visible as dragons, nor as simple to kill, but just as deadly to poor folks. Things like poverty, and famine, and war, and hatred, and prejudice. There will never be an end to all sorts of monsters that have to be slain so that people can live decent lives."

"Then I'll fight against all of those things," Corran said bravely.

"If you do, then you'll be remembered just as proudly as all of your ancestors," Melayne promised him. She smiled up at Bantry. "That was a good story," she said approvingly. "And maybe I'll be the person to write it down one day to pass along."

"Plenty of folks know it," he answered with a shrug. "I don't reckon there's any need to waste paper and time on a task like that."

"Perhaps not," Melayne said, not wishing to argue. "But I still might do it just the same."

"Suit yourself," agreed Bantry. "Well, I'd better be about my business. It's almost time for me to take a watch at the gate again." He gave them both an amiable smile, and then hurried away.

"Is all of that true?" Corran asked her abruptly.

"All of what?"

"What he said about the dragons." Corran frowned. "My father says that dragons weren't horrible, just quiet and cold, and that they were killed because people hated and feared them. He never said anything about them eating people."

Melayne shook her head sadly. "I don't know which is true," she admitted. "Sometimes I wonder if there ever were such things as dragons. People sometimes make stories up, Corran, that don't have any basis in truth."

"That's a wicked thing to do!" the boy exclaimed.

"No, it's called *fiction*," Melayne replied. "People who write it know what they write about never really happened, but they have wonderful imaginations, and they tell stories of things that *might* have happened. And if they're very good, these stories can be marvelously thrilling. But you have to remember that they're not really true. Some people who hear these stories don't realize that they were just invented, and they think they must be true. So they come to believe in something that never really happened. It seems to me that this might be the case with dragons. There may never have been any *real* dragons, but somebody invented stories about them. Then other people believed those stories to have been true, and believed there really were dragons."

"But there weren't?" asked Corran, looking disappointed.

"I don't know," admitted Melayne. "It's just a thought I had. Of course, it could be wrong, and there might once have been real dragons. Perhaps they were horrible and killed people, like Bantry thinks. Or perhaps they were just killed out of jealousy, like your father said. People can do mean, unthinking things sometimes. But I simply don't know what the truth is, Corran."

He nodded solemnly, and went back to his reading. Melayne couldn't help wondering about all the different stories she was hearing. Was it *ever* possible to get the truth about anything? Bantry believed that all dragons had been evil, man-eating creatures. But he also believed that anyone who wasn't from Farrowholme was a subhuman monster! According to Corran, Lord Sander thought dragons were the victims of human fear and hatred. But could she accept that view, when his own ancestor had supposedly been the one to kill them all off? She found Lord Sander interesting and attractive, but maybe he wasn't exactly right in the head. Normal people, after all, didn't usually take walks in the dark with bags of raw meat.

The problem was, a story was only as true as the person who told it wanted to make it. And it all depended, of course, on where he'd been told the story in the first place. The only reliable testimony was that of a witness, and so far Melayne had found none that talked of dragons from firsthand knowledge, since they'd been dead for over a hundred years. The only chance she'd have was if she found a book older than that which spoke about them.

Melayne wondered if she could find one in Lady Cassary's room. She'd only looked through a small number of the books there, stopping once she'd found the books she could use. But who knew what other treasures might be there. After dinner, she decided, she'd go there and check out every book in the place.

Sarrow turned up again a short while later, and he and Corran took a break to play some sort of ball-game. Melayne wasn't really paying attention. She jumped when Bantry suddenly came racing out of the gatehouse, a wild expression on his face, his spear forgotten.

"Whatever's wrong?" she exclaimed.

"There's a Seeker at the gate," Bantry gasped, without slowing down. "He wants to come in. I've got to find Lord Sander."

A Seeker! Panic settled in her stomach, cold and hard. Had she and Sarrow been traced? That soldier, Brant, had said that the Seeker had escaped from the Farrowholme soldiers . . . Could he have followed her somehow? She hurried over to where Sarrow and Corran were playing their game.

"We'd best go inside," she said, shocked at the waver in her own voice. "Playtime is over."

"Slave driver," Sarrow muttered. "We're having fun."

"Do as you're told!" Melayne snapped, harsher than she intended. Couldn't he see that there was trouble?

"You're getting too bossy," Sarrow complained. "I don't see why we have to go in. We're having fun."

Melayne grabbed his shoulders and felt like shaking him. "There's a Seeker here," she hissed. "Do you want him to find you?"

That stopped his protests. He turned pale, and bolted toward the closest door, aiming to hide anywhere he could. Melayne wanted to run after him, but she couldn't let anyone suspect that she was afraid of the Seeker. If somebody saw that, they might figure out why.

Unfortunately, Corran had heard her remark to Sarrow. What was she going to say to explain herself? Melayne struggled to think of a good excuse. Corran surprised her.

"A Seeker?" he asked, shaking. "We've got to hide! Come on!" He whirled and fled after Sarrow.

Stunned by this reaction, Melayne didn't move. *Corran* was scared of the Seeker! That could only mean one thing . . . that *he* had to be a Talent, too. The thought had never occurred to her before, but it made a wild kind of sense. Perhaps *that* was why Lord Sander stayed in his castle all of the time — hiding his son from the world. Being the heir to Dragonhome wouldn't save Corran from serving in the army. Quite the opposite, if anything. The King's Men would want a noble to set a good example for the commoners.

She hesitated a shade too long. Lord Sander

strode out of the tower, and saw her. "Where's my son?" he demanded coldly.

"Inside," she replied. "Sarrow's hiding him."

"Good." The lord nodded. "Make certain he stays there until I send for you all. Now, go!" He strode on, not even bothering to check that she obeyed.

Melayne found Sarrow and Corran, both white and shaking, in her own room. She closed the door. "Your father has gone to speak to the Seeker," she informed Corran. "I'm sure he'll send him away so you'll be safe."

"*He'll* be safe?" Sarrow stared at the lord's son. "You're a Talent?"

Corran nodded miserably. "It's supposed to be a secret," he said quietly. "My father told me never to tell anyone. But if the Seeker's come for me, there's no need to pretend anymore."

"I don't think it's *you* he's come for," Melayne said gently. She couldn't bear to see the small boy so frightened. "One of them has been after us for some time."

Corran's eyes opened wide with surprise. "*You're* Talents, too?" he asked.

"Yes," Melayne admitted. "But you're the only one who knows that. We'll have to promise to keep each other's secrets."

"I promise," Corran said immediately. His curiosity seemed to have gotten the better of his fear. "What can you two do? I don't know what my Talent will be yet."

Of course not; he was much too young to show a Talent.

And that made Melayne stop and think. How did Corran know he was a Talent? Even a Seeker couldn't tell properly with anyone younger than Sarrow. And Sarrow didn't even show his Talent yet. Perhaps there was something she was missing. After all, her own parents had known that Sarrow was a Talent shortly after he was born. Melayne wished she knew more.

Another puzzle. Well, she'd have to find out the answer later.

"We don't know what Sarrow can do yet," she admitted. "He's still a little young. But I have the gift of Communication."

Corran looked puzzled. "What does that mean?"

"It means that I can talk to animals, and they can talk back to me," she explained.

"Wow." Corran looked very impressed. "That's got to be really fun."

"Only if you like animals," Sarrow said, a little peevishly. He didn't like Melayne getting all of the attention.

"It *is* fun," Melayne insisted. "I get to hear all kinds of interesting stories that way, and sometimes animals will help me."

"Can I see?" Corran asked.

"Later," Melayne promised him. "I don't think it would be very wise to use my Talent while there's a Seeker around."

"Oh." Corran looked embarrassed. "You're right. I didn't think of that." He stared fiercely at her. "I don't want them to take you away! I like you too much."

249

Touched, Melayne hugged the boy. "And I like you too much to want to go," she replied.

"Oh, please," muttered Sarrow. "This is getting way too mushy. Can we cut the girl stuff?"

"Perhaps the two of you can play quietly," Melayne suggested. "I'll keep watch, in case . . ." She had been about to say *in case the Seeker comes*, but decided not to alarm the boys further. "Just in case," she finished lamely. She left them together and moved to the front door. Opening it a crack, she peered out.

There was nothing really to see. Hada had come out of the main tower and was standing in the court-yard, staring uncertainly at the main gate. There was no sign of Lord Sander or Bantry. And, more hopefully, no sign of the Seeker.

Why was he here? Was he after Corran? Or her and her brother? Melayne's stomach twisted, and she fought to keep her fears under control. This wasn't the time to panic. Not yet.

Melayne saw Lord Sander striding back from the gatehouse, his face darker than normal. There was anger in the way he moved, Melayne could tell. Hada seemed to sense the same, and she ran across the courtyard to her lord. Melayne couldn't hear what was said at this distance, but the lord sent Hada toward Melayne's room with a few words and a gesture.

Hada moved quickly. Though attempting to re-tain her dignity, she hurried to the doorway, where Melayne met her, not knowing what was about to happen.

"The dark hour has come," Hada said sadly. "The Seeker wants Corran."

Corran. Melayne felt an instant elation. *Not her and Sarrow!* They were still safe! Then she felt horribly guilty for her reaction. The King's Men couldn't have Corran, either. Even if Lord Sander was to agree, Melayne wasn't going to allow her young charge to be sent off to learn how to kill and be killed. She'd take him from the castle and his father before she'd let that happen.

"Our lord wants you and the two boys to come to his chambers immediately," Hada added. "Quickly, quickly! There's no telling what might come next!"

Melayne nodded, and then gathered Corran and Sarrow. The three of them followed Hada back to Lord Sander's room. He was in his large chair again, brooding in a blacker mood than any she'd ever seen him in. He looked up as they entered, and his face seemed to clear a little. Hada closed the door behind them carefully.

"I've sent the Seeker away for now," Lord Sander explained abruptly. "But he won't stay away for long. He wants to see Corran and test him. And I can't possibly allow that."

"Because he's a Talent," Melayne said.

"Yes." Lord Sander gave her a troubled look. "Does this bother you, Melayne? Are you one of those people who think Talents are monsters?"

"I don't think anything of the kind," Melayne replied firmly. "And there is no way I'd ever allow the Seekers to get to Corran while I'm still alive."

Relief washed over the lord's face. "Bless you,"

he said. "I chose more wisely than I knew when I made you his teacher."

"But what are we going to do?" she asked him. "If the Seeker doesn't test Corran, then he's bound to suspect the truth. And then he'll be back, with King's Men to back him up."

"I know." Lord Sander looked thoughtful. "I told him that Corran was sick, with a contagion. The man's very fastidious, and he doesn't want to encounter a sick boy. That will buy me a couple of days. But I have to produce Corran for him then, or else be in serious trouble." He smiled slightly, looking at Sarrow. "Of course, he doesn't know what my son looks like . . ."

Melayne could see where his thoughts were heading, and she shook her head sadly. "It won't work," she said gently.

"I know Sarrow's a little older, but if he were in bed, and sickly looking . . ." Lord Sander looked hopeful. "I'm sure it would work."

"It might," agreed Melayne, wincing. "Except Sarrow's a Talent, too."

"Oh." That wiped the hope off Lord Sander's face. "And he's too young to control himself, isn't he? I suppose it's too much to hope that he has a Talent that might prove useful to us?"

"We don't know what his Talent is," admitted Melayne. Then she realized what the lord had said. *"Control himself?"* she repeated. "What are you talking about?"

Lord Sander looked confused. "You don't know how Seekers can find other Talents?" he asked.

"I don't know much about Seekers at all," Melayne admitted. "Only enough to avoid them."

"Your parents didn't teach you very well, then," he replied.

"They taught me as best they knew!" Melayne protested indignantly. "Just because they didn't know *everything* —"

Lord Sander held up his hands. "Enough! I didn't mean to insult them, and I apologize. But Talents have a special sort of feel to their minds, not like everyone else. Something to do with their abilities. I think It's because Talent is actually housed in an area of the human brain that isn't normally in use. Seekers can tune into this, and that's how they recognize Talents. But it's possible, using special training, for a Talent to clamp down on this part of their brain, and make it seem like a normal human brain. Then they can hide from the Seekers. How do you think *I've* managed for so long?"

It seemed as if the day was going to be one shock after another. "*You're* a Talent?" Melayne gasped.

"Of course I am," Lord Sander replied. "I'd have thought you'd have realized that by now. Anyone born in this castle is."

"Oh." Melayne blinked, confused. "What Talent do you have?"

"Sight," he replied bitterly.

"Sight?" This was one that Melayne had never heard of before. "What's that?"

"All I have to do is to touch someone, and I can See their future," he explained. He held up his hands, showing the heavy gloves. "Why do you think I wear these? I don't want to see what will happen to people."

"Why not?" Melayne asked, confused. "It sounds like a terrific gift to have."

"Because," he replied slowly, "when I held my wife, I could see that she was going to die. And I couldn't tell her, or anyone. I just had to wait, and *know* what was to come."

"You poor man," Melayne said softly. She couldn't imagine the torture he must have gone through, knowing there was nothing he could do to change what was to happen. "Perhaps you're right, and it's best not to know."

"All of this is very well," Hada interrupted, "but it doesn't help us at all. If Sarrow's a Talent, too, then he can't help us. And we can't let them take Corran off to die."

"True." Lord Sander sighed. "But what can we do?"

Melayne gazed at him in sympathy, an idea starting to form. "I think I may have a solution," she replied. As he looked at her in hope, Melayne couldn't help but see how attractive he was. She buried the thought instantly. "You had the right idea, just the wrong person. What you need is a substitute for Corran."

"But Sarrow is the only boy around," Hada protested.

"No, he isn't," Melayne answered. "In the village there are plenty of young boys. In fact, there's a family I stayed with who had one just about the right age."

"I'm sure there are plenty of boys," Lord Sander said gently, though there was pain in his eyes. "But I can't tell everyone that Corran is a Talent. If I did, sooner or later it is bound to get out. I simply can't trust these people, no matter how nice they are."

"You don't have to trust them," Melayne answered. "You don't have to tell them anything at all. Look, the Seeker thinks that Corran is rather ill. He won't get too close. He'll want to check him from the doorway, probably without even speaking. And the boy wouldn't even have to know who the Seeker was."

Lord Sander straightened up slightly. "But how do I get the boy here without him knowing what I'm doing?" he objected.

"*You* don't," Melayne said firmly. "*I* do. I'm friends with his sister, Ysane. If I send word that I'd like to see her and her brother, I'm sure they'd come to visit. I can keep Ysane distracted, while you pretend for the Seeker that her brother is Corran, so he can do a quick check and confirm he's not a Talent."

"It might work," the Lord said, hopefully, stroking his chin. "Melayne, you're a very bright girl."

"There are many ways it could go wrong," Hada objected. "If the Seeker hears a peasant boy talking, he'll *know* immediately that he's a fake."

"Then we'll have to make certain he hears nothing of the kind," Lord Sander replied firmly. "Hada, we have no choice: It's Melayne's plan, or else admit that Corran is a Talent."

"I suppose," agreed Hada reluctantly. "But I still think we're asking for trouble."

"No," Melayne answered. "We're not asking for trouble; trouble has come knocking on our door. We simply have to send it away. Now, what we must do is simple. We have to get Ysane and her brother here tomorrow. We can send Bantry with a message."

"What if they're busy and don't want to come?" objected Hada.

"Not a problem," Lord Sander said firmly. "I can make it *my* invitation for them to come. They're not likely to refuse me, are they?"

"Right," agreed Melayne. "And then you also arrange for the Seeker to visit a little while later. Tell him that Corran's recovered slightly, but is still very sick. Ask if he can make the visit short. If he's as fastidious as you say, he won't want to stay longer than he has to. Then we'll have Ysane's brother for him to look at, and then get rid of the Seeker. Nobody will be any the wiser, except the six of us."

"It might work," agreed Hada.

"It *has* to work," the lord said, a lot more optimistically. "We don't have any other chance." Then he sighed. "The problem is, I'm going to have to make this trip myself. It's the only way to convince the family and the Seeker that these are really my orders. And I don't like leaving the castle for very long. Still, we all have to play our part." He stood up. "Hada, go see to my horse being saddled. It's best that I ride now. Have Bantry and two men go with me. It wouldn't do for me to be without an escort."

"Of course." Hada bowed slightly, and left.

"A good woman," Lord Sander said, smiling slightly. "And very faithful. As for you, young lady." He looked down at Melayne. "I don't know how to thank you. You may have saved my son's life."

"I would never allow anyone to harm him," Melayne vowed.

"No, I don't believe you would." Lord Sander looked at her in wonder. "You're quite a tiger when roused, aren't you? I'd hate to ever come up against you."

"I'm sure you never would, my lord," Melayne answered, blushing for some strange reason.

"There's no need to be quite so formal," he replied. "Except in the presence of others." His dark eyes bored into her own. "Call me Sander when there's nobody else around."

Melayne swallowed, and nodded. "All right," she agreed, a catch in her throat. She couldn't think when he stared at her so intently.

Suddenly, the stare was gone. "I have to leave," he said. "I hope I won't be long. We'll talk some more when I return. I have a suspicion that there's more to you than I ever realized, and I think I'd better get to know this new you." He turned and marched out of the door.

Melayne nearly collapsed into the closest chair. Did he have any idea at all of the effect he had on her when he looked at her like that?

"Dinner's going to be late," Corran said. "And I'm already hungry."

"Me, too," Sarrow agreed. "Why don't we go to the kitchen and see if we can get the cook to give us something?"

"Okay." Corran turned to Melayne, obviously certain that his father and Melayne would fix everything. "Do you want to come with us?"

"No," she answered. The state her stomach was in, the last thing she could manage now was food. "You two go and see if you can convince her that you'll starve to death without a snack. I'll join you later."

"Your loss," said Sarrow without sympathy. The two boys shot out of the room.

Melayne was glad to be left alone. Her mind was in such a turmoil right now. So much had happened, and everything had suddenly changed. Lord Sander and Corran were both Talents! And there was a way to hide out, as the lord had done, to avoid being detected. If she could learn the secret, too, she and Sarrow could be safe forever. Maybe there were more Talents around who did the same thing?

And then she suddenly noticed something.

On the floor, where Lord Sander had been sitting, was a key. It must have fallen while he was talking, and he hadn't noticed.

The key to the west wing . . .

She stared at it for a moment, frozen in indecision. Here was her chance to learn what was going on. Lord Sander was gone for a couple of hours, at least, so she should have time to discover what was happening.

But . . . *should* she do it? This was sneaky and

cheating. To take the key and try to discover Lord Sander's secrets while he was out trying to save his son . . . On the other hand, it was the perfect opportunity, and she might never get a better one.

The struggle in her conscience didn't last very long. Melayne snatched up the key, and hurried from the room.

She would know what the secret of Dragonhome was very shortly. . . .

Chapter Thirteen
The Secret

Melayne was determined, but couldn't help feeling guilty. Was this *really* the right thing to do? Right or wrong, she knew she was going to do it anyway. She *had* to know what Lord Sander was hiding. Even though her conscience troubled her, she moved through the courtyard to the locked door.

There was nobody around. Lord Sander and Bantry had left for the village, and Hada and the others were preparing the late meal. With the two boys occupied, there was nobody left to observe Melayne as she unlocked the door and slipped inside. She closed the door behind her, and stood there, her heart beating fast.

What was in this part of the castle? Could it possibly be a ghost? If it was, would she be able to hide from it, since it was not yet night? Or did ghosts really care what time of day it was? And what if it was a madwoman? Then what? And what if it was something unimagined? Melayne was getting more and more nervous as she hesitated, and she knew she simply had to gather all of her courage and force herself to go on, before she lost her nerve entirely.

Slowly, she moved down the corridor. It looked like the main part of the castle, though there were no lit torches. There was an unlit one, though, which she took hold of and lit with matches she'd been smart enough to bring. This helped her see where she was going.

Which, of course, raised the question: Where *was* she going? The west wing was quite large, and she didn't have hours to spend looking around. She needed some indication of the way to go.

The wing had been abandoned for years, she remembered. Maybe the stories about it being unsafe weren't entirely made up. It might be dangerous where she was going. She glanced at the floor, to see how safe it was.

The place had been abandoned for so long, there was dust all over — except where Lord Sander's feet had trod. There was a pathway leading down the center of the corridor! Melayne grinned to herself. All she had to do was to follow this trail, and she'd discover . . . whatever there was to discover.

Cautiously moving forward, Melayne couldn't help thinking about the melancholy lord. Actually, he seemed to be lightening up somewhat. He'd been really quiet and broody when she'd first arrived, but seeing his son blossom had encouraged a similar reaction in him. He seemed to be recovering a measure of life and humor at last. Not that she could blame him for having been so sad. The gift of Sight that he had might be helpful sometimes, but it was also a curse. To have known his wife was dying, and that there was nothing he could do about it, must have really hurt him. He was obviously afraid of ever getting close to anyone again, in case the same thing happened to him. *That* was why he'd never married again, or even seemed interested in any other woman. If he touched such a person, he'd see their future. And that obviously terrified him.

On the other hand, his retreat from everyone was far too extreme. Yes, it was terribly sad that his wife died and he couldn't alter it — but that happened in life sometimes. To retreat from other people in case you might lose them was understandable, but very, very foolish. You'd never lose anyone you cared about again, true enough — but at the same time, you'd never *gain* anyone you cared about, either. Despite the possible loss, you *had* to live for the more certain gains. Lord Sander needed friends very badly. He needed someone he could talk to, confide in, care for — and someone to love. Cutting himself off from that had made him a shadow of a man.

All he seemed to have was his hidden secret. Melayne frowned. The passage turned, and then there were steps leading downward. To where? The footprints continued downward, so she slowly followed.

Once steps came to an end, there was another corridor—this one quite short. There was a strange smell in the air, one that Melayne couldn't quite identify. It was faint but distinct, pungent and mysterious.

Ahead was a large door, made of very strong oak. There was a lock on it, and for a moment she panicked. Did she need a second key to enter here? She tested the door, and it was locked. The keyhole was too large for the key she'd brought with her, and for a moment she was overpowered by despair. There was a second key! This was as far as she could go.

And then she saw the key, on a hook beside the door. Sighing with relief, she took it down and unlocked the door. Since the key was here, it meant that Lord Sander had something locked inside the cellar. But what? Or who? And why?

Slowly, she eased the door open, and held out the torch to look inside. It seemed to be no more than a dungeon. There was a tiny window high in the wall, about twenty feet from the ground. Even though it was afternoon, virtually no light seeped in. The flickering light from the torch showed her the walls of the room, which had to be about forty feet across in all directions.

Just inside the door were bones. She gave a start, thinking that they were the remains of some prisoner. Was *that* Lord Sander's secret? That he had some enemies chained down here, left to rot and die? Were they the source of that terrible wailing?

Then she realized how foolish she was being, and shook her head, amazed at her own stupidity. These were ham and lamb bones, the remains of the raw meat that Lord Sander had been bringing. Melayne bent to look at one of the bones. It was a shinbone of a cow, by the look of it. She shuddered, because there were sharp gouges in the bone. Whatever had eaten this meat, it had powerful jaws and teeth. They resembled the teeth of a wolf or some other predator.

What was down here with her?

For the first time, she wondered if she'd really been very wise to venture down here. Whatever could shred bones like that could make very short work of one scrawny teenage girl. . . .

But it was too late for her to leave now. She'd die of curiosity if she came all of this way only to retreat before she had the answers that she wanted — and *needed*, she reminded herself. After all, Lord Sander came and went without any problems.

But, then again, maybe the monster — or whatever it was — was used to him . . . and wouldn't harm him. A stranger, on the other hand . . .

Fighting to control her fears, Melayne moved slowly into the room. She left the door open behind her and stared into the gloom beyond the circle of her torch.

There was straw on the floor, and it didn't look or smell like it had been changed for quite a while. There was also the residual stink of dried blood, and then that something else she'd noticed earlier. It had to be urine of some kind, she realized, and that made her feel slightly better. Whatever it was she was facing, at least it wasn't supernatural. Ghosts didn't need to go to the bathroom.

"Is there anybody here?" she called. Her voice was faint and somewhat squeaky from fear, but it sounded horribly loud in her own ears. She stared around, trying to see.

There was a sudden noise, the sound of something sharp scraping on stone. Melayne's heart thundered in her chest as she tried to figure out where the sound had come from. There was what sounded like a sneeze, and then something suddenly reared up in front of her from the pile of straw.

Melayne shrieked and backed against the door, slamming it shut.

A head emerged from the straw, blinking and snuffling. Two large, expressive eyes glared at her from above a large beak. Twin nostrils flared and blew. Two small ears twitched, and the great reptile head glowered at her.

And then a second erupted beside it, and a third. They were all the same — large eyes, beaks, and scales. . . . They looked purple in this light, but it was hard to tell. A fourth head, and then a fifth reared up, staring at her with cold, hard eyes.

Melayne was shocked. She couldn't move, except that the hand holding the torch was shaking badly, making the shadows in the room dance. The five-headed creature stared at her, dark eyes glaring, beaked mouths showing plenty of sharp little teeth.

She realized that she had been wrong: This wasn't some fantastic creature with five heads — it was five separate, but still fantastic, creatures. They started to move in the straw, and she could now see clawed feet, more scales, and then the glint of wings as the creatures shook themselves fully awake.

Dragons . . .

Fear caught at Melayne's throat as she stared at

the slow-moving creatures. Were they as dangerous as she had been told? Were they stirring, hoping to taste her flesh and drink her blood? Melayne had never really been frightened of any animal in her life. Being able to talk to them, she felt comfortable and confident around any creature.

But dragons . . . dragons were different. They were supposed to enjoy killing and devouring, especially maidens! She was their prime source of food, at least according to legend. Her heart beat faster, and she felt slightly giddy. Should she be standing here like this, or running for her life? Fear and uncertainty kept her rooted to the spot. But, as the creatures stirred, her natural optimism managed to keep the fear in check. Surely these were only babies, and wouldn't harm her.

Would they?

Five dragons unfolded themselves from their sleeping straw, staring at her with growing curiosity. Melayne had no idea how they had come to be here, how they had even survived when they were all supposed to have been killed off so long ago. All she knew was that she was staring at five small dragons, possibly even babies.

Of course, *small* was a relative term. Each of them was over six feet long, body and head. Melayne could glimpse sinewy tails from time to time, but couldn't see how extensive these were.

One of the dragons opened its mouth and uttered the horrible wailing sound that had so scared her the night she had first heard it. Now, however, she knew what it was, and what it meant: *I'm hungry*. It wasn't Communication, just obvious, basic baby need.

Hello, she called out to them, gently, not wanting to scare them.

Five pairs of eyes stared at her in astonishment. *You can speak!* one of them said, its voice shaking with wonder.

Yes, Melayne replied. *It's my gift: I can Communicate with all kinds of animals. You can't imagine how stunned I am to see you—I thought all dragons were dead long ago!*

The others are, the spokesdragon replied, bending its neck to sniff at her. *We are the last — as far as we know. The human male tries to take care of us.*

He's a good man, Melayne said with conviction. *But he can't speak to you.*

No, the first dragon agreed. *So he doesn't really know what we need. He tries his best, but it's not enough.*

Meat, Melayne said. *You're flesh eaters.*

Yes, yes, yes, a second dragon piped up, a purplish tongue licking its teeth. *But not dead flesh.* It flexed a claw, showing off the six-inch-long talons it possessed. *We need fresh meat.*

Oh. Melayne was starting to understand. *How do you all feel? Are you well?*

Well? the first dragon asked, snorting. *How can we be well? We're stuck here, in this lightless place, eating only dead meat.* It shivered its wings. *We cannot fly, we cannot hunt.* It shook its head. *We ail. And, sooner or later, we shall die.*

No! Melayne exclaimed, scared for them. *You can't die! Not now I've found you. You must live, and grow and be strong.*

Simple to say, the second dragon answered. *But very, very, very hard to do. The human will not allow us outside.*

He keeps us prisoners here, the first dragon added. *Though not through malice, I don't believe.*

No, agreed Melayne. *He keeps you here because he knows that if you go outside, you will be hunted by other humans and killed.*

Killed? The dragon blinked its large eyes. *Why would people kill us?*

Because they're afraid of you, Melayne explained. *They believe you eat people, and would kill them for food.*

Eat people? The dragon snorted. *Quite frankly, my dear, I wouldn't dream of it.*

Melayne felt a lot happier at that news. *Because you're too kindhearted?* she asked.

No, it answered. *Because, to be honest, you smell terrible. I'm sure you'd give us the most dreadful stomachache. No offense meant, of course. I'm sure you smell quite . . . pleasant to one another.*

Well, that was hardly the answer she'd been hoping for, but it would have to do. At least it meant that she was safe, though she had never really feared any animal in her life. Even carnivores rarely ate prey they'd had a chat with.

The problem is, she told them, *that while I believe you, other humans wouldn't. Most of them can't talk to you, and even if they could, they'd think you were lying to them. They've grown up believing that drag-ons are cold, aloof, and cruel.*

Well, they got two out of three right, the dragon answered. *But we can't help being cold and aloof. We're reptiles, after all. But we're not cruel.* It extended one of its claws, and Melayne gently touched it. The skin was, indeed, cold to the touch.

We need warmth. A third dragon spoke up. Melayne could tell instantly that this one was a female; the first two must have been males, then. This dragon seemed slightly smaller and more delicate. She rustled her wings. *We freeze down here. We need to be in the sunshine. We cannot live like this for long.*

Melayne moved to stroke her scales. *No wonder you cry all night,* she said sympathetically. *You're cold and badly fed. You need room to fly and hunt.* She looked around the dungeon. It had seemed so massive when she had first come in, but that was from a human perspective. From a dragon point of view, this was a small, cold, airless cell.

Will you help us? the first dragon asked. He lowered his head, his large, liquid eyes staring at her. She could see her distorted reflection in the lens.

Any way I can, she promised. *But it won't be easy, and I may not be able to do it very quickly. Can you last a while longer?*

No, the female dragon answered. *We are perishing. Two more years at most.*

The dragon thought that was not long? Melayne was confused until she remembered that dragons were supposed to have very long lives. *There has to be something I can do*, she informed them. *But it may take me a few days to figure out just what.*

A few days? the second dragon repeated. *Well, that's all right then.* He looked up at the tiny window near the ceiling. *I can wait that long to stretch my wings.*

Melayne couldn't help smiling. For all of their bulk and coldness, there was something rather endearing about these creatures. *Do you have names?* she asked them. *I'm called Melayne.*

Do we have names? the first dragon echoed. *What do you think we are, savages? Of course we have names, you dolt. I'm Brek.* He waved a paw at the other male. *This is Shath.* A wave at the female. *That's Tura, and the other two females are Loken and Ganeth.*

Well, I'm very pleased to meet you all, Melayne informed them. *Honestly, you have no idea just how excited I am.*

Yes we do, Brek answered. *You're radiating heat like crazy.* He grinned, somehow, despite his beak. *You could probably warm us all up if we huddled in next to you, in fact.*

Brek! Tura exclaimed. *We'd crush her to death!*

Brek sighed. *I wasn't serious, you idiot.*

Oh. Tura leaned forward, and said, confidentially to Melayne, *He's a bit of a fool at times; don't let it bother you.*

I heard that! Brek snapped.

You were meant to, Tura said primly. *Now, behave yourself, before you scare our visitor off.*

Oh, he wouldn't do that, Melayne said hastily. *I*

know you're all very nice, and I'm happy just to be here with you. But I really think I ought to be going now. I'm not supposed to be down here with you, and if Lord Sander finds out, he's likely to be very mad.*

Is that the human who brings us food? Loken asked timidly. *I always wondered if he had a name.* She seemed to be very shy, at least for a dragon. And Ganeth hadn't even spoken.

He's the one, Melayne agreed. *He's in charge of this castle, and I was forbidden to come down here. Now I see why.* She was reluctant to leave these creatures, but she knew that it wasn't wise to overstay this visit. If Lord Sander returned and discovered she'd been down here . . . How long *had* she been down here, anyway? It couldn't be very long, surely. Certainly not enough time for the lord to have ridden to town and back. Still, there was no point in tempting fate. She should just sneak back upstairs, replace the key, and pretend she'd never been down here.

Then she'd have to think of what she could do to free the dragons and help them. Which would mean coming down again, somehow. Maybe she could get the rat she'd talked to earlier to steal this key after Lord Sander had gone to bed at night. . . . She started to plan what she would have to do to help the dragons.

The plan was dashed from her mind as the door flew open. Lord Sander ran in, a furious expression on his face. Melayne gasped, too startled to move.

"So *this* is what you've been up to!" the lord

cried, his voice thick with anger. "You were forbidden to come down here! I ought to chop you up and feed you to the dragons!"

"They wouldn't eat me if you did," Melayne snapped back, scared of his wrath, but angry in her own turn. "They say I smell bad."

"I don't care what . . ." Lord Sander's voice trailed off. "What did you *say*?"

"You've been abusing these poor creatures!" Melayne yelled at him, blissfully unaware that the "poor creatures" were bigger than either her or the lord. "Feeding them dead meat, caging them up, and not allowing them any sun! How could you treat them so badly? You . . . you monster!"

He actually took a step back from her. "You can *talk* to them?" he asked her, his anger completely evaporated.

"Of *course* I can talk to them, you idiot!" Melayne snapped. "What did you think I'd been doing down here? Didn't you realize that I was a Talent, too?"

Lord Sander smiled hesitantly. "No, actually, it never even occurred to me. I suppose I'm really not too bright. I had just assumed that only your brother was a Talent. I didn't realize it ran in your family." He stared from her to the dragons. "You've been talking to them?"

"Didn't I say so?" Melayne demanded. "And they told me how horrible you've been to them."

"Horrible?" He looked pained at the accusation. "I've been the only one looking after them since my father died."

"Looking after them?" Melayne asked him, crossly. "You've kept them prisoners!"

"I had little option!" Lord Sander said with some heat. "If any of them had stuck their snout out of here, they'd all have been killed. Surely you realize that!"

"Yes," Melayne agreed. "But being imprisoned down here is killing them. They need sunshine, room to use their wings, and somewhere to hunt. They have to chase and catch their food, not eat it cold and butchered."

"I've done the best I can," Lord Sander said sulkily. He looked like a guilty schoolboy, just caught cheating on an exam.

"I'm sure you have," Melayne agreed, realizing he *had* been trying for so long. "But now that I'm here, you can do a lot better."

Lord Sander stared at her in disbelief. "I can't let you know about the dragons," he protested. "I couldn't even trust Cassary with this, and I loved her dearly."

"It's too late for that," Melayne said firmly. "I already know, so you're stuck with it."

"No," the lord replied. "I have a number of options." He laid his hand on the pommel of his sword. "I can always kill you to prevent you from talking."

Melayne felt a shock at these words. "Would you really do that?" she asked, for the first time frightened of him.

He stared back at her, and sighed. "I don't want to," he told her. "Melayne, I like you a lot. I really do.

But I can't allow anything or anyone to endanger the lives of these five dragons. Too much is at stake here."

Melayne didn't have a clue what he was talking about. "Look," she informed him, "I'm with you on this one. I won't allow anyone to harm these dragons, either. And that includes you. I know you're only harming them out of ignorance, but that's not a good enough excuse. Especially not when you could work with me and help them."

For the first time since she had met him, the dark lord laughed. "*You're* threatening *me*?" he asked, shaking his head. "Melayne, I'm stronger and faster than you, and I'm armed while you're defenseless."

"You're quite wrong there," Melayne informed him coldly. Then she called: *Brek — I want you to scare the human. Not much, just enough to worry him.*

Why? asked the dragon.

Because he's talking about killing me to stop me from telling about you five, Melayne explained.

He can't do that! Tura yelled, and she surged forward. Her right forefoot lashed out. Lord Sander leaped backward, shocked, and barely missed having his head slapped across the room. Without his body attached.

Tura, calm down! Melayne called desperately. *I don't think he meant it. I only wanted to scare him a little.* This seemed to calm the dragon down. She settled back beside Melayne, still glowering at Lord Sander.

The lord recovered his wit quickly. "It seems I've badly underestimated you, Melayne," he murmured. "They seem to be rather protective of you."

"I can Communicate with them," Melayne said. "I know what they want. Of course they want to keep me around."

"Far be it from me to argue with five dragons," Lord Sander said. "However, you have to understand that I can't help but mistrust you. Nobody outside my family knows anything about these dragons, for their safety."

"I'm no longer outside your family," Melayne answered. "You took me in, and I promise you that I will not betray their secret."

"And I'm sure you mean that promise," Lord Sander agreed. "But it may not be so easy to keep it as to give it. You may speak accidentally, or in haste, or in a hundred other ways. And then they would be discovered and killed. I simply can't trust *anyone* else to keep their secret."

"You can't stop me from knowing it," Melayne replied. "I'm not some foolish blabbermouthed child, and I resent your implication that I am."

"I *can* stop you from knowing it," the lord informed her. "I have a drug in my chambers that causes a person to forget the events of a day. If I gave it to you, you would remember nothing of what has happened this day. Then you and the dragons would both be safe."

"Perhaps I would be," Melayne answered. "But the dragons wouldn't be. They're *dying*, you fool! Why do you think they've been howling all night?"

"Dying?" He looked shaken at the news. "You can't be serious!"

"Which of us talks to them?" she yelled. "Of course I'm serious! Being cooped up in this cold, smelly, dark dungeon would make *anything* sick. They need to be out in the open."

"And *that* would kill them faster than anything!" Lord Sander growled back. "The moment a person saw them, they'd be dead."

"I know," Melayne agreed. "But there has to be *some* solution to this. And, to be honest, I don't think either of us stands a chance of keeping them without the other. You need me because I can talk to the dragons. I need you because you have the skills and resources that might be able to save them."

He studied her with his own dragon-dark eyes. She was so angry with him that she didn't feel the shudder that this stare normally caused her. "I wish I could trust you," he said finally. "But I simply can't take the chance. To trust you would be to risk their lives."

"Yes," she agreed, "it would be. But you *can* trust me. I would *never* harm them, or allow harm to come to them."

"I wish I could believe that," he said, quite miserably. Melayne realized that he did mean it.

"You *can* believe it," she informed him, moving toward him. Tura hissed out an alarm. *It's all right, Tura,* Melayne said, stroking the dragon's snout as she moved past her. *He won't hurt me. In fact, I think I know how to win him over. Be patient.* She drew closer to Lord Sander. "Take off your gloves," she said. "Touch me. You have the Sight. You'll be able to tell whether I'll betray the dragons or not."

He stared at her in confusion and worry. "But . . . if I do that, there's no telling *what* I'll see. Melayne, I might see your death."

"Well, what of it?" she yelled. "I know I'm going to die some day. So what? I can't go through life being terrified that I might suddenly die. It would paralyze me, preventing me from having a life. Look, I know that your seeing the future is a bit of a curse, but you have to live with it." She held up her hands. "And, in this case, isn't the risk worth taking? To see if I'll keep their secret or betray them?"

"And if I see you betray them?" he asked bitterly. "What then?"

"Then I'll take your sword and kill myself to prevent it from happening," she vowed. "I won't let *anyone* harm them — and that includes myself."

Lord Sander stared at her in amazement. "I do believe you're serious."

"I certainly am."

"But it wouldn't work, anyway," he protested. "If I see you betray them, then it will *have* to happen."

"No it won't," Melayne insisted. "I'll change the future. It hasn't happened yet, and I'll stop it from happening."

"It *has* happened," Lord Sander objected. "For me, at least."

"But not for *me*," Melayne protested. "I refuse to accept that what you see is unchangeable. That would be to insist that your Talent is infallible. That the future is predestined, and that you have, in fact, interpreted what you see correctly." She pushed her hands almost into his face. "Take my hands," she insisted. "Read my future. And *then* decide."

He hesitated, uncertain. She knew that he was afraid of what he might see. Suppose he *did* see her death? It might be today, it might be in eighty years. Whichever it was, she'd had a glorious life, and she wouldn't regret it, even if she died in five minutes. She had a wolf for a friend, and now had met dragons. Nothing could take such things from her.

"As you will," he agreed grimly. "But on your own head be it."

"I agree," Melayne said impatiently. "Just do it."

He stripped off both of his gloves, and started to reach for her. Then he hesitated, obviously having second thoughts. There was a flicker of worry in his eyes. Melayne didn't let him back out — she gripped both of his hands in her own.

Lord Sander gasped slightly, and his eyes went unfocused, as if he were staring at something a great distance away. His fingers shook slightly in her grip. Melayne felt a twinge of anxiety, wondering what it was that he was seeing. She'd managed to sound very brave, but what if he saw something about her that she'd sooner not know? She'd vowed never to harm the dragons, and intended to keep that promise. But what if, for reasons out of her control, he might see her in some way harming them? Would she have the courage to carry out her promise to kill herself?

Lord Sander jerked his hands free, and his eyes focused on her again. He looked shaken by his emotions, and his self-control was obviously badly damaged. Something had caused him great turmoil.

"What did you see?" she begged, scared.

"This," he replied softly. Then he gripped both of her shoulders, leaned forward and kissed her.

Melayne was too stunned to know what to do. Whatever she'd been expecting, this wasn't it. Then her thoughts started to clarify, and she realized what was actually happening — he was kissing her with passion. And she was kissing him back.

She had no idea why he was doing this. The touch of his lips on hers, the strong hands holding her shoulders, the scent of him — all made her giddy with emotion. She stopped trying to think, and simply enjoyed the wonderful moment.

Then he broke free and gazed at her with his dark eyes.

Melayne stared back. "*That's* what you saw?" she asked, breathlessly. "I guess you didn't see very far into the future, then."

Lord Sander smiled back at her. "Further than that," he murmured contentedly. "But that seemed like a good place to start."

"You won't get any complaints from me about that," she agreed. Then she realized that Tura was staring at her. *What is it?* she asked.

The dragon sounded confused. *What were you two just doing?* she asked. *It looked quite disgusting, like you were trading food or something.*

Melayne laughed. *Quite the opposite*, she assured the female dragon. *It's called kissing, and it's what humans do when they like each other very much.*

He should make his mind up, Brek complained. *Does he want to kill you or not?*

I'm pretty sure it's "not" right now, Melayne answered with another laugh.

"Something amuse the dragons?" asked Lord Sander dryly.

"They don't know what kissing is," Melayne explained. "I guess with beaks you can't really get into that sort of thing. Besides, they're probably too young to understand romance anyway."

"I can see that," he agreed. "Look, we have to talk, Melayne. This is very important. I know now for certain that you'll never harm the dragons." He ran a hand through his hair, and then replaced his gloves. "To be honest, it's a relief having someone to help me with them. Keeping them a secret has been a great strain on me."

"I'm here to help," Melayne promised.

"I know. But now we have to talk, and I think it would be best if we did that in my chambers, and not here. I don't normally come down here in the day. I only did so today when I realized that my key and you were both missing."

Melayne nodded. She turned back to Brek. *We'll be back later. We have some planning to do.*

Fine, agreed the dragon. *Um . . . you couldn't manage some fresh food for us, could you? We're not too fussy, as long as it's alive and can run.*

I'm sorry, Melayne replied. *I couldn't bring*

you any live prey. I can talk to all animals, and wouldn't be able to stand it if you killed someone I knew.

Then we'll just have to wait a little longer, Shath said with a sigh. *Hurry back, little human.*

Lord Sander held his hand out for the key, which Melayne gave to him. He led the way out of the dungeon, pausing only to lock the door and return the second key to its place on the wall. He moved quickly, and they were at the outer door in moments. Lord Sander motioned for her to wait. "If people see me come out of here, it's one thing. But they mustn't see you. If they know you've disobeyed my strict instructions, they might be tempted to do the same. As far as anyone in this castle is concerned, you've never been in here. That even goes for your brother."

"I understand," Melayne said.

He nodded, and then stepped outside. A moment later, he gestured for her to follow. "Go directly to my chamber," he ordered her. "I'll be with you in a moment." He turned to relock the door.

Obediently, Melayne hurried across the deserted courtyard and into the main part of the castle. She passed one of the cook's apprentices in the corridor, and then let herself into Lord Sander's room. It was later in the day than she'd thought, which explained why he'd managed to catch her in the dungeon. She'd been down there with the dragons a lot longer than it had seemed.

Minutes later, the door opened again, and Lord Sander entered the room. He closed the door behind

him. "We must talk," he said firmly. "But first . . ."
He pulled her closer and then kissed her again —
longer, slower, and holding her close against his
body as he did so. Melayne simply melted into the
kiss.

Chapter Fourteen
Explanations

Melayne allowed herself to enjoy the moment without thinking about it. She'd been attracted to Lord Sander from the first, and it felt amazing to be held and kissed by him. His hands on her back held her tightly against his muscled body, and her own hands clutched his back just as firmly. She could feel the surge of emotions within as he kissed her.

And then, all too soon, it was over. He pulled reluctantly away. "We'd better talk," he said, his voice slightly husky. "Otherwise I'll forget what it was I had to say."

"And I'd forget how to listen," Melayne murmured. Her heart refused to settle down to its normal speed, and every nerve in her body was tingling. "So, what was it you wanted to say, my lord?"

He sat in his great chair, and gestured for her to sit beside him. He frowned. "Don't start any of that *my lord* nonsense," he told her. "I've noticed that you don't do it normally, and this is definitely no time to start pretending."

Melayne blushed slightly, but refused to back down. "I'm only being accurate," she said. "You *are* a lord, and I'm a commoner."

"Oh, I see." He leaned forward slightly. "And you're wondering what my intentions are. Is that it?"

"To be honest —" Melayne began.

"Please do," Lord Sander said dryly. "Don't break the habit of a lifetime on my account."

"To be honest," she repeated, "I think I *know* what some of your intentions are. Those kisses were quite . . . communicative. But it's the part that they don't tell me that I'd like to know. Where do I stand with you? What are your plans for me?"

He nodded slowly. "Understandable," he agreed. "Well, the first thing is that you can forget this lord and commoner nonsense. There's absolutely nothing common about you."

That made her blush with pleasure. "You, however, are very lordly," she answered. "And lords are known for taking what they want."

He stared back at her, and she had to avoid his dark eyes. They made her too weak when she looked into them. "And you're thinking that I might be intending to take you, whether you like it or not?" he asked.

"The thought had crossed my mind," she admitted. "Powerful lords can take a girl to their bed without facing any consequences. Normally."

"I see." His face was a mask, and she couldn't

read whatever his thoughts might be. "And if I told you that was my intention? That you were to . . . entertain me tonight?"

"I'd decline the honor," Melayne answered truthfully.

"You can't pretend you don't feel the same attraction to me that I feel to you," Lord Sander insisted.

Melayne was squirming. He was right, she couldn't. "No," she agreed. "But that doesn't mean I have to act on it. I won't be a plaything for any man. I'm not that kind of girl."

"And I'm not that kind of man," Lord Sander answered. "I'd be offended that you thought I might be . . . except I know that there are too many men who are." He sighed. "Do you have any idea what I saw of your future, Melayne?"

"Not unless you tell me," she replied. "And if I'm not to address you as *my lord*, what should I call you?"

"Sander should do nicely," he replied, a faint smile on his lips. "It is, after all, my name. Though I suppose you'd better stick to *my lord* when other people are about. At least for the time being."

"The time being?" she repeated, puzzled. "What do you mean?"

"I mean," he said gently, "that I saw quite a bit about you when I held your hands, Melayne. I saw that you would never harm the dragons, which relieved my fears. And then I saw the two of us . . ."

Melayne's face burned slightly. "The two of us *how*?" she demanded.

For the first time, he looked slightly embarrassed. "Ah, well . . ." he hedged.

"How?" she repeated, glaring at him.

"Without our clothes," he admitted.

Melayne scowled, blushing madly. "I *told* you I wasn't that kind of girl," she growled. "And I meant it. If you think you can —"

"Without our clothes," he repeated, slightly louder. "But *with* wedding rings."

That stunned her. "Wedding rings?" she repeated. Her voice was squeaking slightly.

"Wedding rings," he said firmly. "Of course, you *did* say that you thought my visions were not of what *must* be, only what *might* be. So, if it doesn't appeal to you, perhaps you can somehow prevent it from happening. . . ." His voice trailed off.

Melayne's mind was whirling. "No," she murmured. "Maybe I was wrong, and the future can't be changed. . . ."

"I'm glad you think that," he said warmly. He took her hand in his own gloved hand and raised it to his lips, kissing it gently. "I've been attracted to you since I first saw you," he admitted. "But I was too scared to do anything about it. After Cassary, the thought that I might be fated to watch someone else I love die has made me hesitate to show my feelings. But when I saw the two of us in that vision . . . well, I *had* to admit what I felt."

Melayne touched her lips. "You admitted it very well," she said approvingly. "And I was attracted to you, too. But I thought the gap between us was too great to cross."

"You think too much," Sander replied. "It's one of my failings, too. But in this matter, we don't have to think. We simply have to act."

"I'm good at that," Melayne admitted, still trying to get her thoughts into order. She could hardly believe that this was happening to her.

"So I noticed," Sander said. "I want to know all about you. The *truth* this time, not the fairy tales you've been making up. If we're to be married, I want to know what I'm getting into."

Melayne's face fell as she realized what she had to say next. Despite his vision of their marriage, she believed that it was possible to change the future, and her next comment might well do that. "First of all," she said, slowly and reluctantly, but with determination, "I was born in Stormgard. I've been in Farrowholme just a few weeks." There, that said it all: She had just told him that she was an enemy. If he sent her away now, she would understand. How could he possibly love — let alone marry — an enemy of his people?

"Well, that explains the slight accent I detected," he said. "I had wondered about that."

"Doesn't it bother you at all that I'm one of your enemies?" she demanded.

"You're not an enemy of mine," Sander said firmly. "This war has nothing to do with either of us, and I won't let such a foolish thing stand between us. You were born in Stormgard; big deal." He shrugged. "Are *you* upset that *I'm* from Farrowholme?"

"Of course not!" Melayne exclaimed. "I've found

that the people here are just as nice — if not nicer — than the people back home."

"And you think I'm more narrow-minded than to think the same of you?" Sander asked. "Melayne, where you were born is unimportant. Who you *are* is what counts. And that's the person I'm attracted to."

Melayne hung her head guiltily. "I suppose I was expecting less of you than of myself," she admitted. "I'm sorry."

"That's better." Sander smiled at her. "Now, tell me how you came to be here. I want to hear the whole story."

So Melayne told him everything, in as much detail as he wanted to hear. It felt so good to be able to tell someone the complete truth for once. It was as if she'd been carrying huge chains that bound her down, and now she'd been able to cast them off and walk freely again. Sander listened intently, asking questions only occasionally, and took in everything she said. When she was done, he stroked her hand gently.

"You've been through a great deal," he said. "You're a brave and courageous person. But there are some things that you don't quite understand yet that I can explain to you. Now —" He broke off as there was a knock at the door. "Come in!" he called, almost growling in frustration.

Hada glided into the room. "Dinner is ready, my lord," she announced.

"Oh, yes, of course," he said. "Dinner. I'd forgotten all about it."

"Me, too," agreed Melayne. "Mind you, now that I think about it, I am hungry."

Sander nodded. "Well, let's take a break from the conversation for now and get back to it later."

Hada gave Melayne a puzzled look, and Melayne realized that the woman must be wondering what they had been talking about. Well, Melayne had no intention of explaining! She gave Hada a sweet smile and followed Sander to the dining hall. Both Corran and Sarrow were already there, and both of them had brought huge appetites. Hada sat beside Sarrow and gave his hand a pat. Melayne couldn't help wondering why, but then the first of the dishes was brought in, and everyone began eating.

The meal was a strange one. Melayne ate, but couldn't remember what she was eating, even a few minutes after it was gone. She kept stealing looks at Sander, only to discover his eyes on her. Both would then look away, embarrassed. Melayne wondered if their silly behavior was being noticed by anyone else. It seemed so obvious to her! She felt almost giddy, unable to take in what had happened on this eventful day. Dragons, Sander, and his revelations all whirled insanely in her mind. She needed time to think things through, and sort out how she felt and what she should do about it all.

Luckily, Hada kept up most of the conversation. She continually asked one or other of the boys questions. Melayne wasn't really paying attention, so she wasn't sure what was actually being said. Nothing of importance, at least, which was a relief. But it was odd. Hada had hardly shown any interest in either of the boys before, and yet today she seemed to be completely focused on them.

And that bothered Melayne. Even through her own confusion and elation, there was a spike of worry troubling her mind. Why this unusual behavior? Hada was smiling and joking with Sarrow, which was definitely very unlike her normal starched personality. Still, it was probably not really important — certainly not as important as saving the dragons. Or wondering about her own relationship with Sander.

Marriage . . . She'd fantasized a bit about what it would be like to *kiss* him, and fall into his dark eyes, but she'd never imagined more. And her imagination in the kissing scenario had been badly offtrack! It had been a much more intense sensation than she'd imagined. And it had felt so right, as if he and she were meant to be together. . . .

Melayne jerked her thoughts back as she realized her dish had been taken away and that the meal was over. It had all seemed to fly past.

"If you don't mind, Melayne," Hada said, "I'd like to look after Corran and Sarrow this evening."

Melayne blinked and focused on the other woman. "Oh, no, that's fine with me," she said. Then she glanced at Sander. "I have . . . other things to do, anyway."

"Fine." Hada stood up, inclining her head at the lord, and shepherding both boys. "Good evening, your lordship."

"Good evening, Hada," he replied, a smile flickering about his lips. "You, too, Corran. And Sarrow."

Hada led the boys out, and Melayne stared after them thoughtfully. "That's very strange," she commented. "I mean, I like Hada and all, but she's never struck me as the motherly type."

"She normally isn't," Sander said, equally puzzled. "She's barely spoken to Corran since he was born, and she's never offered to take care of him. That's not her job, and Hada's *very* firm about what her job is."

"Then I wonder why she's offered to look after him tonight?" Melayne said, troubled. "I don't think she'd ever hurt him, but there's something not quite right here."

"I agree," Sander answered. "But I think you're asking the wrong question. You should be wondering why she's offered to look after *Sarrow*, not Corran. I think my son's included only because he couldn't be left out."

"*Sarrow?*" Melayne couldn't understand it. "Why would she be interested in Sarrow?"

"You don't know?" Sander examined her with his intense gaze again. "Melayne, you're a bright girl, but sometimes there are these huge gaps in your awareness."

Melayne blushed again. "It comes from growing up alone, I suppose," she said. "I really don't understand people very well."

"You understand some of them well enough. But you can't see the truth about your brother." Sander stood up. "This isn't the place to talk," he said firmly. "We'd best go back to my chamber, where we won't be disturbed." Then he cracked a smile. "Unless you're afraid for your reputation."

"What reputation?" Melayne asked. "I doubt anybody here talks about me at all."

"You're too modest," he informed her. "I'm sure they're all gossiping wildly behind your back."

That was something she didn't even want to think about. Quickly, she followed Sander back to his room. Once the door was shut, she demanded, "*What* truth about my brother? What are you talking about?"

Sander sighed. "Your brother has a Talent all right," he replied. "One of the strongest and rarest I've ever seen. He has the gift of Persuasion."

"Persuasion?" Melayne scowled. "What are you talking about?"

"Haven't you noticed that he always seems to get his way if he's around someone long enough?" asked Sander. "Especially you. You are obsessed with his well-being."

"I'm his *sister*!" Melayne exclaimed. "I love him, and it's my job to look after him!"

"Yes," he agreed. "But he makes you do things. Remember, you told me that you don't eat meat? That you think it's wrong? Yet he *made* you do it."

"He didn't *make* me," Melayne protested. "I had no choice; I had to eat it so I'd be strong enough to look after him."

"That's what you think," he agreed. "Because your mind has to rationalize it somehow. But if you think about what you've been doing all along, you'll see that it's been to make Sarrow happy and comfortable, no matter how dangerous or absurd your actions. Persuasion is a subtle thing — it only works as long as you don't know it's happening. And Sarrow *knows* he's doing it. He plays innocent, but he's aware of his Talent. And now he's using it on Hada, bending her to do what he wants. I think he suspects that he's losing his grip on you, because of your other priorities."

"I wouldn't abandon him!" Melayne protested. But she realized that Sander was correct in at least one thing: She really hadn't been thinking or worrying about Sarrow for most of the day. He'd slipped completely from her mind several times, in fact. "And . . . he can't be doing what you think."

"Trust me, he is," Sander insisted. "Even your wolf friend, Greyn, doesn't trust Sarrow. Yet Greyn adores you. Leaving aside the fact that he's obviously got good taste, why do you think that is? Because Sarrow's Talent works only on humans, and not on animals."

"How can you be so sure?" Melayne demanded. But there was a sinking, uncertain feeling washing through her. "You didn't even know he was a Talent until a couple of hours ago!"

"I watched him carefully over dinner," Sander explained. "And I saw what he was doing to Hada. If you weren't his sister, you'd have seen it, too."

"I thought you were watching *me* over dinner," Melayne replied.

"You noticed that?" Sander asked with a smile.

"Well, I *was* trying to watch Sarrow, but you're quite a distraction, you know." He gently stroked her cheek. Even though he was wearing his gloves, the touch was electrifying. Melayne struggled to stay focused.

"I *did* think it was odd, the way Hada behaved," she had to agree. "And you're right — Greyn doesn't like Sarrow much. But surely that's just jealousy; Greyn's very possessive of my attention."

"Perhaps," Sander conceded. "But I wouldn't want to wager on it. Anyway, let's forget about Sarrow for the moment; we've a lot of other things to discuss."

"Yes," Melayne agreed. "The dragons."

"Those, too," he admitted. "But I was thinking about us."

Melayne colored again. "Well, I couldn't help thinking about us, too," she confessed. "But we really should be thinking about the dragons."

"Yes," Sander agreed. He leaned forward and kissed her lips. "But, as I've already said, you're quite a distraction."

"So are you," she said in a soft voice. Her body felt electrified, her senses heightened, her head giddy. She threw her arms around him and dragged him close for another kiss. It was like fire raging through her bloodstream, and she had no idea how long it lasted. She felt his hands stroking her hair and back, and stopped thinking after that. It was a while before he broke reluctantly away. Melayne gasped, breathing fitfully as she gazed at him.

"I think we'd better take a break for breathing,"

Sander suggested. "I hear it's supposed to be very good for the constitution."

"Yes," Melayne agreed, just as reluctantly. If only her head would keep still and she could think clearly! "Did . . . did you mean it about marrying me?" she asked, still hardly able to believe it.

"It doesn't matter whether I meant it or not," he replied, smiling. "I *saw* it, and I'm absolutely convinced it will happen. Why? Are you having second thoughts?"

"I'm not having many thoughts at all," Melayne confessed. "I'm too overwhelmed."

He laughed. "And you think *I'm* not?" He shook his head. "Melayne, I never imagined I'd ever fall in love again. I did love Cassary very much, you know. When I saw her die, it devastated me. I collapsed inward, convincing myself that I would never open myself up to such hurt again. I know I was an idiot, but it was just too painful. I couldn't even allow myself to get close to my own son, in case something happened to him that would hurt me again. But now, with you . . ."

"You could still get hurt," Melayne said. "I can't guarantee that nothing will ever happen to me. Sooner or later, we all die."

"Yes, I know," Sander agreed. "But, you see, I'd forgotten something in my pain. I'd forgotten that there can be great joy in loving. The pain of loss is terribly real, but it's only so real because the joys are so great. And, even if there is the possibility of loss, the certainty of joy overwhelms it." He stroked her cheek again. "When I first saw you, looking so beautiful and acting so . . . well, wise and forthright, you weren't intimidated by my being a noble, and you were out to get what you needed. I admired that in you. Since then, I've come to see how you've made Corran blossom. He's changed so much under your influence." He grinned. "And he was the first one to suggest that I should marry you. I think he's looking for a new mother more than I'm looking for a new wife."

"He suggested it to me, too," Melayne replied with a smile. "I think you may be right. He's a wonderful child, and I do love him."

"I noticed." He kissed her again. "You're a very loving person, Melayne, and it affects everybody around you. Well, almost everybody. I think Sarrow's immune to your charms. But siblings often are."

"And I seem to have been blind to his faults," Melayne answered bitterly.

"You didn't know," Sander said gently. "But now that you're aware of what he can do, it won't work on you. He can only Suggest, not Control, thank the good God."

"Shouldn't we warn Hada about his Talent?" Melayne asked.

"I don't think quite yet," he replied, considering the matter. "If we do, he might switch to controlling somebody else. Right now we know his target. I'd feel safer that way."

"You make him sound like such a menace," Melayne protested. "He's just a child. I don't think he has any plans as such, beyond staying alive and comfortable."

"He's just a child, yes," agreed Sander. "And that's the problem. He's doing what he wants, without any kind of restraint. And what he does might well be foolish and harmful, simply because he doesn't know any better." He sighed. "I wish he were older. Then we could use him to Suggest to the Seeker that there's no problem here. But he's too young and too untrained to be sure he could do it properly. We'll have to go through with your plan, and hope for the best. Which reminds me — I met your friend Ysane, and she's agreed to bring her brother out in the morning. The Seeker will be here shortly afterward. I hope it will be a very brief visit, because I wouldn't want him to even chance finding the dragons, or any trace of them."

"I agree," Melayne replied. "I'm sure he'd happily betray them to the King's Men. It seems as though everybody hates the dragons."

"In this case," Sander answered, "with very good cause." Seeing her shocked expression, he added: "Of course, you don't know the truth, do you? It's because of the dragons that we Talents exist."

"What? What do you mean?"

Sander chewed his lip a moment, and then leaned forward. "Haven't you ever wondered why there are Talents in the first place? Why some humans develop such special powers?"

"There doesn't seem to be any logic to it," Melayne replied. "And so few of us, really. Since many normal humans hate and fear us, I suppose that's for the best."

"No," Sander answered gently. "There's never any excuse for hatred and fear. People like that are simply scared of their own inadequacies. Talents would never hurt humans unless they are pushed. In fact, many of us are more careful with normal people because we can see and do so much more than they can. Have you ever met a Talent who hated normals?"

"No," Melayne admitted. "But I've not really met many Talents."

"Fair enough," he agreed. "But the fact is that normals have nothing to fear from us. The trouble is that we make them feel inferior, and that makes them fear and hate. None of them really understand that *we're* actually the normal ones."

Melayne was totally confused now. "What do you mean?"

"Hundreds of years ago," Sander explained, "there were many more Talents than there are today. What we call normal humans today were still in the majority, but only slightly so. Then somebody discovered what gave Talents their abilities. It's dragon scales."

"Dragon scales?" Melayne shook her head. "I don't understand."

"Dragons shed their scales as they grow," Sander informed her. "These scales fall into the ground and dissolve. They contain many chemicals, far too complicated for us to understand. These chemicals stay in drinking water, and in the soil, for centuries. If you eat or drink as a child from ground where a scale has fallen, these chemicals cause changes in your body that result in your Talent. Once the normals discovered this, they realized that they had a way to combat the Talents: Kill the dragons, and sooner or later Talents would die out. *That's* the real reason dragons were slaughtered so devastatingly. To prevent more of *us*.

"And it has almost succeeded, too. There have been no dragon scales shed for almost a hundred years, and the chemicals are dying down. Your family must have lived in a concentrated scale site once, because both you and your brother have such strong Talents. But there are so few left. Each year, there are fewer and fewer Talents. And now there are just five dragons left. If they die, then not only dragons die, but so do Talents."

Melayne was stunned; she'd suspected none of this, and yet it did make grim sense. Dragons *causing* Talents . . . normal humans wanting to destroy them both . . . "We'll never be left in peace," Melayne whispered.

"Not if anyone knows," agreed Sander. "That's why I've had to be so secretive for so long. Hada knew for a long time that Corran was a Talent, but even she knows nothing about the dragons."

"I heard that your great-grandfather was a noted dragon slayer," Melayne said. "Bantry told me a story about him and six knights going into the Dragonhome Mountains to kill the last of the dragons."

"It's partly true," Sander admitted. "The six knights went up to slay the dragons. My great-grandfather went up to save any that he could. He's the one who found the five eggs that he brought home and successfully hatched. Dragons take a long time to mature, and my family has been hiding and guarding them ever since. Now ..." He sighed. "The problem is, none of us really knew anything about raising dragons, and we did what we thought was best. Now you tell me that it isn't enough, and the dragons are dying. I can't allow that to happen, both for their sake and for the sake of the Talents. But what can we do?"

"They need to fly and hunt," Melayne said. "That's the only way their vigor will be restored to them."

"But that's impossible," Sander said flatly. "The second one of them tries to emerge into the daylight, their deaths will be sealed."

"Perhaps," Melayne said softly. "Perhaps not. I have an idea for one way to save them. Wait here." She dashed from the chamber to Cassary's room. Grabbing the geography book, she hurried back and then spread it open on the table. "Look at the map," she said, pointing to where Dragonhome stood. "We're fairly close to the sea."

"They'd still be seen flying over the sea," Sander objected.

Melayne hesitated, knowing what she was going to say would be very hard for him to hear. "I was thinking of a trip," she said. "By boat." She pointed. At the edge of the map were several small clumps. "The Far Islands," she explained.

Sander looked stunned. "They've only been sighted twice," he said. "And both times by accident. Nobody knows for sure where they lie, or anything much about them."

"No," Melayne agreed. "So if we went there, we could hardly be followed, could we?"

"Melayne," Sander said with frustration, "there's no guarantee we can get there ourselves! A ship can't navigate properly once it's out of sight of land. If we tried to find those islands, we'd wander at sea, lost, and eventually die."

"But you're forgetting something," Melayne pointed out. "We have dragons. And dragons can fly. They can rise in the air and see what we can't. Besides," she added with a shrug, "don't forget my gift of Communication. I can question the sea birds and dolphins or seals, or whatever there is."

He looked stunned, and then thoughtful. Finally, he broke into a smile. Grabbing her shoulders, he kissed her again. "Brilliant! I *told* you that you were wise. That never even occurred to me. It could be the perfect answer to our needs."

Melayne was pleased by his reaction, but knew she had to point out the major problem with her plan. "If we were to do that," she said gently, "we would have to leave Dragonhome. And I don't know when we could ever come back. If people knew we were protecting dragons, we'd be killed if we ever tried to return."

"Give up Dragonhome..." Lord Sander murmured, looking around his room. His face fell, as the weight of the decision descended on him. "You're right. I'd have to give it up. My home..." He was silent for a moment. Melayne knew that there was nothing she could say or do to help him here. He had to think this through for himself.

Abruptly, he rose to his feet. "Come with me," he said.

Puzzled, Melayne followed him outside. He led her to a part of the castle she'd not been in before. It was close to the west wing, but unlocked. Sander opened a door and gestured her to enter.

It was a small chapel. There were just a few seats, and a small altar at the end of the room with a symbol of the good God on it. Two small windows allowed light inside, but still it was dark and musty.

"I haven't been in here for a while to worship," he told her. "We used to have a household priest once, but I lost interest when Cassary died. It's the family chapel." He led her to one wall. There were carved stones there. "This is where my family is buried," he explained. "The stones are markers. My father, my mother, my aunt . . ." He touched one stone that was more recent. "Cassary herself." He gazed at Melayne solemnly. "They are here, in Dragonhome forever. It is our home."

"I understand," Melayne said gently. How could she have thought he'd be willing to leave a place like this?

"No, you don't," Sander replied. "They are here, and while they are here, this castle will always belong to my family. If Corran and I go, they will remain, and they will possess it." He stroked Cassary's stone again. "Perhaps it's only fitting that the dead lay claim to this place. We, the living, must dedicate ourselves to preserving life, not lifeless stones." He looked at her resolutely. "The important thing is that the dragons should live. If they die, hope dies."

"I was afraid that you wouldn't be able to even think of leaving Dragonhome," Melayne confessed. She held him tightly. "I'm glad I was wrong."

He stroked her hair. "You're making a habit of being wrong about me," he murmured. "One of these days, you're going to have to stop underestimating me."

"I'll try," she promised. "Only I'm not very good at relying on other people."

"Then you'd better start getting good at it," he answered. "Because you can rely on me. Always."

"I know." She kissed him again.

"Besides, I'll be taking everything with me that matters," Sander added. "You. Corran. The dragons. My memories. And, I imagine, anyone here who wants to come with us. Though I doubt many will want to."

She hugged him again. "Thank you for putting me first."

"It's your fault," he complained. "You've made me very dependent on you already. God knows what will happen to me once we're married. I'll probably end up being useless and letting you do everything."

"That's not very likely," she answered with a laugh. "But now we have to make plans. It's one thing to suggest escape to the Far Islands, but there are a lot of practical details to take care of first."

"And that's where I can be useful," Sander said. He held his arm protectively around her. "There's an old friend of my father's in town who owns a ship or two. I can ask him to sell me one. And we'll need some way to transport the dragons there unnoticed. A large wagon, I think." He nodded. "Tomorrow, once the Seeker is gone, I'll go back to town and start making the arrangements. It shouldn't take us long." He sighed. "The only thing that bothers me is that I'll have to start telling some people about the dragons. And if any of them betrays me . . ." He didn't need to finish the thought.

"We'd better pray to the good God for help, then," Melayne suggested.

"After all this time, I don't know if he's still listening to me," Sander replied.

"The only way to find out is to ask." She buried her head against his chest. "Anyway, it's getting very late. You still have to feed the dragons, and I'd better check on the children. They'd better get rested, ready for tomorrow."

He nodded. "Come on." He led her out of the castle, and then stopped. He looked around, but darkness had fallen some time when Melayne hadn't been paying attention. "We're being watched," he said softly.

He's good, Greyn's voice called. *For a human.*

"It's just Greyn," Melayne told Sander, with relief. *Come on out.*

The wolf padded into the faint light and stood looking up at Sander with his interested golden eyes. *So you've decided to settle down and have cubs?* he asked Melayne. *Well, I suppose it was in-*

evitable. And you could have chosen a lot worse. This one's almost as good as a wolf.

From my perspective, Melayne answered dryly, *he's better.*

Yes, I imagine he might be. Greyn grinned. *So, can a wolf still hang around with you, then?*

You might not want to, she replied. Turning to Sander, she said, "Greyn likes you. I think he wants to make you an honorary wolf."

"I'm touched," Sander said with a smile.

"But you'd better go feed the dragons," she added. "I have a few things to discuss with Greyn." He nodded and hurried away. Melayne turned back to her lupine friend. *There are dragons in the dungeons,* she informed him.

Call an exterminator, Greyn said, and then hastily added, *I'm only joking! Well, that explains the strange smells and the weird cries. I'm looking forward to meeting my first dragon.*

That might not be a smart move, Melayne told him. *They're predators, and looking for moving food.*

Greyn inclined his head. *That might be a problem,* he agreed. He looked at her. *Sounds like they're related to humans.*

Melayne explained the situation to Greyn, and finished up: *So, we're going to have to take the dragons across the sea to the Far Islands to live.* She stroked Greyn's neck. *I understand if you feel you can't come. It will be difficult, and we don't really know what we'll meet up with on the journey.*

305

Then it sounds to me like you'll really need my help, the wolf answered simply. *I can't abandon you now, Melayne. Besides*, he grinned, *maybe there will be some cute she-wolves on the islands. There's none around here.*

Melayne hugged him tightly. *Thank you!*

No problem, he answered. *Though there might be if you don't allow me to breathe.*

Melayne let him go, knowing he was still joking with her. It felt very comforting to have him beside her. There had been many changes this day — but at least a few important things remained constant.

And that was encouraging, because there was so much for them to do in the next few days. Transporting the dragons was going to be hard. Getting married . . . Well, she didn't know when Sander might be planning to slip that in, but she was looking forward to that part very much. Knowing that he felt the same way about her as she did about him had changed everything so drastically. And what was she to do with Sarrow? The more she thought about it, the more convinced she became that Sander was correct: He did have the gift of Persuasion. That could cause problems — but it might even make things simpler. There was no way to tell yet.

But the first problem was that of the Seeker. Could they fool him in the morning?

It was going to be a long, worrying night.

Chapter Fifteen
Tricks

Melayne was right in one respect, at least: It was a long night. But, to her surprise, she didn't worry as much as she'd thought. After getting both Sarrow and Corran to bed, Melayne discovered herself absolutely exhausted. The events of the day had taken their toll on her, and she couldn't stay awake any longer. Her dreams were many, varying between dragons and Sander. She would be playing with one of the dragons, only to discover she was stroking Sander instead. Or she dreamed that she was on a beach with Sander, and he somehow had become a dragon. The dreams were strange and somewhat disturbing. But they didn't wake her up. In fact, it took a heavy knocking on her door to startle her awake.

Corran and Sarrow piled in, grinning as she pulled the sheets tight around her.

"Come on!" Corran said, impatiently. "You've been sleeping *so* long, and I want breakfast."

"She was too busy with your father last night," Sarrow said with a smirk. "I think she's soft on him."

"Really?" Corran asked. He turned to Melayne. "Is that true?"

"If you both want breakfast," Melayne said, blushing, "you'd better get out of here so I can dress. Go on."

Laughing, they both shot out.

"And close the door!" Melayne yelled. Corran came back to close it. After waiting a few moments in case the boys came back again, Melayne jumped out of bed and rapidly dressed. *Soft on Sander?* she asked herself. *I should say!* But she wasn't sure that Sander wanted this to be public knowledge yet, so she didn't aim to tell anyone until she'd discussed it with him. The thought of simply seeing him again made her move more quickly.

The boys were playing in the courtyard when she hurried past them. "Come on, lazy bones!" she called. Complaining, they hurried after her.

Hada looked at her, raising an eyebrow as they entered the dining hall. "You seem to be inordinately pleased with yourself, considering the troubles ahead of us," she remarked rather primly. "Or have you forgotten about the Seeker?"

"Of course not," Melayne replied, slightly subdued. "But there are things to be happy about, you know."

Hada glanced at Sarrow, and her frown eased. "Yes," she agreed. "I know what you mean."

No, you don't, Melayne thought. She'd forgotten for the moment the effect that her brother was having on the other woman. Now that Sander had alerted her to it, Melayne couldn't help seeing the difference Sarrow caused.

Sander was there, too, waiting. Melayne hesitated before sitting down with the boys. How would he greet her? Had he had dreams, too?

"Melayne," Sander murmured. "Delightful as ever. Well, now that you're here, let's get breakfast moving. There's a lot to do today."

Hada glanced at Sander curiously, and then turned her attention back to Sarrow. She insisted on him being served before her, even though that wasn't protocol, and she was normally absolutely strict on that. Melayne caught Sander's glance, and nodded slightly. Sarrow's powers were becoming quite clear to her now.

She resented the fact that he'd been using them on her. She tried to excuse him — he was, after all, only eight years old and could hardly understand the consequences of what he was doing. But that wasn't really a good defense for the misuse of his Talent. He seemed to be enjoying exercising his control over the overseer.

Breakfast went quickly, and then Sander stood. "Hada," he said, "please keep both boys out of the way today. I'll have the Seeker come to my chamber to see the fake Corran, and I don't want him to run into the real one by mistake. Or Sarrow, for that matter."

"Of course, my lord," Hada agreed. "That should be no problem. I'll keep them both in the Eagle Tower until you send word that it's safe."

The Eagle Tower stood on the far side of the castle from Sander's room, so it was a good choice. He nodded. "Excellent, as always, Hada. Afterward, we all need to talk. Now, Melayne, you come with me. We have to greet your friend and her brother, and prepare them for the role they must play."

Sander led the way to his chamber. As soon as they were alone, he grabbed Melayne and kissed her. "I wanted to do that all through breakfast," he murmured.

"You'd have gotten porridge all over your face if you had," Melayne replied affectionately.

"It would have been worth it." He gently let her go. "Now, we really do have to prepare. Ysane and her brother should be here any moment. I'll have him stay in here. You'll have to take your friend off elsewhere. We can't chance the Seeker spotting you until you learn to erect some mental shields, as I do."

"How far off could he detect me?" Melayne asked.

"If he's good — and we have to assume he's one of the best — he'd only have to be within twenty feet of you." Sander frowned. "Why?"

"Because I don't want to be too far away," she replied. "In case anything *does* go wrong, I want to be ready to help."

"I don't know how you could help in that case," Sander answered.

"Nor do I," admitted Melayne. "But you know how resourceful I can be. I'd think of something."

"You'd be placing yourself in danger."

"To keep Corran safe, I'd risk it," she said simply.

He kissed her again. "All right. I don't like it, but I have a suspicion that, even if I forbade it, you'd do it anyway."

"Your feelings are remarkably accurate," Melayne answered with a smile. "Besides, I haven't taken a vow to love, honor, and obey yet."

"I knew I should have insisted on an early wedding," Sander murmured. "Well, we'll correct that problem as soon as possible. Though I have another feeling about how likely you are to *obey* me."

"You can always hope," she said with a grin.

"It's about all I can do," he agreed. "Let's head out to the gateway, and wait with Bantry for Ysane." He kissed her, and then led the way.

Bantry was a lot more formal with his lord around than he normally was in Melayne's presence. He was stiff and ill at ease. Luckily, his ordeal didn't last long, as Ysane and her brother turned up very quickly, escorted by Falma.

"I thought I'd come to see how you were, too," Falma said to her. "I thought you weren't staying in the area."

Melayne felt guilty that she'd forgotten all about the young man. "I hadn't planned on it," she admitted. "But things got rather out of hand." This complicated matters slightly, as she wanted time alone with Ysane, who hugged her tightly as if she were a long-lost relative. "Falma, would you mind staying here and keeping Bantry company? I really have to talk to Ysane alone for a while."

His face fell. "If I have to."

"I'm sorry," Melayne apologized. "But you do.

Ysane, would you come with me? And the young-ster." She couldn't remember the boy's name. He seemed a little nervous being in the supposedly haunted castle, and clung to Ysane's hand. The blond girl led him after Melayne and Sander. Ysane couldn't help staring at Sander.

"We really need your help," Melayne said to her friend, trying to stick as close to the truth as possible without giving anything away. "This is Lord Sander, master of Dragonhome."

Ysane managed a very respectable curtsy. "Pleased to meet you, my lord."

"And I you, Ysane," Sander said politely. "Melayne has told me a lot about your kindness, and I want to thank you for befriending her. It shows a kind heart."

Ysane blushed deeply at the compliment. She seemed undecided as to whether she should curtsy again or not. Melayne grabbed her arm. "Lord Sander has a young son, who's been threatened by some men who want to hurt him. We need to confuse the men, and we want your brother to pretend to be Corran for a short while." Seeing Ysane's panicked expression, she said quickly, "He'll be in absolutely no danger, I promise you! The men won't even get close to him. They just have to look at him and think he's Corran. Then, later, Corran will be safe from them. You and I will be very close by, and we can watch what happens. I give you my word that your brother will be perfectly safe the whole time."

"And I give you mine," Sander added. "I would not ask this of you if I weren't certain he'd be safe."

Ysane looked troubled, but then she nodded. "Of course, my lord. I know you wouldn't lie. Nor you," she added to Melayne. "If we can help you, then of course we shall."

Melayne hugged her friend tightly. "Thank you so much! You're so kind. I don't deserve it."

Sander placed a gentle arm on the boy's shoulder. "Come with me," he said kindly. "I have things for you to play with, and I'll watch over you carefully." The boy looked at Ysane, who nodded encouragingly. Then he nodded and went with the lord.

Continuing to another door in the corridor, Melayne led Ysane into the small chamber. It was a tiny room, but from the open doorway they could see the door to Sander's chamber. "We'll wait here, and watch. I'll almost close the door when the men arrive, but we'll keep an eye on them the whole time. Everything will be fine."

Ysane nodded. "I believe you, Melayne. So, tell me — what are you *doing* here? You said you were going to your aunt's."

"My plans changed," Melayne admitted. "We came here, and San ... Lord Sander asked me to look after his son, Corran. He's a little sweetheart, and I became quite attached to him."

"Only to him?" asked Ysane perceptively. "You're on a first-name basis with the lord of this castle?"

Melayne didn't know what else to say, so she nodded.

"Well, you certainly seem to have ambitions," Ysane remarked. "Mind you, he *is* terribly good-looking. If you've got to be somebody's mistress —"

Melayne blushed at the thought. "He's asked me to marry him."

"They all say that," Ysane answered. "Really, Melayne, I thought you had better sense than to fall for that old line."

"He hasn't touched me," Melayne protested. "Well, at least not in *that* way. And I know he means it."

Ysane frowned. "You're serious?"

"Never more so."

Her friend grabbed her and hugged her tightly. "Then I'm very happy for you." She released Melayne, and added, "Though I doubt Falma will be quite as pleased for you. He's got something of a crush on you, you know. You seem to have that sort of effect on men, don't you?"

"I don't know why," Melayne answered. "And I feel guilty about Falma."

"Don't," Ysane advised her. "He falls in and out of love at least three times a week. It's his age and his hormones." Then she frowned again. "Does this mean you're going to become Lady Melayne now?"

Melayne raised an eyebrow. "You know, that had never even occurred to me. But I suppose it does."

"Will I have to curtsy to you, too?" Ysane asked, grinning.

"You even try, and I'll kick you," Melayne promised. "Besides, I'm not sure we'll be staying in the castle anyway."

"The men after Corran?" Ysane guessed. "Are they so powerful that you have to go away?"

"Partly," agreed Melayne. "Look, there's something more, and I think you should know about it. But I'll have to tell you later, okay? Right now, the important thing is covering up for Corran. Then there's so much more happening."

"Including a wedding," Ysane said, grinning again.

"When we have the time," Melayne pointed out. "Maybe you can be a bridesmaid; I'd like that."

"Me, too," Ysane agreed.

There was the sound of the outer door opening. Melayne shushed Ysane, and closed the door, letting only a sliver of light peer through. Ysane came over and pressed close to her so she could see out as well. Melayne felt a twinge of fear: Was this going to work? And, if it didn't — what then?

Bantry came into sight, followed by a tall man in a yellow cloak. It had to be the Seeker. He had a handkerchief pressed against his face, and he was sniffling rather imperiously. Bantry tapped on Sander's door, and then hastily retreated.

"I don't like the look of him," whispered Ysane. "He looks cruel."

Melayne had to agree. The Seeker's face was thin and lined, his eyes cold and gray. His fair hair was thinning, and he had tried to brush it to cover a growing bald spot. Then she felt Ysane stiffen.

"Melayne," she hissed, "that's a *Seeker*! You're trying to hide a Talent!"

"Yes," Melayne confessed. "Corran's a Talent. And the Seeker mustn't find him."

"But ... but hiding a Talent is *treason*," gasped Ysane.

"It's the only way to prevent him from being killed," Melayne answered. "Ysane, think — have you *ever* seen an adult Talent, except for the Seekers? Of course not — because they make sure none live that long." She saw Ysane's troubled face. "Now shush, and listen," she warned her friend. "I promise, I'll explain everything later." And then she'd pray she wouldn't regret it....

Sander opened his door. "Ah, here you are," he said with fake cheer. "My son's feeling a trifle better today, though it may not last. You don't need to get *too* close, do you?"

"Thankfully, no," the Seeker replied. His voice was thin and whiny. "Let's get this over with. I'll stand here and check him."

Sander nodded and opened the door. The Seeker held the handkerchief closer to his mouth and stared over Sander's shoulder. "That's your son?" the Seeker asked.

"Yes."

The Seeker scowled at him. "I know I'm something of a dandy, but don't take me for a fool, Lord Sander. The commonest way people try to evade me is to substitute another child for their own. I obtained a description of your son before I came here, and that isn't him."

Oh, no ... Melayne's heart started to hammer as she realized that her ruse had completely backfired. Now what were they going to do?

"I assure you —" Sander began, but the Seeker cut him off with a swipe of his hand in the air.

"Assure me of no lies," he said coldly. "And don't even think of trying to bribe me; it wouldn't work. Or," he added, eyeing Sander's sword-belt, "of killing me. The King's Men accompanied me here, and they are waiting outside. If I fail to come out, they will come in and kill everyone here in the castle."

"*If* they can get in," Sander said softly.

"They *will*," the Seeker assured him. "The only way to avoid further trouble is to turn over your brat, immediately. He obviously must be a Talent. It will be a marvelous example to the peasants if they see your son going off to fight for the King."

"To be slaughtered, you mean," Sander said darkly. "This is no war they fight — it's simply butchery of the Talents to appease the fears of the so-called normals of this world."

"Call it what you will," the Seeker answered. "It's either your son or else every life in this castle."

"Stay here and listen!" Melayne hissed to Ysane. Then she stepped into the corridor. "You're wrong," she said firmly. "There's another option you haven't thought about."

"Melayne, no!" Sander exclaimed, horrified.

"No, Sander," she said. "I've had more than I can take of people threatening those I love. I'm not going to stand it any longer."

The Seeker stared haughtily down at her. "And what can *you* possibly do, child?" he sneered. "You can't even lift a sword. How do . . ." His voice trailed off, and he suddenly looked uncomfortable. "*You're* a Talent, too! *Another* hidden treason!"

"Yes," Melayne said grimly. "I'm a Talent, too. But the only treason here is yours. How can you do what you do, knowing that the Talents you expose are destined to be murdered? How can you betray your own kind like this?"

"It is my duty," he answered pompously. "And I know my duty. The normals want the Talents found and killed, and they are the majority. The will of the majority rules."

"Not when that will is wrong," Melayne said, her anger growing. "You excuse betrayal and murder of children as the will of the majority. But the majority don't know the truth, do they? Only the king and his soldiers know what *really* happens to the Talents. And scum like you, of course. Well, I've had it. I've had more than I can stomach of betrayal and fear and hiding, and I'm not taking it anymore. The only way you'll take Corran is over my dead body."

The Seeker seemed to have regained some of his courage since Melayne hadn't acted against him. "If that's your decision, then I'll be happy to fulfill your conditions."

Sander grabbed his arm. "Touch her," he growled, "and I'll carve open your stomach and hand you your intestines."

"You can't threaten me," the Seeker blustered. "I'm here on official business. I have the king's authority!"

"His authority is useless here," Melayne replied.

"He betrayed us, and we owe no allegiance to him. It stops here, and it stops now."

"I'll order the gate locked," Sander said. "We can hold off the King's Men for a while, until we can think of something else to do."

"No," Melayne ordered. "Allow them in. There's only one way to beat them, and it's not by allowing them to besiege the castle and trap us all here."

Sander gave her an anxious look. "I hope you know what you're doing," he said.

"So do I," Melayne admitted. "But I *am* sure it's the only way. Let them do their worst." She turned to the Seeker. "If you want that child to torture and kill, you go through me," she informed him. "Fetch your men, and do your worst. But whatever happens is on *your* head, not mine."

The Seeker regarded her with a mixture of contempt and fear. "Brave talk from a small girl," he finally sneered. "We'll see how brave you are against cold steel." He turned to leave.

Ysane stepped out of the other room, and blocked the corridor. "Seeker," she said, her voice tight, "examine me."

Melayne didn't know what Ysane was thinking. Her friend's face was emotionless, her arms crossed. How had she taken all of these revelations?

Puzzled, the Seeker did as Ysane bade. "You're no Talent," he said. "I have no quarrel with you, unless you try to interfere with my duty."

"No, I'm no Talent," Ysane agreed. "I'm one of the *majority* you're supposedly defending from them. And you know what I think?" She suddenly swung her right hand, clenched in a fist, and punched him across the face. The Seeker staggered, and whimpered, blood flowing from his nose. It looked to Melayne as if it was broken. Ysane's years of chores on the farm had certainly given her some power in her punch! "I think you're a disgusting little creep if you want to take a poor child off to be killed just because he's a Talent! And so would everybody I know! And you can be sure that I'm going to make certain that they all know the truth of this."

The Seeker didn't even try to reply. He dabbed at his nose with his rapidly reddening handkerchief and dashed past her to safety. Melayne hurried to her friend.

"Ysane! Thank you."

"My hand hurts," Ysane complained. "But it was worth it. Melayne, *you're* a Talent, too?"

"Yes," Melayne confessed. "I'm sorry I didn't tell you before, but I didn't know how you'd react. I *know* what they do to Talents because I escaped the fate myself."

"Thank the good God you did," Ysane said fervently, hugging her tightly. "It doesn't bother me, honestly. I'm not one of those idiots who thinks Talents want to rule the world, or hurt the rest of us or anything. I know *you* would never hurt anyone."

Melayne was so touched at Ysane's faith in her. She wanted to cry, but there was no time for that now. "You're wrong about that," she apologized. "Ysane, I *am* going to hurt someone. But only if I'm forced to do so. I won't let the King's Men take Corran. Or Sarrow."

"He's a Talent, too?" Ysane laughed. "Is *everybody* here a Talent but me?"

"No," Sander assured her. He took Ysane's hand and kissed it. "Thank you for your support." Ysane blushed. "But now, Melayne, you'd better know what you're doing."

"I think so," Melayne answered. "I think it's time to let all of our secrets out into the open. *All* of them," she stressed.

"Melayne . . ." Sander said in alarm.

"I know what I'm doing," Melayne promised him. "It's time to stop hiding. We have a great weapon against the King's Men — their own fear. I think it's time to use it."

"But the consequences!" he protested.

"We'll deal with those later," Melayne answered. "It's time to act, and you know what to do." She turned to Ysane. "You should take your brother and Falma and get out of here now," she told the other girl.

"You're right, I should," Ysane agreed cheerfully. "But I'm not going to. What kind of a friend would I be to abandon you when you need all the help you can get?"

"The sensible kind," Melayne answered, as they strode toward the courtyard. "There are more secrets that you don't know yet."

"I *love* secrets," Ysane answered. "And this is just starting to get interesting."

"It may soon be too interesting," Melayne said dryly. But she realized that Ysane was not going to leave. "Well, just stay back," she suggested. "This could get rough. In fact, I'm almost certain it will."

There was no sign of the Seeker when they reached the courtyard. Melayne hurried toward the gatehouse. The portcullis was down, and beyond it she could see the Seeker and the King's Men advancing on horseback. Bantry and Falma were in the gatehouse, looking scared.

"Open the gate!" Melayne called. "Let them in!"

"But . . . but . . ." Bantry protested.

"Do as she says!" Sander roared, as he headed across the courtyard to the west wing. "Obey her as you would me!"

Bantry hurried to comply, engaging the mechanism that raised the creaking portcullis. The King's Men were obviously surprised, but they seized their chance and rode into the courtyard. Melayne felt a moment of insecurity, as their huge horses stormed inside. There were eight of the men, all armed and looking ready for battle. One of them was Brant, which disappointed her.

"Melayne," he called, puzzled. "What is this? What are you doing here?"

"Defying the king, I'm afraid," she replied. "The only way your lot are going to get out of here unhurt is if you give up this mad mission and leave now."

"You can't seriously be threatening *us*," Brant protested. "Melayne, you must be ill or something."

"She's a *Talent*, you moron!" the Seeker howled. "She's evading the draft! It's your duty to take her in."

"Actually, it isn't," Melayne said, with a slight smile. "You see, I was born in Stormgard, so if I were drafted, it would be to the other side."

"Get her!" the Seeker ordered. "And then we search the castle for any other Talents. If anyone tries to stop you — kill them."

Brant looked terribly confused, but he moved his horse closer to Melayne. "I'm sorry, but I have my duty . . ."

"And so do I," Melayne replied. "Brant, this is your last chance."

He drew his sword, and Melayne sighed. She had hoped he'd be reasonable about this, but that was apparently impossible. Now she had no option.

It was simple for her to use her Talent to order insects about, but the higher animals were not so simple to control. Unless she caught them by surprise . . .

Buck! she screamed at the horses.

They, of course, were not expecting anything of the kind. Her scream affected them at a primal level, overcoming all of their training and rational thought. All nine steeds shied, whinnying in terror, at the same moment.

Eight soldiers and the Seeker were thrown from their saddles, flailing and yelling. None of them had been prepared for any trouble, of course, and had thought they were in perfect command of their steeds. All the men went down heavily, and Melayne winced as she heard the cracking of bones. Two of the men had broken legs, and one had shattered his shoulder. Unfortunately, the Seeker was unharmed.

Calm, she called to the horses, who immediately settled down again. They seemed to be confused about what had happened. Melayne stared at the men, who were shaking themselves and starting to rise to their feet. The captain drew his sword, an ugly expression on his face.

Greyn! she called. She had expected to be panicking by now, but a surprising calmness descended over her.

As the captain moved forward, his sword ready to attack, a gray blur flashed from the stones. The soldier barely had a second to register this new attack when lupine claws and fangs slashed across his arm. With a scream, the man dropped his sword and clutched his shredded arm. Blood flowed freely over his fingers, and he collapsed to the ground.

"Don't try anything else," Melayne advised the stunned soldiers. Greyn padded to join her, and she stroked his fur affectionately. "I really don't want to hurt any of you. But I will, if I have to. Stay still, drop your weapons, and you'll be fine."

"Don't listen to her!" the Seeker yelled. "She's trying to bluff you!"

"Bluff us?" Brant turned on him. "We've four wounded in twenty seconds and she hasn't even worked up a sweat. She's not bluffing."

"Coward!" The Seeker wrenched the sword from

Brant's fingers, and turned to face Melayne. "I'll kill you myself for what you've done!"

Melayne sighed. Some people simply refused to learn. Without turning, she knew that Sander had done what she'd suggested. *Brek*, she called, *be gentle.*

The five dragons erupted from the west wing.

Chapter Sixteen
Changes

All sense of control was lost at that second. The soldiers howled as the dragons surged from the doorway. The horses screamed and bucked, panicking at the sight of the predators. The dragons roared in anticipation.

Melayne couldn't follow what happened next. The screams of the horses enveloped her mind so that she couldn't think straight.

The dragons were starving, cold, and in desperate need of exercise. Their instincts possessed them, and they immediately attacked the frightened horses, ripping into the animals with claws and teeth. The stench of blood overwhelmed Melayne, and the screams of the dying animals nauseated her. But there was nothing she could do now. Five horses were down in seconds, and the dragons ripped at their steaming carcasses as the other three steeds turned and bolted out of the open gateway.

The soldiers were just as stunned as their

mounts, but they, at least, hadn't been attacked. Ysane was screaming in fear, and holding tightly to Melayne. It wasn't easy to break her grip.

"They're on our side," Melayne promised Ysane. "They won't hurt us."

"They're *dragons*!" Ysane burbled in fear.

"Yes. And they're really cute when you get to know them." Melayne shook her friend. "Snap out of it, and trust me on this." She turned to survey the scene.

The five dragons were ripping greedily at the dead horses, scattering entrails and blood all over. There was an air of immense satisfaction and happiness coming from them. They were, however, keeping very wary eyes on the humans in the courtyard. Starving they might be; stupid they weren't.

The humans were all pale and shaking. Especially Bantry and Falma, who were staying very close to the walls, ready to bolt for cover if it was needed. Aside from Melayne, the only one not panicking was Sander, as he strode back from the west wing.

"Be good, and you'll be fine," Melayne called out. "They won't harm anyone unless they're provoked. So I strongly suggest that you not provoke them."

The Seeker finally found his voice again. "Dragons," he said in a very squeaky voice. "You're consorting with *dragons*! You're more disgusting than I imagined. You've betrayed the whole human race!"

"Stuff and nonsense," Melayne insisted. "You've nothing to fear from them if you behave yourselves." She shook Ysane off her arm and walked over to Tura. The bloody-snouted dragon looked up from her gory meal. Melayne stroked her head. "They're very sweet, really."

"They're *dragons!*" the Seeker screamed. "They have to die!"

"You know," Melayne informed him, "you could really improve your personality if you developed a little flexibility in your thinking."

The Seeker simply screamed and threw himself toward Melayne, with his sword held ready to spear her.

He didn't stand a chance. Greyn leaped for him at almost the same second as Sander. But neither of them were as fast as Brek. Despite his bulk, the dragon threw himself at the Seeker, his head snapping forward. The Seeker didn't even have time to scream before his head was no longer attached to his collapsing body. Brek spat the head across the courtyard. *That tastes disgusting*, he complained. *I think I'm going to throw up.*

The soldiers shook where they stood or lay, expecting to be the dragons' next victims. Melayne moved to stroke Brek. *You'll be fine. But I'd finish that horse before one of the others gets to it.* She hated that the horses were dead, but she knew that the dragons were only doing what came naturally. And they really had to feed. Brek hurried back to his meal.

Melayne moved to where Brant was standing. He was staring at her in a mixture of fear and horror. "We don't want to hurt you," she said gently. "But we cannot allow you to hurt us. Or the dragons. So you're going to have to be our prisoners here for a while. Once we leave, you'll be free to go."

"Prisoners is fine," he said faintly. "It beats being dead and devoured."

"Good," Melayne said. She really hadn't wanted to hurt the soldier; he'd been very good to her, in his own way. "Make sure your friends understand and agree, and we'll all be happy." She turned to Sander. "I think we'd better explain everything to your employees about now," she said. "We're going to have to ask them to make some tough choices."

"I'll get them all together," he said. Then he looked down and kissed her. "You were magnificent," he told her.

"Actually, I'm sick to my stomach," she admitted. "But we didn't have any choice. I'll do what I have to, don't worry." He kissed her again, and then left.

Melayne turned to Ysane. "Are you all right?" she asked the blond girl anxiously.

"I think so." Ysane was a little pale, but she'd rallied her emotional reserves. "You're sure the dragons are okay?"

"Absolutely," Melayne assured her. "My Talent is Communication, and I can talk to them. They're a bit full of themselves, but they're nice."

"Can I . . . can I stroke one?" Ysane asked.

"Of course." Melayne led her over to Tura. "This is Tura. She's a sweetheart. Say hello."

"Hello." It was more than a little squeaky, but Ysane did manage it. Then she reached out with a shaking hand and stroked Tura's neck. The dragon almost purred, and rubbed her head against Ysane. It left a bloody streak down Ysane's blouse, but Ysane smiled anyway. "She's kind of nice."

"Yes, she is," Melayne agreed. "Now, we have a lot to do, so maybe you'd better get Falma and your kid brother together. We're up to the sitting around and talking a lot phase, I'm afraid." She glanced at Sander. "Is there anyone in the castle who can look after these soldiers' injuries?"

"Yes," he replied. "But it might be better to leave them as they are. They'll be less likely to cause trouble."

"I don't want anyone hurting if I can help it," Melayne answered. "Not even our enemies. Let's treat them well, even if they wouldn't do the same to us."

Sander smiled affectionately. "You've a kind heart. I'll get help."

"You'd better get Hada and the boys while you're at it," Melayne added. "They're going to have to know the truth as well." He nodded and hurried off. Melayne felt exhausted from all that had happened. And it was still early in the day, with lots more to do. All of her plans had unraveled, so it was up to her to come up with new ones. She wished it wasn't all on her shoulders, but there didn't seem to be a lot of options.

She crossed to the soldiers, and bent to examine the captain's arm. The blood was starting to congeal, but the limb was a mess. The man was pale, and looked on the verge of fainting. "Brant," she called, "come here." Nervously, the soldier obeyed. "I don't think your captain's really in any frame of mind to listen to me right now. I'm getting medical help for him, and I figure that leaves you in charge of these men for now." She gestured at the dragons and at Greyn, who was watching them carefully. "I imagine you can see that you'll be in serious trouble if you try anything, so please be smart. We'll let you go once we're sure that you can't hurt us anymore."

Brant nodded slowly and carefully. "What do you plan to do?" he asked. There was fear and a measure of respect in his eyes.

"I'm sick of having to hide," she answered, considering her own motives. "I've done nothing wrong, and yet people like you force me to lie and hide away. Well, no more. I'm a Talent, and I'm not going to hide any longer. It's people like you who can't accept that we have as much right to live as anyone else who has the problem. Well, now you'll have to deal with it. You can't just cart off helpless children, to train them to die in a pointless, bloody war that's designed only to kill Talents. I'm going to make sure that everyone knows that this is the *real* purpose of the King's Houses. Keeping quiet about it helps only the abusers, not the victims."

"Melayne," he said, "I want you to know that I had no idea that was what was happening. I genuinely believed that the Talents were fighting for a just cause. It wasn't until the Seeker admitted your accusations that I knew better." He swallowed. "If I'd known earlier, I would never have worked with him. I don't care if you believe me or not, but it's the truth. And I will never help bring in a Talent again."

Melayne touched his arm. "I believe you," she said simply. "The truth is that there are many good people who have been duped by this story of what happens to the Talents. If they knew, I'm certain that most people would not turn the Talents over to the King's Men. But they don't know."

Gripping the handle of his sword, Brant said solemnly, "Melayne, I swear to you on my honor that from today, I will tell everyone I can the truth. I have to make up for what I've done."

"Well said," she congratulated him. "Start spreading the truth — it's the best antidote to the lies that have ruled everyone for so long. This plot only works because of the silence of those who know the truth."

"And I'll make certain everybody knows, too," Ysane added. "We'll stop this terrible practice, I know."

"I'm sure," Melayne said, much encouraged. "But it's not going to be easy. People aren't going to want to believe you."

"You can come with us," Ysane said eagerly. "Tell them what you know. Once they see what you can do and hear your story, I'm sure they'll believe."

"I can't come," Melayne said sadly. She gestured at the dragons. "People might be able eventually to accept the Talents as having a right to their own lives. But everyone is still too terrified of dragons to ever allow them to live. Right now, I have to make certain that they're safe. They've become my responsibility."

She saw Sander returning with a couple of his

servants, who hurried across to the wounded soldiers — skirting as far from the feeding dragons as they could. Hada, Sarrow, and Corran were in tow, all staring nervously at the dragons, too.

"It's all right," Melayne called to them. "They're harmless."

"They don't *look* harmless," Hada muttered. "Those poor horses."

"I know," Melayne agreed. "But they needed to feed, and they have to build up their strength. We've a long journey ahead of us."

"What are you talking about?" asked Hada, confused.

"We have to take the dragons away from here," Sander explained quietly. "They will be killed if they remain."

"Let them be killed!" Hada exclaimed. "They're dangerous, man-eating creatures!" She clutched Sarrow to her protectively. "They'll kill everyone if they're left alive!"

"No, they won't," Melayne said firmly. "They don't want to eat anyone. That's just a silly superstitious tale. They're very gentle, really, and they have to be able to live."

Sarrow glared at her. "That's typical of you," he complained. "You're always looking out for animals! Well, what about me? I'm your brother! I'm the one you should be caring for — not those monsters. And not *him*." He gestured at Corran.

With a sigh, Melayne studied her brother. "Sarrow, you're being selfish and silly. Of course I'll look after you. I always have. But these dragons need my help, and so does Corran. I don't love you less simply because I love them, too. But Sander and I must take these dragons away from here."

Hada looked incensed. "That's *Lord* Sander, you disrespectful girl!" she snapped. "Remember your station!"

Sander put an arm around Melayne's shoulder. "Melayne has it right," he said gently. "We're to be married."

"*Married?*" Hada went pale, and gasped. "My lord, think of the consequences! She's nothing, a nobody! You should marry an equal, not a peasant!"

"Melayne *is* my equal," he replied evenly. "If not my better. And she's the one that I want."

Hada shook her head firmly. "I cannot allow you to do it, my lord! To allow this little . . . *tramp* to take the place of Lady Cassary is unthinkable."

Sander gave her a furious glare. "If you ever say another word against Melayne, you shall be out of this household in a moment," he growled. "I don't care what your snobbery may lead you to believe. I shall do as I please. And it pleases me very much to marry Melayne."

Not ready to give up, Hada wrung her hands together in despair. "She's a pretty enough girl," she conceded. "I can see that you might be infatuated with her for the moment. Nobody would fault you for bedding the . . . girl. But to *marry* her!"

"You're treading very dangerous ground," Sander said coldly. "I would never offer such an insult to Melayne. She will be my wife, and that is final. I will not hear another word from you on the subject." He whirled and stalked away.

Hada glowered at Melayne. "You've done something to his mind," she accused. "Bewitched him or something. He's not acting sanely."

Ysane pushed forward and glared at Hada. "Yes, she's done something to his mind," she agreed. "She's engaged it. He's looked at Melayne and fallen in love with her. And who could blame him? She's a wonderful person. If you weren't so prejudiced, you'd have seen that for yourself."

Melayne glowed at her friend's praise. "It's all right, Ysane," she said gently. "Hada's simply . . . very traditional. I know it must upset her sense of stability that Sander wants to marry me. But she'll get over it sooner or later."

"Never," Hada vowed. "You're a wicked girl, whatever these people may think of you. I know you've done something to affect my lord's mind, and I'll stop you." She clutched Sarrow to her. "Anyone who would abandon her own brother is a devil!"

"I haven't abandoned him," Melayne said, starting to lose her temper. "He's a spoiled brat, if you want to know the truth, who's too used to getting his own way. And a lot of that is my fault, because of how I've treated him for years. Sarrow, you have to learn that I have to share my attention and my concern. I don't love you any less, but I have other responsibilities now."

"Yes," he snarled. "Getting yourself a rich husband and looking after monsters! And abandoning me. I hate you!" He turned and buried his face in

Hada's side. "You won't ever abandon me, will you?" he begged her.

"Never," Hada promised. "Though your own flesh and blood has rejected you, I never shall. You'll be safe with me, I promise."

Melayne threw up her hands. "Idiots, the both of you!" she exclaimed. Their accusations stung and hurt her, and she didn't want to let them poison her mind. Not now, while she had so much work to do. "Look, I'll talk to the both of you later, and we'll try to straighten things out. Until then, I've got a lot of work to do." She turned to go.

"That's right!" Hada sneered. "Abandon him again!"

Ysane raised her fist under the other woman's nose. "Melayne might be too polite to punch you out, but I'm not," she warned. "One more nasty remark out of you, and you'll be the next person with a broken nose." Hada subsided at the threat, though she didn't look repentant.

Melayne examined the injured soldiers. The servants had done a fine job in patching them up. Even the captain's arm had been treated, and was wrapped tightly in bandages. They'd either given him a sleeping draught, or else he'd fainted. Melayne encouraged the servants, and then moved on to the dragons. They had all just about finished their gruesome feasts, and were cracking the bones for the marrow.

Are you feeling better? she asked them.

This was more like a meal, Brek answered

happily. *This is how we should feast. I feel much stronger now.*

Good, Melayne answered. *Because you may have to be ready to move very shortly. I think we may have found a solution to your problem — if we can figure out how to get there.*

You'll manage, Tura said, chewing on a thigh-bone. *We have faith in you.*

Thanks. Melayne moved on, Ysane sticking firmly by her side. She crossed to where Sandor was talking to some of his men. They were looking nervously at the dragons, but paying attention.

"The choice is yours," Sander said. "Either stay here or come with us. It's purely voluntary, and I shall not hold it against any man or woman who decides that they'd sooner remain behind. Just think it over." He turned to the two girls. "I've spoken to everyone, and made certain that they all know about the dragons and the choices that must be made. I don't know how many — or few — will be coming with us, but we should know soon." He ran a hand through his hair. "Incidentally, now that we've won the battle, what's the plan?"

"Why does everyone always assume I know what to do?" Melayne complained.

"Because you always do," Sander answered simply. "You're the smartest girl I have ever known, and I'm happy to follow your plans."

"The last one didn't work out too well, did it?" Melayne asked glumly. "Using Ysane's brother to fool the Seeker . . ."

"It worked out fine," Ysane assured her. "Just not quite the way you'd expected, that's all."

"Not quite?" Melayne echoed. She flopped onto a stone seat in the courtyard. *"Not at all* is more like it."

"Maybe," Ysane agreed, joining her. "But you did stop the Seeker, you've disabled the King's Men, and even won some over onto your side. You've helped the dragons, and you have people listening to you. That's not bad so far, is it?"

"Ysane's right," Sander agreed. "You've done very well so far, even if it's not going quite the way you anticipated. So — what now?"

Melayne gave up. They insisted on her leading them, so she really had no other option. "I think you'd better get in touch with that sea captain you mentioned. We're going to have to get moving very soon. These soldiers will be missed by the end of the day, and there will be others along. I'm sure we won't be in any real trouble yet — but it won't be long in coming, and we must be gone by then."

"Agreed," Sander said, nodding. "I'll take my fastest horse. With luck, I'll be there and back by nightfall, and have transportation ready. I'd also better see to wagons to carry the dragons."

"No," Melayne replied. "I don't think there's really any point in hiding them now. Too many people already know about them for them to be kept a secret for much longer. Just get the ship ready, and then come back." She grabbed him and hugged him. "I'll miss you."

"I *already* miss you," he replied, and gave her a

kiss. "I've told everyone that you're in charge after me here," he added. "They'll all listen to you while I'm gone, whatever needs doing." Then he hurried away.

"Well, that's another thing you were right about," Ysane commented with a grin. "I'd never have believed you'd landed yourself a noble for a husband if I hadn't seen it. I'm starting to believe that there isn't much that you can't do."

"I didn't exactly land him," Melayne protested, blushing slightly. "More the other way around, if anything. He's very hard to refuse."

"Like you tried!" Ysane laughed. "Well, your ladyship, now what?"

Melayne looked around and saw Corran standing with Falma and Ysane's younger brother. "I think you'd better meet Corran," Melayne answered. "And we'd better see what he knows about what's happening." As they headed to join the boys, Corran rushed over, jumped up, and hugged her.

"Father said you're going to be my new mother," he said happily. "I like that."

"So do I," Melayne answered, hugging him back. "And it's probably all your fault, too. You kept saying we should get married."

"And I was right, too," he said smugly.

"So you were." Melayne and Ysane met up with Ysane's two brothers. "Falma," Melayne said gently, not sure how to break the news to him.

"I hear you're getting married," Falma said, a slight catch in his voice. "I'm glad for you, honest." Then he pouted. "I just wish it could have been me, though. Mind you, a lord's a pretty good second best."

Melayne grinned. "Yes, I think so," she answered. "And I'm sure some other girl is going to snag you soon. You're a good person." She touched his shoulder.

"Hey, I'm going to play the field before I get caught," Falma vowed.

"Well, the first thing you're going to do is to take your brother home," Ysane said firmly. "I don't think hanging around with soldiers and dragons is really the best place for him to be."

"I like it here," the boy protested.

"I bet you do," Ysane said, glaring down at him. "But do as you're told, and get along home. You've got a lot to tell your friends, haven't you?"

"That's right," he agreed, realizing he was going to be very popular with this story. "Come on, Falma, let's go." He grabbed his older brother's hand urgently.

"What about you, sis?" Falma asked. "Aren't you coming?"

"No," Ysane said. "I'm staying here to help Melayne. She can't do *everything* herself, and she'll need someone to keep things running. Besides," she added with a grin, "until she gets married, she's going to need a chaperone. I wouldn't trust her alone with that lord of hers for a second otherwise."

Melayne giggled. "You've got a filthy mind."

"True," Ysane agreed. "And if you're thinking even half of what *I'm* thinking, you ought to be ashamed of yourself."

Melayne was glad that Ysane was staying, at least for now. It felt good to have someone with her whom she could confide in, and who knew the whole truth about her. There was nothing, she realized, like having a good friend. Except, of course, having a good husband and family. She hugged Corran to herself again. It looked as if she had all three. She glanced around for Sarrow, but he and Hada had vanished. No doubt they were off sulking about her. Right now, she couldn't see a way to change their minds. She'd just have to hope that they'd come around and see that they were wrong.

One of the cook's assistants came running over to her. He looked uncertain, as if wondering whether to bow, curtsy, or whatever. "Uh, ma'am . . ." he said nervously.

"What is it?" she asked.

"Begging your pardon, but it's almost noon, and the cook was wondering how many people there are to feed."

Thank goodness cook had retained her senses! "I don't know," Melayne answered. "Everybody who's here, I suppose. I don't think everybody will fit into the dining hall, though. Do you think it would be possible to bring the food and plates out here?"

"Yes, ma'am," he agreed. Then he glanced nervously at the dragons. "Um . . . they won't eat it, will they?"

"No, they like their food very raw," Melayne explained. The boy paled. "Not quite as raw as you," she said kindly. "Don't worry, you won't be hurt, I promise." He nodded, and ran back to pass along the instructions to the cook. "There are so many details to take care of," Melayne said with a sigh. "Castles are complicated places."

"Get used to it," advised Ysane. "Once you're Lady of Dragonhome, you'll be in charge here, you know."

"I don't know if that will ever happen," Melayne answered. "We have to take the dragons away from here. I was planning on the Far Islands. They should be safe there."

"If you ever reach them!" Ysane exclaimed. "Is that why Lord Sander's gone to arrange for a ship?"

"Yes," Melayne explained. "And I know we can reach them. The dragons can fly high, and spot the islands far out to sea. Once we're sure that the dragons can live there and thrive, we can come back. I have no idea how long that will take. And by then . . . well, Sander and I aren't likely to be very popular around here for what we've done. Dragons aren't exactly well liked. I don't think we'll ever be allowed back."

"You're probably right," Ysane agreed. She looked around the castle grounds. "So you're prepared to give all this up, then, just to look after a handful of dragons?"

"A handful of dragons, Sander, and Corran," Melayne answered. "Oh, and Sarrow, of course. But what else can I do?"

"Nothing, I suppose." Ysane smiled. "Well, at least you know what you're doing with your life. Anyway, here's the food. I'm starved after all of this action." She grinned at Corran. "Race you to the cauldron!" He grinned back and they shot off together.

Melayne couldn't help smiling. She might not have known Ysane for very long, but there was no doubt of the other girl's sincerity of friendship. She thought for a moment about the people she'd met since she had left her home. Perhaps she hadn't been trained to make friends, but somehow she'd done fine. Corri and Devra ... Brant, Ysane, and Falma ... Bantry, Corran and, especially Sander ... They were all good people in their own ways, and she felt blessed to have been allowed to be their friend. But it highlighted what she had missed for so many years. If only she could have known people like this from her childhood. But her parents had been forced to hide her away, for fear of the Seekers.

Well, she decided, that was going to have to come to an end. She'd made two small starts already, by helping to free Corri and the others, and by making Ysane and the King's Men here aware of the truth of what the Seekers were doing. Bit by bit, she thought, they could start to spread the truth. And, once people knew it, they would stop the horrible practice of sending the Talents off to die. The kings and some of the nobles would undoubtedly try to cover up their lies by violence, but that would only serve to validate the message that what they were doing was wrong. Melayne could only hope that the Talents would be entirely freed in her lifetime.

But they were dying out, anyway, without fresh dragon scales. Saving these five dragons was a start for the future, but if they were isolated on the Far

Islands, away from man, then so also would be their scales. Eventually, then, the Talents would cease to exist.

Was that a bad thing? If every human was the same, would that make things better? Melayne reluctantly realized that the solution wasn't that simple. Without Talents to pick on and victimize, the cruelly powerful would simply find some other targets. Eliminating the victims wouldn't help; there were always more victims. What had to be eliminated were the persecutors. But was that even possible? She didn't know, but she knew that she'd have to try, even if it was futile.

Bantry wandered over to her, with a plate of some kind of vegetable stew. "No meat," he assured her. "I know you don't eat it. But you need to keep up your strength. You have a lot to do."

"Thank you, Bantry." She took the meal gratefully, and started to eat. He looked uncomfortable. "Is there something you want to talk about?"

"Well, I don't know as I should, ma'am," he said, nervously. "After all, what with you being the next lady, almost, so to speak . . ."

"If you call me *ma'am* again, I'll hit you with this spoon," Melayne threatened. "Bantry, you're my friend, and that won't stop no matter what rank I do or don't have. So, stop being silly, sit down, and tell me what's on your mind."

He looked relieved, and sat on the stone bench beside her. "I'm glad you feel like that," he said. "I was sort of nervous. Anyway, I've made up my mind: I'm coming with you and Lord Sander. You're going to need someone you can rely on to help stand watches, and to look after those ..." He eyed the dragons. ". . . babies."

She felt a glow of pleasure. "Thank you, Bantry. You'll be very welcome with us. But it's not going to be easy."

"Not as cushy as guard duty here, eh?" he guessed. "Well, I really think I need some exercise. I've been getting lazy." He nodded, and then moved off.

Melayne was grateful to him. He was their first volunteer. Honestly, she didn't expect many, but she was glad he'd chosen to come along. She cleaned her plate, amazed at how hungry she'd been. She took the plate back to the cook's apprentice, who had made sure that everyone had been fed, even the captive soldiers.

The dragons had been watching all of this from perches on the walls. They had spread their wings to make the leap, and all five were sunning themselves happily, warming their chilled blood and bones. Melayne gave them a smile and a wave as she helped to clean up from the meal. Most of the servants were very nervous around her. Obviously the news about her change in status had spread quickly!

Ysane and Corran joined her again. They seemed to have become friends already. "So," the blond girl asked, "how's it going? Do you have any other volunteers yet?"

"Only one volunteer so far," Melayne answered. "Bantry, the guard."

Ysane frowned. "What do you mean *only one*? Don't I count?"

"You?" Melayne stared at her. "But I thought you were just talking about staying here until Sander got back. I mean . . ."

"You're not getting rid of me that easily, you know. You're going to need my help."

"Well, yes," Melayne agreed, bemused. "It's not that I'm not grateful, but what about your family?"

"I told Falma to tell them what I was doing," Ysane answered. She shrugged. "They always said I should get a good job, and I figure being your lady-in-waiting should count as the best job I could ever get."

"Lady-in-waiting?" Melayne snorted. "On a sea voyage, some lost islands, and then maybe in exile somewhere. I wouldn't call that much of a career."

"Hey, you take the bad with the good. Besides, if Bantry's coming along, then I'm interested. He's pretty cute, isn't he? And I wouldn't exactly have a lot of other girls to fight off for him."

"If he looked at another girl with you around, he'd have to be crazy," Melayne assured her friend.

"Oh, he can *look*," Ysane replied. "But that's all he'd better do, if he knows what's good for him."

Melayne laughed. Somehow, Ysane always managed to cheer her up. To be honest, she was really glad that Ysane wanted to come along with them. It was still a small party, but at least it was very select. "Can you ride a horse?" she asked.

"You ask a farm girl *that*?" Ysane demanded.

"Sorry," Melayne apologized. "Well, we'll need to

get some ready, and some traveling things. A little food and water, and maybe some changes of clothing for us all. Normally, I'd ask Hada to do it, but she seems to have gone off somewhere sulking. She really hasn't taken either the dragons or the news about Sander and myself very well."

"That's her problem," Ysane answered. "She's just jealous of you. I'll bet she had her sights set on Lord Sander for herself."

"That's silly," Melayne replied. But then she considered it. "She *did* say she was waiting for the right man, though . . . maybe she had designs on him, after all."

"She probably did," Ysane said. "Well, tough. You won. Anyway, I'll see about getting things ready. How many horses will we need?"

"Well, there's the two of us . . . Corran can ride with me. Sarrow and Bantry . . . and I think we'd better plan on a fresh one for Sander. That's five, at least. I don't know if Hada will come, but we'd better be ready, just in case. I wouldn't want to insult her by leaving her out."

"I would," Ysane said. "But I won't, for your sake. Six it is." She grinned and hurried away.

Melayne wasn't sure what to do next. Everything seemed to be in hand. Maybe she could take a quick break and just relax a while. Her head was spinning from everything that had happened, and she badly needed to catch her breath and just do nothing. She climbed up to the wall top where Tura was sunning herself.

Can I join you? she asked. *I need to calm down.*

It's being around humans too much, the dragon answered, flexing her wings and spreading them to gain the maximum warmth. *Of course you can join me, you poor thing.*

Gratefully, Melayne settled down beside Tura. Her skin was slightly warm to the touch now, and felt good. *I'll just stay a little while*, she promised, and laid back against the dragon's stomach. It was so good just to do nothing, to have nothing demanded of her. She wished she could stay like this, but she knew she had duties, things to see to . . .

Tura nudged her awake, and Melayne blinked as she opened her eyes again. *How long have I been asleep?* she asked.

Several hours, the dragon answered. *You needed the rest, so I wouldn't allow anyone near you. However, since Sander is now approaching the castle, I thought you'd probably want to see him.*

You should have woken me earlier! Melayne exclaimed, jumping to her feet.

No, I shouldn't, Tura answered primly. *You've a lot to do, and you need your rest. You're not a dragon, and you're considerably more fragile and less enduring than we are.*

Melayne wasn't going to argue. She hurried down the steps to the courtyard, where Ysane joined her.

"The horses are ready," she announced. "Packed and provisioned. We can start out when Lord Sander gets here."

"He's on his way, according to the dragons," Melayne replied. "They're on the walls, and can see farther than we can. Let's see about getting things into motion. Have there been any other volunteers wanting to join us?"

"Not one," Ysane said cheerfully. "So it'll be a nice, cozy party."

"Okay," Melayne agreed. She hurried to the captives. The captain of the King's Men was awake again, though still pale. Brant was by his side. "How are you doing?" she asked.

"I understand your people saved my life," the captain answered. "And Brant tells me that we were in the wrong, after all. I'm sorry for the distress we caused you."

Melayne was touched. "Thank you," she replied. "But you couldn't have known then. Now you do. Look, we're going to be leaving. You and your men are free to go, and I'm not placing any conditions on it. But I'd really appreciate it if you decided not to report in for a while."

"To give you a head start?" The captain looked at Brant. "I have a suspicion we may have to stay here the night. My wounds are really giving me grief." Brant grinned back at him.

"Thank you," Melayne said, grateful. "I'm sorry about your arm."

"Better that than my throat." He eyed Greyn, who was still keeping his eyes on the soldiers. "Though I'm not sure he'd agree."

"Greyn's a predator by nature," Melayne apologized. "But he has a good heart." She hurried over to greet him. *It's all right,* she assured him. *They won't harm us now.*

They won't while I watch them, he agreed.

They won't anyway. Melayne ruffled his neck fur affectionately. *I hope you ate well; it's almost time for us to be on our way.*

Well, I just hope you don't hold me up, then, Greyn answered, showing his teeth in a grin.

Typical. Did every creature think they were the best in the world? Melayne was starting to believe so. Well, she could handle that. She headed across to where Ysane had the horses waiting, stroking them as she passed, and then entered the gatehouse. Bantry was there, keeping watch.

"It's almost time to go," she informed him. "Sander will be here any minute, and Ysane has horses ready. It'll be a small party."

"Is she coming, too?" Bantry asked. "The pretty blond?"

"Yes," Melayne answered. "And she's glad you are." She grinned. "I think you've got a good chance there. She likes the look of you."

"And I like the look of her," Bantry answered. "She's the prettiest girl I've ever seen." He colored slightly. "Not that you aren't, of course, but . . ."

Melayne laughed. "Thank you, kind sir. But I'm glad you find her prettier than me. You should tell *her* that, though. Go and get ready; I'll watch the gate." He nodded and hurried off.

Everything was coming to fruition now. Melayne stared out of the stone dragon's eye, watching for signs of her love. They'd be forced to leave in a few minutes, but at least they would all be together.

Except, she realized, that she hadn't seen Sarrow

or Hada for a few hours. She'd have to have Ysane go look for them. Did she have time to run to do that now? No. Sander's horse appeared, racing toward the castle. Melayne frowned. True, they were in a bit of a hurry, but surely he was overdoing it. She opened the gate, watching carefully as the portcullis rose.

Sander reached it, barely slowing, and ducked under. "Lower it, immediately!" he called out.

Melayne didn't know what was happening, but she could hear the urgency in his voice. She kicked out the restraint, and the portcullis crashed down. She hurried out of the gatehouse and into the courtyard. Sander's horse, panting and sweating, had come to a halt. Brant held its reins as Sander jumped down and hurried to her. He hugged her tightly, and then released her.

"Trouble," he said, panting almost as much as his steed. "There's a large party of soldiers approaching the castle. I managed to skirt them as I came in. At least a hundred, maybe more. Too many for even your powers to take out."

That wiped out her good mood. Her stomach sank like lead. "They'll be here soon?"

"Fifteen minutes," he answered. "And we'll never get past them on horseback. I was lucky."

"Then we'll have to hold them off until I can think of something else," Melayne answered. She didn't have a single idea, but something would have to come to her. "Let's get everyone ready for the journey, so we can slip out as soon as possible. Bantry and Ysane are going with us, along with Corran and Sarrow. I don't know about Hada. I've not spoken to her."

"I know about her," Sander said grimly. "And Sarrow. You won't find them in the castle." He gestured back the way he had come. "They're out there, leading the soldiers here. They've betrayed us."

Chapter Seventeen
Flight

Melayne gasped and staggered, as if she'd been punched in the stomach. Sarrow had *betrayed* them? How could he? How could Hada have turned against them? Well, that was easier to answer — Sarrow had turned her. But why had her own brother done this?

He was hurt, of course, and felt that she had abandoned him. But to turn around and do this ... that was insane. "What can we do?" she asked, bitterly. "You're right, I can't take out that many people. Not before they could do us some serious damage, at any rate."

"Well, we can buy a little time by negotiating," Sander suggested. "After that, all I can suggest is that you'd better apply that brilliant mind of yours to coming up with a new plan."

So it was all on her shoulders again ... wonderful. Still, she'd simply have to cope, that was all. Even with Sarrow's betrayal. She turned to Brant. "I can't ask you to go against your friends out there," she said. "If you want to join them, though, we'll let you go."

Brant scratched his neck. "The captain's not feeling well," he reminded her with a grin. "And I don't have the authority to act without him. I think we'd best stay here until he's well enough to tell us what to do. And you don't have to worry about your backs; none of us would harm you."

"Thank you," she said. She turned to Ysane. "I don't know if we can use the horses to get out of here," she said. "But we ought to have them ready, just in case. Maybe I'll be able to think of a way."

Ysane nodded. "You'll do it," she said confidently. "I know you will."

I wish I were as sure, Melayne thought. She hurried back up the steps to the top of the wall, beside Tura.

And now she could see the approaching soldiers. If anything, there were more than a hundred of them. Sander hurried to join her, and gestured at the front of the troops. Beside the captain rode Sarrow and Hada, their faces grim. "They're not prisoners," he pointed out sadly.

"No," she agreed. "They slipped away to fetch the soldiers. And I just slept, like a fool!"

"You couldn't have guessed," Sander said sympathetically. "You had no reason to mistrust them. In fact, I still don't know why they did it."

"I'm sure we'll soon find out," Melayne answered. The troops had drawn to a halt, completely encircling the castle. The captain, Sarrow, and Hada rode forward, and leaned back on their horses to look up at them — and the dragons.

"You are Lord Sander of Dragonhome?" the captain called loudly.

"That I am," Sander agreed.

"Then I call on you to surrender immediately, and open your gates to my men," the captain shouted back. "If you do not, I will be forced to attack."

Sander glanced at Melayne. "What do you think?" he asked quietly. "We could keep them outside for a long time, but that would only make them annoyed. They'd be likely to kill everyone when they broke in."

Melayne agreed with him. She leaned across the wall, and stared down at Sarrow. "Why are you doing this?" she asked him.

"You betrayed me," he replied coldly. "Those dragons are dangerous and must be killed. The captain will let you go if you help to kill the monsters."

"*They're* not monsters," Melayne said firmly. "And I don't think the captain will let us go. You seem to forget that we're Talents, and all we're good for is murdering."

"You're *useful* Talents," the captain said suavely. "There's no need to treat you like the common herd. I can guarantee you, the king will find useful places for you both at his palace."

"Can you indeed?" Melayne asked coldly. So *that* was it — Sarrow had sold them out for a promise of security. And, given his powers, he'd probably be granted it, too. "And how about you, Hada? Why did you betray your liege lord?"

"You have him bewitched, girl," Hada answered. "I have to get him away from you, so he'll return to his proper senses and marry someone of his own station."

"*You*, perhaps?" Melayne shot back. Hada colored, and Melayne saw that the barb had struck home.

"I would never consider someone like you," Sander said firmly. "Even if there were not Melayne. I could never love anyone who would betray me like this."

"Enough of this," the captain called out. "I don't care why any of you do whatever you do. All I demand is your surrender, and the death of those creatures."

"Never," Sander answered firmly. "You will harm them only over my dead body."

"*Our* dead bodies," Melayne corrected him. She glared at Sarrow. "Are you prepared to kill me to destroy them, Sarrow?"

"They threaten me," her brother replied. "Their scales can make more Talents, and Talents are dangerous. I can control humans simply enough, but Talents are harder. *You* slipped out of my control without even knowing it. I can't chance more Talents being born."

Melayne stared at him in horror. Greyn had been right — Sarrow was a little monster. He *knew* what he'd been doing to her all along. He'd been using her to stay alive, as he was now using Hada and the captain of the troops. He'd do *anything* to stay alive, and comfortable, and he'd figured out the best way to do it. But his plans called for no living dragons . . .

"I won't allow you to do it," she warned him.

"Then I'll have to kill you," he replied. There was no affection or softness in his voice at all. He turned to the captain. "They aren't going to surrender."

The captain laughed. "Then they're trapped inside that castle. They can't get past us." He turned to his men. "Archers!"

Down! Melayne called urgently to the dragons. Their skins were thick, but an arrow might just penetrate and harm them. The five dragons immediately spread their wings and glided serenely down to the courtyard. They seemed to be a lot stronger and more comfortable now. Sander grabbed her shoulder and jerked her down.

Arrows slammed into the stones, and some flew up above her head. She'd been stupid to just stand there, and Sander had saved her life. She still found it hard to believe that her own brother would want her dead. But she had to face reality. He *was* doing it.

"I can't fight Sarrow," she said, her heart aching. "No matter what he does to me. I won't hurt my brother."

"I wish he felt the same," Sander answered. "Come on." He hurried her down the steps. "Those men have no siege equipment, but they can probably send for some to be here by the morning. Or they could construct ladders, to come up the walls. We don't have the men to stop them, and I wouldn't want to ask anyone to risk their lives to stop the attack. We can't fight back without a lot of my people dying, and that's unacceptable."

"I agree," Melayne said. They had reached Ysane and Corran by now. The arrows had stopped flying, thankfully. "So, if we can't fight, we have to escape."

"Horses would never get past them," Sander pointed out. "Let alone the dragons."

The dragons . . .

With a cry, Melayne rushed over to Brek. *How are the five of you feeling?*

Wonderful! he exclaimed. *Soaking up the sun was what we needed. And the food, of course.*

Strong enough to fly? she asked him.

Fly? He laughed. *Up to the sun itself, if we have to.*

Now came the tricky part. *Could you take passengers?*

Brek eyed her thoughtfully. *You and the others?* He considered the question. *We could each take one passenger, I think,* he said finally. *But nothing else. We are not yet up to our full strength.*

Melayne sighed with relief. *One passenger each will be enough. We can leave everything else here.* She turned to Sander and the others. "The dragons will take us out of here," she announced. "On their backs. We will have to strap ourselves to them somehow, so we don't fall."

"Fly out of here?" Sander paled. "Melayne, is that really a good idea?"

"No," she admitted. "But we don't have any other

choice right now. We have to escape, and that's the simplest way to do it. Did you arrange the ship?"

"Yes," he agreed. "The captain's willing to take us and the dragons. He didn't seem happy about the idea, but the thought of being one of the few people to get out to the Far Islands intrigues him. He's getting ready to sail right now, if we can get to him."

"With the dragons, we can," Melayne said firmly. "Corran, will you be all right?"

His eyes danced. "Flying?" he asked. "You bet! Which one's mine?"

"Ganeth, I think," Melayne decided. "She's the smallest."

"All right!" Corran shot over to the dragon and patted her head.

"Well, he seems happy enough," Sander said dryly. He turned to Bantry and Ysane. "How about the two of you? You don't have to come, you know."

"To be honest," Ysane admitted, "I'm scared stiff at the thought of riding a dragon. On the other hand, how many people get a chance to do it? And Melayne's going to need my help. I'm in."

Bantry looked troubled, but he nodded. "Ysane's promised me a date tonight, and I'm not letting her get out of it."

Sander smiled. "Thank you both. Then I guess that makes it five maniacs. Well, I'd better see about getting harnesses or whatever. Come on, Bantry." The two men headed for the stables.

"All my hard work loading the horses, too," Ysane sighed. "Oh, well."

Melayne went to the captain and Brant. "We're

leaving on the dragons. Yes, I know," she added as they opened their mouths to protest, "it's crazy, it's suicidal and it's way too dumb for words. But we're doing it anyway. As soon as we do, you can open the main gate and let in the soldiers outside. Promise me that you'll make sure they understand that nobody else here had anything to do with the dragons except for Sander and myself. I give you my word that nobody else here even suspected they were alive."

"Everyone here will be treated well," the captain answered. "I give you *my* word. May the good God go with you — I certainly wouldn't!"

Sander and Bantry came hurrying back with harnesses. The dragons didn't like the feel of them, and they grumbled fiercely as they were fitted. Melayne was glad that she was the only one who could understand what they were saying. And she had her hardest task to perform. She went to where Greyn was waiting.

I have to go, she told him sadly. *And this time, you can't come.*

On the back of a dragon? he asked. *Even for you, I wouldn't.* He lowered his head. *It's a shame, though. I was looking forward to meeting some nice she-wolves on the Far Islands.*

Did it ever occur to you that there might not be any wolves there? she asked him.

No, he admitted. *So I'd have been wasting my time anyway if I'd come with you? Then it's a relief I'm not.* He couldn't pretend anymore. *Melayne, I'm going to miss you.*

And I'm going to miss you, too, she replied, hugging him tightly. *You were my first and truest friend.*

I still will be, he assured her. *Only I won't be as close. But I've got a feeling you've not seen the last of me.*

I hope not, Melayne answered. *One day . . .*

More than one, Greyn answered soberly. *But less than a lifetime.*

Will you be all right? she asked him, anxiously.

Of course, he replied, his usual cocky self. *I'll just have to find me a nice she-wolf in the neighborhood here. Not a problem. Take care of yourself. I won't be able to watch your back for you.*

I will, she promised. *Be good.*

Greyn laughed. *Not a chance!* Then he whirled, and was gone.

Melayne stared sadly after him for a moment. She would really miss him. They had been very close. But she would always have the hope that he was right, and that they would meet again, one day. . . . She moved back to the dragons.

Sander had managed to fix several straps around their bodies. "You'll have to sit in front of the wings," he explained to her, Corran, Ysane, and Bantry. "Grip the reins tightly, and don't let go." He smiled ruefully. "I'd tell you not to look down, but that's probably pointless. You can fasten your legs to the straps, and that should keep you in place. I don't know how fast the dragons can fly, but it's only about twenty miles to the ship."

I don't know how fast we can fly, either, Brek offered. *After all, we've never tried this before. The only way we'll know is to do it. I suppose I'd better take Sander, since I'm the biggest. Shath, you take the other male.*

I'll take Melayne, Tura offered. *Which leaves Loken for the other female.*

Melayne passed on their instructions, and each of the five moved to their respective dragons. Tura lowered her head, and Melayne clambered onto her back, just in front of the wings. She found the straps that Sander had fixed, and had to pull her skirt up to midthigh to get them fastened. She was a bit embarrassed showing so much bare skin, but that was the least of her concerns right now. She noticed that Bantry was helping Ysane to strap herself into place, and he certainly seemed to be enjoying touching her long legs in the process. That made Melayne smile. Sander was fixing Corran into place, making sure he wouldn't fall. Then the two men went to their own dragons.

Taking hold of the reins, Melayne wound them around her left hand. As soon as the others nodded to her that they were ready, she swallowed her panic and tried to be brave about this. But she'd never flown before, and the prospect scared her. She wished she'd taken time to go to the toilet before starting, but it was too late now. She could only pray it would be a short flight.

"Good luck," Brant called. "Though I suspect you make most of your own."

"If I did," she replied, "I'd have made it less terrifying." Her voice caught, but she made herself go on. "Brant, can I ask one further favor of you?"

"Anything," he replied promptly. Melayne was grateful, and more than a little amazed.

"My brother," she said sadly. "I know that he's betrayed me, but he's still very young. He's scared, and he wants protection. Can you tell him . . ." She tried to clear her thoughts. "Tell him that, no matter what, he's my brother and I will always love him."

"Of course," Brant agreed gently. "And I'll do my best to stay close to him and watch over him for you. Though he doesn't deserve it."

"It doesn't matter if he deserves it or not," Melayne answered. "He's my only sibling, and I hate to desert him."

"You haven't deserted him," Brant replied. "He's left you."

"Perhaps," she agreed, unsteadily. Then she pulled herself together. This was no time for her to fall apart. She would see Sarrow again one day, she was certain. And, until then, he would be fine. Perhaps he would come to his senses while she was away and become again the loving younger brother she missed. Only time would tell. "Everyone," she called, "ready!" To the dragons, she called: *Let's go!*

Tura gave a cry, and started forward. She took several steps, and then her wings spread wide and started to beat. It seemed impossible to Melayne that these would be large enough to lift both her and the dragon from the ground, and her stomach knotted in fear. The draft from the beating wings slapped her hair around, and she wished she'd thought to tie it up. Another two steps, and then Tura sprang upward. The wings beat faster, and there was a curious and unpleasant rise in Melayne's stomach. Her head spun, and then she realized that Tura was no longer on the ground.

The wings moved faster, dipping further, as the dragon scrambled to gain height. In a giddy moment, Melayne saw the castle walls pass below them, missing the edge by only a couple of feet. Tura was rising, but sluggishly. And then they were outside the castle walls.

She heard the scream of an oath from the soldiers outside the wall, and then the captain there yelled: "Archers! Kill them!"

Melayne reacted instinctively. *Buck!* she screamed down at their horses, putting all of her fear into the call. She gazed down, and saw every horse outside the walls rear, legs churning, nostrils flaring, whinnying with fear. The riders couldn't stay in their seats, let alone fire arrows. They all tumbled from their steeds, even Hada and Sarrow.

Serves them right, Melayne thought vindictively. Then she felt guilty. Whatever he had done, he was still her brother. She glanced back, but couldn't see him in the throng. Well, he'd survive. His Talent would ensure that. There was no need to worry on his behalf. What she did worry about was those whose lives he would affect. He was going to be a serious problem — but right now he wasn't her problem, and she was glad of it.

Tura was several hundred feet in the air now, and

Melayne realized she was staring down at the ground without fear. In fact, she was starting to enjoy this sensation. The dragon's flight was quite smooth, and she seemed to have leveled off. Melayne looked around the sky. Loken was close to her, with an ashen Ysane on her back. The other three dragons were a little above them, all flying strongly.

"Are you all right?" she called to Ysane, worried.

"Fine," Ysane answered in a shaky voice. "As long as I keep my eyes closed."

Melayne felt sorry for her friend, but she was enjoying herself almost as much as Corran. She could hear him whooping for pleasure. The wind buffeted her hair, making it stream back, except when it puffed forward from the wing-beats. But the experience was exhilarating, and the view stunning. For the first time in her life, she could look down on the hills and trees, seeing them from a unique perspective. She wasn't afraid of falling, tied as she was, and she had absolute faith in Tura.

This is wonderful, she said to the dragon.

How do you think I feel? Tura replied. *This is what I was born to do, and I've been locked up forever in a smelly old dungeon. For the first time in my life, I'm free. I'll never forget this, Melayne — and dragons have very long memories.*

Melayne was overjoyed that the dragons were so happy. Whatever happened now, everything she'd suffered had been worth it.

They passed over forests, and roads, and trails that were just thin lines below them. There was a village, and a few isolated farmsteads with fields,

365

but Melayne couldn't see any people. She was probably too high for that. Everything looked so peaceful from up here.

Then she could see, ahead of them, a thin line of blueness, and she realized that they were approaching the coast. It seemed to be barely minutes since they had taken off, and they would soon be reaching the end of the flight. Melayne felt disappointed, then realized how selfish she was being. Tura and the others were probably tired after flying all this way. They'd never flown before, and it couldn't be easy on them, carrying people on their backs.

"To the south a little," Sander called, and Melayne passed along the instruction to the dragons. They veered in the air and soared toward their destination. Melayne could see they were bypassing a town on the coast, and realized that Sander had arranged for the ship to pick them up outside of the town. A smart move — taking the dragons into a human town would have certainly invited a lot of trouble.

And then they were over a bay. Below them was a three-masted ship, quite large enough for the five dragons. Tura spiraled downward, aiming for the deck. Melayne heard Ysane give a strangled squeak of terror as they descended, but she concentrated on watching their approach. Tura moved easily and confidently, and the ship below grew larger. Melayne saw startled sailors moving out of the way as the dragons gently settled down onto the planks of the deck.

"Again!" Corran said eagerly.

"Not just yet," Sander answered firmly. "We've got work to do, son."

Melayne hugged Tura's neck in silent gratitude, and then unstrapped herself. As her feet hit the deck, they wobbled a little. But then she steadied, and moved to help Sander release Corran.

The captain came to greet them — a tall, thin man with a wispy beard and an amazed expression on his face. "I don't know quite what I was expecting," he confessed. "But seeing you riding dragons down out of the sky wasn't it!"

"We weren't expecting it, either," Sander confessed with a laugh. "It was, as usual, last-minute improvisation. We're likely to be hunted, Tamin. Can we get under way?"

"As soon as my men recover their wits," Tamin promised. "Look lively, lads!" he yelled. "You'll have plenty of time to gape at the dragons later. There's a good breeze rising, and I want to be well on the way in five minutes! Move it!"

The sailors pulled themselves together and started working. Melayne had no idea what they were doing. No doubt it was all very technical, and perhaps she could learn it as they went along. For now, though, she was simply relieved that they had escaped, unharmed.

Ysane was holding tightly onto Bantry. "Don't let me go," she begged him. "I can hardly stand up."

"Don't worry," he promised her. "I won't." He looked very happy at the prospect of holding the blond girl, and Melayne grinned.

Sander joined her, and the two of them started to

strip the harnesses from the dragons. It felt good simply having him beside her, with no real need for words.

Brek looked at her. *That was glorious*, he informed her. *I can't wait to go flying again.*

As soon as we're clear, you can probably go off again, Melayne suggested. *As long as you stay near the ship, I don't think there'll be any problems. Besides, you might be able to catch some fish.*

The thought made him happy. *Thank you, Melayne. You've proven that some humans can be trusted.*

She liked the thought, but she knew their troubles weren't over yet. In fact, they might just be starting.

With a creak of deck planks and the sound of ropes being hauled, the sails were unfurled, and they caught the stiff breeze. The ship sighed through the waves, heading away from land. Melayne looked back at it, her feelings mingled.

"Sorry to see it go?" Sander asked her gently, as they leaned on the rail together, looking back.

"Not really," she admitted. "There are a lot of bad memories there. But some really good ones, too. And unfinished problems. Sarrow, for example."

"He'll be fine," Sander assured her, placing his arm about her shoulder and drawing her close to him.

"Oh, *he* will be," Melayne agreed. "It's everybody else around him that I'm worried about. And I can't help thinking about Greyn, and Corri and Devra, and all of the rest."

"We'll be back," he promised her. "As soon as the dragons can survive, we'll come back and settle some of your doubts. And there are a few other things to do, too, that we probably can't get done on the Far Islands."

"Like what?" she asked.

He reached into a pocket, and pulled out a small box. When he opened it, she could see that there were two rings inside it. "Like getting married," he said. "These are family treasures, worn by my ancestors for hundreds of years. They're the ones I saw on our fingers."

"They're beautiful," she said honestly.

"As are you." Sander bent to kiss her. "And we'll be wearing them just as soon as we can, I promise."

"Good," Melayne answered. "Because I really don't want to wait too long." She kissed him back.

"Isn't this great?" asked Corran, happily.

Melayne looked around. Sander was next to her, holding her tightly. Corran was helping one of the sailors. Ysane and Bantry were still clinging to one another. Brek, Shath, Tura, Loken, and Ganeth were staying out of the way and staring longingly at the sky. The sails billowed as the ship was driven along.

"Yes," Melayne answered. "Yes, it *is* great."